*For Michelle, for getting me through some of my darkest days, and for sharing some of my brightest*

Special Thanks to *Brock Hunter* for his tireless efforts on behalf of wounded veterans facing criminal charges, and for his work reforming the criminal justice system to account for war trauma in the sentencing of former soldiers.

Visit veteransdefenseproject.org or brockhunterlaw.com for more information.

# Table of contents

# The Ghost
# Of Fort Leavenworth

# Part One:

# Old Wounds

# Chapter 1
## Mosul, Iraq (2008)

"Captain, is it true about the kid?"

Captain Casper glanced up from his weapon, his hazel eyes lost in the glare of the mid-day Arab sun. He wore a subdued American flag on his right shoulder, hovering above his unit patch for Explosive Ordnance Disposal (EOD), a blackened bomb facing downward and surrounded in a periphery of flames. They'd rumbled through that arid country too many times, baking in the back of an up-armored Humvee, the blinding sun seeping through the windows and cooking the metal panels like the inside of an oven. Sweat lined the insides of his palms and underarms. A quiet trickle dripped from his temples, slickening his skin under the weight of his Kevlar.

The captain loaded and reloaded his magazine in a well-practiced rhythm. "What's the matter, Sergeant? You haven't seen enough dead kids yet?"

Staff Sergeant Khoury lowered his eyes. They were set deep into his skin and half hidden by shadows. "I'd just like to be prepared, Sir."

Casper went back to inspecting his weapon. He was tempted to not even respond. "You can't prepare for this shit Randy. Whatever we find at the blast site, the sound, the weight, the smell, it's going to stay with you. That won't ever wash off."

Sergeant Khoury tightened his grip on his own weapon, trying to settle the shaking from the rocky terrain below them. "What do you think happened?"

"I think they stopped the damned convoy."

Casper continued to check the functions of the M16 in his lap, the clicks and snaps were a welcome distraction, keeping his mind and his fingers occupied.

"Who was driving the lead vehicle?"

"Sergeant Hestler. Lieutenant Adams was ordered not to stop the convoy for anything. You stop the convoy you're as good as dead, along with everyone you're transporting. If there's a kid in the road, so be it. You can't save him anyway."

"Hestler has a kid at home." Khoury mouthed the words, more than spoke them. "A boy. If there was a kid in the road, I don't think he could've . . ."

"Neither do I." Casper looked up for the first time, his fingers still fiddling with the safety on his weapon, switching the firing mode from single to burst. "I think he disobeyed the order and stopped long enough for the triggerman to take him out."

"If they had run the kid down . . ."

"If they had run the kid down it would've been one dead kid instead of Hestler and his entire crew. The kid is just a pawn for the insurgency. That's how these assholes operate." Casper spat. He scanned the dusty landscape that surrounded them, barren and full of unseen hazards. Nothing to guarantee that they wouldn't be rolling over their own hidden explosives somewhere en route to Hestler's grave. He just hoped that Hestler had enough foresight to put his dog tags in his boots, or they weren't likely to find what was left of him. The head and torso would have been incinerated if he was too close to the blast. Hands and feet seemed to be the only parts that survived that kind of a wreck.

Casper turned his head towards the interior of the Humvee. Sergeant Khoury had set aside his M16 and was loading a few rounds into an unidentified 9 millimeter.

"What's the 9 Mil for?" Casper's eyes hardened on the beat-up hand gun.

"Crawford told me to take it along." Khoury had loaded three rounds in the magazine before he placed the gun on safe and hid it away in the holster on his flak jacket. "Just in case."

"Just in case?" Casper eyed the young Sergeant. "Is that a drop gun Sergeant?"

"I'm not sure what you mean Sir."

"You know damn well what I mean. It's a drop gun. Just in case one of the locals gets a little too close and you pull the trigger a little too quickly, you've got an ace up your sleeve to make it look like it was a legitimate kill. Am I hitting close to the mark?"

3

Staff Sergeant Khoury reclaimed his M16, the barrel sticking to the insides of his palms. "Sir, there's a dead kid. We're heading into a firefight."

"I know that." Casper nodded.

"I just think that . . ."

"Hand it over Randy. Now, you hear me?" Casper looked at the kid sitting across from him. His Kevlar and body armor rattled as the Humvee closed in on the kill zone, where they'd be forced to sort through the liquified remains of former soldiers, and the skinny legs and arms of the boy who'd taken them out.

Sergeant Khoury looked his captain dead in the eye, a nervous shake stirring through his pupils. He reached into the holster on his hip and pulled out the gun. He squeezed the heavy metal grip one last time before turning it over.

Captain Casper fastened the weapon to the outside of his body armor. "I get that you're scared, alright? You should be. But you don't want to start a habit like this. Killing assholes is one thing. Hell, making a mistake is just one more part of the bullshit. Look at me Randy."

Sergeant Khoury raised his anxious eyes towards the captain. He was too damn eager. He hadn't been worn down yet and numbed from so many months of wading through the gruesome remains of IED blasts.

"We've all done it." Casper tried to console him. "Made mistakes. But planning on it is another thing entirely. You take that weapon to the blast site you're going to be far too tempted to shoot the first guy that looks your way, and you don't want to go home with that hanging over your head. You don't want to start fighting this war like you're not going home."

The trembling beneath them slowed as the Humvee rolled to a stop and crouched in the shadows of a string of abandoned buildings. Captain Casper crawled out of the vehicle, stepping into the hot wind that carried the unmistakable smell of burnt flesh. The streets were too quiet to be secure. Somewhere in the mess of destroyed buildings around him, someone was watching and waiting to take them out of this world.

A second Humvee pulled up behind them and the infantry team disembarked from their vehicles. They were covered in full body armor with their M16s drawn. Casper laid a hand on the drop gun fixed to his vest as Staff Sergeant Khoury descended from the vehicle, a thin film of sweat coating his forehead.

"Hey Khoury." Casper laid a hand on the kid's shoulder. The Staff Sergeant turned around, his weapon aimed at the captain's center mass.

"Easy there." Casper pushed the muzzle out towards the empty streets surrounding them. "You're going to be okay Randy. I wouldn't have you out here with me if I couldn't count on you to do the right thing."

It was something that commanders and platoon leaders said to their soldiers. It helped take some of the edge off. But it only took one accident or disastrous firefight to convince them otherwise. There really was no 'right thing' in certain situations. There was just surviving and not surviving. And even surviving had its costs.

The staff sergeant nodded and his helmet slid down his forehead.

"Wipe the sweat from your forehead. You can't shoot if you can't see. This way." Casper took a few steps in the direction of the smell in the air and pointed with the muzzle of his M16. Staff Sergeant Khoury shuffled up beside him, hanging off his right elbow.

The infantry men moved ahead of and behind them. Bravo team took the lead while Alpha team assembled in a wedge formation behind them. Casper watched the windows and the rooftops of the buildings as they stepped into the miserable heat, the muzzle of his weapon bounding between empty corners and doorways. It wasn't long before he started catching glimpses of heads and scarves. A few stragglers and vagabonds lining the streets. He kept steady count of the soldiers ahead of him, their names sewn into the backs of their patrol caps. Lewis. Brandt. Kauffman and Sinclair. He focused on the steady breathing of the others, Johnson, Vang, Crawford and Alonso just a few paces behind.

They moved through the streets without speaking, just listening to the shuffle of their heavy gear and the clinking of metal as weapons knocked against hooks and plates. Each man guarded his own dread as they inhaled dust and charred debris.

Casper noticed the moment the terrain changed. The dirt underfoot mixed with moist, black tar, and the sound of heated metal popping and sizzling buzzed in his ears. The squad rounded the corner and collided with the thick stench surrounding the stalled convoy. The MRAPs snaked through the narrow streets, with a large hole blasted through the head, leaving behind a mass of twisted metal.

They approached the wreck with steady strides, their eyes and weapons trained on the handful of onlookers that had gathered after the blast. Seemingly innocent faces, all lined with some bitter emotion. They were old before their time, hollow and burdened with grief. Casper felt the blood pulse in his throat and hands, waiting to hear the whiz of bullets coming from behind the shattered walls around them.

He broke away from the formation and moved towards a trained squadron of soldiers, forming a security ring just beyond the perimeter of the destroyed MRAP. Their platoon leader, Lieutenant Adams, was waiting inside.

"Are you the one they call the Ghost?" The lieutenant lowered his rifle as Casper approached.

"I am." Casper nodded.

"We're sure glad to see you Sir." Lieutenant Adams relaxed without smiling.

"Wish I could say the same." Casper stepped inside the security ring. "What's the situation?"

"Kid ran in front of the convoy. The lead vehicle couldn't have stopped for more than 15 seconds Sir."

"That's all it takes. How many dead?"

"Four Sir." Lieutenant Adams responded with a dry throat. The moisture in his lips and eyes was all but gone. "The truck commander was medevaced out."

"Let's hope that's all for today. Any other explosives in the area?"

"None that I've seen."

"I'm going to send Sergeant Lewis and his men through to clear you. Once we give you the all clear, you can drive on, head back to the FOB."

"What about the vehicle Sir?" Lieutenant Adams avoided looking in the direction of the wreck. "With the bodies?"

"Won't be any bodies to recover LT. We'll gather up what's left. But I guarantee it won't be much."

Casper stepped outside the security ring and motioned to both teams. "Brandt, go left, Alonso, you and your team take the right. Lewis, pull security for me. I'm going to see if I can find the IED."

"What are you thinking Sir?" Sergeant First Class Lewis stepped up beside Captain Casper, his M16 raised and directed outward as he walked.

"I'm thinking we have a dead kid in the road and no one's taken a shot at us yet." The captain made a quick sweep of the area with cool eyes. The horizon blurred in the heat and he picked up on the impossible scent of lilacs, distant and sweet. "Makes me uncomfortable. Fan out." Casper called to the crew, motioning to the surrounding streets on either side of the convoy. "Since the main road's cut off, we'll have to divert the convoy down another road. Make sure we're not being forced into another set of explosives. Let me know if you find anything even remotely suspect."

The squad fractured off, making a broad sweep of the area surrounding the convoy, looking for any irregularities in the street that could be hiding explosives.

Captain Casper headed in the direction of the charred MRAP with Sergeant First Class Lewis focusing his rifle on any movement in the streets surrounding them. Casper avoided what appeared to be a pool of fresh vomit on the ground, some poor soldier's reaction to the sickening smell. Or the fact that he'd narrowly escaped being incinerated.

Casper breathed through his mouth to take in less of the fumes and used the muzzle of his weapon to sift through the smoking wreckage. He waded through boiled metal coated in blood, and picked apart ribbons of seared flesh and human bone. He lowered himself to his knees and reached for a standard issue military boot, most of the foot still inside. With a singed ankle bone poking through the charred meat. Possibly Hestler, or what was left of him. Casper spotted a small glint of silver tucked into the laces and pulled out a pair of bent and blackened dog tags. He could barely make out the last name, and the religion engraved at the bottom, "Hestler. Lutheran." A 240 pound man reduced to a mess of raw scum burned to the floor of a destroyed MRAP.

Casper pocketed the dog tags and dropped the boot, continuing to breathe in through the mouth. He moved more debris from his path and noticed a half disintegrated hand in one corner near what would've been the front door. The brittle finger bones of the thumb and index finger had snapped off. The remaining fingers were black and shriveled, with the mushy remnants of a melted wedding band blended into the remains.

Casper stood in place and moved to the front of the vehicle, looking for what was left of the IED that took out the MRAP. All he could make out was the blackened outline of a small, mangled pair of legs, skinned to the bone and barely recognizable, smoldering in the desert heat and already beginning to attract flies.

He heard the deep vibrations of laughter, and the hair on the back of his neck stood straight and rigid. He turned his head to the right and fixed his eyes on a large man with a dark face, half hidden in an empty doorframe along the road. Casper was close enough to stare into the eyes of the wicked soul. His skin was tanned and leathery, covered by a thick beard and a reddish head scarf. He flashed a smile, bold and incriminating. His teeth were perfect, aligned in a malicious curve, brilliant and white. He laughed again, cool and hearty.

"Stop laughing." Captain Casper felt the earth move under his feet. He lunged for the man's throat and wrestled him to the ground, the laughter replaced with panicked gasps for air. Casper anchored himself against the doorway with his elbow tight around the man's neck. He ripped the drop gun from his outer vest and held the barrel against the man's neck, feeling the demented pulse of his blood flow beneath the cold metal.

8

"You think this is funny, you sick fucker?" Casper screamed into the dusty air.

"Let go!" A weak protest escaped his constricted airway. He pulled at the thick arm that was wrapped around his neck and his voice broke in terrified and perfect English. "What's wrong with you, let go!"

Casper heard the shuffle of boots and mix of voices as the rest of his squad ran towards him. He looked up into the glare of the sun where their heads bobbed and swayed. Their faces unrecognizable. Their eyes glowing behind their helmets.

"Jesus Sir, what's got into you?"

"My God, let him go!"

A warm hand settled against his shoulder and the smell of lilacs swept across his palette. "Ben, look at me."

He turned his head towards the soft voice drifting in with an unexpected wave of cool air. The rumbling of boots and guns nearly drowned out the sound, but he heard it. As faint and poetic as a whisper. The subtle hint of lavender broke through the toxic smoke and filled the air around him. He loosened his grip on the trigger well of the gun in his hand and focused on the blurred outline of the face in front of him.

"Ben, let the captain go. Give me your hand. Give me your hand." The sound lifted above the roar of the Humvees and gunfire snapping in his head.

The haze settled around the edges of his vision. He found himself staring into a pair of crystal blue eyes that didn't belong in the desert. Didn't belong anywhere near the bombs and mortars and dead children. She was lost and wandering unarmed through a war zone.

Or maybe it was him.

"Drop the weapon Ben. You don't need it here. Take my hand instead."

"Jamie?" He almost whispered her name as her face came into sharper focus. "Jamie is that you?"

"I'm here." She extended her hand towards him, her perfumed wrist moving beneath his nose and drawing him back from the Middle East.

The foggy outlines of the soldiers around him morphed into the stricken faces of bystanders, watching with tight lungs, their eyes wide and their hearts racing. The Humvees and falling structures along the road, everything down to the sand beneath his boots faded and disappeared. He was surrounded by nothing more than old tables and chairs and the sweet smells of amber ale and red wine. His back was pressed up against a wall, and one of his classmates was locked beneath his left elbow. He looked down at the man's frightened expression, his hands pulling at the arm that was cutting off his oxygen, and his eyes trained on the broken piece of glass in Casper's right hand, inches from his chin.

## Part Two:

## Veteran's Day

# Chapter 2
## Fort Leavenworth, KS (2014)

Benjamin Casper opened one eye and took in his surroundings. His head was reeling. The sound of shouts and gunfire still ricocheting through the sticky gray matter in his brain. He was comforted to find himself in his own bed. He felt precious seconds ticking by, suspended in a state of painless delirium before he fully regained consciousness. His head was unsettled, like something was sure to sneak up on him after the morning fog cleared.

He climbed out of bed and fell to the floor, diving into his morning routine of planks and push-ups. His blonde hair settling across his forehead as he moved.

His head swelled as the blood started feeding into his brain. He memorized the pattern in the carpet threads under his nose. He picked up the smell of bacon warming up the room. He recognized the sound of his wife's soft feet, moving across the kitchen tiles down the hall.

He lifted his lean body up and down until his muscles burned. He felt a dull ache in his chest and abdomen. A scattering of tender spots around his ribcage. He glanced down at his sore body and noticed that his entire torso was bruised and swollen. Some of it was coming back now. He'd been hit by someone with small hands and fierce fists. He reached towards the left side of his head and felt an obnoxious lump just above his ear.

He pulled himself off the floor with some minor discomfort and stepped in front of the bathroom mirror. He was older than he remembered, with new creases forming around his mouth and eyes every day. But his chest and shoulders were still defined and healthy. He splashed some water on his face and checked his head and upper body for any signs of distress. He found another less obvious lump below his right eye.

It was possible, if Grace had worked the night shift that she would be too tired to notice. But he had no memory of her schedule anymore.

He pulled on a pair of jeans and reached for a discarded sweatshirt in the pile of dirty clothes on the bedroom floor. He felt it, before he saw it. A crisp stain alongside the zipper, just below the U.S. Army logo. A dark blotch that could only be one thing. He looked down at the gray tee-shirt that he'd worn the night before, dotted with freckles of dried blood that he could only hope was his own. He reached a hand up to his face to feel for any signs of dried blood. He inspected his shoulders and upper body for any open wounds, and was disappointed to find nothing. He dropped the sweatshirt back into the pile, picked out a clean tee-shirt from his dresser drawer and headed towards the smells and sounds coming from kitchen.

He moved stealthily through the house, an old habit he couldn't seem to break, and watched his wife from the open entrance to the kitchen. She was standing at the stovetop in one of his oversized T-shirts, scrambling eggs. She moved from the stove to the cutting board to slice the ham and green peppers, and then back again to throw it all together. Her blonde hair was piled on top of her head. Not in a neat, orderly fashion like she used to do. And not in an untamed, sexy sort of mishmash. She looked more worn down and defeated. There was a used wine goblet on the counter at her elbow, with about an ounce of red wine wasting away in the bottom of the glass.

Casper slunk into the room and reached for a pack of cigarettes on the small table behind her. He flicked the lighter and Grace jumped at the noise, turning around with a solid grip on the steak knife in her hands.

"Easy baby." Casper took in his first stale breath of chemicals for the morning. "It would seem, against all odds, that I still have a wife."

She made a noise that might have been a weary laugh, and lowered the kitchen knife. Then looked at him with the saddest nod of recognition, and turned back towards the stove. "Is that what you're aiming for? To come home one night and wake up to an empty house?"

"I take it you didn't work evenings last night?"

"It's cruel Ben." She started beating the eggs with an aggressive roll of her wrist. "If you don't want to do this anymore you could at least have the decency to say so."

"I come home to you every night Grace." He pulled out a chair and took a seat at the table, watching her as she moved about the kitchen. "Maybe a little worse for the wear, but I come home."

"Where were you last night?"

"Does it really matter?"

"You tell me." She stared at him from across the room, tired circles under her eyes. "You look sick."

He wondered how much wine she had had while he was out. How well she slept in the room down the hall. "I think I was in a fight last night." He exhaled a long plume of smoke.

"You think?" She glanced back at him, a dull pain in her voice. "With who?"

"I don't know yet. Another officer. Someone I don't care much for."

"I should hope not." She approached the table with two healthy plates of scrambled eggs and bacon. "But then with you, one never knows."

"I may have hurt him." He put out his cigarette in the ashtray under his fingers. "You won't be able to protect me this time."

He watched her set a warm plate in front of him with the salt and pepper shakers off to one side, like she had been doing for most of their turbulent life together. He reached for the pepper shaker and sprinkled his eggs in a familiar and heartbreaking pattern. He stopped when he saw her stretch her fingers towards the small lump under his eye.

He froze as he felt his wife's fingers against his skin, relishing the little slivers of pain that pulsed each time she touched the inflamed tissue. He closed his eyes and held his breath, searching his distant memory for an appropriate response.

"Does it hurt at all?" Her face softened as she touched him.

"I don't mind the hurt." He exhaled, then picked up his fork and dug around in the yellow eggs. "At least it's something."

"Did you sleep at all last night?"

"How is anyone supposed to sleep with gunfire going off all night?" He shoveled a few steady mouthfuls of eggs into his mouth. "I thought they were through with training around here."

"You mean the fireworks?"

"Fireworks?"

"The Veteran's Day celebration. You were supposed to meet me at the high school." He watched the disappointment break across her face. "You never came."

"Veteran's Day." Casper set his fork down and brought a napkin towards his mouth, fragmented memories swirling to the surface. "I have a flight this afternoon. I have to pack."

"Ben."

He got up from the table and headed back towards the guest room. He began digging through his drawers for clean clothes and tossing them into a beat up duffle bag. He opened the closet and glanced up at the empty shelf, looking for an old shoebox that was supposed to be nested in its usual corner. His palms began to sweat and his fingers tingled. He opened drawers and swept shelves, pressing his memory for the last place he'd seen it.

Grace was in the doorway watching him, her green eyes full of concern. "What are you looking for?

"The shoebox. The one I brought back from Iraq, have you seen it?"

"I don't know what you're talking about. That was ages ago."

He stood and looked about the cluttered room, his eyes settling on the pile of dirty clothes in the corner. He wondered if he should tell her about the blood. If there was any sense in trying to explain himself now.

"I know this is important to you. But do you have to go this time? Do you have to go now?"

"I made a promise Grace." He picked up the duffle bag at his feet and brushed past her.

"Why won't you talk to me? Why won't you tell me what's happening with you?"

There was a loud knock on the back door.

"Leave it Grace," he warned her as he headed into the bathroom and began rifling through drawers for toothpaste and shaving cream. "It's not going to be good news."

Grace shook her head headed back towards the kitchen.

"Grace." He stuffed a handful of items into his bag and followed her as far as the end of the hallway. He froze in place as she opened the door, and he saw two men standing outside on the porch.

They were dressed in civilian clothes, like all special agents from the Criminal Investigation Department. A simple and effective trick to insulate them from the influence of rank. A cool chill rippled through Casper's veins.

"We're here to speak with a Major Benjamin Casper." The young man on the left spoke smoothly and predictably.

Grace stepped back and opened the door. "He's in here somewhere. If you're able to find him you let me know."

The two men stepped into the kitchen. Casper entered the room with his packed duffle bag in hand. The special agents stood by as he set the bag on the floor and lit another cigarette. He took a quick drag and waited for them to do what they'd come to do.

"Major Benjamin Casper?" The trim man in the white collar shirt spoke first.

"You've found him. What can I do for you so early on a Saturday morning?"

"I'm special agent Redding, this is special agent Fox. We're with CID."

"I know who you are. Your reports are routed through my office. I'm the one who prosecutes all the soldiers you investigate."

"We're aware." The shorter agent responded.

"Is there an immediate problem that can't wait until the holiday's over?"

"We received a report this morning that you were personally involved in an altercation last night with a Captain James Mann."

"Captain James Mann." Casper took in another slow drag as the name swirled around his cloudy memory banks. "JAG officer?"

"Roger. According to police reports you were involved in an assault against Captain Mann outside the Eagle Lounge last night at approximately 9:45 p.m."

The face of the man with the small hands and the fierce fists was coming into focus. The bar room lights, the music, that stale stench in the air. The scuffle in the parking lot, the lumps on his face and head, the ache in his chest, the blood on his sweatshirt. The queasy anger was beating at his temples.

"Well I can only assume that you've been properly trained to read a soldier his rights in the event that any sort of criminal charges might be forthcoming."

"If you'll accompany us to the CID office, special agent Hartman is prepared to administer the rights warning for the article 118 charges."

"I think you mean article 128, Sergeant." Casper took another tight pull from the cigarette between his fingers. "Assault is article 128."

"To the contrary, I meant article 118."

Major Casper removed the cigarette from his lips and stared perplexed at the two men standing so still and severe in his kitchen.

"Captain Mann is dead."

# Chapter 3
## Fort Leavenworth, KS (2014)

Grace could smell her own fear. It overpowered the fading smell of pepper and eggs on the stove behind her. The minor comforts that gave the place a semblance of a home.

She was stalled in front of the used dishes in the sink, wondering if her time had finally run out. She felt the first signs of regret tingling through her nose and throat. All the missed doctor appointments and sample medications that she'd tossed down the drain at her shaking fingertips. All her good intentions dissolving at her wobbly feet. She felt the silent seconds tick by, waiting for Ben to respond. She was prepared for just about anything they might have brought into her kitchen. Anything but what they'd just said.

"Dead?" Ben's one word response echoed off the empty kitchen walls.

"We've been asked to escort you to the CID office to answer some questions." The thin agent's voice was deep and surreal and penetrated into the thick of her bones.

"I see." Ben practically whispered.

The worst had finally come home – just as she imagined it would, on a dark evening somewhere between her first and second glasses of wine. While she sat tipsy and alone, nursing some dark and terrible mood, Ben had been swallowed by the dust and sand. Only it wasn't her that had been throttled by his dangerous memories. The brittle truth broke against the back of her throat.

She watched her husband absorbing the news that he had killed someone, wrestling for some blocked memories that would refute it. She thought she saw him reach for a weapon on his hip that was no longer there. It was a subtle movement, something she'd only picked up on after years of looking. A tell-tale sign that he felt threatened. Blood beat at her temples like racing thoroughbreds.

"You're not being placed under arrest at this time. But it would be in your best interest to come with us now." Agent Redding's words were like canned lines from an old cop movie, without much purpose or meaning.

She tried to pinpoint the moment she realized there was still something dangerous inside him. Something that had followed him home from the desert and wouldn't let go of him. The special agents standing in her kitchen were just the most recent incarnation of everything she'd been sweeping under the rug. All the warning signs that she'd patched over with temporary solutions. All of it becoming more real and irreversible with every passing breath.

"I see." Ben echoed again. He took a last pull from his cigarette and left it smoldering in the ashtray. He seemed to look right past her and she immediately thought about the steak knife that she'd left out from that morning's breakfast. It was easily within arm's reach, but it was too late for her to lunge for it without exposing her deepest fears.

"Ben." She wrapped an anxious hand around her throat and used the other to steady herself against the counter. "Tell me what's happening."

"Shhh. Grace. I need you to stay calm okay." He stepped towards her, slow and bewildering. He extended his arms as if he might embrace her, but then placed his restless fingers along the edge of the old countertop, trapping her inside his firm arms. He stood for a moment, staring into her eyes and processing what was left of the oxygen in the air.

Her face and hands went hot as his empty eyes searched the countertops behind her. In one swift motion he pitched forward and gripped the stem of her abandoned wine goblet, throwing back the lingering drops of the red wine.

A simple shiver moved down her spine. She let go of a tight breath as she watched him lift his left hand off the counter and pick up a discarded set of keys beside the sink.

"Those are my keys Ben." She murmured.

He looked at her with sharp, unfamiliar eyes. He gave a soundless nod that sent a chill into her bloodstream, then dropped the keys where he'd found them and moved towards the door.

Grace reached behind her and grabbed the knife from the counter, casually placing it in the skillet on top of the stove and burying both in the sink under stacks of used dishes.

Ben grabbed his own keys from a hook near the door and slid them into his pocket. He kept his eyes on the special agents in the center of the room as he crouched to the floor and pulled on his shoes. "I have a flight at 1300, agent Redding. As long as I'm not officially under arrest, I intend to leave the CID office in time to make my flight."

"That's something you'll have to sort out with Agent Hartman."

Grace watched the delicate way he laced up his shoes. His toned body was still so much muscle and grit, with a gorgeous softness buried in his ever-changing eyes. He was still as fierce and sexy as the day she'd married him, only broken into a thousand jagged splinters on the inside. She wondered if she'd ever see him again. If he would find a way to board his plane to Minneapolis like he'd planned and disappear from her life. She searched for something to say, everything she should've told him when he left for Mosul so long ago, if she had only known he would never come back the same.

"It's Veteran's Day." He spit the words with the only bit of passion he seemed to have left in him. "I have an obligation that I have to keep."

Ben stood upright and headed back towards her, setting his calloused fingers in the quiet safety of her hands. She held tight to his wrists, but felt him slipping away from her. She focused on the wrinkles around his eyes, his unshaven face and the few gray hairs mixing with the dirty blonde covering his forehead. She took everything in with an uncommon surge of tenderness.

He kissed her quietly on the cheek and she felt a million strands of sensation tingling through her skin. The pepper from his eggs that morning, the nicotine from his last cigarette, the dryness of his lips and the bullish words that seemed to linger between them.

*"You won't be able to protect me this time."*

He'd underestimated her before. She wasn't going to let him go that easily.

"Call me when you can." Her attempt at a casual goodbye was spoiled by the tremor in her voice. She squeezed his hands one last time before he pulled away, wondering what those hands had done while she was sleeping.

# Chapter 4
## Fort Leavenworth, KS (2014)

"I can't help him this time Grace." Agent Hartman rifled his fingers through his silver hair. He pressed his cell phone against his ear, as if he could quiet her voice or drown out their curious phone call by muffling the heavy sounds against his cheek.

"You said you were his friend." She snapped.

"I am his friend!" His voice rose and then fell again. He closed his eyes against his cluttered desk, buried in investigation files. Each one of them a testament to the dark potential of human beings. "You said you would get him some help."

"I don't know how to help him!" Her voice was shrill and mean. "You don't have to do this Leon. You didn't arrest him last time."

"Last time I didn't have a dead body on my hands!" He pressed his lips together and tapped a pen against the manila folder in front of him, trying to curb the swelling in the back of his throat. "I want to help him Grace, I do. But if he did this, he'll be charged with murder. There's nothing I can do about that."

"Is it still murder if it was all just a terrible dream?" Grace's frightened voice brought back memories that he'd promised to forget. Echoes of a far more disturbing phone call during the hottest part of August.

"I'll do what I can for him Grace. But I can't make it disappear this time. I wish I could." There was a knock at the door and he looked up to see Casper step into the room, a packed duffle bag slung over his shoulder. He wondered how much of the person he once knew was still operating behind those distant hazel eyes. "I have to go now Grace, I'll call you as soon as I can. Take care."

Ben took a few steps forward and began sizing up the room like there were still insurgents lurking around every corner. Noting all the entrances and exits, windows, fire extinguishers and a million potential threats that were no longer there.

"She's called you already, has she?"

Hartman nodded towards his old friend, a waxy dread building in his palms and fingers. "What's with the bag?"

Casper let the bag slide off his shoulder and deposited it on the floor at his feet. "Aren't you supposed to read me my rights before you start asking questions?"

"Your rights warning is on the desk." Hartman pointed towards the blank form on his desk and a sour spot swelled in his stomach. He sank into his chair and felt his own weight creak beneath him. All the years behind a desk had added an extra layer to his old ranger physique. He dressed in dark blues and grays to hide the bulge in his midsection.

Casper fell into the empty seat across from him. He picked up the familiar form and glanced over the top of it with sharp eyes. "So this is what it's come to?"

"I don't want to treat you like a criminal Ben." Hartman folded his hands in his lap, his tongue starting to feel heavy in his mouth. "But you've put me in a hell of a position."

"Sorry to drag you out of bed on your day off." Casper leaned back in his chair and waved the rights waiver back and forth between them. "So you want me to sign away my rights as a favor to you? As a friend?"

"I want you to tell me what happened." Hartman folded his hands across his desk. All he had to do was exclude him as a suspect. Pull enough information to negate any motive, to give him even the weakest alibi and he could put an end to the questioning. The uncomfortable suspicion. The guilt. "Between the two of us. Off the record."

Casper looked back at him with sullen eyes, filling with a quiet resentment. "It's not admissible in court."

"I don't give a shit about that Ben!" Hartman reached across the desk and tore the empty form from Casper's hands, tossing it in a drawer. He flipped through the folder on his desk and pulled out a standard Army photo of the victim. The perfect image of a proud soldier in his dress uniform. An African American with a clean shaven head, a chestnut complexion and deep set eyes. His uniform was decorated with ribbons from overseas tours and a captain's rank on his shoulders.

"You want to tell me who this guy is?" Hartman handed the photo to Ben and saw a quiet flicker of anger spark in his eyes. Hartman's chest muscles tightened.

"He's a colleague of mine." Casper set the photo on the desk. "I met him in Charlottesville, about two years ago."

"This morning a jogger found him dead in the woods near the rec center."

Casper kept his eyes trained on the image in front of him. A gray wave seemed to wash over him, transporting him to another time and place.

"He had a broken jaw, shattered ribs, and three bullet holes in him." Hartman pulled the crime scene photographs from the folder. The same captain was dressed in a white t-shirt and faded jeans, sprawled on the dirty ground and bleeding from three angry red wounds. Two in the chest just above the heart and one to the middle of his forehead. He had large glossy eyes and a twisted mouth, and looked a little desperate, even in death.

Hartman set the grisly images on top of the previous photo and waited for Ben's reaction, hoping for a simple explanation that would satisfy both mercy and justice.

Ben picked them up with both hands, his expression more curious than shocked.

"There was a police report that you assaulted this guy about 8 hours before his body was found." Hartman stalled, caught up on his own suspicions. The rest of his question lay in the pit of his stomach, churning over itself like bad meat. "I'm asking you as a friend, not as a cop or a soldier or anything else, did you do this to him?"

Ben looked up from the photographs, edgy and confined in the small, cluttered office. "I don't remember much about last night Leon. It's still coming back in flashes. I remember there was a fight. I probably broke his jaw and his ribs. I don't remember much else."

Hartman brought his hands to his mouth and pushed out a volume of trapped air, unaware that he had been holding his breath.

*"I don't remember much else."*

24

It wasn't much of a defense, and might even be enough to tie him to this poor captain's death. To convince generals and prosecutors that he had lost himself in a recycled war and taken out an innocent somebody.

"What was the fight about?" Hartman needed details, anything that might break up the scattered trail of evidence, or trigger fresh memories.

Ben set the photos on the desk in front of him, his hazel eyes turning from green to blue in the fluorescent light. "It had something to do with a girl."

"What girl? Who?" Hartman's questions started breaking across each other with increasing urgency.

"Someone I haven't thought about for a long time." Ben played with his silver wedding band, sliding it up and down the ridges on his finger.

"Did you screw around on Grace?" Hartman looked at Ben with an arch in his eyebrows, clinging to the first substantive answer he'd given him since he came into the room. "Was it this guy's wife or girlfriend?"

"It was nothing like that." Ben looked at his hands, playing with an old scar that ran down the middle of his left palm.

"Listen, Ben." Hartman picked up the photos from the desk and buried them inside the folder on his desk. "If you're hiding something because you're afraid of adultery charges . . ."

"I'm more worried about the assault charges."

"Adultery and assault charges are better than homicide charges!"

Ben closed his eyes and shook his head. "Does it really matter? My career is over either way."

"I'm not worried about your career, I'm worried about you spending the rest of your life in Leavenworth!" Hartman raised his voice, trying to penetrate the thick cloud that had formed in Ben's head. Trying to convince himself that Ben Casper wasn't just another violent soul hiding behind a military uniform. "You're in some shit here! This man was murdered! I'm trying to help you, but I can't eliminate you as a suspect if you can't even offer me a simple explanation as to why you attacked him!"

"I didn't know him that well."

"But you knew him well enough to break his face!"

"I don't want to talk about this anymore." Ben gripped the arms of the chair, a cool defiance building in the tenor of his muscles. "Am I being arrested?"

Agent Hartman glanced at the duffle bag in the corner, his face tightening into hard knots. "Not yet. But I'm going to recommend that your leave be suspended."

"Don't do that to me Leon."

"You're not really giving me much of a choice."

"I have a flight at 1300." A ripple of hot energy crept back into his cheeks. "It's Veteran's Day."

"This is a criminal investigation!" Hartman spit back. "You're under suspicion of killing a fellow officer! I don't think I have to tell you how serious that is!"

"I made a promise, Leon." Ben leaned into the desk as if he were ready to confide some desperate truth. "If it comes down to it, I can live with the murder charge. That's not what's keeping me up at night."

"Look, I'm sorry that you lost someone." Hartman stood up from his desk, steadying himself against the worn furniture. He wondered how long he'd been falling apart like this. How many red flags he'd missed, or ignored, or avoided. "But a lot of us have lost someone. It's not worth throwing your life away."

"That's not for you to decide." Ben sat back in his chair again, staring back with clean, honest eyes. "Why don't you tell me what's really on your mind?"

Agent Hartman tightened his fists on top of his desk, blood running from his heart to his hands. He closed his eyes and swallowed hard before he spoke. "I'm going to request a warrant to search your house this afternoon. And I'm afraid of what I'm going to find." He opened the folder in front of him and stared down at the photos of the murdered captain, the contorted body and the caked blood on the man's chest and face. "You've got a history with this sort of thing. And you and I both know I can't sweep it under the rug this time. I think you should find a good lawyer."

"Anything else?" Ben looked up at him with deadened eyes.

Hartman wrestled against the swirling in his gut and forced out a heavy and terrifying truth. "I think you should consider a sanity board."

"A sanity board?" Ben grunted in his chair. He reached for his neck as if the barbs had cut into his throat on the way out. "Is that what you think of me?"

"You can't even remember enough about last night to defend yourself Ben." Hartman shook his head, the weight of all those red flags bearing down on him as he closed the folder for the final time. "You refused to get help when you had the chance. And now you've got some innocent captain's blood on your hands."

Ben nodded as the blood drained from his face and his hot eyes cooled. "I have go Leon." He stood up from his chair and headed for the door.

"Don't get on that plane Ben." Hartman called after him. "I can't do anything to help you if you if you go AWOL now."

Ben picked up the duffle bag near the door and slung it over his shoulder. "I'm looking at homicide charges, assault charges, possibly even adultery charges. And you want me to break a promise to a dead friend because you're threatening me with an AWOL?"

"And what about the people who care about you Ben? What about me? What about Grace?"

Ben paused in the doorway, lifting his heavy head from the floor. "We both know that she's better off without me." Ben stepped through the doorway and turned the corner, letting the heavy wooden door fall back on its casing, rattling the foundations of the old room.

# Chapter 5
## Minneapolis, MN (2014)

Benjamin Casper felt the snow crunch as he walked, his feet finding their way through the sloppy paths. He held a fresh handful of red and gold blossoms sprinkled with baby's breath as he headed towards the lonely plat at the far end of the cemetery. The flowers were a sad substitute for everything that kept him coming back. For accomplishing a five year old mission that was still lingering in his head.

The sun had slipped behind a row of barren trees, throwing jagged streaks of burnt orange across the cemetery. Rows of tiny American flags lined the headstones, sagging in the wet November air. Casper brought his last cigarette to his parched lips and pulled in an unhealthy drag. He exhaled and watched the ring of smoke uncurl into the late afternoon.

For the first time since Randy's death he was distracted by a more urgent tragedy. The images of Captain Mann's broken body left a permanent imprint on his psyche. They mixed with flashes of genuine recall, angry eyes and flying fists. His imagination filled in the blank spaces, producing synthetic memories that were indistinguishable from hard facts. He gripped the cold steel of an unregistered firearm in his fists, until the thorns dug into his fingers.

He walked past a pair of weary stragglers, shifting uncomfortably at the grave of someone they once loved, not sure how long to stay or how to walk away. They looked for cues from the strangers around them, people who understood the protocol. Casper nodded to them as he walked on by to let them know there was no judgment here. Solace, if you could find it. But coping wasn't something to be criticized, no matter how unconventional or undignified you went about it.

Randy's marker lay just a few yards ahead at the end of a long line of simple, unadorned stones. He could just about make out the place from the path he was on, just behind the next row of headstones. He honed in on a small tuft of pale blue flowers, laid delicately in the snow in front of Randy's stone.

"Looks like she beat me again." Casper shook his head as he shuffled forward, leaving large prints in the snow as he went. He glanced around him, to see if there was still some trace of her. Only footprints. Small feet. The woman he'd been searching for had kneeled in this very spot, only a few hours ago.

Casper kneeled beside the marker and brushed the snow from the engraving. SSG Randy Koury. 1976 – 2008. He set his trim bouquet of red and gold beside the blue carnations left by Randy's unknown visitor, leaning the simple arrangement against the cold stone with a tiny American flag sagging in the middle.

"I'll catch her one of these days Randy." Casper addressed the headstone in front of him. He took another drag of his cigarette. "Whoever she is. I won't give up on you."

Casper straightened the tiny American flag that was stuck in the snow beside the flowers. Pressing out the wrinkles in the wet fabric.

"I can't wait to meet her. I'm glad you found someone who loves you so much. Maybe the two of you can come down to Leavenworth sometime. Grace will make us dinner."

Casper sat back, sucking on his cigarette and staring at the display in front of him. He reached inside the lining of his coat and pulled out a flask of whiskey. He took one biting sip and held the container close to his chest.

"Grace doesn't believe me you know. She thinks I'm imagining things. Seeing ghosts in graveyards." Casper took another hard swallow from the flask in his hand. He took another deep tug on the cigarette in his mouth and thought about the charges against him. The possibility that he could find himself in Leavenworth Penitentiary before another year passed. That he might never find the woman with the blue carnations.

"I'm going to need a good lawyer if I'm going to find her for you."

Casper glanced up from the cold snow crunching beneath him. His eyes followed the mysterious set of footprints as they left the headstone and wound their way back to the main path. He distinguished them for as long as he could, before they blended in with the footsteps of a hundred other lost souls, saying their goodbyes and re-opening scars that never seem to heal.

He sat quietly, his cool flask of whiskey still pressed tight against his chest. He still didn't know if he had pulled the trigger. If he had lost his head long enough to take Mann out of this world. He searched his soul for some sliver of remorse, wondering if it were possible to regret things he couldn't remember.

He lifted his cigarette to his lips for another quick puff, staring into the cold engraving on the stone in front of him. He remembered a soft face and a familiar scent that had saved him once before. A swirl of precarious faith filled his heart.

"I don't know if I can face her again, Randy. I don't know if I have that kind of courage left in me." He took another small sip of liquor that burned his throat as it slid down into his chest. "But she might be our only chance."

# Chapter 6
## Minneapolis, MN (2014)

"This isn't me, Ma'am. This is all a big misunderstanding."

Lieutenant Sharon watched Sergeant Matthews paw at his hands. He had mechanics' hands, coarse and stained. His eyes wandered around the room, anywhere that he wouldn't have to look her in the face. He raised his head just long enough to check her uniform, staring at the empty right shoulder under the American flag where a deployment patch should have been.

Sharon looked at him with a pair of crisp blue eyes, her expression both patient and controlled. She swept a stray strand of her dark hair into the thick bun at the back of her head and scanned the paperwork in front of her. It was always the same, formalized to the point of absurdity. Leaving just the thinnest imprint of uniqueness that was buried in every soldier's case.

"How often do you use cocaine, Sergeant Matthews?" She was sensitive, but direct.

"That's just it Ma'am. I don't." His bowed body pulsed with life.

"You tested positive for cocaine and marijuana on your last urinalysis."

"That was one time Ma'am. I swear to you." The sergeant shook his head as he spoke, repeating a familiar phrase that lost more meaning every time she heard it. He looked directly at her for the first time since walking into her office. Their eyes met briefly, before she noticed him staring at the bare spot on her left shoulder again. "I don't have a drug problem."

Lieutenant Sharon watched the sergeant slink back into himself, defensive and tense. She paged through the file again, sorting through deployment dates and family history, searching for some clue as to what she was dealing with. Whether this was just another reckless kid with an aversion to responsibility, or something a little more fragile. "How many times have you deployed Sergeant Matthews?"

"Twice Ma'am."

She nodded quietly, underlining the dates in front of her. "One of them was a pretty long one, wasn't it?"

"22 months in country. That was during the surge. We were supposed to be there 18 months. Our tour was extended."

She nodded again, making absent-minded notes in the margins of her notebook. "And other than the extension, how was the deployment for you?"

"How was the deployment?" His lips curled into sarcastic smile. "Well it wasn't a damn vacation, but it was nothing I can't handle."

"You had some problems at work when you came back?"

"Yeah, my boss demoted me, moved me to another office, cut my hours. They swore it had nothing to do with the deployment, but I doubt that."

"Did you talk to your commander about that? Anyone from JAG?"

"No need. I quit after a few months."

"You were unemployed for awhile?"

"Yes, Ma'am. I eventually found another job, but then I got deployed the second time."

"How about your family? Were the deployments pretty hard on them?"

"My wife and I had some issues, yeah. We were separated for awhile, but she's back home now. We have a baby. I don't mean any disrespect Ma'am, but I don't see what this has to do with my case. Can't you just tell me where I stand with all this?"

Lieutenant Sharon put her pen down and directed her full attention to the sergeant sitting across from her. He had a red bull emblem fixed to his right arm, a solid black oval with a silver cow skull in the center. He'd put in almost four years overseas, when the entirety of her career had been spent behind desks. She stood up from her chair and walked in front of her desk, leaning against the dusty furniture with Matthews's file and her notepad in hand.

"Well, the Commander is looking to separate you from military service, but I think you already knew that."

"Yes Ma'am."

"I think if you hadn't been promoted during your last deployment, we might be having a different conversation. But you're not a new soldier, you're a sergeant. You're supposed to be setting an example. If the Commander retains you after you tested positive for cocaine use, what kind of a message does that send to the unit?"

"The Army is my family Ma'am. It's the only thing I have left that I'm proud of. Look, I know I screwed up bad, but they have to give me another chance."

Sergeant Matthews looked directly at her for the second time. He held his gaze steady in spite of the slight tremble in his voice. That barely perceptible sliver of fragility that Sharon had been looking for. She took a quick breath and looked the soldier straight in the eye.

"Well, you have over 6 years of commendable service. You can request a board. The Brigade lawyers will put on evidence that you tested positive, that your drug use is incompatible with military values and that you need to be removed from further service. We'll put on evidence that you've served your country honorably, that you're an asset to the Army and you ought to be given a second chance. The board, rather than the Commander, will decide whether what happens to you."

"And what are my chances if we go before a board?"

Lieutenant Sharon glanced down at her notes, scribbles mostly, rough ideas of what she might say when this question came up, as it inevitably did. Getting the truth out of him may very well hinge on how she phrased the next few sentences. "I'm going to be straight with you."

"I would appreciate that Ma'am."

"I don't think you're being honest with me about your drug use. And I don't think the board is going to think you're being honest about your drug use. I think you're a good soldier. Remarkable, actually. But in my experience, good soldiers don't just wake up one day and decide they're going to try cocaine. There's usually something else going on that's maybe a little more than they can handle at the time."

Sergeant Matthews stiffened in his seat, trying to keep his composure. "With all due respect Ma'am, you don't know enough about me to make that call."

"That may be true Sergeant. But that's not the sort of argument that's going to keep you in the Army." She kept her eyes pinned on him.

"So what am I supposed to do?"

"We have seven days to submit a rebuttal statement to the Commander, asking him to reconsider his decision to separate you. We can write that letter one of two ways. That letter can explain how the deployments have affected you. How they've affected your job, your financial situation, your marriage. You can admit to having a substance abuse problem, meet with a counselor, tell the Commander that you're doing everything you can to overcome your addiction and to meet the standards expected of the Army. Or your rebuttal can say that you only tried cocaine one time and this is all a big misunderstanding. It's up to you."

He looked down at his hands again, losing himself in the web of grit and sweat lining his skin. "Can I think about this for a little while?"

"Of course. I'll request an extension so you can take a few days to think about it." Lieutenant Sharon reached behind her and pulled out a small card. She glanced over the information and passed it to the soldier sitting across from her.

"What's this?" He took the card between his fingers.

"This is the name and number of our substance abuse counselor and the chaplain, should you decide you need to talk to somebody."

"Thank you Ma'am." The sergeant nodded his head as he stood up from his chair.

Lieutenant Sharon followed Sergeant Matthews out of the office. He didn't seem to appreciate her time or shake her hand, but he did take the card she had given him and tucked it safely inside the chest pocket of his uniform.

Sharon watched him step outside the office door, then turned towards her paralegal at the computer to her right.

"Sergeant Anthony, I'm going to need you to request an extension on Sergeant Matthews's rebuttal statement to the Commander."

"Yes Ma'am." The young woman extended one arm to accept the file without diverting her eyes from the computer screen. "How long of an extension would you like?"

"Seven days should be enough."

"Not a problem Ma'am."

"Sergeant Anthony." Sharon paused in front of the young woman's desk, waiting for her to look up from her computer. "I really appreciate you coming in today. I know this isn't how you planned on spending your Veteran's Day."

"Somebody's gotta do it." Her lips curled into a rough smile. "Just part of defense work, right? I clipped an article from this morning's paper for you. It's sitting on top of that stack on the table."

Lieutenant Sharon picked up the clipping from atop the disarranged paper. A short expose on a local bridal shop that had been cut from its tiny space between stories of the drawdown and personnel cuts.

"What is this?" Sharon twisted her eyebrows.

"It's a bridal shop up in Blaine. They're giving away free wedding dresses to military brides. All you have to do is write in and tell them your military love story."

Sharon smiled as she skimmed through the first few paragraphs of the article. She quickly got the idea and put the clipping down. "That's a pretty gesture. You know we're not really doing the big show, we're just going to go down to the courthouse and signing the papers."

"How incredibly practical of you, Ma'am." Sergeant Anthony took her eyes from the computer screen, unsurprised. "Obviously, you don't have to have a big fancy wedding, but you should at least have a dress."

"There's not much sense in getting a dress to wear in front of the mirror and then pack it away in the closet for 20 years."

"I did mention it's free, right?"

Lieutenant Sharon smiled again, a sad sort of smile as she glanced down at the article one last time. She played with the simple engagement ring around her finger, running her thumb along the smooth silver and jagged stones. "What if I don't know how our love story ends?"

"No one knows Ma'am. That's part of the adventure." Sergeant Anthony swung her chair back towards her computer monitor. "Are you about ready for lunch?"

"Yes, I'm starving."

The phone rang as Lieutenant Sharon reached for her patrol cap.

"Trial Defense Services, this is Sergeant Anthony." The sergeant answered the phone with a sour grin. "There's no Captain Sharon here, we have a Lieutenant Sharon."

"Take a message." Sharon rolled her eyes.

"She just stepped out the door Sir, can I have her call you back?" Sergeant Anthony grabbed a pen and began jotting down a phone number. "And you're calling from where again, Sir? I'll let her know. You too Sir."

"Who was that?" Sharon lifted her head at the gratuitous "Sirs."

"That was the Chief of Military Justice from Fort Leavenworth. Major Benjamin Casper." Sergeant Anthony finished scribbling the information on the slip of paper.

Sharon paused where she stood. "Major Casper?"

"He says he knows you from Charlottesville. He's in town for a few days, wants to know if you'll meet him for coffee."

Lieutenant Sharon stepped across the room to Sergeant Anthony's desk and took the message in her fingers. Just a name and a number that didn't belong in her hands. She was tempted to tear the thing to pieces.

"If you don't mind my asking Ma'am, why haven't you been promoted to captain yet?" Sergeant Anthony got up from her desk and pulled her own patrol cap out of her cargo pocket.

"My promotion was suspended for a year." Sharon looked up from the note in her hands, searching for the best way to explain the lieutenant rank on her chest. "Someone from our class was involved in an article 134."

Sergeant Anthony looked up intrigued, though her raised eyebrows suggested that she wasn't familiar enough with the UCMJ to get the reference.

"Adultery." Sharon explained. "The guilty parties never came forward, so they punished the entire class."

Sergeant Anthony's jaw dropped. "I'm so sorry Ma'am. I had no idea."

"The suspension was lifted last month. My promotion packet is being processed, it shouldn't be too much longer." Sharon folded up the phone number as trepidly as Sergeant Matthews had treated the phone numbers she had given him, and tucked it away in her uniform pocket.

"Did they ever find out who it was Ma'am? The adultery?"

"No, they didn't." Sharon shook her head as she and Anthony headed towards the door. "But everyone has their suspicions."

# Chapter 7
## Minneapolis, MN (2014)

Benjamin Casper stared into the amber brew in his pint glass, wondering how many he could suck down before the room went dark. He sat at a small table in a quiet coffee bar with yellow lights and shiny wood paneling on the floor and walls. He sat with his back to the wall so he could see and hear everything around him, but the alcohol was already blurring the edges.

He took a quick, cowardly swallow. He needed the alcohol to get him through this conversation. Whatever dark turn it might take. She should have been married by now, with another name, another rank, no trace left of Lieutenant Sharon. She should have been Captain Chase or whatever the hell that Sergeant's last name was. He tempted fate by picking up the phone and asking for a shadow. It wasn't the first time that fate called his bluff.

He spotted her about a hundred feet in the distance. A resolute woman in a long winter coat. Her shape and stature were familiar. The way she tilted her head to embrace the cold air. She swept the deep brunette hair from her face, revealing a pair of glassy blue eyes. She flashed a faint hint of recognition.

Casper felt as if the wind had been knocked out of him. She had seen him, just as the memories started bubbling up, disconnected and trivial. It started with the subtle tingling of her first name, gently brushing the tip of his tongue. Jamie.

The little bells of the coffee shop door jingled as she stepped inside, a gust of cold November air coasting in with her. She gave him an uncomfortable smile as she moved past him, heading towards the counter to put in her order. He followed her with his eyes, already picking up on the comforting smell of coffee and lilacs.

The fact that she was here gave his heart relief, and yet, he couldn't shake the feeling that he had hurt her somehow. He had almost forgotten how it felt to hurt something that was innocent. That didn't deserve it.

She took a seat across from him, balancing a hot cup of dark roast in both hands. His pulse slowed the moment she was near him. Her cool blue eyes like a powerful sedative.

"I thought you wanted to meet for coffee." She motioned to the amber brew in front of him.

"I figured you were more likely to accept the invitation if it was coffee." Casper rested his hands on the security of the bitter ale in front on him. She was unlikely to come at all if she knew the disturbing truths he had to tell her, carefully corralled just underneath his skin.

"With all due respect Sir," Jamie stirred a packet of sugar into the warm drink in front of her, watching the crystals melt and spin in the swirling brew. "You drink far too much."

"So I've been told." He took another defiant swallow from his pint glass, trying to hold on to that addled feeling in his brain when he was too numb to sense danger.

"What brings you to town?"

"Visiting an old friend."

"Anyone I know?"

"No. No one you know." Casper shook his heavy head, still surprised at how much a simple phrase could injure him. The more time passed, the more friends he collected that didn't know Randy. That would never know Randy. Life kept moving at the same pace, ignorant to the fact that he was still stuck in a time and war that wouldn't end. "Why haven't you made Captain yet?"

Sharon looked up with a stilted glare. "You know perfectly well why I haven't made Captain yet, Sir."

"The rest of the class has been promoted."

"The rest of the *active* army has been promoted. The National Guard has a few more hoops to jump through. The paperwork is being processed."

Most of the people he'd met in the military were a little broken on the inside. They craved chaos because it was where they'd come from, and where they felt the most comfortable. They came into the Army because they were drawn to the idea of having some control over that chaos. Of confronting it on their own terms.

Guardsmen were a different sort of lost soul. They had to possess enough of a taste for stability to hold down a civilian job between deployments. To masquerade as whole people. They were damaged, to be certain, but they were either in denial about it, or there was something in them that was still fighting for some shred of normalcy. Jamie Sharon was National Guard. He could see it in the way that she walked. There was a lot of fight in her step, and a lot of apology. And as much as he needed answers about this girl, this woman, he was terrified of what he might find if he pried her open.

Jamie brought the coffee cup to her lips, barely wetting her mouth with the steaming brew. Casper watched her pull in the drink with soft lips. He fought the urge to take the cup and kiss her the way he'd meant to do for so long. "I feel like I owe you an apology."

She shook her head and set down the coffee cup. "I can't take any more of your apologies Sir."

Her response was so painfully ambiguous. Somewhere between 'you have nothing to apologize for' and 'no amount of apologies could excuse what you've put me through.'

"I don't even remember what happened that night." His head shook under the weight of the pronouncement. How could he not remember if he had kissed her? If he had touched her hair? If he had undressed her? Made love to her while his wife called his cell phone over and over again? Had he told her he loved her? He couldn't bring himself to imagine anything else.

"Perhaps it's for the best."

Her simple, direct statement was far worse than having her tear into him. He'd rather she slap him, hold up a vile mirror and show him what he really was in her eyes. "Is there anything I can do?"

"You can forget about it." She looked at him with those pale blue eyes, the scent of lilacs coating every sharp word. "I've given up enough over what happened in Charlottesville, I just want to let it go and move on."

She stirred her coffee with a little more purpose. Casper was captured by the strength of her fingers. The glint of silver that was wrapped carefully around her fourth finger. There were only two logical explanations for the ring. Either Sergeant Chase was uncommonly understanding about the episode in Charlottesville, or Sharon hadn't found the nerve to tell him.

"Looks like your sergeant finally put a ring on your finger."

Jamie glanced down at the ring, almost as if she were making sure it was still there. "We haven't settled on a date yet."

"Congratulations. He's a lucky man." He took another cool swallow from the pint glass that was draining in front of him. She took another guarded sip from her hot cup of coffee.

"And how are you, Sir?" She seemed genuine, though she might have been simply digging for something substantial to fill the empty air. "What's it like to be the Chief of Military Justice?"

"I'm being court-martialed." The words slipped past his filter.

Jamie's eyes widened behind her cup of coffee. The news rattled her. Broke past the disturbing, collegial façade and found some hint of concern buried underneath. "What did you say?"

"I haven't officially been charged yet. But it's coming." Casper leaned into the table, hoping to grasp onto that hidden shred of concern for all it was worth. "As soon as I return to base I'll be placed under arrest."

"For what?"

He soaked in the scent of lilacs coming from the woman across from him, anticipating the change in her expression, the change in her voice, the change in her posture the moment he said the word out loud. "Homicide."

Sharon's grip on her coffee mug tightened until a tiny splash of the heated brew spilled across her hands. Her fingers and face muscles flinched. "Homicide?"

"I was in a fight outside a bar." He felt a terrible sucking, like the pressure being drained from the air. She stared at him, waiting, he could only assume, for something to keep her from getting up and walking out the door. He focused on Jamie's pale fingers against the table. She still hadn't wiped the spilled coffee from her hands. "I hurt the guy. Eight hours later, he was found dead on post with three bullet holes in him."

He swallowed another taste of bitter ale and felt the weight of all the hidden details burning beneath his skin. He didn't volunteer the dead man's name, or the fact that his memory was in shreds. He didn't tell her that he'd gotten on a plane against orders and was AWOL as he sat across from her, sipping his beer.

Just like Grace and Leon, she already thought he was guilty.

"What about the gun?" She slipped into character without missing a beat, as if defending the powerless was a natural instinct. "Did the police find a weapon?"

"They're still investigating." He shook his head, still coming to terms with the fact that CID was probably rifling through his house as he sat there, chasing down ghosts and sifting through the cinders of old flames. "I had a gun in the house for a while. It was purchased illegally. Unregistered. I don't know where it is now."

"Is this the gun you brought home from Iraq?" Jamie lifted her wet fingers from her coffee cup, finally registering the fact that she had spilled.

"How do you know about that?" He reached for a napkin and handed it to her. She let go of her coffee cup and began to sponge the spill from her fingers.

"You told me Sir."

The certainty in her voice restrained him in his seat. He ran a hand over his chin and mouth, trying to call up more lost memories.

"What do they have on you?" She interrupted.

"Not much, that I'm aware of. I may have his blood on my clothes from the fight."

"What was it about?" She asked quietly. "The fight?"

"Just a girl." He seemed so sure when he answered Leon, but things seemed foggier now. Messier. As if his mind was protecting him from truths that were too sharp, too vicious for him to process all at once.

"Are you sure they'll charge you?" She lifted her blue eyes from the dark coffee that remained in her cup, piecing together fragments of evidence from thin air.

42

"Fairly certain."

"What can I do to help?"

"I need a lawyer." The words slipped from his lips before he had a chance to prepare for her response. But he couldn't see himself facing a court-martial without the comfort of those pale blue eyes, or that warm scent of lilacs.

"You want me to defend you?" She glanced up from her slick fingers.

"You're defense counsel, are you not?"

"I've never done a court-martial Sir." She protested as she continued to pat down the mess on the table in front of her. "I've never handled a homicide."

"I trust you Jamie." He reached for what was left in his pint glass and swallowed a dose of lukewarm security. "You were the class honor grad, if I remember correctly."

"Are you sure they'll even allow me to defend you?"

"Will you take the case if they do?"

Sharon glanced down at the silver ring nestled in between her sticky fingers. He saw the discomfort lining her face and he prepared to write her off as another traumatic loss for which he'd never find closure. He thought about how much he still hadn't told her. Everything that Leon was passing off to some junior prosecutor, who was already preparing the case against him.

"I'll help you Ben." His first name rolled off her tongue and bit into the phony formality between them. "How far is Fort Leavenworth?"

# Chapter 8
## Fort Leavenworth, KS (2014)

Pamela Hunt sat in an uncomfortable chair, staring at her hands. She was absorbed in her long white fingers, that had become so capable and so daring since she'd joined the military. She was comforted by the sight of her clean, smooth skin. Her thick red hair was pulled back into a tight bun and her grey eyes were accented with green eyeliner. She needed the subtle splash of color to give her some sense of femininity, all of it masked in the genderless camo print uniform with the captain bars on her chest.

"Did your office tell you what this is about?" Agent Hartman finally spoke to her. He had an old face and white hair, and wore a worn flannel shirt that almost covered the pudge in his midsection. He leaned against his desk and folded his arms over his chest like he had something difficult and shocking to tell her, though there wasn't much that would shock her these days.

"They didn't." She noticed a small increase in her blood pressure. She didn't like the fact that he wore no rank. That there was no clear indication of who was in charge of the conversation.

"Did you have a chance to look at the police blotter this morning?"

"I didn't." She tried to keep a cool expression. She calmed her breathing and waited for him to get to the point.

"Maybe you should do that now." He reached for a thick accordion file on the desk behind him and brought it in front of her.

Pamela Hunt looked at the file with curious eyes. She reached to take it from him and he glanced at the sheen on her fingernails, well-manicured and clearly out of regulation. Hunt stared back at him, defending her indiscretion with perfect resolve. She waited for him to correct her, but he simply stared, disapproving. It was enough to confirm that he was likely some warrant officer who should be addressing her as Ma'am, civilian clothes or not.

She closed her fingers around the file and took it into her lap. She opened the end and pulled out a stack of paperwork. It felt heavy enough to be a serious charge and her throat tightened. She paged through the file and reached for the police blotter, glazing over the black and white print. An icy dread filled her veins as she recognized the name in the third line of the report.

> Victim is a black male, 5'10," 173 pounds. Identification found on the victim indicates that the victim is a captain in the United States Army by the name of James Anthony Mann. Victim is 31 years old. Victim is dressed in civilian clothing, consisting of jeans and a white tee shirt. There are two gunshot wounds in the left chest cavity and one in the forehead. Victim had on him a cell phone and a set of car keys that appear to belong to a silver Corsica parked a few yards from the running trail where the body was found.

Pamela Hunt froze in her seat, still absorbing the facts, dates, details. She flipped through the paperwork and pulled out the photos of the crime scene, her fingers tingling as she focused on the images. His body was laid out in the dirt, a pained, almost remorseful look frozen into the contours of his face. There was a dark hole in his forehead where the bullet had struck, leaving a whimsical pattern, almost like a star.

She remembered, vividly, the last time she saw him, and was surprised at how little she felt as she stared at the photos. Perhaps there wasn't that much to cry over. He had been full of lies and ego, like half the officers she knew. And yet she couldn't seem to calm her racing heart.

"Everything okay, Ma'am?"

She took no notice of the fact that he had addressed her as 'Ma'am.' She was still negotiating the adrenaline in her face and fingers. She tried to swallow her nerves and looked up at the special agent with a forced calm. "Shouldn't Major Casper be reviewing this?"

"Major Casper is our main suspect." Agent Hartman closed his lips over his teeth as if it pained him to say it. He directed her back towards the file in her hands. "There's another police report in the file. From earlier that evening. You should take a look at that next."

Captain Hunt paged back towards the beginning of the file with a bit more urgency, sorting through the layers of documents for something that looked like another police summary. She found the one page report near the front of the file. Another small, simple paragraph with overwhelming implications.

> Officers responded to a call involving an altercation between two bar patrons at the Eagle Lounge in downtown Leavenworth. The individuals involved were no longer on the premises when the police arrived. Eyewitness reports indicate that a tall white male assaulted and severely injured a black male of medium build in the parking lot behind the establishment. One eyewitness recorded the license plates of the subjects' vehicles before they left the scene. The vehicle belonging to the alleged assailant was traced to a Benjamin Lee Casper. The vehicle belonging to the alleged victim was traced to a James Anthony Mann.

The temperature in the stale room rose. The air felt heavy and uncomfortable. She found herself sifting through a stack of evidence against the Chief of Military Justice, who had gone to bed last night with liquor on his breath and blood on his hands. She felt the pulse of her racing heart pounding in her fingertips. A rare opportunity had fallen into her hands. To see to it that there were consequences for his actions. Even if it was years later, there was still a chance to force justice to correct an unfortunate mistake.

"How well did you know Major Casper?" Agent Hartman asked her over his tense fists.

"Not well." She lied with wide open eyes. "We went to school together in Charlottesville. He was a colleague. So was the victim."

Hartman leaned forward, taking his hands from his chin and posting them on the desk behind him. He looked straight into her grey eyes. "How well did you know the victim?"

"The JAG Corps is fairly small." She nodded, poised as glass. "Most of us have crossed paths at some point. But few of us are close."

"You seemed a little upset when you pulled out the pictures." He raised his eyebrows, still looking for something a little more intimate.

"This is my first homicide." She heard the words echo in her own ears.

"Are your prior relationships going to interfere with your ability to be impartial in this case?" Hartman looked down at the floor as if he were hiding his own secrets. As if he were asking the question of himself as well as her.

She bent her eyes on the case file under her glossy nails. "I didn't care for either of these men enough to jeopardize my career."

"Just so you understand, we don't have much to go on at this point. It all depends on what comes back from the crime lab."

"There may be more here than you think." She reached into a cargo pocket and pulled out a small brown notepad. She took a pen from her left sleeve and scratched out another familiar name in shaky letters, Aaron Cade, CPT. She tore the page from her notebook and handed it to the CID agent.

"What's this?" Agent Hartman glanced at the name on the slip of paper.

"A lead on a witness. I don't know where he's stationed or how to contact him. Can your investigators track him down?"

"If he's still in the military, we can find him." Hartman nodded as he folded up the slip of paper and hid it in his wallet. "What I need from you is an honest assessment of the evidence."

She could feel the suspicion in his eyes. It wasn't the first time a seasoned soldier had underestimated her. They had a hard time envisioning her with a ruck sack strapped to her back and an M-16 at her side, doing time in the trenches like the men. But she was every bit as lethal as they were, and would have no problems putting Casper away.

"What evidence have you collected so far?" Captain Hunt began paging through the report, searching for specific slivers of data.

"We searched the Major's house this afternoon. We found some bloody clothing that was sent to forensics. We don't know yet if it's the victim's blood. Even if it is, it could just be from the assault at the bar. You should know that he's not contesting the assault. Only the homicide.

"Why the homicide?" Hunt's grey eyes flashed.

"Because he doesn't remember anything after leaving the bar."

"So we may be looking at a sanity board?"

Agent Hartman shook his head, tugging at his bottom lip and staring at the floor again. "I doubt he'll be requesting a sanity board."

"You must have found something else on him besides the assault?" She continued to page through the file in her hands. She came upon the autopsy report and glanced over the front and backside diagrams of the body, trying to glean something from the illegible notes in the margins. She flipped to the next page and scanned a short synopsis about trace amounts of pepper spray discovered in the victim's mouth and throat.

"We recovered a small canister of pepper spray from Major Casper's home." Hartman responded before the questions reached her lips. "It was one of those key chain attachments that they sell at the shoppettes. His wife insisted that it was hers. It's being analyzed for fingerprints."

Hunt drew in a long swell of air and continued paging through the report. She flipped forward to more drawings and diagrams of human anatomy, identifying the entrance and exit wounds of each bullet. "How about the weapon?"

"Nothing so far. We were able to find some casings and a fragment of a bullet that was lodged in the victim's head. Forensics should be able to tell us the caliber of the weapon that was used, possibly even the make and model, but without a test fire, we can't tie it to a specific firearm. The victim did have a personal firearm registered to him at Fort Riley that seems to be missing."

"What about witnesses?" She paused to review a cold list of phone numbers, incoming and outgoing calls dating back to early October.

"There's very little." Hartman crossed his arms and leaned back into his desk. "The victim called his wife shortly before he was shot. I spoke to her personally. She said he was drunk and rambling about losing his career. They'd had an argument that evening and he took off, but she didn't know where he had gone. Fort Riley's only about a 2 hour drive from here. We haven't been able to confirm why he was here on post."

Captain Hunt spotted the highlighted phone number in the phone log, noting the very time and place where Captain Mann had spoken to his wife for the very last time.

"There was also an unanswered phone call to the CID office at 11:28." Hartman's voice was muted and terse. "The office was closed for the holidays, but something stopped him from leaving a message."

"Something like a bullet?" She arched her eyebrows.

"Possibly."

Captain Hunt closed the file in her lap, confident it contained at least the raw elements she needed to prove he was guilty. "Where is Major Casper now?"

Hartman stiffened against the old desk, the truth hanging like a weight on the back of his tongue. "He's AWOL. He took a flight to Minneapolis against orders. We'll place him under arrest when he arrives at the airport tomorrow afternoon."

"Are you sure he'll be on the plane?"

"He'll be on the plane." Hartman glared again at her painted nails.

She stood up and stared back at him, her hands resting on the back of the uncomfortable chair. "I'm going to recommend that the command place him in pre-trial confinement."

"Do you really think that's necessary?" Hartman lifted his chin and narrowed his eyes.

"He's already proven that he's a flight risk and you're missing a murder weapon. Every hour he's not in custody is an opportunity for him to destroy evidence." And just like that, she changed the trajectory of the conversation. Took a man's life into her hands with little more than raw suspicion and made a move to place him under lock and key. "Has defense counsel been detailed?"

"Major Casper's made a specific request for representation. A First Lieutenant from the National Guard by the name of Jamie Sharon. You know her?"

Captain Hunt heard the name ring between her ears, breaking against an old wall of suspicion and blame. "Yes, I know her." Hunt bit her bottom lip and squeezed the damning file between her fingers. "As I said, most of us have crossed paths. But few of us are close."

# Chapter 9
## Minneapolis, MN (2014)

It started with a simple whimper that grew into a low moan and a constant scratching.

Matt Chase was crouched on the floor near the head of the bed, trying to coax out the panicked dog with a broken piece of hot dog. He wore an old pair of jeans and a faded t-shirt, his dark hair still well within Army regulation. An old habit that he hadn't been able to shake.

"C'mon Reese." He called to the Border Collie under the bed. "Take the hot dog. You know you want it."

He heard a comfortable click as a key turned in the front door and he knew she was home. He listened for the sounds of her familiar routine in the kitchen. She was probably pulling off her shoes, setting her things on the table, and spotting the pan of half eaten lasagna that had been waiting for her.

"Matt?" Her voice bled through the hallways.

"In the bedroom." He called back.

He watched Jamie step into the bedroom and absorb the scene, releasing a tired breath as she moved. "What happened this time?"

"Veteran's Day." Matt looked up with a shrug and a smile. He watched Jamie make her way near the bed, an alarmed crease folding over her eyes. He winked to set her at ease, and continued to wave the hot dog into the empty space under the bed while the scratching and whimpering continued. "Some kids were setting off fireworks down by the park. They spooked him."

"Did you give him some Benadryl?" She crouched down on the floor and lifted the comforter to peek at her dog holed up under the furniture.

"It's in the hot dog. But he doesn't seem to want it."

"He's probably getting sick of hot dogs."

"Can't say I blame him." Matt stood up and stepped away from the frantic scratching under the bed, uneaten hot dog in hand. "Maybe we should try to sneak it into a piece of lasagna?"

"Matt, I'm so sorry." She closed her eyes and sat up on her knees, biting into her bottom lip. "I should've called."

"No harm done." He brushed through her hair with the tips of his fingers and she lifted her blue eyes up towards him. "I'm sure you will next time, right?"

She nodded and stood up beside him, wrapping her arms around his waist and laying her heavy head against his chest.

He kissed her forehead softly, his free hand nested at the nape of her neck. The scratching and groaning filling up the empty space around them.

"C'mon, let's see if we can take care of him."

Matt rubbed her back and separated himself from her loose embrace. He headed towards the kitchen, digging the dog's medication out of the uneaten hot dog. He set the powdery pill on the countertop and tossed the hot dog in the trash.

He turned and saw Jamie come into the kitchen behind him and take a seat at the table. She massaged little circles in the front of her scalp, staring into the drying pan of lasagna, the sauce and cheese already setting and crusting around the edges.

"I didn't know you were planning on making dinner."'

"Well, I wasn't. I wanted to take you out for Veteran's Day. But Reese heard the fireworks go off and started tearing apart the carpet." Matt caught her staring into the abandoned pan and reached across the table to take it out of her line of vision. "Don't worry about dinner Jamie. That's what we have microwaves for right? Are you hungry?"

"Yes."

"Good. We'll make one for you. One for the head case under the bed." Matt cut two generous pieces of lasagna and slid them onto a large plate. He set the microwave to re-heat and put two minutes on the timer. The buzz of the microwave finally cancelling out the noise of the frightened dog in the next room.

"So what's the deal, you're not only working Veteran's Day, but you're working late too?" He meant to change the subject. To find some way to put a smile back on her face. But she seemed worn. From something a little more significant than an unpleasant workday.

"Not quite." She took her hands away from the soreness in her scalp and began examining her fingers, casually checking the silver band on her finger. "An old friend from JAG school is in town. He asked me to meet him for coffee after work."

Matt raised his eyebrows at the vague reference to Charlottesville. "Anyone I know?"

"Major Casper."

Matt tried to nod without letting the fever creep into his face. The same faceless major that had interrupted their phone call, just as he was telling her he loved her. She had no idea how much he'd overheard of their conversation, or how much sleep he'd lost over those desperate, whispered words. How many times he'd bit his tongue when too many questions crossed his mind or how often he wondered why a married man had come to her room so late at night. Drunk and burning to apologize for something rash and cruel.

She seemed uncomfortable bringing up his name, like she was concerned she might give herself away. By emphasizing the wrong syllables, stretching out uncomfortable sounds, fidgeting, avoiding eye contact. There was a story and a lesson hiding behind that discomfort. But he knew better than to ask for specifics.

"The bomb technician? How's he adjusting to life behind a desk?"

"He's being court-martialed. For murder." Jamie seemed to have a hard time getting the unpleasant news past her throat, but she didn't seem surprised. If anything, her cold stare told him that she knew he was guilty.

He stared back at her with wide, sober eyes.

"He wants me to defend him." Jamie turned towards him and brushed a tired hand through her thick, dark hair. "Down in Fort Leavenworth."

"Are you going to do it?" Matt stumbled.

"I don't know." She shook her head and glanced down at the floor. "I don't know what kind of evidence they have against him. I haven't even seen the file yet."

"You don't know if he's guilty?" Matt leaned back against the counter, hoping for an honest, authentic reaction.

"He's unstable at times." She tried to hide her suspicions from him, but an unmistakable fog had formed in her eyes, hiding some crucial dark matter from him. "But that doesn't make him a killer."

"He's a soldier, Jamie." Matt stared into the floor, struggling to lift his head and look her in the eye. "That's what soldiers do. Only difference between a war hero and a murderer is instability."

Jamie went still in her chair. A quiet descended and the sound of Reese's breathing and scratching took over the room.

Matt almost felt guilty breaking her phony resolve. She somehow managed to put the whole ugly business of war out of her mind when she was defending her alcoholics and AWOLs. But whether she recognized it or not, most of her clients had taken a life at one point or another. Even he had fired his weapon at someone who got a little too close to the wire in Iraq. It wasn't something they talked about, but he felt the need to make a point and it sunk in like lead.

He watched her massage her palms, ironing out the stress.

"Something tells me you'll take the case regardless." He wrestled with how much he could truly blame her for whatever had happened in Charlottesville. They might not be caught in another twisted conversation about Benjamin Casper if he had been clear from the beginning about how much she meant to him. "You're not the type to say no to a friend."

The microwave beeped. Matt turned to open the door and pulled out the plate of re-heated lasagna. He transferred one slice to a clean plate and brought it over to Jamie, making it a point to squeeze her hand before he turned away, trying to communicate something that kept getting lost in translation.

He turned towards the kitchen counter and hid the Benadryl deep inside the warm layers of pasta and cheese that remained.

54

When the medicine was completely covered, he headed down the hallway towards the soft cries and scratching.

He crept into the bedroom and lowered himself to the floor near the head of the bed. He lifted the comforter and glanced at Reese, curled into a ball of nerves with hurried breathing as he tried to burrow his way into the floor. The carpet beneath him was shredded into a hundred strands.

"Take it easy Reese. You're not in any danger here." He set the plate of lasagna on the floor and slid it under the bed. The frightened dog caught the smell and turned his head. He watched the plate slide closer and his breathing slowed. He looked up at Matt with lonely eyes, and then back down at the plate of food. A momentary calm settled over him and he edged towards the plate. He snuck the first few bites, cautious and timid, until the pleasure reflex snapped on. For a few fragile seconds he forgot his fear and wolfed down the food in front of him.

Matt felt a surge of hope for the lost animal.

"There you go buddy." He reached his hand under the bed and rubbed the dog's soft head. "You're going make it."

He let the dog lick the sauce off the plate and then took it back. He made his way back to the kitchen with the empty plate in his hands, and a relieved sort of quiet settling through the house.

Jamie looked up from her own re-heated dinner as he set the plate in the kitchen sink and sprayed it down.

"He ate it?"

"Every last bite." Matt was satisfied. "He should calm down soon."

"I'm sorry you have to put up with this."

"It doesn't bother me."

"It started with the fireworks." She put her silverware down and leaned back in her chair, her eyes wide and somber. "Then it was sirens. Then thunderstorms. Now it seems like anything will set him off. The Benadryl doesn't help like it used to. I just wonder if it's right to keep him living this way."

Matt shut off the water and grabbed a towel for his hands. "Jamie, I took care of that dog for 6 months while you were in

Charlottesville. If I was going to give up on him, I would've done it then."

"Why didn't you?"

"We came to an understanding." He pulled out a chair and sat down across from her.

"What was that?"

"That as long as he has more good days than bad days, as long as he has one person who loves him, to comfort him when he's terrified, we don't give up on him. Alright?"

"Alright." Jamie forced a smile.

Matt moved as if he might reach for her hand, but then stopped himself as she picked up her silverware again and started pushing the sauce and noodles around on her plate. He glanced at the stack of paperwork that she brought home with her every drill period. Legal forms, counselings, the remaining pieces of some soldier's life. Like Major Casper. She was tasked with somehow putting it all back together.

He noticed a small, greyish newspaper clipping poking out from in between the stack. He could make out the grainy image of a woman in a wedding dress and his curiosity got the better of him. He pulled the clipping out from the stack.

"What is this?"

Jamie looked up from a mouthful of pasta, her eyebrows curved into a look of surprise. "That's something Sergeant Anthony gave me this morning."

"Free wedding dresses for military members?"

"You have to send in your military love story to win."

Matt raised an eyebrow as he reviewed the short article in his hands, considering how he might describe what they had to a stranger. How their love story had started with a goodbye. How their first kiss was both forbidden, and perfect.

He knew that her initial training would change her. He hoped that she would come back stronger, surer. But he also knew there was a chance that he'd lose her. That things happened when military couples were separated for long periods of time. Thrown in with a group of strangers, living together, sleeping together, training together. An intimacy develops that can easily be misinterpreted. Mistaken for something more substantial and permanent than it really is. Fidelity had more flexible boundaries in the military, especially on deployments and long training periods. He knew what they were up against. He took it on faith that she'd come back to him. And yet here he was, preparing to say goodbye a second time, wondering if she'd ever really come back.

"Are you going to do this?" He lifted the newspaper clipping between his fingers.

"I thought we talked about that." Jamie finished her last bite and set her silverware on top of the used plate. "We're not going to have a big wedding."

Matt shrugged his shoulders. "I don't care about the dress Jamie, as long as there's a wedding." He folded the news clipping in half and buried it deep into the stack of papers where he had found it. As he did, Jamie slid her hand across the table and meshed her fingers with his.

Matt felt their fingers intertwine, almost struck by the soft, familiar motion. She had always kept her distance. He had been patient, watched her soften at the edges and grow more tender, more attached. But she still wasn't his.

He'd given up his sergeant stripes for her. The proud world he'd built for himself in the Army. He didn't regret it for a moment. He just hoped he wasn't wrong.

He squeezed her hands softly, the pressure both genuine and surreal. He was taken with memories of the last time he'd said goodbye to her, as a loud growl rang through the halls, and the scratching continued.

# Part Three:

# The Oldest Law Firm

# Chapter 10
## Minneapolis, MN (2012)

*"We need to talk."*

Jamie stared at the cryptic text message as she waited in Matt's driveway, wondering what sort of surreal conversation she was walking into. Matt was either going to break up with her or tell her he loved her. Maybe even coax her into making a silly promise that she wouldn't fall for any of the captains she met in Charlottesville. She tried to smile at the simple idea, but she wasn't able to shake off the uneasiness.

She sat in her car in front of the olive house, building up the courage to knock on his door. The outside was simple and inviting. There was a scattered rock garden leading up to the red door, and the paint was old enough to be charming, without looking shabby. The windows on either side were wide like storybook windows.

She saw the curtains move as Matt passed between rooms and her blood stirred into dizzying eddies. This would be their last moment together. Before she left for Virginia and their accidental romance became a whole lot more complicated. If it was to survive at all.

She turned off the ignition and looked in the mirror, adjusting a thick swath of dark hair behind a silver barrette.

"This is crazy."

Reese whimpered from the back seat. The Border Collie raised his ears and turned in tight circles. Jamie adjusted the rearview mirror and saw that he'd shredded another floppy animal, the stuffing lying about the seat and the strings hanging from his mouth. He cried a second time and pawed at her headrest.

"It's not forever Reese. Just six months." Jamie gave the dog a tired smile and nodded at the mess. "Hopefully Matt won't change his mind when he sees what a mess you are."

Jamie dug the dog's leash out of the glove compartment and stepped out of the car. She opened the back door and hooked the leash around Reese's collar. The nervous dog picked up what was left of his torn rabbit and jumped down to the pavement, sticking close to her heels. They made their way up the steps and Jamie tapped on the door.

Her heart pounded in the pristine silence that followed. She tried to keep her head low and her runaway heart at bay.

The front door opened and Sergeant Matt Chase stood in front of her in a tan t-shirt and a comfortable pair of jeans. She loved seeing him out of uniform. Recognizing how strong and tan he was, with the same welcoming eyes that had reeled her in before she noticed the enlisted rank on his chest. Before she fully understood how off-limits he was.

"Hey LT." There was a dull note behind his smile as he opened the door wide and invited her in. "C'mon inside."

Jamie felt her heart pound as she stepped through the crowded doorway. Goodbyes were always difficult. But secret goodbyes were completely foreign and unpredictable. She took a cautious step inside with Reese trailing close behind her.

She closed the door and looked for subtle cues in Matt's patient expression. He didn't press her up against the wall and kiss her like he'd done before. He didn't look her over with relief and amazement the moment they were alone and free to indulge in all the complicated pleasure that was swarming just beneath the skin. She should've known that you couldn't get away with violating centuries of code and tradition forever.

"I take it this is Reese." Matt reached down and patted the dog's neck. Reese allowed the soft touch, still clutching his torn doll in his teeth.

"He's a little nervous." Jamie explained, trying to read the curious waves behind Matt's eyes. "It's like he knows I'm leaving him."

"I'm sure he does. They can sense these things." Matt held his hands in front of Reese's nose, allowing the dog to take in his scent. He established some loose trust with the anxious animal, then stood upright, opening a strange open space between them. His warm expression was tempered with something heavy and uncomfortable.

"Thanks for agreeing to look after him." Jamie removed Reese's leash and let him wander through the open kitchen, taking in the mixture of new smells. "I know it's a lot to ask."

She looked around at the signs of a disciplined soldier, the clean countertops and the organized cereal boxes lined up against the walls. There was a can of dog biscuits left out in front of the sink, and a large bag of dog food propped up against the fridge. Reese would be safe here. At least she could take comfort in that.

"It's not a lot to ask." Matt moved into the kitchen and reached for a dog biscuit, offering it to the uninterested dog who pranced around in nervous circles. "I'm happy to do it for you."

He kept his eyes pinned on Reese, or the floor, or his own nervous fingers. Anywhere but in her general direction. He was distracted and distant.

"Tell me what's happening Matt." Her words were sour and quiet and felt like the beginning of something being severed. "Did somebody say something to you? Did somebody see us together?"

"No, no it's nothing like that." He answered quickly, but wasn't able to fill in the empty space that followed.

Her heart grew a touch colder in the thin October air, and before she could shake off the chill, the moment was broken by the sound of glass shattering.

Jamie turned towards the sound and saw Reese snatch a half-eaten sandwich from the floor beside the kitchen table. He disappeared down the hall, leaving behind the fragments of a broken plate.

"Reese!" Jamie shouted after him.

"Don't worry about it Jamie, I'll take care of it." Matt moved to pick up the mess. She crouched to help him, but he lifted a hand to stop her. "You warned me he was a little temperamental. I knew what I was signing up for."

He stacked the pieces of broken glass and threw them in the trash, then turned towards her with his steady, enduring patience. "Come with me. I have some things for you."

He reached for her hand and she felt his fingers dance across her palm, loosely holding on to the slippery intimacy between them. The simple way their fingers meshed felt natural and pre-determined. It was just this sort of touch that had broken down her defenses to begin with and made the arbitrary distinction between officer and enlisted give way to basic human nature. She squeezed his smooth fingers and clung to the improbable delusion that just this once, the rules might be set aside.

Matt led her into his bedroom, where an assortment of socks and clothing were laid out on the bed. And just underneath the bed was the hushed sound of Reese's breathing.

"Looks like Reese found a place to hide with the rest of your sandwich."

"Wouldn't be the first roommate to steal my lunch." Matt dropped her hand and reached for a camo print bag at the heel of the bed. He held it up and showed her the name and the unit patch fixed to the large pocket. "I got you a pack with your name and rank on it. And an extra Red Bull patch, just in case you get homesick."

There was a genuine tenderness in his eyes. Something that told her he still had a real weakness for her, that there was still some possibility he wasn't about to break her heart.

"You're going to need socks." He unzipped the bag and set it on the floor at the foot of the bed. "You can never have too many pairs of green socks."

He picked up some rolled socks from the bed and tossed them into the bag. Jamie reached for a pair that had fallen from his fingers, inspecting the obvious wear on the toes and heels.

"Are these your socks?" An involuntary surge of color crept into his cheeks and she went warm at the idea of slipping her feet into his oversized cotton socks.

"They may be a little big, but trust me, they're comfortable." He took the socks from her and tossed them in the bag with the others, trying to ignore the familiarity they carried. "And you're going to need some snivel gear."

He unfolded two pairs of tan undershirts and long underwear. "Don't worry, these aren't mine. I picked up some surplus from supply. You wear these under your uniform when you're out in the field. It's going to get cold down there. You'll want to have these." He refolded the clothing and set it in the bottom of the bag. "I also got you some extra rank for your uniforms, some patches and flags." He pulled the items from the bed as he spoke, packing everything inside the bag at his feet. "Some moleskin for your feet. You'll be doing a lot of ruck marches. If you don't cover your feet you're going to get some pretty awful blisters. Make sure you use this."

Jamie nodded quietly as he packed up her supplies, still waiting on the harsh words that he was saving until the bitter end. "You pack a bag of supplies for all your soldiers?"

Matt gave her a thin smile as he loaded everything into the bag and zipped it closed. He leaned into the bed with a strange and unreadable softness in his eyes. "Just the ones I care about."

There was a subtle invitation in his posture and Jamie stepped into it. She wandered into his guarded space and placed her fingers around his neck, feeling the sleek comfort of his shorn hair. He closed his eyes at the soft touch and she placed her lips inside his, drawing them into a deep, familiar kiss. It began as a small, simple pleasure and quickly turned into a dark tempest. He pulled her hips against him and a cool tingling took over. Within seconds she was dizzy and unmoored, floating out to sea with no way back to shore.

Until he broke his lips from hers and looked at her with an unsettled expression, awash with every sacred line that they'd crossed from the first secret kiss to the last.

Matt slowed his breath and casually slipped out from under her, moving away from the bed and out of her reach. "I can't do this with you anymore."

"Why not?" Jamie forced the words past her lips, her blue eyes hardening as they followed him around the room.

"Because you're an officer." He lifted his heavy eyes towards her, open and sincere. "And we both know I have no business thinking the things I'm thinking about you."

"None of that matters Matt." Jamie's voice cracked under the loaded words.

"This is the Army, Jamie. It's not high school. There are consequences when you break the rules." Matt pulled at the tension in his jaw, wrestling against something rebellious and strange. "People lose their careers over this."

His words cooled the fever brewing in her. She had lost herself in him just as he was pulling away. Because the Army had rules about who you gave your heart to, and there was no compassionate exception for circumstances that looked and felt like love.

"I should've stopped this a long time ago." The words were almost lost under his breath. "Someone's going to get hurt."

"It's a little late for that, don't you think?" Jamie felt an angry mess of emotions rolling through her veins.

He looked both hurt and embarrassed, but there was nothing in his face that suggested surrender. He'd given himself just enough time to come to terms with his decision, then sprung it on her without any warning, just as the Army was about to take her away from everything that was comfortable and familiar.

"What made you change your mind?" She started reaching for details. Irrelevant nothings that might turn the hurt into a more manageable anger. "Why did you wait until now to tell me?"

"I never meant to hurt you Jamie."

The steady peal of low moans and scratching built from under the bed. Jamie crouched on the floor and lifted the sheets, overwhelmed by so many unexpected heartaches hitting her at once.

"Reese!" The Border Collie stopped scratching and looked up at her, his thin body curled into an impenetrable knot on the floor. "There is nothing to be afraid of. I wish you'd come out of there." She dropped the bed covering and left the dog in his makeshift cave, an awful swell of helplessness filling her lungs. "I can't stand to leave him here like this."

"Jamie." Matt sat down on the bed and stared down at her. His voice was soothing and calm. "I'll take good care of him."

"Why are you doing this?" The words themselves were far fiercer than her tone, but they had the intended effect, landing swift and severe.

"It may not make sense right now, but you're going to learn things in Charlottesville. About duty and sacrifice and courage."

He ran a tense hand through his regulation haircut, hesitating over every loaded word. "All of this will feel very different in a few months."

"You don't know that."

"I care about you a lot." He intentionally stopped short of love. Stopped short of giving her any real answers. "That's why we have to stop this."

"What about Reese?" Jamie listened to the sad cries of her lost dog under the bed. She looked at him with clear blue eyes that gave everything away.

"I told you I'd take care of him. This doesn't change that." He dropped his calm eyes towards the bag on the floor. "Please take the bag with you. I know you're angry right now, but I don't want you to find yourself freezing in a field come December because you were too proud to take it from me."

Jamie glanced towards the camo print bag at the foot of Matt's bed. She wasn't so afraid of freezing, but she could still taste his last kiss on the edge of her lips. She still wanted to feel her toes in the warm folds of his socks. She pitched forward and pulled the pack into her lap, hoping she might learn to be the sort of officer that didn't let bullish emotions like pride or heartache dull her senses.

"Promise me you'll be careful out there." Matt looked at her with heavy eyes, still drawing her in, even as he was pushing her away. "You can't trust everyone in uniform."

# Chapter 11
## Charlottesville, VA (2012)

Lieutenant Sharon found her classroom just before the 0500 start time. She was dressed in a simple gray t-shirt and black shorts, with the bag that Sergeant Chase had given her slung over one shoulder.

She snaked through the array of folding chairs and long tables looking for an empty seat. The class was dressed in identical PT uniforms with the same bland Army logo. No ranks. No names. Just a sea of unknown faces.

Most of them were male. Some of them sported toned chests and biceps under their cotton shirts. Some had joined the JAG Corps straight out of active Army combat positions. Others came from law firms with no prior military experience, their bodies far less defined and carrying a little more weight around their mid-sections.

She headed for an empty chair in the fourth row, but didn't reach it before an oversized man dropped his bag in front of it.

"Sorry, taken." The man shrugged as he sat down.

Sharon took a step backwards, surveying the room for an empty space.

A bald man in fatigues and captain's rank brushed past her, making his way to the front of the room. He glanced at his watch as he looked over the handful of stragglers.

"Alright, alright, grab your seats. Quickly. Start time is 0500. Which means you are in your seats and ready to begin at 0500. Not milling about the room looking for a chair."

The rest of the class began moving down the aisles into their seats, some of them looking tired and groggy from the early morning wake-up, wrestling with paper cups of black coffee as they stepped around each other in a controlled hurry.

"This seat's empty."

Jamie Sharon turned to towards the baritone voice. He was one of the leaner men, his shoulders built and his arms and face an even tan. He had a head of dirty blonde hair that fell across his forehead and tapered off in back. A pair of distant hazel eyes looked up at her with bewitching curiosity.

"Thank you."

She sat in the chair beside him and set the bag at her feet. She reached into the front pocket for a notebook and pen, and heard the familiar tone of her cell phone's text message alert sound across the crowded room.

"Shit." She mumbled under her breath, reaching for the phone and silencing the volume.

The bald captain looked in her direction.

"That was my phone Captain Fassbender." The man with the hazel eyes covered for her before she had a chance to open her mouth. "It won't happen again."

The captain nodded and turned to speak with another member of the cadre, a shorter man with jet black hair and more sergeant stripes than she'd seen in her short military career.

"You'll want to silence that or they'll confiscate it." The man with the hazel eyes warned her.

"It was a stupid mistake." She pulled out her phone and checked the screen, pulling up a new text message from Sergeant Chase. A grainy picture filled the tiny pixels, of him and Reese curled up on his bed in the house on Olive Street. In the very same room where he'd kissed her with so much sincerity and still found the courage to break himself free of her. She hit the home icon and the photo disappeared, along with all her speculations about her short-lived affair with Sergeant Matthew Chase.

"Boyfriend misses you already?" The man with hazel eyes watched her as she powered down her phone and zipped it in the corner pocket of her bag.

"He's not a boyfriend." Sharon corrected him with a knot in her voice. "He's just taking care of my dog."

"That's pretty gracious of him." There was a lift in the man's words that fell somewhere between curious and shrewd. Almost as if he could read the whole hidden history between her and Sergeant Chase by seeing his photo flash across the screen. "You sure you don't have a sergeant with a little crush on you?"

Sharon wrinkled her mouth at her brutal memories of Sergeant Chase still churning through her guarded heart. "That would be pretty inappropriate, don't you think?"

"It would. But stranger things have happened." The man had a sweet spark in his voice that reminded her of summer. Warm and drifting and perfectly elusive. He gave her a sly wink that left her feeling transparent and exposed. "But for what it's worth, your secret is safe with me."

She might have found him charming under the right circumstances. And for a moment, she was almost grateful that she hadn't made any promise not to fall for the rugged captains she met in Charlottesville. A pleasant chill ran across her neck as the man leaned closer and extended his left hand.

"I'm Ben."

The first thing she noticed was the ring on his finger. Charming or not, he wasn't safe. Or at least, no safer than Sergeant Chase had been. Just another instinctive human bond, capable of inspiring feelings that could end her career. Even now it seemed so unreal that the military had found a way to criminalize the most gratifying emotions. That they taught you to bury your feelings so early on.

She took his hand with a confusing mixture of relief and disappointment. "Jamie."

"You're a Red Bull." Ben pointed to the black patch with the silver cow skull on the bag at her feet.

"Yes, for about six months."

"I was a Red Bull for about 4 years, before I went active duty." He took his hazel eyes from the horned bull on her bag and stared straight ahead at some invisible memory. "Some of my best friends are Red Bulls."

The bald captain wrapped up his conversation with the impressive sergeant at the front of the room. He took the sergeant's clipboard and headed back down the center aisle, stopping and leaning into the table in front of her and Ben.

"Major Casper. We're going to have you head up 2nd Platoon when we head out for formation. Will that work for you?"

"Be happy to Captain."

68

The captain handed the clipboard over to Ben and moved back towards the front of the room.

Jamie felt a steep rise in adrenaline as it occurred to her that she'd been chatting with a major all this time. She hadn't once called him 'Sir.'

# Chapter 12
## Charlottesville, VA (2012)

Captain Mann took a seat in the back of the room, running one hand over his smooth bald head. He was dark and polished, with a cutting sort of confidence behind his crystal brown eyes. He glanced around the room at his new colleagues, amazed by the amount of women.

He tried to count them all. Damn near 20 women, with breasts and thighs and soft necks, mingling among the hundred or more male attorneys filling up the room. He was worlds away from the infantry, where catching sight of a woman was something worth reporting to your buddies. Where word would circulate for weeks that a female soldier was sighted over in supply and hundreds of canteens would go missing just so guys could go have a glimpse of her. In the infantry you lived, ate and slept with nothing but crude men, surrounded by testosterone and horseplay. And here he was sitting in a classroom with damn near 20 females, enough to actually discriminate between the good looking ones and the ones that wouldn't even set off a chain reaction in supply.

"Welcome, Ladies and Gentlemen to the oldest and largest law firm in the country, the United States Army JAG Corps." The company commander stood at the front of the room, the only officer with any rank on his uniform. A tall white captain with a shaved head and an impatient stare. The sort of guy that might have intimidated him years ago. But he'd been a company commander himself. He'd earned his own captain bars.

"My name is Captain Fassbender and I will be responsible for you for the duration of your legal training at the JAG School. It is my intention to ensure that by the time you leave here, you are prepared for the challenges that await you, whatever they may be. You were recruited into this organization for you legal knowledge and skills. But you are also required to conduct yourselves as Soldiers. You are not only expected to learn the mechanics of conducting a court-martial or the international treaties behind the laws of war, you are also here to learn the basic skills necessary to fight and survive in a battlefield environment. If there is any one of you who believes that you do not need to learn these skills, then you are sorely mistaken. If there is any one among you whose recruiter told him that you do not need to worry about such things, because you're JAG, I hate to be the one to break it to you, but your recruiter was dead wrong. You are not simply staff officers and paper pushers. That's not what we do here. Can anyone give me the Army's Mission Statement?"

Captain Mann lifted his hand and waited for Captain Fassbender to zero in on him. "You in the back. Stand up, give us your name."

"Captain Mann, Sir." Mann got to his feet and placed his hands behind his back.

"And what is the Army's mission statement Captain Mann?"

"To fight and win our nation's wars."

"Dead on. To fight and win our nation's wars. So if you're not on board with that, I'm afraid you're not going to like the JAG corps very much. You can have a seat Captain."

Mann eased himself into his chair at the back of the room and smirked. He'd made it a point to let the commander, and the rest of the class know his rank, despite the PT uniform. He had no intention of being mistaken for a lieutenant. After three years of law school with ordinary civilians he was ready to re-immerse himself in a properly stratified environment.

"This is not your typical law firm." Captain Fassbender continued his address. "You will learn to fire a weapon. You will learn to navigate unknown territory with nothing more than a map and a compass, you will learn to perform emergency first aid, you will learn the taste and smell of poisonous gases. I have news for you ladies and gentlemen, there are no front lines anymore. Roadside bombs don't discriminate. You can and will be targeted and you can and will be asked to perform investigations outside the wire. If this is not for you, I'm sure there are plenty of fancy law firms back home you can apply to, do I make myself clear?"

Mann glanced around the room at the sea of matching uniforms and haircuts, their exteriors offering only the smallest clues as to the mettle of the individuals hiding beneath. The next six months would test them. Their endurance, their determination, their sense of right and wrong. The Army would find a way to expose their true characters, and single out the leaders from the dead weight.

The incoming class was rumored to be brilliant. The economy had collapsed and law firms had folded, driving scores of unemployed lawyers to sign up with Uncle Sam. But brilliant meant nothing if they couldn't be molded into warriors.

Mann watched their expressions as Fassbender spoke, to see if the idea of a deployment or a roadside bomb rattled them. He wanted proof that they weren't just an assorted group of opportunists riding out the recession. He looked at the women in particular. Having something pretty to look at during the day didn't necessarily make up for having to pull someone else's weight for the next 6 months.

Mann cracked his knuckles, glancing at the silver wedding band on his left hand. Of course, there was always the possibility that some of them were up for more than just looking. He toyed with the silver band on his finger for a time, weighing his options. He wasn't likely to find himself in this kind of training environment again for quite some time. He may as well enjoy it. Without another thought he slipped the wedding ring off his finger and buried it deep in his pocket.

"By my count there are 112 of you, from all across the country." Fassbender continued. "You come from different states, different religions, different politics, different ethnicities, that all ends here. You're a team now. Some of you were business owners in a previous life. Some of you may have been politicians. Here you're soldiers. Plain and simple. Some of you are brand new to the Army and the Army way of life. Some of you are Reservists or Guardsmen who have civilian jobs to return to when this is over. Some of you were raised on Army bases and have been serving your country since you turned 18. Most of you are lieutenants, but we also have a good number of Captains and for the first time we even have a Major in this class."

This turned a few heads. Captain Mann glanced around with the rest of the class in quiet curiosity. There were rumors, before he even left his home base, that some unknown character had been recruited into the JAG Corps from an EOD unit. The one classmate with enough experience to outrank all of them, including Fassbender. He imagined that this major, whoever he was, would give himself away through a subtle nod, or other sign of indifference. But he remained perfectly blended into the mass.

"I expect you to learn from each other. To take care of each other. Some of you have led men in battle. You've diffused roadside bombs, you've flown combat operations. I expect you will learn from our new recruits as much as they will learn from you. I expect you will work together."

Captain Mann continued to scan the crowd as Captain Fassbender spoke, trying to place some of the anxious faces with the impressive backgrounds that were mentioned. Most of what he saw was out of shape tax attorneys and unemployed lobbyists. Pampered civilians who'd never once handled a weapon or suffered long term exposure to the desert sun. He didn't see the potential that Captain Fassbender saw. A few laps on the track outside would make that abundantly clear.

"For those of you who are interested, there will be an opportunity, once your required training is complete, to go on to Airborne school at Fort Benning. This is a unique opportunity, since lawyers aren't generally selected for this type of training."

Captain Mann shifted forward in his seat, suddenly alert and hungry for information. He had attended Airborne school a lifetime ago, when a fractured ankle prevented him from earning his wings. He'd spent too many years of his career explaining the empty space on his uniform. Crafting his ego around a common and lackluster excuse. His chest inflated at the opportunity to redeem himself.

"There are only 20 seats available and you will have to compete against your fellow classmates to earn a seat. Rank is not an eligibility factor. How hard you work will determine whether you will be considered for Airborne school and we will make that determination at the end of your legal training. We will begin the selection process at 0430 this Saturday morning. If you prefer to stay in bed, by all means. Take the day off. We are only looking for serious competitors. How many of you are interested? Show of hands."

Captain Mann lifted his hand before any of the others, casually taking stock of the competition. Hands went up across the spectrum of body mass and stature. Bulky men with obvious strength, but no speed. Thin, tall men with impressive reach and stride. In the front row, a short, Asian man with horn-rimmed glasses and little muscle or height, possibly banking on determination alone. Off to the side, an older gentleman, with a hardened jaw and a sun-damaged brow. And then, the one hand that no one expected. The long, slender fingers and well-manicured nails of the stern redhead in the middle of the class, who was bold enough to think she could compete with the men.

"Very well." Captain Fassbender smiled for the first time. "Go ahead and put your hands down. Captain Mann."

"Yes Sir." Captain Mann stumbled as he stood, still a little rattled at the sight of the pale white hand in the air. Without knowing it, she had raised the stakes and upped the tension. Because no infantryman, no soldier for that matter, would live down the tale that he lost a physical competition to a woman.

"Those of you who plan to compete for a slot in Airborne school, please see Captain Mann after this morning's PT session. He'll take down your name and two mile run times. Can you handle that Captain Mann?"

"Yes sir." Captain Mann watched the heads of his classmates turn around and he took stock of their faces. The girl turned a pair of grayish eyes in his direction. He flashed her a salty, mocking smile and put her out of his mind.

# Chapter 13
## Charlottesville, VA (2012)

Lieutenant Pamela Hunt pulled her hat over her red hair and stepped outside. There was still frost on the ground and the air was sharp. The class had pulled gray windbreakers and long pants over their t-shirts and shorts. They covered their heads and hands in wool hats and black gloves. They were assembling into platoons in the open field just down the hill from the classroom. Three standard formations in front of a dimly lit track.

She covered her ears and tightened her gloves, receiving more than a few curious stares as she headed towards the field. A cold wind brushed against her face, sending a rustle through her clothes as she walked. She would have to run hard to stop the staring. She was still sullen over the fact that she'd been singled out so soon.

She reached the field and lined up with the other officers, trying to remember how it was that she ended up here, standing perfectly still in the darkest hours of the morning, freezing in silence beside a row of disconnected strangers. She imagined that they'd all been driven here by individual strings of life's cruelties. Fresh wounds that needed time and distance to heal. She was here because she'd lost her appetite for being weak. The Army was the fastest way to cut ties with that forgotten life.

She stepped into position next to a thin brunette who was shoving her hair into her wool cap, shivering in the cold. She wasn't tall, or sturdy, but she was fit and probably capable of out-running some of the larger men around them.

"What's your two mile run time?" Hunt glanced out at the empty track, preparing for the barrage of tears and sweat that were about to hit the pavement.

"Around 15:50. 15:30 on a good day."

Hunt balled her fingers inside her thick gloves. She knew she could beat 15:30 even on a bad day, but not by much.

"You could've raised you hand." She found herself reaching out to someone she had no reason to trust. Someone who could keep her motivated when things got difficult. Out of solidarity or defiance, or whatever it was that made her tick. Whatever it was that brought her here. "Even if you didn't make the cut, you could have tried."

"I'm National Guard." The brunette was distracted by a tall officer heading towards the formation. His head was covered in a wool cap like all the others and he carried a clipboard in his gloved hands. "I can't volunteer to spend three more weeks out here. I have a job waiting for me back home."

Home. Reservists talked about home like it was an actual place. Like it wasn't something they'd all given up when they raised their right hand and signed on the dotted line.

Home had become a concept, rather than a place. From here on in, she went where the Army needed her, whether it be Fort Sill, Oklahoma or Okinawa, Japan. She'd packed up her belongings, sold what she couldn't carry and was ready to make her way to her next duty station.

"Second Platoon, Attention!" The officer with the clipboard shouted to the group, and necks and limbs straightened in perfect sync.

"What's your name soldier?" The officer with the clipboard addressed the lieutenant at the front of their squad. His breath making billows of white heat in the cold morning air.

"Lieutenant Randall." The solider responded.

"Lieutenant Randall. I'm Major Casper. Where are you from?"

Pamela Hunt glanced at the man who had managed to hide himself so well in the midst of a classroom looking to ferret him out. He was tall and focused, and appeared well-practiced at giving orders. The mere mention of the major's rank seemed to gum up Lieutenant Randall's response time. A brash example of the effect that power can have on a person's psyche.

"Kentucky Sir." He finally spouted.

"And where are you headed?"

"Fort Belvoir Sir."

"That's in D.C. How the hell'd you get that assignment?" Major Casper glanced up from his clipboard, jotting down the information as he spoke. He moved through his questions quickly, biting his bottom lip as he picked through the details.

"Got lucky I guess."

"Well don't get used to it. Social Security Number?"

"495-87-0987."

"Blood Type?"

"AB Negative."

"Religion?" Major Casper gave the kid a serious stare. "This is for your dog tags LT."

"Catholic, Sir."

Major Casper took down this last bit of information. He lowered his clipboard and glanced over the lieutenant in front of him, focusing on his exposed head, his hair blowing about in the cold wind.

"You got a cap Randall?"

"No Sir."

"Why not?" His voice dropped an octave and sounded a little less kind.

"Haven't had a chance to pick it up yet Sir."

"It was on your packing list soldier, everyone else seems to have one." Casper motioned to the rest of the platoon, heads covered in their regulation wool caps.

"I'm sorry, Sir." Randall seemed to grow colder as he stood before the major.

"Don't apologize to me, apologize to your classmates."

Hunt saw the subtle way that the major glanced over the platoon, and realized that he was about to make their morning a hell of a lot worse.

"We all wear the same uniform here Lieutenant Randall. I want you to understand what that means. If you don't have a cap, and everyone else does, we're not in uniform are we?"

"No Sir." The lieutenant shivered.

"But, if everyone else takes off their caps?" Major Casper removed his own cap and secured it in his jacket pocket, a gust of cold air whipping through his dirty blonde hair. He looked out across the platoon of distressed faces, silently waiting. One by one, the soldiers in Second Platoon removed their caps, exposing their heads to the frigid air.

Hunt watched as the brunette beside her removed her cap and stowed it away. The cool air whipped a few strands of loose hair across her face, but she stared straight ahead, unflinching. Major Casper watched the group out of both corners of his eyes, a guilty grimace lining his jaw. He focused his attention on Hunt, who had yet to remove her cap.

Lieutenant Hunt sucked in a tight breath of cold morning air. She removed the cap and shoved it deep into her pocket. She could practically feel her temperature drop.

"Are we in uniform now LT?"

"Yes Sir."

"Alright, and what about gloves, do you have gloves?"

"No Sir." Randall had a hard time getting the words out.

"Don't have that either, huh? Well, then, we know what to do, don't we?" He removed his gloves and a bevy of unintelligible cuss words escaped from the ranks. "Hey, hey hey. What does this tell us? We're a team here. We rise together, we fall together. We sweat together. We freeze together. Take off your gloves, all of you."

Hunt looked down at her gloves. A raw defiance was already setting in. She was a grown woman, being asked to do something absurd and unsafe because some idiot couldn't follow instructions. Again she watched as the woman beside her struggled with removing her gloves, her fingers already white and frozen.

For the first time since she signed her paperwork, Pamela Hunt started to wonder if she'd made the right decision. If the Army could truly teach her anything about strength and courage, rather than raw obedience.

She'd had her fill of obedience. Obedience was something that was sold to young girls - to keep them quiet when boys took things from them without asking. She'd come here to rise above all that.

Lieutenant Hunt had no intention of flirting with majors or generals to keep her hands warm or her belly full. Everyday she would wear her rank on her chest, and everyday it would make her just a little bit stronger. She was drawn to the law to get just a taste of justice. She was drawn to the Army so she wouldn't need it.

She clenched her fists where she stood and hid her hands behind her back, her first small act of rebellion as an officer in United States Army.

# Chapter 14
## Charlottesville, VA (2012)

It started with a slight tingling in the back of his brain, his synapses firing as if he'd overdosed on stimulants. It had followed him out to the field, some cannibalistic energy that fed off broken details and minutiae. He saw their birthmarks and scar tissue, he heard them popping gum and biting into breath mints, he smelled their body odor and shampoo. He struggled to record only the data he'd been sent to collect. Social Security Numbers, religions, home states, duty stations, filtering out the irrelevant debris.

He couldn't shake the feeling that he still belonged out in the field, pulling wires on homemade explosives and breaking in new soldiers. The mess in his head hadn't started until they moved him into the classroom and the bombs had stopped. Where he was forced to sift through the ashes of all those life or death decisions. The silence of ordinary life was swallowing him.

He stepped down the line and found himself facing the brunette from the classroom. The Red Bull that smelled of lilacs and shared a curious history with some sergeant back home. She stared straight ahead with glassy blue eyes and an eerie stillness to her. She had a soothing sort of presence that calmed him, drowned out the steady noise in his head. Perhaps it was the way she was standing perfectly poised and determined, despite the cold beating against her temples, refusing to acknowledge any discomfort or vulnerability. That kind of strength was far more appealing than a short skirt and a laundry list of petty vanities. It was nearly impossible to come across as either feminine or beautiful in an oversized Army uniform, but something about her moved him.

"Name and rank?" He spoke to her like any one of his soldiers, dismissing the memory of her first name and quieting the illicit fondness that was stirring.

"Lieutenant Sharon Sir."

"You cold Lieutenant Sharon?"

"Yes, Sir."

"It'll get colder. Make sure you stay hydrated. Aren't you from Minnesota LT? You should be used to this by now."

"We wear caps and gloves in Minnesota Sir." She seemed to snap off the reply before it occurred to her to filter her words. Casper watched her eyes widen at her own brashness and he flashed a quick smile.

"That's a fair point. You going active LT, or are you headed back home?"

"Back home Sir."

"What's your social security number?"

"459-08-9858."

"Blood type?"

"A positive."

"Religion?"

"None, Sir."

"None, huh?" Casper glanced up from his clipboard. Her eyes were steady and clear. "This is for your dog tags LT. You sure you don't want me to put you down as Muslim so the terrorists treat you a little better if you're captured?"

"From what I can tell Sir, they don't treat Muslim women much better than Christian women."

Casper flashed another brief smile. Usually the thought of dog tags was enough to scare some weak trace of spirituality out of new recruits. Of course, lawyers were a completely different breed of soldier. More logic than emotion. And a lot less likely to end up blown into several pieces by an IED. The second the thought hit his temples, the innocent smile faded. His voice went as cold as his fingers.

"Also a fair point. More than likely you end up in a situation where someone's reading your religion off your dog tags you're beyond the point of prayers any way." He looked down at her hands, restraining a surge of tenderness as he looked over her frozen fingers. "You think you might be in danger of a cold weather injury you see me immediately, alright?"

"Yes Sir."

He forced himself away from the simple warmth she gave him and stepped towards the next solider in line, letting his head

81

grow dizzy again with the names and numbers sliding through his head. A persistent anxiety crept along his spine.

He lowered his clipboard and looked down at the red-haired lieutenant in front of him. The bold woman who'd raised her hand to compete with a mass of men larger and stronger than her. She was standing before him with perfect military posture, aside from her arms, which were casually secured behind her back.

"Name?" Casper waited for her to correct her stance. But the look in her eye told him it was something more than a confused lieutenant adjusting to protocol. It was both intentional and defiant.

"Lieutenant Hunt."

"Where you from Lieutenant Hunt?"

"New York, Sir."

"New York. Should have known you came to us from someplace where it pays to be a little cutthroat. Where you stationed after training?"

"Fort Leavenworth, Sir."

"Same here. Looks like we're going to be seeing a lot of each other. Social security number?"

"545-09-9879."

"Blood type?"

"O Positive."

"Religion?"

"None, Sir."

"None." He recorded the answer then stared back at her. She was still standing with her hands behind the small of her back. "Got a lot of independent women in Second Platoon. Perhaps a little too independent. Show me your hands Lieutenant Hunt."

She froze in place, staring back at him with cold eyes.

"I asked you to show me your hands lieutenant." He repeated.

Without a word, the lieutenant disengaged her gloved fingers from behind her back and presented them to him.

"I told you to take your gloves off LT."

"It's freezing, Sir." She locked eyes with him.

"I know that." His response was slow and firm. "I'm not doing this to be an ass, I'm trying to make a point here."

82

He'd dealt with insubordination plenty of times, but it didn't usually come from officers. He had a limited opportunity to drive home a point to a platoon full of adults and professionals. Individuals who had made their careers out of arguing against authority, insisting upon civil rights and free speech. They weren't conditioned to take orders based on hierarchy alone. They needed a reason. For a brief moment, he felt relevant again. He had a small, but intense sense of purpose.

"I want all of you to understand what I'm trying to do here." He took a step back and addressed the entire platoon, walking in front of the rows of soldiers so that each of them could hear him. "All of you are coming from a world in which you were individuals. If you stayed up too late drinking or zoned out in front of the TV and you're not well rested at work the next day, no one suffers from that but you. In the Army, it's not that simple. If you come to the mission without enough sleep, chances are someone is going to have to carry your rucksack for you. Your lack of discipline, slows the group down. And on the battlefield, it may even get someone killed. So we need to drill it into your heads, from day one, that you are not just responsible for yourselves anymore. You are responsible for each other. And if one of you comes to class without a cap," Casper motioned to Lieutenant Randall. "You need to be concerned about that, because it's going to affect the entire group and it's going to affect the mission."

He looked over the rows of soldiers in front of him, the cold wind breaking against their stoic faces in the dark morning. He pivoted at the end of the formation and headed back the other direction.

"This is the only way I can teach you to make the right decisions, not just for yourself, but for the group. Because we're only as strong as the weakest among us. We have to make the weakest links stronger. Everyone suffers the consequences when someone isn't where they're supposed to be or doing what they're supposed to be doing."

He paused in front of Lieutenant Hunt, her hands still buried deep inside her PT gloves. "Now if I let Lieutenant Hunt wear her gloves this morning, she's not going to get that message, are you Lieutenant Hunt?" He stared into her fierce grey eyes. "But if I make you take your gloves off and your hands freeze all morning, you're going to make sure Lieutenant Randall has his gloves tomorrow, aren't you?"

She glared back at him, a crisp venom building in her motionless stance.

"That's what this is about. This isn't some senseless power grab. If you think you're getting frostbite, that's a different story. I can always send you in to see Doc Morgan, get you on a medical profile. But that would pretty much ruin your chances of going to Airborne school. You don't want to go out like that do you?" He finally pinched a nerve and he could see the bitter energy course through her face.

"No Sir." She spoke out loud.

"Take the gloves off. Now."

Lieutenant Hunt glared back at him. She removed the gloves in an act of angry surrender, and stowed them away in her jacket pocket.

"You owe your classmates 20 push-ups." He pointed to the ground and she lowered herself into position, her pretty fingers sinking into the cold dirt.

"Make sure you go all the way down LT." He watched as she began the movements, lifting her body up and down as her classmates looked on with frozen fingers. "Your hands are going to warm up real soon anyway, because we're hitting the track as soon as I have everyone's information. We'll see if you run a little better than you follow orders."

# Chapter 15
## Charlottesville, VA (2012)

Captain Mann leaned into the railing in front of a stack of old bleachers. He took a swallow of tinny water from his camelback and watched the rest of the class darting around the track. His forehead was coated in a thin film of sweat and his body was still warm from the run. His ankle still bothered him, but even before the injury, he was never a strong runner. He spent more time in the weight room than he did on the track. All that extra muscle slowed him down.

He watched for the slim redhead who had raised her hand in class that morning. She was trailing one of the overweight tax attorneys by almost half a lap. He shrugged his shoulders, unsurprised. By the time she finished he would have enough names to fill two Airborne classes. It was bold of her to volunteer, he gave her that. But boldness didn't necessarily make up for brute strength.

He exhaled slowly, turning his eyes from his classmates to the clipboard in his puffy hands. He read through the names on his roster, noting their ranks and run times. He recorded his own time at 13 minutes and 6 seconds. Thirteen men had finished ahead of him, two of them were Lieutenants. He would have to spend a lot more time on the track if he wanted to stay in this thing.

"Captain Mann."

"Yeah." He looked up from his notes to see another winded soldier standing in front of him, with fresh sweat dotting his hairline. The low light almost concealed the outline of a pink burn that ran down the left edge of his face. The rough skin covered his chin and dipped down his neck, disappearing into the neckline of his gray shirt. He had dark wavy hair that curled under the sweat, hugging the sides of his narrow face.

"Put me down for the Airborne competition. Captain Cade. Aaron Cade."

Mann tried not to stare at the man's singed skin, focusing on the arms and legs he would be competing against. He wasn't built or intimidating, but he wasn't scrawny either.

"What's your run time?"

"13:34."

Captain Mann nodded and started flipping through the roster. Captain Cade's long limbs suggested that he could shave a good two minutes off his time if he put in a little more effort, but he didn't seem ambitious enough to try. Mann fumbled through the pages, eventually finding Captain Cade's name near the end of the second page. "Got you down."

"The cold is killing me this morning." There was a subtle lift in his voice, something like an East Coast accent.

"It's not getting any warmer." Captain Mann jotted down the captain's time, putting him at number 19, the last of the serious competition. Of course, the two mile run was only the beginning. There would also be longer runs, ruck marches, unending push-ups, squats, sprints, testing the limits of their strength, speed and endurance. Injuries would happen. Illness. Fatigue. In the end it would all be about mental stamina. Those who could stick it out to the end without knowing what was being thrown at them next or how long it would last. The rest was just sore muscles and strained tendons.

Mann looked out at the remainder of his classmates, some of them barely lifting their tired ankles from the pavement.

"Where do these people come from?" Captain Mann shook his head as he leaned against the bleachers,

"Law firms." Cade shrugged his shoulders, taking a large pull of metallic water from his own camelback.

The cold was already biting back into Mann's fingers as he turned the pages on his clipboard, making a loose effort to account for all the social security numbers he'd collected from third platoon. "What are they doing here is a better question."

"That's the mystery. What makes a person want to join the Army at 30 years old?" Cade took another swallow of water, swished it around in his mouth and then spit into the ground.

"A hundred grand in law school debt?" Mann was still distracted by the captain's jagged burn, an uncomfortable reminder that bombs were still detonating, halfway around the world. "Finding out billing hours in a fancy law office isn't as glamorous as you'd think. Some of them'll wash out. Like this guy right here." Mann pointed to a roundish man barreling across the track in front of them. "He's a tax attorney from Georgia. Looks like he's never run a day in his life. Even if he makes it through JAG school he'll never survive Fort Benning."

"So what do you think of the girl?" Cade nodded towards Lieutenant Hunt as she rounded the bend, pushing her way into the cold morning air.

Mann paused as he watched her, weaving her way through the crowd of stragglers, steadily building momentum. She lifted her head and locked eyes with the two captains watching her from the bleachers. Something in that look caught him off guard. She lunged into the pavement, her legs gliding across the track, heat and sweat churning from her skin.

Mann bit into his pen as he watched her glide by, breathing heavily, lungs about to burst. He saw the effort lining her face and it hit him that she might not be trailing the overweight tax attorney at all. It was possible that she'd lapped him.

"What lap is she on?" He asked with his teeth still clenched around his pen.

"This is her final lap. She was on my heels the whole time."

She stretched her legs wide and drew up a final burst of energy as she crossed the finish line, ambling off the track a full lap and a half ahead of the shuffling tax attorney.

Mann flexed his eyebrows as he watch her walk off the track, her legs shaking from the pitch in adrenaline. He glanced down at his clipboard. She had come in at number 20.

She used her shirt sleeve to wipe the sweat from her forehead and headed towards the bleachers, still collecting her breath. Her face was red and slick, with hair slipping from its bonds and sticking to the sides or her cheeks. She looked miserable, but proud, some hidden reserve of strength keeping her collected and upright.

She ambled towards him with his name already waiting on her dry lips. "Captain Mann." She was clearly struggling to get the words out without sounding the way she looked.

Mann pretended to look up from his clipboard, gnawing on his pen and watching her pant.

"I want to be added to the list." She heaved. "For Airborne school."

"You're still stuck on that?" He removed the pen from his mouth and paused, waiting for a response.

"Yes." She coughed.

"What's your name?"

"Hunt. Lieutenant Pam Hunt."

"Pam Hunt." He began paging through the roster again, a slight smile forming on one edge of his mouth. "What's your run time LT?'

"14:39."

Mann found her name on the third page of the roster and penned in his notations. Airborne candidate. 14:39. Number 20. He glanced up at the sweaty Lieutenant, growing paler as she stood in front of him. She shivered slightly in the cold and he knew how hard she had worked to get that time. He'd been where she was and he knew what was coming. How hard she was still working to hold it in. "Looks like you came in at number 28. You're going to have to go a lot faster than that if you want to make it to Airborne school."

"That would've been a perfect score if this were a record test." She mumbled.

"On the women's scale maybe. On the men's scale, you're just average."

Her eyes filled with heat and she turned away from him, clearly looking for a discreet location to empty her stomach. She hurried around the corner to the opposite side of the bleachers, where it was still dark enough to obscure her face as she bent over. But the sound of the retching was unmistakable.

"Nice push Lieutenant Hunt." Mann called after her. "Make sure you stay hydrated."

"Captain Mann." Another stiff voice came out of the cold.

Mann looked up to see a tall, lean soldier standing in front of him, with dirty blonde hair falling over a dry, white forehead.

"Ben Casper." He introduced himself and stretched out his arm for a cold handshake. "I'll be running with the Airborne crew in the mornings."

"That depends on your run." Mann laughed to himself, glancing down at his clipboard.

"I'm not competing for a slot." He took a sip from his camelback as his eyes followed the remaining runners along the track. "I've been to Airborne school. Fassbender wants me to tag along and make sure the competition's clean. How's Lieutenant Hunt?"

"She's not doing so well. That's her wretching behind the bleachers." Captain Mann bit down on his pen a second time, already disliking this guy. "So you gonna tell me your run time Casper?"

"11:49." The blonde man gave him a sticky grin, like he was hiding some inside joke, then turned back towards the track. "I'm surprised you gentlemen aren't out there cheering on the rest of your classmates."

Mann rolled his eyes as he struggled to find the guy's name on his roster, his stiff fingers fumbling to get a grip on the slippery pages. "A few laps around the track isn't going to turn them into soldiers."

"They've got some work to do." The blonde man watched as the new attorneys rounded all four bends on the track, stumbling awkwardly into the new life that they'd chosen. "You do have to give them one thing though."

"What's that?" Mann shook his head.

"They signed up after the war." The blonde man took a short swallow from his camelback, holding the end of the tube in his mouth like an old cowboy sucking on the end of a broken cigarette. "They knew exactly what they were getting themselves into and they took the oath anyway. People like us? We joined right out of high school. Pre-Afghanistan, pre-Iraq." The smug officer looked down from the few solid inches he had on him and raised an eyebrow. "You sure you would have made the same decision if you knew you were headed over to the sandbox for a few deployments?"

"Fuck you, man." Captain Mann dismissed him with a loose wave of the arm.

The blonde man narrowed his eyes as Mann continued to fiddle with the clipboard, finally flipping to the second page of the roster where the "C" names began.

"You find my name on there yet Captain?"

There was a subtle shift in the man's tone. Something authoritative. Mann felt a quick prickle at the back of his neck. The sort of alert he hadn't felt since he'd mouthed off to his drill sergeant in basic training. He glanced down at the roster in front of him and spotted the name he was looking for at the top of the list. Major Benjamin Casper. The one fucking major in the class and he had just told him to fuck off.

"Yes Sir." Mann answered with his eyes forward.

"Glad to hear it." Major Benjamin Casper turned his eyes towards the remainder of the class as they pushed along the track, pointing towards the struggling tax attorney. "Who is this guy here? Is he in your platoon Captain?"

"Yes Sir, that's Lieutenant Peterson. He's from Georgia." Mann pushed out a humble answer, already feeling the pain of whatever was coming next.

"Well it looks like he could use a little encouragement, wouldn't you say?" Major Casper turned his attention on Captain Cade. "And how about you? What's your name?"

"Captain Cade Sir."

"Captain Mann, why don't you hand your clipboard off to Captain Cade and come with me, we're going to run in with the rest of the class."

"Yes Sir." Mann spit into the ground and went for one last sip of water.

"Put your camelback down, let's go." Major Casper dropped his gear and began making his way back toward the track. "Let's go Lieutenant Peterson." The major hollered out as he re-entered the track behind the struggling Lieutenant.

Mann handed off his clipboard to Captain Cade and tossed his camelback to the ground, trotting back towards the track on the major's heels, already feeling the stress in his thighs and swollen ankle.

"Just imagine you've got a corporate client from a fortune 500 company at the end of this lap," Casper shouted and every word, every breath burrowed its way under Mann's skin. "He's looking for the most lucrative tax shelter you can create for him. Don't want to keep him waiting, let's go."

Casper sped up alongside the struggling lieutenant as Captain Mann fell further and further behind. His muscles were already spent and wasted. And all for a two mile run that only put him 93 seconds ahead of that stubborn redhead.

# Chapter 16
## Charlottesville, VA (2012)

Captain Cade held the clipboard in his hands. He watched the stragglers on the track for a brief spell before his eyes dropped to the roster of names. A quick wind ruffled through the pages and he took the opportunity to sort through them. He scanned Mann's handwritten scribbles next to the Airborne candidates, their run times and rankings. He found himself on the second page. Number 19.

A gruff laugh passed through his lungs. It could only mean one thing.

He flipped towards the middle of the alphabet, looking for the name of the redhead who'd finished behind him. First Lieutenant Pamela Hunt. Airborne Candidate. 14:39. Number 20. Cade glanced over his shoulder at the sick lieutenant hiding behind the bleachers. He'd felt her steady breathing the entire time as she ran behind him. Determined and fierce.

Mann lied to her about her chances. He was just another empty ego, hiding behind his classic cheekbones and his dimpled smile. From the moment she raised her hand, he'd been concerned about her stealing his wings.

All Cade could think about was what she looked like under her clothes. Even covered in sweat. Even smelling of sickness. He liked the idea of her. A fierce redhead who wasn't easily intimidated. He never would have volunteered for such a needless body-breaking if he hadn't seen her slim white fingers dancing in the air.

He reached a hand towards his left cheek and felt the scarred flesh between his fingers. His face had morphed into something strange and unappealing. They'd given him a bronze star and a purple heart. All he wanted was his skin back. He cherished the rare moments when he forgot about the burns. When he still pictured himself with the same sleek smile he grew up with. The sort of face that could churn the heart of a new lieutenant.

He secured the clipboard under one arm and searched the bleachers for a camelback with her name on it. He laid eyes on her gear and picked it up, making his way behind the bleachers to where she was sitting, knees tucked against her chest. She was resting one ear against her drawn-up knees and staring towards the bright gray stripes on the horizon that signaled the edge of dawn. He was at his best in these early morning hours, when the sky was still dark enough to hide his discolored face.

"You okay LT?" He extended a long arm and offered her camelback to her. Pamela Hunt looked up at him with red eyes. She reached for the camelback and set it on the ground beside her.

"Thank you." Her response was quiet and cold.

"I know nothing feels good right now, but you need to stay hydrated and get back on your feet." He crouched down beside her and brushed the dark curls from his sweaty face. Without smiling, without condescending, without insulting her, he gave her a small and palatable sliver of encouragement. "Don't let Mann get to you. You've got a much better chance than you think." He got back to his feet and turned to leave, throwing one final comment over his shoulder for her to digest.

"Believe it or not, you do have some friends here."

*Part Four:*

*The Ghost of
Fort Leavenworth*

# Chapter 17
## Fort Leavenworth, KS (2014)

"Captain Hunt's office is just down this next hallway."

The word "captain" bit into Sharon's ego. She had returned to her combat boots and Army fatigues, with the obnoxious lieutenant bar still pinned in the center of her chest. She hadn't seen or spoken with Pamela Hunt since their last days together at Fort Benning, wandering through the ugly swamps in the mid-summer heat. The thought of revisiting all that unanswered resentment was unpleasant enough, without having to swallow the embarrassment of calling her Ma'am.

Sharon followed a young sergeant with a pixie cut through the open corridors outside the legal office. She glanced over the old paintings and memorabilia that lined the hallways, paying tribute to the long, uneasy history of law and warfare.

Her heavy boots echoed against the linoleum as she twisted and pulled at the ring on her finger. Some days it was tighter and heavier than others. Some days it was just another reminder of everything she kept hidden about those final days in Charlottesville.

Matt had his suspicions about Casper, she could sense that much. But he kept them to himself for reasons she couldn't quite grasp. Some days she was grateful for the silence. That she was able to hold on to their make-believe romance for just a bit longer. Other days it was worse than being interrogated and accused of all kinds of ugly betrayals. Because she had no idea how close she was to losing him.

The sergeant with the pixie cut pushed open the office door and stepped inside.

"Ma'am, there's a Lieutenant Sharon here to see you."

Pam Hunt looked up from behind an old desk, the gray morning breaking through the long window behind her. She had the same vibrant red hair and sharp grey eyes, and wore an identical pair of combat fatigues, with the exception of the captain bars sewn on the center of her chest.

"Thank you Sergeant Cole."

The sergeant walked out of the room to the heavy sound of the door closing behind her. Sharon was left staring across the layers of distrust between her and the woman on the other side of the cramped room.

"Looks like someone called in the National Guard." Pam dropped her fingers on the desk. Sharon shrank at the thought of all the bitterness hidden beneath those perfectly trimmed nails.

"How've you been Pam?" Sharon stepped across the room, taking a seat across from her former classmate.

"I've been well." Hunt looked her over and dropped her grey eyes towards the lieutenant rank on her chest. "Looks like they still haven't made you captain."

"The paperwork is being processed." Sharon responded.

"Isn't that always the case with the National Guard?" Hunt leaned back in her chair, still too sober and awkward to offer anything resembling a smile. "I never did get my wings, but at least they promoted me as soon as the suspension was lifted."

"I didn't come here to fight with you." Sharon tried to stop her before she went too far down old, forgotten roads. "I just need a copy of the CID report."

She had no delusions that Casper was innocent. The missing gun and the blood on his sweatshirt was enough to remind her how dangerous he was. And certainly enough to secure a set of handcuffs around his wrists. But she needed to see the file before she could judge what he was up against. To see for herself, in black and white police data, what he had done that he couldn't seem to remember.

Hunt opened her desk drawer and pulled out a copy of the investigation file. She dropped it on the desk and stared at the thick folders. "You're not going to like what's in it."

"You're really going to prosecute him without a murder weapon?" Sharon stayed focused on evidence. The physical traces and objective facts that weren't tainted with memories or emotions.

"You're really going to defend him?" Hunt lifted her eyes from the file, staring back at her with a troubled look that was both indecipherable and severe. "Knowing everything you know about him?"

"You had no reason to arrest him." Sharon swallowed her doubts and trained her eyes on the thick folder under Hunt's painted nails.

"He was also AWOL Sharon. The day that he was brought in for questioning on a homicide investigation, your client got on a plane and left the state against orders." Hunt tilted her head to one side in a display of mock sympathy. "And you still think that he's innocent?"

She knew that Casper had kept things from her. They always did. Petty things like AWOLs and bad debt. Things that prosecutors would use to question their integrity and taint juries. It didn't change things. But it made her temperature rise and her stomach uneasy. "Leaving the state against orders doesn't make someone guilty of homicide. Bad judgment perhaps, but not homicide."

"He has you completely brainwashed, hasn't he?" Hunt leaned against the desk, aiming straight for the softest, must vulnerable flesh she could see. "I'm trying to help you Sharon. I'm trying to save you from yourself."

"And who's going to save Casper if I walk away?" Her voice sounded loose and uncontrolled in her own ears.

"You really believe in all this? God and Country and Valor?" Hunt shook her head in pained disbelief. "You're willing to put your own safety at risk to try to preserve this image of some great war hero? You know what they call him in the MP Brigade?"

"It doesn't matter what they call him." Sharon set her jaw.

"They call him the Ghost of Fort Leavenworth. Because he died in the desert and he never came home." There was nothing resembling gratitude or reverence in her voice. Only naked, unadulterated hostility. "The person you're trying to save is gone."

"You don't know that." Sharon was losing the battle to keep her whirling emotions deep inside her core. All the love and fear and regret was slipping to the surface, and Hunt could sense every tremor.

"You know the worst part about your sad little affair?" Hunt bit her lip as if trying to get the hideous words past her tongue. "I could never really tell if you were actually in love with him or if you were just following orders."

Sharon felt each word sink into her skin. The nauseous feeling they gave her was both familiar and strange. She closed her eyes until the wave passed, then shook her head in a tired motion. "You can't really think he meant to do this."

The awful words slipped past her throat, exposing her own misgivings in a single traitorous sentence.

"If you want to cry PTSD you need to request a sanity board." Hunt directed her eyes back to the file beneath her fingertips. "Otherwise he's at the mercy of the panel."

"You're making this personal." The words came out a bit crisper and thicker than she'd intended. "You're not thinking like a prosecutor. You don't have the evidence for a conviction."

"You don't think so?" Hunt raised her eyebrows.

"One bar fight and an AWOL is not enough to charge someone with a homicide. If you weren't so bitter you could see that."

Hunt bit her lip again, a small puff of air escaping from the sides of her mouth. "You don't even know who the victim is, do you?"

Sharon's lips parted as some awful thought died in her throat. A cold, distant memory hit her like ice water.

"The crime photos are just past the police reports." Hunt loosened her grip on the investigation file and slid it across the desk.

Sharon took the accordion file in her uneasy hands. She fished through the intake forms and general reports, her fingers stumbling through the piles of data until she came upon the hard edges of a series of photographs.

She saw the familiar face first. The brown skin and dark eyes, the shaved head and perfect white teeth. She recognized the completeness of his face before she focused in on the bullet holes and the blood. The lifeless gaze, the stiff limbs. Her breath was caught in her windpipe and her mind seized up around the one toxic detail that Casper had failed to disclose.

"Oh god." She brought one hand to her mouth and buckled. She could hear the squeak of Hunt's chair as she sat back and rolled across the plastic mat beneath her desk.

"Jamie." Hunt used her first name for the first time in a long string of hostile months, her voice vibrating with what sounded like genuine alarm and concern. "You don't have to show up for the confinement hearing on Tuesday, we will get him another lawyer. The man is a danger to himself and whether you realize it or not, he's a danger to you. I'm doing you a favor. Withdraw from this thing now before it's too late."

# Chapter 18
## Fort Leavenworth, KS (2014)

Ben Casper walked ahead of his police escorts, his dog tags jingling against the laces of his combat boots. He stood tall in his Army fatigues, with pieces of his military career decorating his uniform. His major rank, a solid gold leaf, was centered on his chest and a pair of Airborne wings were sewn above the words U.S. Army, just above his heart. His EOD deployment patch was fixed against his right arm and his ranger tab was proudly displayed on his left.

He felt the soft tingling moving through his head again, the way it always did when he'd gone too long without a drink. He needed one now. To keep the past where it belonged and to help him digest the heavy details that would eventually take his future from him.

He stepped over the threshold into the courtroom and was met by the shine in the wood paneling that covered the high walls and severe angles. The American flag and the emblem of the United States JAG Corps were centered on the back wall between the empty judge's platform and the witness stand. At the far end of the room were twelve vacant seats, waiting for the panel of officers that would determine things he couldn't remember. The room was full of formality and the busy sounds of the judge's staff moving about the enclosed space. The shuffling of papers, clicks on keyboards, heavy combat boots on hard linoleum, hushed conversations.

He'd spent plenty of time in this very room, and yet it had never seemed so cramped. He stepped through the gallery, wincing at the creak of the swinging door. He focused on the red hair of the woman seated at the prosecutor's table, her face was hidden in her notes and all he could see was the thick bun on the back of her head. He looked to his left and his eyes fell on the empty defense table, making the room seem very, very small.

"We have to keep moving Sir." The MP behind him edged him forward.

Major Casper set his stomach and walked the final few steps into the courtroom. He forced himself to sit at the empty table and his bones grew heavy. When at last he dared to take a glance at the prosecutor's table, he saw the familiar frame of Pamela Hunt. The shiny nails and coiled bun perfectly positioned behind her ears.

She looked up at him, a glint of vindication in her eyes.

She still blamed him for the adultery. For the suspended promotion and the fact that the Army had clipped her wings. She dropped her eyes back to the file in front of her, tapping her nails against the desk in an obnoxious rhythm, scribbling out her strategy for keeping him under lock and key.

"All rise." The bailiff behind him made the announcement.

Casper rose to his feet with the rest of the room as the military judge stepped through the chamber door. He entered the raised platform, his name and rank obscured by his black robe. He had a stern face. A long square jaw framed with thin gray hair and eyes full of difficult history. He seated himself and hid his eyes behind a stack of paper.

"Please be seated."

The courtroom filled with the sound of shuffling as the assembly took their seats. Casper glanced up at the clock on the wall, the seconds ticking by like the sound of an impending explosion. He glanced at the closed door behind him, the vacant chair where Sharon should have been.

She wasn't the sort to disappear without formal notice. Without offering up her petition to withdraw from the case and making a clean, unsuspicious exit. By now she knew more than he did. She had seen the file and made up her mind. It was possible he really was a monster. That he'd taken up all the forgiveness she had to give.

Judge Bradley looked at the empty defense table. He shuffled the papers in front of him, then looked up at the clock. "Major Casper, will your defense attorney be joining us today?"

Casper stared back at the judge, afraid of putting his thoughts into words. He would never truly know if it was the lies that lost her, or the truth. "It doesn't appear so Sir."

Captain Hunt raised an eyebrow, her fingers curling around her pen.

Judge Bradley folded his hands on the desk in front of him. "Unfortunately, if she isn't here, momentarily, we will have to proceed."

"I understand Sir." The message seemed to catch in his throat. For the first time since he'd learned that Mann was dead, it occurred to him to run. To take his life back. To find a way to the safety of the days before the war started. He could still outrun the enemy. He could fight and claw his way to freedom, outperform, outlast, survive. He sat silently assessing his situation, muscles clenched, eyes focused, heart rate rising. Searching frantically for just one concrete reason to do the honorable thing.

Then he heard the heavy creak of the door behind him. He closed his eyes and listened for the sound of her combat boots stepping into the gallery.

"Glad you could make it Lieutenant." Judge Bradley spoke across the room.

Casper heard the tread of her feet and the creak of the hinges on the gallery door. He took in the comforting smell of lilacs and his heart relaxed.

"We were just wondering if we would be forced to proceed without you."

"I apologize, your honor. I had some unfinished research to do this morning, but I'm ready to proceed."

Casper opened his eyes at the sound of her voice. He looked up in time to see her set a thick binder full of the evidence against him on the table. She avoided his eyes and concentrated her attention on the military judge staring back at her.

"Have a seat counselor."

Sharon sat down at the long table and opened the file in front of her.

"I didn't think you were coming." He spoke to her in a hushed tone.

"That makes two of us." Her voice was terse, her eyes buried in the notes under her fingertips.

"You didn't return any of my phone calls."

"When were you planning on telling me about Captain Mann?" She managed to lift her head and her eyes tore into him. "Why the hell would you keep something like that from me?"

"I have my reasons." He tried to soften the sting in her voice.

"The entire time," She shook her head with an angry breath. "You sat there in that coffee shop sipping your beer as if this was all just a big misunderstanding. You lied to my face, Sir."

"I couldn't tell you everything right away."

"Why is that?"

Judge Bradley cleared his throat and sorted his papers on the desk in front of him. He opened a pair of wire rimmed glasses and balanced them on his nose.

"Because you wouldn't have come if I had told you." Casper's voice dropped. "That's perfectly obvious."

"Are you ready then counselors?" Judge Bradley addressed the attorneys before him.

"Yes, your honor." Sharon stood in response.

"Yes, your honor." Hunt stood as well.

"Alright then. Please be seated." Judge Bradley adjusted his glasses and began reading from the script in front of him. "This hearing is a pre-trial confinement review of Major Benjamin Lee Casper. This review will include an examination of the relevant facts surrounding the offense for which you have been accused, specifically, one count of homicide in the shooting death of Captain James Anthony Mann." Judge Bradley glanced at Casper over his glasses. He tightened his jaw as he flipped a page in his notes. "This hearing is not a trial, but is solely to determine whether you should remain in pretrial confinement until such time as a court-martial can be convened. Do you understand the purpose of this review?"

"I'm the Chief of Military Justice." Major Casper responded from his subdued position behind the defense table. "I'm familiar with the process, your honor."

Sharon glared at him with her glassy blue eyes.

Judge Bradley looked up from his script, his response grotesquely formal. "I understand that Major Casper. Just the same, I intend to follow the required procedures the same as I would for any other defendant. Is that clear?"

"Say 'yes your honor." Sharon directed him.

"Yes, your honor." Major Casper echoed.

"Very well then. I will now advise you of your rights." Judge Bradley returned to the script in front of him. "You have the following rights granted to you under article 31 of the Uniform Code of Military Justice. You do not have to answer my questions or say anything . . ."

"Do not make this any worse for yourself." Sharon whispered.

"I don't need him to read me my rights off a piece of paper." Casper responded.

"Anything you say or do can be used as evidence against you in a criminal trial." Judge Bradley continued.

"That kind of bravado may work when you're the prosecutor, but over here it just makes you look reckless." Sharon continued. "They expect you to appear a little more subdued when you're being charged with a homicide."

"You have the right to talk privately to a lawyer before, during and after questioning and to have a lawyer present with you during questioning. This lawyer can be a civilian who you arrange for at no expense to the Government or a military lawyer detailed for you at no expense to you, or both." Judge Bradley concluded. "Do you understand these rights?"

"Yes, your honor." Casper nodded with a thick resistance in his throat.

"You have been charged with the offense of Homicide in violation of Article 118 of the Uniform Code of Military Justice."

Casper sat in silence as he listened to Judge Bradley's emotionless reading of the charges against him. Every meaningless word another weight pressing down on him, confining him to his chair. The cold reality of the situation becoming more clear with every heartbeat. He glanced at the woman sitting beside him, who was only marginally aware of the how broken he was. He caught the glint of the ring on her finger and a solid knot filled up his lungs.

"Do you understand the nature of the proceedings as I've described them?" Judge Bradley's voice echoed through the cold room.

"Yes, your honor." He responded.

"By whom do you wish to be represented during this pretrial confinement review?"

"First Lieutenant Jamie Sharon."

"The government representative in this hearing is Captain Pamela Hunt, who is also present. I have before me the report of investigation, which I intend to consider in making my determination. Is there anything else that you wish me to consider Captain Hunt?"

"Not at this time your honor." Captain Hunt stood to answer the judge. Her voice stirred the air in the stale room, indicating that the preliminary instructions were coming to a close.

"Defense counsel, do you desire to make a statement on behalf of the accused?" Judge Bradley turned his attention towards Lieutenant Sharon.

It wasn't until that moment Casper realized what little chance he had of walking out of that courtroom. He listened to the creak of Sharon's chair as she stood to face the judge. She squared her shoulders and cleared her throat.

"Your honor I'd like to make a motion to have my client released from custody pending trial. There is no evidence that Major Casper was involved in Captain Mann's death. He *was* involved in an altercation with the victim the night that he was murdered. The government intends to use this simple assault as evidence that he later committed a homicide, but they have no eyewitnesses, no physical evidence, they haven't even articulated a plausible motive for the crime."

"Your honor, if I may." Captain Hunt stood to object.

"Proceed Captain." Judge Bradley nodded in her direction.

"The altercation by itself is not evidence of a homicide, it is, however, evidence that Major Casper is inclined to violence and that the victim was a target of that violence not more than 8 hours before his body was discovered. I also think it needs to be noted that the altercation at the Eagle Lounge was not a 'simple assault.' The victim had a broken jaw and three cracked ribs."

Casper balled his hands in his lap. He could picture the soft flesh in Mann's face and midsection giving way beneath his tight fists.

"Major Casper's been trained in hand to hand combat," Hunt continued. "He's proven that he's willing to use this specialized training against other soldiers when provoked."

"Your Honor, I would remind you that my client has already received an Article 15 for the assault against Captain Mann. If the government intended to use it against him like this, they should have brought the appropriate charges." Sharon stood and interrupted. "Captain Mann left the bar around 10:10 p.m. He was recorded entering post at the front gate fifteen minutes later. At that point we lose sight of him. No one sees him, no one hears from him until his body is found on the running trail near the gym at 5:30 a.m. Somewhere between the front gates and the running trail, Captain Mann was murdered. But the government has no evidence, other than the altercation at the Eagle Lounge, tying Major Casper to this man's death."

Judge Bradley straightened his glasses as he paged through the CID report. "What physical evidence do you have Captain Hunt?"

"Your honor, CID recovered a large black sweatshirt from the defendant's home. The sweatshirt was covered in blood spatter that DNA analysis confirmed belonged to the victim."

Casper opened his hands and examined the creases in his palms, running one finger along the pink scar that filled his right hand. Mann's blood was all over his sweatshirt. And all over his hands. He felt a cold shiver as he tightened his fists again, trying to hold onto some sense of stability.

"Your honor, the victim's blood was likely transferred during the assault at the Eagle Lounge. The DNA test doesn't prove that Major Casper was involved in the homicide any more than the assault itself."

"The autopsy report indicates that trace amounts of pepper spray were found in the victim's nose and throat." The pitch in Captain Hunt's voice rose. There was a sense of urgency in her arguments that Casper found unnerving. Something cutting and ruthless. Bordering on unhealthy. "CID agents recovered a small canister of pepper spray from the defendant's home. They also pulled two clean fingerprints from the canister, both belonging to the defendant."

Casper closed his eyes and brought his closed hands to his lips.

"The pepper spray was fixed to a key ring that belonged to Major Casper's wife." Sharon responded for him. "There is nothing inherently suspicious about the fact that my client's fingerprints were found on a common object in his own home."

"Please, be advised, both of you that this is not a trial on the merits." Judge Bradley raised his voice to interrupt the exchange. "This hearing is solely to determine whether there is probable cause to keep Major Casper confined until a court-martial can be convened. Captain Hunt, is there any other statement that the government wishes to make in support of *confinement*?"

Hunt tapped her nails on the desk, marking the room with a repetitive click, soft and simple. She had a calculated warning nestled behind her grey eyes. "Your honor, it needs to be recognized that the defendant is an obvious flight risk, evidenced by the fact that he went AWOL shortly after being questioned by CID."

"Your honor," Sharon's voice broke, a subtle clue the she felt her advantage slipping. "Major Casper boarded a flight that he had arranged months in advance. He returned willingly, and knowing full well that he was likely to be arrested the moment he returned to base. His behavior was rash, inexcusable and definitely a mistake, but does not, by itself, render him a flight risk. I would request, at the very least, that you consider putting him on house arrest. There is heavy security posted at all entrances and exits to the base. He poses no risk to anyone in the confines of his own home."

"Your honor, I strongly urge you to consider the fact that the weapon has not yet been recovered." Hunt didn't pause to breathe. Casper heard a thin stretch in her vocal chords as she forced out each syllable. "Ballistics testing has confirmed that the victim was murdered with .45 caliber handgun, however, no further testing can be performed until CID locates a suspect weapon. If the defendant is allowed the freedom to move about the base we run the risk that he will influence witness testimony, or worse yet, succeed in destroying critical evidence. We can't guarantee he hasn't already disposed of the weapon that killed Captain Mann."

He tried to remember where he'd last seen that cursed drop gun from Iraq. He closed his eyes and felt the solid weight of the weapon in his hands. He heard the clicks as his fingers spun the chamber, confirming the rounds were still loaded. He knew it by sight and smell, but everything else was cloaked in a grim fog.

"Your honor, if Major Casper had intended to dispose of any evidence he would have destroyed the bloody sweatshirt the night of the assault." Sharon threw an impressive energy behind every argument. She was adept and convincing, well skilled in hiding her own misgivings from the court. "We would have evidence that he headed out the front gates with a firearm that very night."

"He's a lawyer, your honor. He understands evidence." Hunt demanded, calm and rational. "He was stealthy enough to wait until the following day when he had a flight out of town. He was ordered confined because he is unpredictable and dangerous."

Judge Bradley raised one hand to stop the arguments. He pivoted in his chair and turned his eyes on Major Casper.

Casper watched the painful evaluation unfolding behind the judge's concentrated stare. He knew he was guilty of things he didn't remember, and things he couldn't forget. The hearing was little more than a formality. A game to see if some robed academic could see past his stoic exterior to the caliber of the man inside. He was still a soldier. Someone who didn't back down. Who was not easily threatened.

But there was something about the very fabric of a soldier that also made him dangerous, and discerning the difference between a soldier and killer wasn't as easy as it might seem. Within the span of 20 minutes Judge Bradley was expected to detect the subtle warning signs that he had lost his ability to contain the very impulses that the Army had trained him to hone and embrace.

"Very well." Judge Bradley adjusted his glasses one last time. He returned to the familiar script before him and read through the pre-packaged language that was designed to impartially deal with the impossible question before him. "Having heard both your arguments and taking into consideration the investigation before me, I have determined that continued pretrial confinement is warranted under the circumstances."

Casper felt the hard exhale of the woman beside him. He closed his eyes and clung to the invisible scent of lilacs that fell from her wrists as they dropped to the table.

"I have reached this determination because there is probable cause to believe that the defendant, Major Benjamin Lee Casper, did commit the crime of homicide and because it is foreseeable that the defendant will not appear for trial or will engage in serious criminal misconduct pending trial."

Major Casper opened his eyes. He turned his head and watched the blood return to Captain Hunt's face and fingers. She exhaled softly and the fierce energy behind her eyes calmed to an undetectable pulse.

"This hearing is now adjourned." Judge Bradley confirmed his decision.

Sharon bit her bottom lip. She turned towards him with a heartfelt grimace. She seemed to be searching for some minor words of comfort. Something from her stockpile of anecdotes that she gave to previous clients on similar occasions.

"I'm sorry, Sir." Was all she could manage.

"Nothing to be sorry about." He shook his head, trying to decipher her flutter of nerves. It was clearly more substantial than simple performance anxiety. It had the look and smell of fear.

He wondered if he even knew what it meant to be afraid anymore. If there was anything left that he loved enough, that he was afraid of losing, to actually scare him.

"You'll need to come with us Sir." The MPs that had escorted him into the room were now standing behind him, crowding at his elbows as if they half expected him to bolt for the nearest exit.

"No need to worry Sergeant. I'm not going anywhere." Casper got up from his seat and straightened his posture, glancing back at Sharon with a question in his hazel eyes. "And how about you?"

"I'm not going anywhere either." She echoed.

He nodded as he grabbed his patrol cap and turned towards the exit, preparing for the short walk back to his holding cell. He had only taken a few short steps when he spotted Grace at the back of the hearing room. Her blonde hair loosely pulled away from her face and falling around her worn cheekbones. She was dressed in an old black jogging suit that hung around her thin hips and shoulders. Her green eyes looked soft and tired as she watched his escorts saddle up beside him, gauging his every movement.

"If I didn't know better, I'd say that was my wife." Major Casper murmured out loud to his escorts. "I may be seeing ghosts after all."

# Chapter 19
## Fort Leavenworth, KS (2014)

The old stones of reeked of distasteful history. Men had been imprisoned in this old building for both clinging to their consciences and for abandoning humanity. From the pacifists who were beaten and starved during World War I, to the Nazi killers who were hanged and unceremoniously buried in the cemetery down the road. The military's answer to tragedies like Abu Ghraib and Kandahar, most of it ended at the front gates of Leavenworth. Major Benjamin Casper found himself living in these men's shadows.

He was escorted through the halls of the old U.S. Disciplinary Barracks. His combat boots and fatigues had been exchanged for a gray jumpsuit and a pair of soft running shoes, with his dogtags now hanging uselessly about his neck

The halls were quiet and smelled of mildew. His footsteps echoed in his ears as they ushered him into the yellowed room. The door swung wide enough to reveal Grace's pretty shape, seated in a folding chair in front of an old table.

He couldn't look at her for long.

The tingling in his head had followed him from the courtroom, building momentum as he was ushered into obscurity. Old habits were emerging from deep inside his wasted brain. He counted the steps it would take to get him from the door to the table, from the table to the wall. He took stock of all the entrances and exits, the lighting and heating sources. How many keys he could hear on the MPs keychain behind him. How heavy were the chairs, the table, how high, how wide. He was vigilant to the point of exasperation, intent on knowing his environment better than the enemy. He surveyed the room for anything that would give him an advantage. Aside from the basic table and chairs the room was empty and uninviting, a perfect breeding ground for the ghosts of old war criminals.

Grace stood as he stepped around the old table and sat across from her, his eyes raking the contours of the walls around them, pulsing as they absorbed details that were both invisible and irrelevant. Casper slipped into his chair and glared into the ceiling lights above him, breathing in the same stale air as the men who'd come before him, some of whom he'd put away himself.

Grace was still standing, watching him through pale eyes. She wiped a wet spot from her right cheek, leaving a small mascara smudge under her right eye. Her nail polish was chipped and her fingers were thin, but she still wore the ring he had given her, all those years ago.

"I didn't want you to have to see me in here." Casper was still lost in the ceiling lights overhead.

"I couldn't leave you alone in here." She hugged her midsection and held tight to her soft sleeves, as if trying to find comfort in the smell and feel of earlier memories. "I found someone to take my shift for me."

"You told work about the hearing?" Casper dropped his eyes from the ceiling and began cracking his knuckles, surprised that he took any concern in petty neighborhood chatter.

"Everyone knows where you are. They all read the paper." Grace took in a shallow breath and looked at him closely. He imagined what he must look like to her, draped in a gray jumpsuit like a violent criminal. "They don't say anything about it. Not to me. Not out loud. They just stare with this sort of pity and confusion."

He dropped his eyes to the scratched furniture in front of him, distracting himself with the grooves in the wood. Measuring their length, curve and depth, imagining the mental state of the man who had dug his nails into the grain, at the end of his rope with no words of comfort to offer to those who'd once cared for him. "I wanted to protect you from all this."

"Your lawyer." She turned her eyes downward, digging into something meaty and puerile. "The first lieutenant. She's a lot prettier than she is effective."

"There aren't many lawyers who would've won that hearing." Casper watched his wife pace back and forth in front of him, unable to look him in the eye.

"I don't know why you didn't run when you had the chance." She gasped into the open air. "You could be halfway to Singapore by now."

"I needed answers."

"Answers to what?"

Casper leaned back in his chair again, cruel thoughts running through his head. He wanted a drink. To drown her out. To stop the questions. To dull the edges and break his furious concentration.

"Do you think I belong here Grace?"

Grace stared at him for a cold minute, on the verge of letting out a confession or something black. "I don't know if you belong here Ben, but as long as you're in here I know that you're safe."

He watched the bulge in her neck as she swallowed. "Why don't you tell me what's on your mind?'

"You don't want to know."

"I need to know." He focused on her nervous hands, the way she couldn't keep them still when she wasn't speaking. The tense energy that pumped through her wrists and fingers as she curled and uncurled them into inefficient fists. "I may be stuck in this jumpsuit in this prison, but I need you to treat me like it's still me, alright?"

"Am I going to lose you?" She brushed a strand of yellow hair from her face and looked at him with hot tears burning the pits of her eyes. "When I think of all the time I've spent worrying about you. Every one of your deployments. There were times I didn't hear from you for weeks on end. I would see something on the news about a roadside bomb going off and I would wonder, is that it? Is he gone? How long will it take the Army to tell me? How long will it take to pick up what's left of him and identify the remains? What will they even send home to me? What could they possibly send home? Are they going to call or will they come to the door? There were days that I pulled all the shades and didn't answer the phone because I didn't want to know what had happened to you. As if I could keep you alive by not answering the door."

"I'm sorry you went through all that." Casper felt his stomach turn. The phrase felt so commonplace and hollow.

"There are days that I think Randy's the lucky one."

"You really shouldn't say things like that." His voice dropped a full octave.

"At least his family knows Ben. At least it's over for them. Me, I'm living with a phantom. I hear the shower running in the mornings and I notice that someone's been drinking the coffee, but you're still stuck over there, in that desert, and every day I wait for you to come back to me." She leaned over the table and he tried to focus on the lines in her face, to feel what she was feeling. His body was shackled to his chair. His mind was distracted by the lines on the floor and the footsteps in the hallway, and hundreds of other details that didn't matter.

"I love you Ben, but I don't love watching you destroy yourself. You have to do something about whatever it is that's tormenting you before it eats you alive. Before it eats me alive."

Her skin had grown pale, as if all this heavy truth was stopping her blood from circulating. Her restless hands, finally lay still on the table between them. Perhaps she was right. His demons were doing more of a number on her than they were on him.

He heard footsteps in the hall, the steady tread of multiple pairs of combat boots, keys rattling and soft voices before the door creaked open and a young Staff Sergeant stepped inside. "Sir. Your attorney is here to see you."

Her boots hit the concrete as she stepped into the room, the crisp sound of her uniform moving in time with her walk.

"Funny how they still call you 'Sir' as they're about to tie a rope around your neck." Casper's eyes were caught on a tiny square of light in the hallway directly behind the staff sergeant's feet. Somewhere beyond the tiny yellowed room, was a window to the outside, conveniently catching the rise of the midday sun.

"Thank you Sergeant." Sharon's voice echoed in the chilled room and the guard stepped outside with the same bullish stride as before.

Grace stared at the young lieutenant with frost forming in her green eyes. She was obviously more concerned with Sharon's cheeks and hips then her intellect.

Lieutenant Sharon extended her hand to introduce herself. Her voice and handshake full of caution, as if preparing for recoil.

"Mrs. Casper, I'm Jamie Sharon. I went to school with your husband."

"Of course." Grace accepted the uncomfortable contact and offered Jamie a simple nod.

"Would you mind if we had a few moments?" Sharon's eyes shifted towards Casper and he felt the weight of the gray jumpsuit close around him.

"Not at all." Grace looked back at him with recycled sadness in her eyes. "I've said enough for one day."

"I'm glad you came." Casper stopped her as she headed out of the yellow room. She turned around with one hand on the door, a whisper of hope brushing the lines of her face.

"I'll keep waiting for you Ben. As long as it takes." She mouthed the words more than spoke them, then walked through the door in the span of a heartbeat.

Casper turned towards Lieutenant Sharon. He scanned the creases in her combat uniform. The Red Bull on her left sleeve and the missing deployment patch on her right. The single lieutenant bar on her chest that should have long ago been replaced with a captain's rank. He noted the arch in her neck, the solid chin and jaw, the crease in her forehead and the unmistakable discomfort in her eyes.

"Why don't you just say it Jamie? I know you're thinking it. You might as well get it out of the way."

"Have you considered requesting a Sanity Board, Sir?" The words rolled effortlessly from her tongue.

"It's not happening LT."

"Why not?"

"Because I'm not crazy." He raised his voice and saw a noticeable drop in her shoulders. "I'm not going to go out like that. If I killed the man, I'll take the punishment, but I'm not pleading for mercy because I've seen too much blood and severed limbs to make my own choices. I'd rather be labeled a killer than a head case."

"It's your decision, Sir." The message sunk in and she took a seat across from him. He hoped it would be the only time she'd ask. "I'll stand by you either way."

Her eyes were the same shade of cool blue. A temporary harbor where he could hide from the hurricane closing in on him. They weren't as warm or welcoming as they had once been, but they were familiar. Far from untroubled, but dedicated and strong. "Why didn't you leave when you found out it was Mann?"

"That's not who I am. That's not what you taught me."

"What I taught you?"

Sharon reached into the stiff collar of her uniform and fished for the beaded chain that held her dog tags. She pulled them out and held them between her fingers, slowly turning the thin metal plates to find the familiar engraving on the back. "I will always put the mission first. I will never accept defeat. I will never quit." She looked up at him with her liquid blue eyes. "I will never leave a fallen comrade."

"So that's what I am? A fallen comrade?"

There was concern in her eyes and she reminded him, for a brief moment, of an earlier, stronger version of Grace. Before the worry had weighed down the skin behind her eyes and mouth. Breaking her charm and everything he'd once loved about her.

Casper watched her drop the dog tags back under her collar. He listened to the small clink as they settled under her shirt and rested, somewhere between her breasts and her heart.

"You need to tell me what happened between us."

She shook her head. "My only concern is to keep you out of prison."

"Even if I belong there?"

"What do you remember that you're not telling me?" Her eyes bored into him and she scraped the legs of her chair against the cold cement floor. "I was late this morning because I went and pulled your bar tab from the Eagle Lounge the night you attacked Mann. You only had three beers. You weren't so drunk that you lost everything."

"I wouldn't put too much faith in that bar tab Jamie. It was Veteran's Day, I'm sure someone bought me a beer or two."

He watched the possibility sink into her tender resolve, forcing her to step back and start again.

"The unregistered weapon you brought home from Iraq?" Her soft eyes burrowed into his skin, tempered with a bit more caution. "What caliber was it?"

"It was a .45. The serial number's been filed off and it had 3 rounds in the chamber."

"Did you kill him Ben?"

He felt the soft sound of his first name roll off her tongue and his defenses relaxed. He was almost drawn into an involuntary confession. Almost spilled how he was responsible for the dead staff sergeant buried under all those pounds of earth. That he failed to do his job and pull the trigger that could've saved him. "I don't know if I killed Mann. But I've done other things. We're not always charged with the crimes we committed."

Sharon's jaw tightened and she shook her head in controlled anger. "If you're so hell bent on self-destruction then why in God's name did you bring me down here to defend you?"

He couldn't find the nerve to answer her. His eyes combed the contours of her face like he were looking for something. A key in her expression, her movements, her body language. A clue to some riddle that he wasn't able to answer. The tingling in his head was waning. He could feel the sharp edges of something dangerous, moving along the perimeter of the thick fog.

"There's obviously something still inside of you that wants a way out of this." Jamie continued. "I'm here for him. The part of you that isn't afraid to hope for a normal life again."

"He's not long for this world Lieutenant. The clock's ticking."

"I'm going to make you an appointment for a substance abuse evaluation."

"Forget it." He shook his head in defiance.

"It is the only way to defend your behavior that night."

"Jesus you defense attorneys are all the same. Is that the only thing you can come up with? He has a drinking problem, he couldn't help himself."

"You have a drinking problem, Ben." Sharon insisted. The chain of her dog tags still visible under her collar, and the simple words of the Warrior Ethos pinned against her chest. "And with all due respect I think you've been fighting a pretty serious case of PTSD since your last deployment."

"Based on what Lieutenant? Because I got into a bar fight with an asshole?"

"It's been more than one fight. You may not remember the last time, but I do. You nearly killed him." She set her palms down on the table between them, the brilliant stone from her engagement ring the only bright spot in the whole of the worn down room. "What was the fight about? You told me it was over a girl, I want details. What was it really about?"

He stared at her hands. The white skin and thin fingers. Soft, delicate and deceptively lethal. He felt the sharp edges closing in. Names and faces cutting painful new groves into his membranes. The smoke cleared and he could finally hear the ugly words Mann threw at him. The accusation that brought his closed fist across Mann's chin. The recall burned and swelled. And sentenced him to a punishment worse than any judge could levy.

"I don't remember any of it." The awful lie grazed his lips.

"The only way I can defend you is if you get a substance abuse assessment." She shook her head again. "Because if you don't have a drinking problem, if you don't have some form of trauma associated with your last tour in Iraq, then this is just bad behavior. And I can't stand before a court-martial with a straight face and convince them to trust in your good character and reputation if this was a deliberate choice. You can't keep all this pain and guilt bottled up like this. It's going to destroy you."

There was a loud knock on the outside door, followed by the baritone voice of the staff sergeant in the hallway. "You got two more minutes."

Sharon stared across the table at a sober man in a gray jumpsuit. Someone unrecognizable and strange. "I'll set up the appointment Ben. The rest is on you."

She pushed herself away from the table to stand, when he brought the unmistakable heat of his fingers on her wrist.

"I'm not the only one hiding things Jamie." He looked up at her with a dark despair flooding through his temples. "I'm entitled to at least one honest answer before you leave."

"What's that?" Her fingers twitched involuntarily and his grip tightened.

"Was it just my imagination?" He looked up from the table, anxious to see some trace of warmer memories in her eyes. "Did you ever want me the way that I wanted you?"

Sharon dropped her eyes to their intertwined hands on the table. His pulsing fingers spread around the sharp edges of Matt's ring. The tender touch interrupted by the cool metal.

"You know I did." She kept her eyes hidden from him, buried deep behind dark eyelashes.

There was a slight tightening in his chest. An ugly feeling of vertigo as if he were standing on the edge of chasm being pulled towards the precipice. Waiting for the air to hit him, the weightless freefall that would finally accept his surrender. "When did it end?"

He felt a tremor run through her fingers. She let out a long breath and re-opened her eyes. "That's two questions."

The staff sergeant knocked on the door a second time. The door opened and Sharon pulled her hand out from under his strong hold. "I've got to go, Sir."

Casper listened to the cold return to formality and the tread of her boots against the cement floor, his eyes still planted on the empty space on the table where her hand had been, losing himself in the steady rhythm of her leaving.

"I'll take the assessment." The voice came from some small, buried place in his chest that was hidden and bruised, still remotely pulsing with life. "I'll do it for you."

He looked up just in time to see her turn back towards him one last time. His vision was blurred and he wasn't able to make out her expression. Her voice was far off and echoed through his head, as if she were shouting down at him from the top of a disappearing cliff.

"I'm going to get you out of here."

# Part Five:

# *Love and Adrenaline*

# Chapter 20
## Charlottesville, VA (2012)

Ben Casper stood in line to pay for his breakfast and coffee. He felt as if he'd been swallowed by the University of Virginia cafeteria. He was mesmerized by the smells and colors of the fruit trays, shuffled among the lines of students with their cell phones lit up in their hands, distracted by the constant beeping behind the register. All of it blended together and fused into the background. He was still remembering ghastly things from the war. Unsavory images lighting up abandoned regions of his brain. This wasn't the first time he'd felt it. That tingling sensation that wouldn't go away.

"Next." The woman at the register called his attention back towards the line.

"Yes Ma'am." He moved his tray down the line and handed her his credit card. She swiped it once, then handed it back to him with a paper receipt, pointing to the dotted line for him to sign.

He was still adjusting to normal. Still ignoring the warning signs that surfaced when life got too quiet. When there weren't enough distractions to keep him from dwelling on old mistakes. He signed the short slip of paper and handed it to the woman behind the register, picking up his tray and weaving about the crowded tables.

"Thank you for your service." He thought he heard her say it, but couldn't be sure if it was real or in his head. Her voice drifted behind him, blending in with the mix of other common noises.

He couldn't trust the daily rhythm of life without war. Standing in lines and picking through fruit with no sense of meaning or purpose. Life was not fragile here. Time was not precious. Happiness was not a rare trinket that he recognized only when things didn't hurt. It had a substance and form of its own and he was expected to find it again.

He glanced at the wedding ring on his left hand, and felt distant memories of Grace merging with that incessant tingling. There was no simple solution for them. No clear strategy to right all of those wrongs.

He watched the civilian students mingle around him. He was drawn to the colors in their clothing. The silky fabric of their scarves and jackets. The sweaters and skirts, light shoes and painted lips. The individual arrangements of hair, loose or layered to one side. The headphones and rebellion.

His boots felt heavy on his feet and for a small moment he was envious of their freedom. Their sense of belonging and peace. The uniform gave him away as an outsider. Some of them looked at him with curiosity as he passed. Some with sympathy. Strings of peers who found it difficult to understand that this life was a choice.

He spotted only one uniformed soldier on the far side of the cafeteria, the brunette with the Red Bull patch on her sleeve, sitting alone in front of a bright window. Seeing her gave him a strange sense of peace. And a muted stirring of guilt. He could envision some form of happiness living in her shadow. Because she had yet to discover all of his faults and frailties. He saw in her the opportunity to pretend to be the person he remembered himself to be, instead of the broken thing that Grace had welcomed home from the war.

He moved towards her, watching the way she spread a layer of cream cheese around her bagel and bit into the warm bread. She picked up a cell phone from the table and began scrolling through the screen. Her eyes went cloudy as she flipped through the pale lights, as if she were looking for a friendly communication that was lost between the circuitry.

He stepped towards the table in front of the unguarded window, directly challenging the early rays of the morning sun. "Waiting for a phone call?"

The lieutenant looked up from her phone and offered him a simple, almost sad smile. "Just hoping for some news from home, Sir." She motioned to the chair across from her. "Would you like to sit?"

He stared out the large window, his eyes fixed on the gathering of birds and breezes in the open space. Simple joys that had been consumed by so many years of deserts and shrapnel. His heart thumped an irregular beat. The tingling in his head swelled and expanded.

He placed his tray on the square table, feeling reckless and unpredictable. He pulled out the chair closest to the lieutenant, and faced the window instead of her. He picked up a bruised orange from his plate, tempering his anxiety with a slow infusion of grit.

He breathed in the peculiar scent of lilacs, surprised at the way it comforted him. He watched the lieutenant hide her eyes behind a long sip of lukewarm coffee and slip her phone back into her pocket.

"Dogsitter again?" Casper tossed the ripened fruit from one hand to the other, keeping his eyes on its yellowing skin.

"Just wondering if Reese has torn apart enough pillows and clawed through enough doors for Sergeant Chase to regret taking him in." She hesitated over the sergeant's name, practically confirming that there was something more familiar hiding behind the uncomfortable formality. She took another bite of her bagel, her eyes glazing over as if her mind was still fixed on the warm phone in her pocket.

"If he's a good soldier, he'll keep his word." Casper responded. He was able to watch her refection in the glass. To see the clouds gathering in her eyes while leaving her some sense of privacy. "You sure he's just a friend LT?"

"He's a good soldier." She nodded as her hands embraced the warmth of her coffee cup. "Which is exactly why he's only a friend."

She looked up at him with clear blues eyes, unashamed of the sudden confession. More relieved to be rid of the burden than frightened of the consequences.

"We were only together for a short time." She continued, her eyes buried in her coffee cup once again. "He ended it. Just before I left for Charlottesville. Strange that you can become so attached so quickly."

"Distances are hard on relationships." Casper nodded blindly. He stopped tossing his fruit from side to side and dug his nails into the tender orange flesh, peeling the skin back and releasing a strong smell of citrus. "It tests people. It tests trust. It tests commitment."

"Your wife must be a pretty strong person." He took his eyes from the window just in time to catch the delicate shift of her eyes towards the silver band on his finger.

"She was." Casper looked up from peeling his orange, without offering any details as to how he'd ruined her. He tried not to question why she had asked about his wife. If it was possible that she was fighting the same gravity that he felt in his own bones.

"Are you going home for the holidays?"

"We make it a point not to see each other during training periods. It just makes things harder. Too many goodbyes in too short a time. It can mess with your sense of permanency. You always think you're living on borrowed time." He tossed a piece of fruit in his mouth and quickly worked it over until it was fit to swallow. "I've worked it out with Fassbender to see an old friend for Veterans Day instead."

"This must be a pretty tame environment compared to EOD." She took another long sip from her coffee cup, filling the empty spaces with pretty sounds and syllables. "What drives someone to give up being a bomb technician to study law?"

He was grateful for her simple presence. Every word and every breath keeping the long silences at bay. It was in those infinite stretches of time, between the bomb blasts and the shrapnel, that people went mad. Fell into cycles of abusive thinking. Of rage and blame.

They were wrong to send him here. The simplicity and solitude would break him faster than the rigged explosives.

"I didn't give up being a bomb technician." Casper put another orange slice in his mouth and waited for its thin skin to disintegrate on his tongue. He rolled it around with his imprisoned thoughts, eventually taking its tangy skin in his teeth and forcing it down. He felt a dangerous urge to open up to her. To create an intimacy where there shouldn't be one. "I was given a choice between the warrior transition unit for wounded veterans or the JAG Corps. My commanders have been around enough explosives to recognize a ticking-time bomb when they see one."

Lieutenant Sharon let go of her coffee cup and the warm smell of lilacs followed her wrists. Her eyes were calm and reassuring, free of judgment or surprise.

"Normally I wouldn't tell people that. But it seemed only fair. You let me in on your secret with the dogsitter. Now you know mine."

"It won't leave this table Sir." Her voice was sweet and strong.

He couldn't imagine a situation where he would regret confiding in her. She might be the first version of normal that was appealing enough to compete with the explosions. And to numb, at least momentarily, the growing tingling in his head.

# Chapter 21
## Charlottesville, VA (2012)

The rope dug into the meat of her palm, deep and painful. The cold rain came down above and below her, and all she could see was the coarse section of tweed in front of her. The thick knotty fibers that kept her suspended above the muddy ground. Her red hair was caked with mud and sweat, and she had been hanging there for far too long.

"Lieutenant Hunt!" Captain Fassbender called to her from the ground below. "You go up or you come down, you hear me! You dangle there much longer and your strength will give out! Now move!"

She could already feel it. Her arms had gone limp like jelly, twitching in the vile rain. She'd forced an unlucky 13 pull-ups from her underworked muscles that morning. Nearly broken herself to keep up with the men. She heard their tired voices all around the soggy mats below her. Felt the rain lick her face with jealousy and malice. She wasn't going down.

"Use your legs Hunt!" It was a voice she might have recognized if she wasn't so desperately hanging there. "Your arms are useless to you now. You need to propel yourself up with your legs, take a bite out of the rope and push."

Her arms still had to hold her long enough to secure the rope around her feet. She sucked in the cold air and wrestled for a foothold, fighting for whatever shred of strength was left in her sagging arms. She pinned the rope under her boots just as the trembling started again. She pushed herself up another quarter inch, then moved again before her arms could give out on her. She fought for every step, eying the top of the climb as if it was a vaulted sliver of heaven. She moved again, the miserable rope slipping between her boots, her weary arms and shoulders hoisting her heavy body 30 feet in the air. When without warning, her arms surrendered. The vile rope ripped itself from her clenched fists and she fell towards the muddy mats below.

***

Lieutenant Hunt could already feel a deep pain spreading across her chest and shoulders. A tightening of the raw muscles that weren't able to hold her up that morning. The sprints, the pull-ups and the disastrous rope climb had all followed her into the mock trial that morning. Every week she fell further behind the Airborne crew. The fatigue was starting to hurt and bristle.

"Exactly what was the nature of your relationship with Sergeant Farrell?"

She found herself on the receiving end of a cross-examination at the indelicate hands of Captain Mann. The same smiling face that had picked her out of the mud that morning, after her strength had failed and her hopes of reaching Airborne school had broken on the drenched mat beneath her. He hid a goading smile behind his perfect white teeth, as if he knew just how much she hurt under her stiff uniform. She felt herself weakening under the weight of that perfect smile. Afraid that she might never be more than prey to such selfish men.

"He was my platoon sergeant." She pushed a mechanical answer through her teeth. "He said he would teach me everything I needed to know about the Army."

The practice courtroom was lined with light oak furnishings and the heavy feel of formality. The instructor, Major Adams, sat behind the judge's bench, with a firm hand on his chin as he waited for Captain Mann to continue with his cross-examination.

Lieutenant Hunt was confined to the witness stand in the center of the room. The large box made her feel small and exposed, threatening to bring back so many feelings of contempt and regret. She fought back shadowy images of hateful hands, holding down a drunk and limp body that was too lost and confused to find her way home.

Captain Mann seemed bent on making the exercise as uncomfortable as the instructor would allow. He set his fists against the defense table, pitched his weight forward and read through the highlighted sections of his open textbook. An immature smile playing across his lips.

"Private Duncan," he used the fictitious name and rank she'd been assigned, trying to work out a confession to a fictional encounter with some fictional swaggering nobody. To taint her reputation and paint her as something dirty and undeserving. The questions he'd planned were invasive and puerile, as if he really were trying to tear out her most closely held secrets. "You said on direct examination that initially you didn't mind the platoon sergeant's advances?"

She wouldn't let him see her fall apart a second time. She'd sworn off any memories that made her feel weak or inferior. Her body might succumb to a few involuntary tremors. A thin layer of sweat under her arms or an undefined nausea in the pit of her stomach. But her mind refused to go back to that place.

"I said that I appreciated the attention he'd given me." She fought to keep the oversized chair from swiveling beneath her. The jury box to her left was full of large men in uniform, captains who outranked her and had seen her fall in the mud that morning. All suddenly suspecting her of something they deemed distasteful and overtly sexual. "I appreciated the guidance. I trusted him."

There was a sharp insult in Mann's strategy to make her break. A predictable unfairness that she couldn't reverse. He would try to coax her into admitting to private thoughts, private moments, vulnerabilities like love and desire. Legitimate human traits that he could turn against her. Cheapening her most intimate moments into something meant for public consumption.

"You trusted him enough to let him into your barracks room?"

Her chair moved beneath her as he twisted her words. Her muscles ached and her fingers trembled as he skated dangerously close to her tangled nerve center.

"He was my platoon sergeant." She buried a more aggressive response, resisting the urge to make this personal. "I didn't think I had a right to tell him no."

Mann pinned his wicked brown eyes on her, and she could see his flawed measure of her reflected back across the sullied air.

The weak thing he thought she was, spoiled in the mud and gasping for air. "But that wasn't the first time you'd let another soldier into your room at night?"

"Objection." Lieutenant Hunt snapped.

"Objection, your honor." The prosecutor echoed on cue. "That's rule 412 evidence, which is specifically prohibited."

"Approach the bench counselor." Major Adams sat upright and turned towards Captain Mann, an obnoxious crease in his forehead. "Were you sleeping through my lecture yesterday or are you legitimately confused?"

"I'm not confused Sir." Captain Mann ambled towards Major Adams. "I'm familiar with rule 412. I just don't agree with it."

"So that gives you the right to ignore it?" The major stared at him with jaded eyes.

"It gives me the obligation to test it, Sir."

"You do so at the risk of losing your case. Do you pull this kind of experiment with every rule you dislike?"

"Only rules that keep relevant facts from the jury, Sir."

"A rape victim's sexual history isn't relevant." Hunt interrupted from her obscure position behind the witness stand. She couldn't suppress the vitriol in her words any more than she could force out a 'sir' to someone who didn't deserve that kind of respect.

"The witness's past sexual history is not admissible in this context." Major Adams flipped to a worn page in the front of his textbook that outlined the controversial provisions of Rule 412. "We went over this yesterday. By trying to introduce this as evidence you've just compromised the entire panel."

"But character is supposed to mean something." Mann responded with the sound of loose gravel in his voice. "Especially in the military. If a woman has a reputation, if she's flirtatious or aggressive, that has some bearing on how the men in the unit interpret her behavior. I don't see the harm in putting it before the jury and letting them decide."

"Because they'll use it against her, Sir." The 'sir' came across as little more than an unimpressive tag at the end of a smart remark, designed to mask the obvious lack of sincerity. Nothing about his attitude was surprising. He seemed just the sort of man that might have trouble grappling with the hard boundaries of sexual consent. The more he was exposed to the idea that women had autonomy and power, the more he'd be forced to question intoxicated encounters from his infantry days. It was easier to question the law than his own troubling behavior. "They always use it against her."

"Did you hear that ladies and gentlemen?" He turned towards her with a vicious twist in his lip. "I actually got a 'Sir' out of the young lieutenant. At the very least we don't have to worry about you letting someone into your room because you were just following orders."

The sting in her chest was overwhelming her. She could feel her muscles flaring just below the skin, pulsing from the strain of that vile morning. She was still fighting the shock of that jarring fall. Her back and shoulders still absorbing the force of her hard landing.

"The military can be a scary place for women." Hunt raised her voice a second time, staring him down with her cool grey eyes. "They're outranked and they're outnumbered, and the Army doesn't exactly hand out ribbons for tearing down war heroes."

"Do you have a problem following instructions, Captain Mann?" Major Adams lowered his eyes at the young captain. "Do you feel that you are so enlightened on the matter of identifying sexual predators that you know better than the Commander in Chief, the Department of the Army and the United States Jag Corps?"

"No, Sir." Mann pressed his lips together in frustration.

"If you cannot defend your client without attacking the victim's sexuality, then perhaps the Jag Corps isn't the best place for you. Perhaps you'd be more at home returning to the infantry?"

"I'll follow the rules Sir." Captain Mann spit.

"I certainly hope so." Major Adams turned his eyes towards the witness stand, a curious and tempered reprimand hanging on his lips. "Lieutenant Hunt, while I appreciate your enthusiasm, I'd like to remind you that you are the witness for today's exercise.

You will have your turn as counsel, but for the time being, please refrain from making further objections while you're on the witness stand."

"Yes, Sir." She nodded quietly, trying to calm the wild trembling in her fingers.

# Chapter 22
## Charlottesville, VA (2012)

Pamela Hunt removed the pins from her hair, letting it fall loose around her back and shoulders. She brushed through the creases that the bindings had left and washed the make-up from her face. She changed into a pair of loose pants and a t-shirt and collapsed on her bed.

Her body was weary and sore. She could feel the lactic acid throbbing through her muscles as she lay there. Recovering. Healing. Despite that morning's fall and despite the pain, she could feel herself getting stronger. Perhaps not fast enough to survive the ruck march tomorrow or earn her place in Airborne school. But little by little, she was leaving behind fragments of the soft girl that was still caged behind her ribs and bones.

She heard a knock at the door and sat upright in her bed, brushing the red hair from her face. She stepped across the floor in her bare feet, following the bright violet sheen of her toenails. The only spot of color she was able to hide from the United States Army.

She opened the door to find the lanky captain with the dark curls standing outside. The curious man who had brought her camelback to her when she was curled up on the ground next to a pool of her own vomit, twisted and vulnerable. She remembered the swath of patchy skin on the edge of his face. The harsh outline of a burn that must have followed him home from the Middle East.

"How are you feeling LT?" He stood outside her door with a slim smile that seemed overbroad and peculiar. Or perhaps she had simply grown too skeptical of kindness. She looked past the damage and saw nothing more than a man, wanting what men want.

"Better than this morning, Sir." She tried to sound gracious, but heard the cynicism echo in her ears.

"I heard you had a Rule 412 argument with Captain Mann this morning." He leaned against her doorframe as he spoke, relaxed and comfortable as if he'd been invited to lurk just outside her door. She curled her fist around the doorknob, waiting for him to cross some invisible line. "I hope he didn't rattle you too bad."

"I don't rattle easily." He smelled of dark spice and Italy, with a dying New Jersey accent that reminded her of home. His face seemed far more pleasant than the morning they'd met. But that could be because she was standing firmly on her feet and not beside herself in the dirt.

"I hope you've had time to recover for the ruck march tomorrow." The captain's words were strong and secretive at the same time. She concentrated on the salty tones, suddenly recognizing the invisible voice that had called to her from 30 feet below that drenched piece of rope, urging her to keep climbing. "It's going to be longer and faster than usual. We're heading out at 4 a.m. instead of 5. Did your platoon sergeant tell you?"

"My platoon Sergeant is Captain Mann." She looked up at him with loaded eyes. "If you thought he had told me, would you really be standing here?"

The captain offered her a hidden smile, as if they were sharing an intimate joke. "You should try to take it as a compliment."

"That he wants to sabotage me?"

"That he's threatened by you." Captain Cade looked at her with hungry eyes and she caught a glimpse of the hidden carnivore lurking behind his innocent smiles. "He wouldn't feel the need to put up obstacles if he didn't think you had a chance of making it. There's a form of flattery in that."

Hunt offered him an ironic smile. She refused to accept Mann's abuse as anything but cruelty. But in spite of her best efforts, she felt her defenses soften. "It hardly matters now. Tomorrow will be my last march with the Airborne crew."

"You've come too far to give up on this LT."

"There are 21 of us left and only 20 slots." The admission stung more than the long fall and abrupt impact with the solid ground. She found herself struggling to keep her emotions in check. "Fassbender's ending the competition tomorrow. He doesn't want to take the chance that I hurt myself trying to keep up with the men. The next person to fall out is eliminated. No exceptions."

"It doesn't have to be you."

Hunt pictured Captain Mann's bullish eyes wearing her down from across the courtroom, an unshakable smile filling up his cheeks. She shook her head as a weary feeling of defeat settled under her skin. "I appreciate the encouragement." She offered Captain Cade a thin nod of thanks before she moved to close the door. "But he's beaten me."

"Wait." Captain Cade blocked the door with his foot, glancing down at her with his curious brown eyes and seared skin. "You don't trust me much, do you?"

"You haven't given me any real reason to trust you Sir." She stared up at the lanky captain, who at least had enough sense not to order her to open the door.

"I'm the only one who bothered to give you the right time for the march tomorrow. Shouldn't that count for something?" The captain offered her a subtle wink, and an unmistakable smirk lined his lips. She took her eyes from the melted flesh and concentrated on his fluid brown eyes. And for a brief moment, she wanted very badly to believe in him. "If you can stick with Mann until the end tomorrow, I'll see to it that you don't get cut."

"How can you possibly guarantee something like that?"

"You'll just have to trust me." She felt his large brown eyes slip over every inch of her, and an intense chill ran down her spine.

"Why are you doing this for me?" Her whispered suspicion formed its own words and broke across her slackened lips.

"Because Mann has one of those pretty faces that women love, despite the way he treats them." It was the first time he'd revealed any insecurity over his scarred face. The human jealousy and spite hidden beneath the burns. "If you let him think he's beaten you, it will only be that much easier for him to tear down the next woman who threatens him."

She remembered the way he'd tried to embarrass her on the witness stand. The way he'd dismissed the rules and worked so hard to demean her in front of the judge and jury. In time he would be advising commanders. Shaping policies and helping men make decisions based on how he believed women ought to behave. Based on what he considered an acceptable abuse of power.

"I'll keep up with him tomorrow." The words felt and sounded like a promise.

"Glad to hear it." The captain's wide eyes filled with a sense of simple satisfaction that easily overpowered the imprint of Captain Mann's plastic smile. "Get some sleep LT."

He turned and walked down the hall with a terrible confidence. Lieutenant Hunt watched him with the sinking feeling that she was trapped between two wolves, each vying for a chance to devour her.

# Chapter 23
## Charlottesville, VA (2012)

Jamie Sharon tugged hard on the straps to her ruck sack, working to flatten out the lopsided bulges and snap the buckles into place. She hadn't made the most efficient use of space, and she wondered how badly she would regret it in the morning. It was too late in the evening to knock on the Casper's door. And there was too much room for misinterpretation. Too much potential for making lonely decisions she might regret. She would have to trek the four miles with her lopsided pack and hope her back and shoulders could take the strain.

Her cell phone rang from the edge of her nightstand. She reached towards the phone and glanced at the glowing screen, a familiar face staring back at her through the pixels.

"It's been a long time Sergeant Chase." The greeting was formal and stiff, the memory of his first name stalled on the back of her tongue. She was still angry, and her heart was still consumed by a soft, hollow ache. She fell back on the floor, letting go of a timed sigh that she wanted him to hear, but didn't care to explain.

"It's good to hear your voice Ma'am." His voice crackled from the heart of the Midwest, a touch more familiar than it should've been. "How are you?"

"Mostly good."

"Mostly good?"

She could hear his breath against the receiver. She wondered if he would probe any further. If he would make it his business to learn what it was that was holding her back from good. What sliver of disappointment had edged its way under her skin and was keeping her from happy. "I was just closing up my rucksack for the march tomorrow."

"Make sure you put the heavy stuff on the bottom towards the frame. You don't have much shoulder width, you want to concentrate the weight against your lower back."

"Now he tells me." She played with the taut strings of the overstuffed rucksack, trying to remember if she had bothered to waterproof her socks and undershirts, or where she finally found room for her combat boots.

"What time is it out there?" He asked.

"9:00." She glanced at the alarm clock beside the bed, watching the minutes creep by, giving her fewer and fewer opportunities for meaningful rest. She hoisted the heavy sack from the middle of the floor and moved it aside, clearing a path from the bed to the bathroom. The alarm would go off well before sunrise and she had no intention of stumbling over the pack before the march had even gotten started.

"What time is your ruck march?" His voice echoed through the receiver like he was worlds away.

"We push off at 5:00." She thought about the long march through the empty streets at dawn with a heavy load strapped to her back. Hoping the challenges and the discipline could help her find a stronger, healthier version of herself. One that didn't bend under so many heavy emotions from so far away. "I just hope I can keep up."

"It's not supposed to be easy." She thought she heard a simple smile in his voice. Something between encouragement and pride that he always pulled together so well. "I wanted to call sooner. But I thought I should give you some time."

Time, she smiled at the simple solution. Time to bury her emotions like he had, pretend she didn't feel the things she felt. Something in the echo of his voice told her they were still playing with fire. Juggling forbidden instincts and secrecy. Spread across states and time zones and still hiding in plain view.

"How's Reese?"

"He's been good." The sergeant's voice broke for a moment, getting lost in the void between the past and the present. "We went for a run in the snow last night. That seemed to calm him down."

Jamie slipped off her shoes and fell backwards onto her bed. The comforting image of falling snow fizzled on the fragile line between them. She could have dropped the receiver and drifted to sleep without much effort.

"He loves the snow." She smiled as she replayed forgotten images of Reese burying his face in the snow. Before her sweet dog's mind started melting with the stress of all the loud pops and shakes around the fourth of July. "Hopefully that means the panic attacks are done for the winter."

"I'm taking good care of him LT. I promised you I would." The line went quiet for a moment, long enough to seem as if the connection had been lost. He sounded, at times, close enough to touch, then drifted further and further away.

"They're letting us come home for the holidays." Jamie spit out the words before she could stop herself, still hoping she might catch a trace of regret or loneliness in his response.

"I'd love to see you Jamie." The words caught in his throat, lingering in the powerful gravity between them. He sounded sincere, but too much hesitation broke up the sentiment. "But I can't kiss you again."

His words were intimate and soft. But at the end of the day they were just words. Ephemeral and wholly inadequate.

"Are you really so afraid that the Sergeant Major will find out?" The anger bubbled towards her lips again, hot and unrestrained.

"Are you really ready to resign your commission over this?" His words were a little too clipped and stern. The phone receiver felt warm against her face and she felt her heart starting to pull away, losing interest in something that was too distant to touch. It was almost poetic how simple it was, to let go of expectations and return to a state of hollow independence.

"I still owe the Army some time. About 9 more months before I have to decide if I'm going to re-enlist." He started an uneasy string of hard, unflinching facts. "But you're an officer Ma'am. You can walk away at any time. All you have to do is turn in your rank and tell them you're out. You just have to be sure that's what you want."

She closed her eyes, trying not to let any of it sink in. She was close enough to that salty edge of consciousness that she could dismiss all of it. Still cling to the broken idea that she could keep him and her rank. The military was forcing them to choose. An unwholesome decision between love and duty. He'd chosen duty. She had yet to make a choice.

"I should get ready for bed." The line filled with another ambiguous silence and Sharon's tired brain cycled through the muddled conversation, wondering what cues she was missing in the unacknowledged silences.

"Make sure you wrap your feet tomorrow." His voice began to break and tremble again, slipping between variations of apology and concern. "Even a short march can give you some pretty nasty blisters. Use that moleskin I gave you. It helps."

"Thanks Matt." The familiarity slipped and she winced at the subtle mistake. "Take care."

"Talk to you soon, Ma'am."

Sharon tapped the screen in her hand, and just like that, he was gone.

She lay in bed holding the phone against her chest, a thick burning filling up the back of her throat. She could already hear the sound of her feet hitting the pavement. She didn't see how she could possibly march four miles through the city streets under all that weight, when everything was already starting to feel so heavy.

# Chapter 24
## Charlottesville, VA (2012)

Lieutenant Pamela Hunt moved through the school parking lot in the black morning, her gear weighing her down. She headed toward the handful of bodies already assembled in the yard, their faces muted by the dark and their frames disguised by hulking sacks and Kevlar helmets. They exhaled puffs of white breath as they milled about, trying to shrug off the cold.

She felt a heavy tug on her shoulders and turned to see the faceless major cinching up her rucksack and adjusting her camelback.

"What are you doing Sir?"

"Just checking to make sure your camelback is full. You may not want the weight now, but three miles into this thing you're going to wish you had it. Here, take this."

He handed her a long plastic firearm, the full size and weight of an M16 rifle, with a sling attached to either side. She took the extra weight in her stiff fingers and slung it around her neck and shoulders. She assured herself that it wasn't enough to break her resolve.

"Get in line behind me." Casper motioned towards the front of the formation. He slipped into the dark with a single glow stick tucked inside the straps of his rucksack. Hunt swallowed a long breath and followed the bouncing light.

She passed by Captain Cade's tall shape and wide eyes, lingering near the back of the unruly squads. His uneven skin was smoothed over by shadows, the treacherous flames reversed by the forgiving darkness. She couldn't see his full expression, but she imagined she saws his sultry wink and signature smile just beneath his Kevlar.

She turned forward and noticed a second neon light making its way to the front of the formation. Even in the dark of the early morning she caught sight of Mann's white teeth, blowing long breaths into the cold air as he lined up beside Major Casper.

"There you are LT, I'm a little surprised you made it out of bed on time." He turned an ingracious smile towards her.

Hunt didn't respond. She stared down at his thick boots and wondered if she might be lucky enough for him to break his ankle a second time. For him to step too quickly into an unseen pot hole or tree root as they stumbled about in the miserable dark. She turned around to look for Captain Cade's wide eyes again, but he had disappeared into the back of the crowd.

The Airborne candidates settled into a somber hush as Captain Fassbender stepped in front of the formation. He was bundled in a thick winter coat and his head and hands were covered in his wool hat and black gloves. He looked over what was left of the competition and rubbed his hands together against the biting cold.

"Group, attention!" He shouted into the air and the group fell in on cue. "Glad to see everyone made it here on time. As you look around you, I'm sure you've noticed that there are still 21 of you in this thing. You've fought long and hard to keep your position, and many of you have proven yourselves well beyond expectations. But unfortunately, I can only send 20 students to Airborne school. We have one too many. I expect that we will lose that one today. Whoever it is, I want you to walk away from this competition with your head held high, proud of all you've done and with the respect and good will of your classmates."

Hunt drank in the speech with a hard heart, knowing that his conciliatory praise was intended for her. She could hear Captain Mann's cocky breathing behind her, every mouthful feeding her new adrenaline.

"You're going to go six miles today." Fassbender continued. "You're also going to make it back in time to shower and grab breakfast before class starts at 8:00. That means once you get moving, you don't slow down, you don't stop. Everybody understand?"

"Yes Sir." Was the automatic response.

"Major Casper will be your pacesetter. Stay on him. Stick with the group and be safe. Whatever happens out there today, remember that you're a team. Look out for each other and do your best. The only way you fail is if you give up. It's as simple as that." Captain Fassbender glanced over their tired faces, then nodded silently to Major Casper. "Major Casper, they're all yours. We'll see you when you get back."

"Airborne crew, right face!" Major Casper hollered above the wind and the formation pivoted on command.

"Forward, march." Casper bellowed through the cold and the group began the steady shuffle through the empty parking lot. Heavy boots and bodies hit the pavement in a coordinated rhythm, waiting for the next command. "Double time."

"Double time." The huddle echoed.

"March!" Major Casper picked up the pace, legs and hips lurching forward into a soft trot. Rucksacks jostled up and down, camelbacks bounced and dripped, soldiers inhaled and exhaled quickly, descending en masse through the empty city streets.

They passed the usual markers, the frat houses and footballs fields surrounding the university campus. The boutiques and trails that dotted the quiet neighborhood. The stoplights, bridges and hills that broke up their route.

"Road guards, post." Casper called out as they approached the first street light. Captain Mann and one of the lieutenants fell out of formation, hustling into the upcoming intersection. The glow sticks strapped to their packs swayed from side to side as they moved into position, warding off traffic as the group shuffled towards the other side of the street.

Hunt caught the flash of Captain Mann's teeth as he sprinted back to the front of the formation. He maintained his stride as he slid in place beside Casper, pushing ahead into the darkness.

"Keep pace with me Mann, this isn't a race." Casper called to him to fall back.

"We only have three hours before class starts Sir," Mann answered over his shoulder, contining to push ahead. "We need to move this thing along."

"Our pace is fine. We'll make it back in plenty of time. Fall back."

The flash of white disappeared as Mann closed his smile and slowed his pace, matching the major's even tempo. Hunt could see Mann shaking his head. He took a small sip from the hose of his camelback, swished the water from side to side and spit into the uneven ground.

"Major Casper Sir." Hunt's voice was broken by hard breathing. Her Kevlar sat low on her forehead and she struggled to keep a hold of her plastic weapon as they shuffled forward.

"What is it LT?"

"With all due respect Sir, you do not need to slow this thing down on my account."

"I'll take that into consideration LT. In the meantime, why don't you save your breath and keep pace with Captain Troy. We will make it back on time."

She closed her lips around the hose of her camelback and swallowed. She hated both of them. The condescension stung as much as the hostility. She took advantage of a brief downhill stretch to free one hand from her weapon and adjust her Kevlar. All she could see was the blurred outlines of two steadily fading glow sticks, cinched into the sacks of the men ahead of her, bobbing up and down to a predictable gait.

Her body was still twisted and strained from yesterday's fall, but she carried enough anger in her veins to keep her promise.

# Chapter 25
## Charlottesville, VA (2012)

Lieutenant Sharon stepped into a fresh snap of cold air and blinked off the fog. She hadn't slept well. She moved through the damp air with her body armor snug and uncomfortable around her chest, and her ruck sack already dragging down her shoulders. She could feel her spare pair of combat boots jabbing her in the back. That stretch of skin just above her heels was already slipping out of the moleskin she'd slapped on her feet that morning.

She looked for a friendly face that might have some last minute tips on how to how to handle a loose and lopsided rucksack. But the Airborne crew had left an hour earlier, and Major Casper was already a few miles out. She had no choice but to carry her weight with her, despite how poorly she had managed it.

She made her way towards the uneven formation assembled near the track, the water in her camelback sloshing from side to side as she trekked through the wet grass.

"What do we have here?" One of the dark figures squinted towards her, lifting a neon glow stick to read her face. "Is that Lieutenant Sharon?"

"Hey Garcia."

"So you finally graduated from the women and old men's group?"

"Yeah, we'll see how long it lasts." She stepped towards the front of the formation, preparing herself for the next 4 miles of steady marching. "You mind if I head up Bravo squad? If I get caught behind some of the taller guys, it's going to be a struggle."

"Yeah, go ahead. We've got another woman who heads up Alpha squad. She's a bit taller than you though. Lieutenant Cramer"

Sharon tightened the Kevlar around her chin as Lieutenant Cramer appeared, her neon glow stick bobbing in and out of the darkness. She was taller than Sharon by a solid foot.

"So much for avoiding a struggle."

"You'll do fine. Just keep your eyes front, make sure to hydrate and keep moving."

Sharon slid into position just as a booming voice interrupted the early morning chatter.

"Group five, attention!"

The formation snapped to attention and Sharon lumbered below the extra weight on her back and shoulders.

"Alright group five, are you ready?"

Sharon couldn't see the man's face from where she stood. She didn't recognize the voice or even notice the direction the orders were coming from. She would follow them until it hurt. That was all that she had strength for.

"Yes Sir!" The group responded in perfect uniformity.

"Right, face!"

On command, the group turned from the track and faced the parking lot. The faceless voice merged with gusting wind.

"How many miles are we going today group five? Anyone? Speak up."

"We usually go four miles Sir." Lieutenant Garcia answered.

"Who wants to go five miles? Can we do that group five?"

Sharon's heart sank. She felt a tug on her ruck sack as Lieutenant Garcia slid a glow stick into place, her combat boots jabbing into her back again.

"Yes Sir!" Sharon belted out the answer along with the others.

"Your ruck's a little loose." Garcia warned her.

"It's too late to fix it." She felt the weight shift as Garcia pulled on her shoulder straps, the heavy boots lifting and then dropping against the center of her spine.

"I didn't hear you group five, I said do you want to go five miles this morning?" The faceless voice boomed again.

"Yes Sir!"

"That's what I like to hear. You want to go five miles and still make it back in time for a shower before class, we're going to have to do some running. Can we do that group five?"

"Yes Sir!" Again, Sharon joined in the automatic response. A steady flow of dread filling her lungs. The build-up was accumulating in her fingers, pulsing under her black gloves.

"Outstanding group five. Right face!"

The group pivoted towards the road out of the parking lot and waited in the darkness for gruff voice to move them forward.

"Forward, march!"

Sharon stepped into the empty parking lot alongside Lieutenant Cramer. She yanked the straps on the front of her rucksack in one final attempt to shuffle the weight off her lower back. The weight shifted left and fell against her hip, pulling hard against her neck and left shoulder.

"Double time!"

"Double time!"

"March!"

The group surged forward without warning and Sharon's feet hit the pavement at twice the pace, with an uncomfortable load digging into her back and shoulder. She struggled to match Lieutenant Cramer's long strides, taking one and a half steps for every one of hers. She sucked in a panicked breath. She'd never make it five miles.

She knew by now that endurance was more mental than physical. She knew that the second she allowed the doubt to creep into her head she was lost. And yet she couldn't seem to recover her thoughts. They had only run a few yards and already her muscles were pleading with her to stop, her shoulders dragged, and she couldn't find the stamina to prop herself back up. She felt the weight on her back grow heavier with each push. She watched Lieutenant Cramer inch ahead of her, one giant step at a time, and her mind betrayed her body. Worse than saying it to herself, she said it out loud. "I can't do this."

"Don't start that Sharon, you're fine."

Sharon had fallen back enough to hear Garcia's heavy breathing behind her. Another misplaced step and he would be stepping on her heels.

"You can do this. Just keep moving."

She kept moving. She followed orders and kept moving. Shuffling through the empty streets with the fear of failure eating into her muscles.

"Alright group five, recover." That gnarly voice from somewhere behind her gave the order, and all at once, the running stopped. Her blood kept pumping, the oxygen kept flowing and her feet kept moving. She stepped quickly and gained the ground that she had lost between herself and Lieutenant Cramer. For a few short minutes, the doubt let up. She could see herself holding steady until the end. Through every turn and every shuffle, pushing herself past the fatigue and the discomfort. For a brief, pristine moment, it was possible.

"Alright group five, hydrate. When we get to the stoplight at the end of this street, we run again."

And then it was gone. If the reprieve had lasted just a bit longer, she may have been able to regain her mental foothold. But the sight of the stoplight only a few yards ahead broke her composure. She could no longer talk herself into the idea of finishing with the group, it was now a matter of how long she would last before she broke formation. She sucked down some water and prepared for her first real failure. The taste in her mouth was sour and lingered all the way down the empty street.

"Alright group five, we're moving again, let's go."

She felt a surge of hot anger bubbling up. She heard Matt Chase whispering through the air as she tried to run from him. *"I'd love to see you Jamie. But I can't kiss you again."* Her feet were heavy and her body armor was weighing her down. Her ruck sack jerking up and down as she ran, tearing her down with each step. It was getting harder and harder to match Lieutenant Cramer's long strides. She slipped behind. She let herself slip behind.

And then, out of nowhere, just when she felt she couldn't run another step, relief.

"Alright group five, recover."

Sharon kept formation for two solid miles. She fell further and further behind during every run, then caught herself up during the brief intervals of steady marching. But her weary legs knew the halfway point. Her neck and shoulders bent under the weight of all that body armor and extra gear. Her muscles gave in after they had covered enough distance to preserve some semblance of dignity, just as the first streaks of gray were beginning to form along the bottom edge of the black night sky. Lieutenant Garcia stepped on her heels. She didn't have the fortitude to push herself forward. She stepped to the side and he shuffled past her, taking her place at the head of Bravo squad. Now it was only a matter of time.

She seemed to fall behind another squad member during each running interval, finally finding herself at the very back of the formation, where she might be able to drop off into the darkness, unnoticed.

"Alright group five, when we hit the bridge we're moving again. Shuffle."

Sharon moved her legs, trying to keep up with the group but falling further and further behind, to the point where she'd never be able to take that distance back during the short marching reprieve. They shuffled across the bridge and ran past another run group rumbling through the intersection. Sharon saw Lieutenant Hunt near the front of the formation with the rest of the Airborne crew. She felt defeat creep into her bones and her legs slowed, shuffling towards the next streetlight where the ugly truth broke through the fog and beat at her temples.

*"You can walk away at any time. You just have to be sure that's what you want."*

# Chapter 26
## Charlottesville, VA (2012)

Casper kept the Airborne crew moving at a controlled run. He'd had to rein in Mann a few times, but by this point, the captain clearly got the message. He kept pace. The sweat broke at his temples halfway into the first mile. He must have been every bit as tired as the rest of them. But still gunning to prove a point. He had no legitimate concern that they wouldn't make it back in time. Only a primal urge to break the only female in the group.

The glow sticks cinched to the rucksacks were fading as the light was leaching up at the edge of the horizon. They had another 45 minutes at best. He could still hear Lieutenant Hunt struggling behind him. The few times that he'd noticed her breathing getting dangerously hoarse, he reminded her to hydrate and left it at that. That was all the help she would accept, and it seemed to be all that she needed. Four and a half miles in and she was still there, holding steady behind him. Barring any unforeseen circumstances, she would make it.

"Road guards, post." Casper gave the order as the formation approached another stoplight.

Captain Mann and the lieutenant moved forward into the intersection before the bridge and again held traffic while the crew shuffled across. Traffic was getting heavier. Lights were coming on in the houses along the streets. A few scattered civilians were leaving their homes, getting into their cars and beginning their daily commutes, staring at the odd assemblage of weary soldiers with plastic rifles jetting through the city streets.

Across the intersection, another group of soldiers was shuffling towards them, with one smallish soldier falling behind the ranks. Perhaps it was the dawn breaking that allowed Casper to recognize her amid the multiple hulking bodies that criss-crossed the streets this early in the morning. Perhaps he would have picked her out even in the darkest hour of the day. But he knew her, without looking twice.

He waited until the crew reached the other side of the bridge, and the road guards had taken up their positions once more. He glanced behind him once, maybe twice, trying to keep an eye on the passing formation that was fast disappearing into the city streets. He listened to the steady sound of Hunt's breathing behind him. Glanced at the sweat treading down Mann's temple. He'd made the decision before he knew there was a decision to make. It was just a matter of getting the message to the rest of his body, which was working on nothing more than adrenaline and muscle memory.

"Lieutenant Hunt!"

"Yes Sir." She somehow found the breath to answer him.

"I'm going to step out of formation, I need you to take my place."

"What? Why?"

Casper glanced behind him. Strands of loose red hair had fallen out of her Kevlar and stuck to her sweat-lined face. Her cheeks and forehead were almost the color of her hair, with blood pulsing just below the surface of her skin. "You got this, you hear me. Just keep pace with Captain Mann. Don't look behind you. Don't quit. If you get winded, remember to hydrate. You got this. You have less than two miles to go. Hang in there."

Major Casper took a quick sideways glance at Mann. He was still recovering from his sprint to the front of the formation, but not so tired that he might restrain himself. His ego was still more tender than his muscles.

"They're all yours Mann." Casper handed him the reins as he broke formation and headed in the other direction. "Try not to fuck this up."

# Chapter 27
## Charlottesville, VA (2012)

"Lieutenant Sharon!"

The voice echoed from somewhere behind her and she tuned it out. Her neck was too sore to turn towards it. She concentrated on keeping her feet moving under all the weight she was carrying.

"Lieutenant Sharon!" It was louder the second time. It buzzed in her ears and evaporated around her, absorbed into the sound of her steady marching and thick breathing. She trampled the sound of her own name underfoot and beat it into the pavement.

"Lieutenant Sharon!"

She lifted her head under the heavy Kevlar helmet. Major Casper was marching beside her, a plastic rifle hanging around his chest and shoulders and sweat collecting in the worn contours of his face.

"Sir. What are you doing here?" She barely recognized her own voice, saturated in embarrassment and heavy breathing. "You need to stay with your group."

"No, I need to make sure you stay with yours. Why did you stop running?"

"I can't anymore."

"That's bullshit, Sharon. You don't fall behind. You hear me?"

"I can't." She heard the strain in her own voice, her resolve cracking and breaking in front of him. A dense loneliness had followed her out of bed that morning. And the hidden reserve of strength that she wanted to show him was bending under the weight of her heavy heart.

"You say can't one more time and I'm going to see to it you go an extra mile after we get back to class, you hear me?"

"Yes, Sir."

"Your rucksack is loose and it's hanging to one side."

"I know. I haven't been able to adjust it."

Casper looked up the street to where the rest of her formation was nearing a corner.

"Alright LT, I'll tell you what's going to happen. We're going to run and catch up to your group. You're not so far behind that you can't make up the distance, but you're going to have to push hard and you're going to have to get your head back on track. I'm going to lift your rucksack to take some of the weight off, but you're going to have to do the rest. You got that?"

"Sir." It came out like an abandoned protest. A heavy resignation. Anything but the commitment he was looking for.

"On my count. One, two, three."

Casper lifted the weight from her shoulders and pushed her forward. Sharon's legs pitched forward to keep from being pushed face first onto the pavement. Her legs were racing under her as Casper propelled her forward, against everything in her that told her she had to stop.

"I'm going to fall!" She shouted at him.

"Not if you keep moving your legs."

"Just let me fall out!"

"You're not falling out Sharon. You keep moving. We're going to run until that post up there. Then we'll go back to marching so you can recover."

Sharon focused on the post up ahead. She was both insulted and embarrassed by his simple strategy. Breaking up the distance into smaller, more palatable pieces that her mind could digest. Trying to break through the mental block that might get her body moving again.

They started closing the distance between themselves and the trailing squad members of the sloppy formation ahead of them. Major Casper pushed her forward and her legs kept moving, straining against the weight holding her body down until they reached the post marking her relief point.

"I know it hurts." He was almost apologetic, but he kept his left hand firmly positioned on the back of her lopsided rucksack. "You're just going to have to work harder than the rest of us. I'm sure you knew that when you came down here. You're smaller

153

than the rest of us, but you gotta carry the same weight. You gotta take two steps for every one of our steps. That's not an excuse, that's just fact. You know what the loneliest feeling in the world is?"

When they set out that morning, she believed that she did. But the conviction in his voice told her that Casper had known a sadness deeper than she could comprehend. "No I don't Sir."

"It's when you're patrolling through the desert and you look up and you realize there isn't anyone ahead of you and there isn't anyone behind you. I don't want you to ever know that feeling Lieutenant Sharon, you hear me?"

"Yes Sir."

"Alright, we're running again, on three, you ready?"

"No Sir."

"You're running, let's go."

He pushed her forward again and her legs raced forward to catch her. They rounded a corner and closed the distance further. The sky was brightening and the roads were becoming more and more familiar. They were on the last mile. Sharon could see the formation she'd left only a few yards away, and beyond that, the last few turns that would take them back to the JAG School.

"We're almost there. You can do this."

"Please don't make me run anymore Sir." Her neck and shoulders ached. She could feel the thin skin on the back of her heel sliding and tearing as she pushed forward, the moleskin now completely peeled and useless at the bottoms of her boots.

"That's bullshit LT, you want to give up, you want to quit the Army, is that what you want?"

"No Sir." The words came out stronger than she thought possible. Without a note of hesitation.

"Why the hell'd you join the Army if you're not willing to push yourself? This is a team Sharon, I thought you understood that. We start together, we finish together. Are you going to let down your squad because your legs are tired? You keep moving. Don't disappoint me. We're going to stop at the next curb, you take a short break, then you catch up to the group on the next run, you hear me?"

154

"Yes Sir."

"Tell me you can do it."

"I can do it."

"Tell me again."

"I can do it!"

"That's it, take a break."

Sharon's legs were shaking. There was a dark, metallic taste in the back of her throat. Her body ached. Her mind was spinning. Casper's hand was still on her rucksack and she hated him for it. She breathed in and out, quick and erratic, hating him more with each halting respiration.

Her formation had slowed their pace and they were absolutely within reaching distance. If she could bear to keep going. She thought about fighting him this time. About grounding her heels and letting him push her face down into the concrete.

"Alright, this is it Sharon. You're going to do this last stretch on your own, you got that? They're only a few feet away. You can catch this up right here. I'm not going to push you on this one, but you're going to do it on your own. Don't you dare give up, you got that?"

"Yes Sir." She spit.

"Alright, its right here, you take it."

Sharon found some forgotten sense of purpose, some untapped drive from the banks of her childhood and ran. She ran on instinct. On desperation and a teeming sense of duty. She turned into the final hill that would bring her to the JAG School and she felt the incline slowing her down, biting into her thigh muscles as she pushed her way up, closer and closer to her squad members. She could feel a surge of relief brush over her as she zoned in on the boots of Lieutenant Hawthorne at the very end of Bravo squad. She was there. Back in rank, right as the group was turning into the parking lot at the end of a five mile march through the city streets.

"Great job group five, fantastic push toward the end. Outstanding. Now get out of here and hit the showers. You got one hour before class starts. Make use of it."

She honed in on the wrinkled face that had sent them running through the streets only a few hours ago. A weathered

Lieutenant Colonel from the Marine Corps, standing aside and watching as the squads disbursed.

"I'm sorry Sir." She gasped through a dry mouth.

"Nothing to be sorry for LT." That same raspy voice took on a warmer tone as the sun was starting to feel its way into the crisp darkness. "Every time I thought I was going to have to turn the group around, I glanced back and there you were. A little behind, but still with us."

"I kept up because Major Casper pushed me." She huffed again, fighting off a growing swell of relief.

"That's called teamwork." The Lieutenant Colonel gave her a condescending smile. "That's what we do here."

"I gave up, Sir." Sharon's heart was still thumping in her ears and fingers. She was still waiting to be broken and torn apart. Looking for a reason to give up on something that had fused with her blood and was racing through her veins. Everything had become perfectly clear when Casper asked her if she wanted to quit. Her breath caught up with her and her muscles pulsed, suddenly grateful and well fueled.

"Everybody loses their motivation at one point or another." The Lieutenant Colonel was convincing and sincere. Not full of false promise or praise, but real, true assurance. "How you handle it is what makes a soldier."

Sharon let the calm satisfaction wash over her. Something deeper than pride that could only be found in this awful, bowled over position when she'd gone further and harder than she believed she could go.

"As far as I can tell, you finished that last stretch on your own. With no Major or anyone else behind you." The Lieutenant Colonel's rough voice split through the cold, his large body receding as his voice grew thicker and stronger. "Something inside you must have wanted to stay with us pretty bad."

156

# Chapter 28
## Charlottesville, VA (2012)

The moment Casper stepped out of formation, Hunt was forced to step up her pace. She closed the gap between herself and Captain Mann, only to have him push ahead of her, hard and unforgiving. She pulled on her fatigued muscles and continued to match his lengthening strides. Every time she caught him, he picked up the pace again, trying to stay ahead and trying to make her drop. She could tell he was struggling to keep pushing ahead. He'd been sprinting off and on throughout the morning and he was losing steam. It showed in his face. But still he drove on, determined, ruthless, mean.

"You can't keep up Hunt." Mann belted out as he slid from a quick jog into an all-out run. "Just let it go."

"I'm finishing with you Sir." She gasped in response. "Get used to it."

"Hey Mann, ease up, will you?" Captain Troy called from behind them. His protest was lost in the rustling of limbs, weapons and rucksacks barreling down the road.

"Even if you make it to the end with us today, you're not going to make it tomorrow, and the next day, and the next." Mann huffed. "It's over."

"I'm not quitting Sir!" She responded.

"Mann, seriously, you need to slow it down, someone's going to get hurt back here!" Captain Troy shouted again, his voice slipping further behind them as they tore ahead of the group.

"You might want to slow down Sir, you don't want to break an ankle again." Hunt warned him as he pivoted around an uneven split in the sidewalk.

He regained his footing and pressed ahead. She could hear the breaks in her own breathing. Almost a crackling in her words as the wind whipped in and out of her lungs.

"You're getting tired, drop."

"Go to hell, Sir."

They rounded the last corner and she saw the entrance to the JAG school, awash in the heavy gray color of early morning. The sound of the formation speeding towards the gate was furious, the weight in their packs slamming down on knees and other fragile joints. She and Mann sprinted ahead of the rest of the group. She could hear them trailing and scattering into sloppy squad lines. She forced her way up the final hill into the parking lot, boots and plastic weapons flying.

She zeroed in on Captain Fassbender, standing in his puffy coat and hat at the top of the hill. He looked alarmed at their breakneck pace, at whatever loose elements remained of their scattered formation.

She saw Mann sprint into the middle of the parking lot. He stumbled off to the side as he passed Captain Fassbender, wandering in tight, broken circles. Hunt stopped her racing legs without slowing and nearly dropped to the pavement beneath her. She unbuckled her Kevlar below her chin and watched the heavy helmet drop to the ground as she pitched forward, heaving in and out with blood rushing to her temples. She uprighted herself only to drop her rucksack and weapon to the ground, then bent over again, with tiny spots of light dotting her vision, trying to slow her thundering heartrate. She saw Mann through the corners of her eyes, still stumbling in undisciplined circles, biting his lip as he watched her recover.

"What the hell is going on here?" Captain Fassbender approached the distorted group as they assembled in a broken mass in the middle of the empty parking lot. "Where's Major Casper?"

"He stepped out of rank Sir." Hunt gasped despite her desperate need for oxygen. "We passed someone who had fallen out formation. I think he went to help her." Captain Fassbender didn't respond, but paced about the beaten formation as he took stock of their ranks. "And where's Captain Cade? What happened to him?"

Hunt craned her neck at the mention of his name. She hadn't given any thought to the lanky captain since they'd set out that morning.

"He fell out Sir." A weathered voice came from somewhere in the midst of the breathless soldiers. "About half a mile back."

Mann looked up at the unexpected news. He reached for his chin strap and removed his Kevlar, still spewing hot air through exhausted lungs.

Hunt caught sight of Captain Cade in the distance, making his way up the last wretched incline towards the parking lot. He weaved towards them with his rucksack and his plastic rifle still biting into his stiff muscles.

She didn't have the energy to feel much, but she recognized the creep of adrenaline in her veins. The slow suspicion building in her gut, swirling and stewing and playing with her mind.

"Shit." Mann puffed as he dropped his rucksack to the cold pavement.

Captain Fassbender turned towards Mann, an irritated glare contorting his slender face.

"Is there a reason you came flying in here like a bat out of hell Captain Mann?"

"Just wanted to make it back in time Sir." Mann insisted through broken breaths. "That's all."

"Is that all?" Captain Fassbender glanced about the remaining candidates, slowly gathering their composure and settling the momentum in their chests. Lieutenant Hunt finally pulled herself upright and began gathering strands of loose hair from her face. She pressed the tangled mess into the knot at the back of her head, counting on the sweat to hold it in place until she was released to go shower. Captain Fassbender nodded once and turned back towards Mann.

"Well it looks like your mad dash for the finish line cost Captain Cade his slot." He glanced about the sloppy lot of exhausted soldiers, pausing with a strange sense of surprise and approval at Captain Hunt. "Congratulations to the rest of you. You're going to Airborne school!"

Lieutenant Hunt collapsed and wheezed among the celebratory shouts, altogether spent and bewildered.

"Go ahead and hit the showers. And make sure you're in the classroom by 0800."

Captain Fassbender turned and headed towards the doors of the JAG school, just as Captain Cade made his way into the thick of the group, slamming his pack into the pavement and gasping for breath like the rest of them.

"Was that Fassbender?" Cade barked as the company commander slipped into the warmth of the old building. "What did he say?"

"You're out." Captain Troy spit between sips from his camelback. "It's done."

"Are you fucking serious?" The subtle touch of Jersey slipped out as he shouted. He removed his Kevlar and shoved it into Mann's chest, heavy sweat beading across his hairline. "What the hell was that all about Mann? What the hell is wrong with you?"

Mann shoved the helmet back at Cade and made his way towards Lieutenant Hunt. Her breathing had slowed and the pink color in her cheeks was fading. A slight shiver rushed through her shoulders as her body cooled, and the sweat was no longer welcome.

"Let me see your rucksack." Captain Mann demanded.

"Why?" She brushed another loose strand of hair from her face. The day had brightened just enough for her to see the cruelty in his eyes.

"Your rucksack! Now Lieutenant!"

"C'mon Mann, don't be an asshole." Captain Troy reached for Mann's shoulder, but Mann shook him off.

"I'm not being an asshole, I'm just trying to figure out how the hell she kept up when Cade couldn't. Is this it?" Mann grabbed the rucksack in front of her. He checked the name, lifted it with one arm to test its weight, and without another word, worked loose the straps and dumped the contents onto the pavement at her feet.

"Seriously, Mann!" Captain Cade interrupted this time. "Haven't you done enough? Leave her alone."

The gray light on the horizon was building. Hunt's heart was still pounding, feeling the undeniable flex and pull of invisible strings. She watched Cade's wide eyes. She remembered his

160

cryptic promise from the night before and the suspicion swelled. She tried to bury it. Disown it.

"Then you won't mind if make sure she's carrying everything on the packing list."

"For Christ's sake, Mann." Captain Troy shook his head. "Can we just drop this and go inside already?"

Captain Mann dropped to his hands and knees and begin combing through the inventory he had spread out on the blacktop in front of him.

"You're making a damn fool of yourself you know that." Captain Cade hollered over him. "I fell out! That's on me! This girl earned it, let her have it!"

"You guys have about an hour before class starts." Mann turned an impatient look on the two captains hovering over him. "I recommend you hit the showers if you want to grab breakfast before class."

Captain Troy and Captain Cade stood for a moment, watching Mann rummage through her excess gear. He was beyond the point of backing down. He would sit out here for another 20 minutes if he had to, looking for evidence that she hadn't truly earned her place.

Captain Troy walked away first, with the rest of the Airborne crew splintering off and following after him. Captain Cade looked at her for the first time that morning, and for the first time that morning, she saw the unsightly scar bent across his face.

"Nice push LT." His wide eyes filled with a mesh of pride and hunger, something her body recognized before her mind. He gave a lurid wink and the rough edges of his skin disappeared, confirming the deep rumbling in her chest. He turned and followed the rest of the class inside, leaving her and Mann to shiver in the graying morning.

Lieutenant Hunt said nothing as Mann dug through her equipment, taking stock of the extra combat boots, uniforms and equipment spread across the pavement. It was all there. Every last item. He counted and re-counted, finally looking up at her stern expression. The dried sweat lining his face and torso sent an ugly chill through his bones.

"Hit the showers LT." He reached for the discarded rucksack and one by one, began tossing her displaced items back inside the sack. "I'll bring you your things after breakfast."

Hunt dropped to the pavement and reached for her combat boots.

"I said I got it Lieutenant." Mann continued to collect her things. He reached for her discarded Kevlar and handed it off to her, with a sullen and silent apology in his fingers. "I'll see you in class."

# Chapter 29
## Charlottesville, VA (2012)

Lieutenant Hunt stepped into her room and tossed her Kevlar on the floor, the rest of her equipment still spilled out over the concrete in the parking lot. She pulled open the Velcro on her body armor and lifted the heavy load from her shoulders. She was covered in sweat, sore and disordered.

She'd never asked him to fall out for her. She'd never asked anything of anyone and still she found herself in a tangled mess of unacknowledged debt. The injustice of it all swirled through her head like miniature hurricanes.

She stripped down and stepped into a hot shower, letting the steam settle into her tender muscles. She dug her fingers into her scalp, working the dirt loose from her skin, a vicious energy still pulsing through her.

She toweled off and pulled on a pair of gym shorts and an old T-shirt, suddenly frightened of the suspicious eyes and incredulous stares she'd face over breakfast. She reached into her mini-fridge for a cold bottle of water and emptied half of it in a long set of swallows, replacing the fluids she'd spent on that last painful sprint.

She looked herself over in the mirror. Her red hair was washed and wet, leaving a pattern of cool water drops all along her neck and shoulders. She was still hot from that last half mile, with a nasty sting to her ego that she couldn't get back. She reached for the door and headed down the hall towards his room. A raw energy burning against the tip of her tongue.

She knocked hard at the door, trying to form words for the heat that was barreling through her. She stood outside waiting for him to answer, still feeling angry and played.

She knocked again and pulled her hand away just as the door swung open. She saw him standing in front of her, undressed with the exception of a loose pair of sweat pants. She followed the line of his scar down his neck and across his chest. He was surprisingly cut and vital, despite the raw skin wrapped around his midsection. She took her eyes from the melted flesh and concentrated on his fluid brown eyes. He must have been devastating once. Cruel.

"Let me in." She demanded.

He nodded and stepped back from the doorway. She stepped inside and closed the door behind her. The blood in her veins pumped with a new sort of energy, hot and strong.

"I suppose you think I owe you something for this?" Her breath was splintered with hostility. A smothering resentment she had to break into manageable pieces that she could swallow. "I never asked you to do that for me. I wanted to earn this! For me!"

"You don't owe me anything." The words billowed over his tongue, opaque and alarming. She watched a sleek shiver moved through him. Then felt something deep and hungry building in her veins. "That's not why I dropped out."

"Then why?" The words fell with a dying animosity from her tongue. He had taken a slice of power from her hands just as she was ready to taste it, and placed her in his shadow. A tremor worked its way through her spine and she was surprised to find she was more grateful than humiliated. "Why would you drop out now if not to hold it over me?"

"Because I want to see you get what you came for." His eyes moved across her with a morose sense of longing. "That's all."

She felt a dark fire in her chest, burning away the thick nettles and thorns. The smoke billowed up through her throat and checked her breathing. She'd been with men since she was assaulted. So many troubling years ago. But always sober. Always when she felt she was in control. She didn't feel in control now, swimming in adrenaline and toxic pheromones, and still found herself inching towards him, alone and wet in his room.

She lifted her fingers towards the dark skin on his face, close enough to feel the nerves pulsing under his skin, without actually finding the courage to touch him. "What happened?" She whispered.

164

"Kandahar." Was his only answer. He took her hand in his and pressed her warm fingers to the braised skin.

"Can you feel it?"

"I can feel this." His answer was tempting. Liberating.

"We all have them." She set the whole of her palm against his face and the pressure transformed his injury into something sacred and useful. Something she could understand. "They aren't always this real."

Her bitterness turned into something exhilarating and unrestrained. There was no more struggle. No more words. She wrapped her long fingers through his slick curls, pulled him towards her and sunk her lips into his open mouth. The sensation made her dizzy, overpowering the dull pain in her legs and shoulders.

His reaction was smooth and spontaneous. He circled her warm hips and thighs in arms that must have ached as much as hers, pulling her against his stiff body. There was a fierceness in this that she was craving. The perfect fit of their lean bodies together, soft and firm in all the right places. She tasted his wet lips and he lifted her against him, carrying her to the bed and tossing her on top of the mattress, stumbling over the spilled equipment from the forgotten ruck march. A devilish smile crossed his lips as he reached for the elastic waistband on her shorts.

"You're going to be sore tomorrow." He warned her.

She traced his scar with her delicate fingers, building a beautiful association with the knotty skin along his ribcage. She reached for his free hand and guided his fingers under the loose folds of her T-shirt toward the most sensitive parts on her own smooth skin. "I don't care about that."

She hadn't had this kind of freedom for a long while. She was too obsessed with getting back everything she had lost to enjoy moments like this. But at least this morning, they would both get what they wanted.

# Part Six:

# Calling Cadence

# Chapter 30
## Mosul, Iraq (2008)

Captain Casper leaned into the Humvee and lit a cigarette. He held his rifle steady in his large fingers, sweaty and stained with grease and charcoal. He stared across the empty road at the explosives hidden in a plastic bag, rustling under a hot breeze. The sky was a seasoned gray and the buildings around him were worn and abandoned. There was a peace that came with early morning in the desert, with nothing but crickets and spiders for company.

Staff Sergeant Khoury approached him from the right, his Kevlar snug around his forehead and his eyes hidden behind a pair of dark glasses. He leaned up against the Humvee next to the captain and removed his glasses, wiping the sweat from his brow.

"You oughtta quit smoking Sir. That stuff'll kill you."

Casper smiled as he took another drag and exhaled rings of smoke into the air.

"You're sure you wanna take this one?"

"I'm sure." Casper nodded. "It's my anniversary."

"Your wife might have other ideas for celebrating your anniversary." The kid shook his head.

"Not that kind of anniversary." Casper kept his eyes on the menacing bag blowing in the wind, less than 100 meters from where they were standing. "This is my 900th IED. I'm planning to make 1,000 before this deployment is over."

"Jesus Sir, you're counting?" Khoury raised an eyebrow.

"They ever talk to you about Murphy's Law when you were in school Randy?" Casper took another long drag from his cigarette.

"If something can go wrong it will?"

Casper nodded as he exhaled, keeping his eyes firmly planted on the bag across from them. "I keep track because this is all just a numbers game. We like to think we're in control, but in the end it's up to Murphy how each of these things ends. There's a bomb out there that has my name on it. Maybe this one here."

"Is that why they call you the Ghost, Sir?" Sergeant Khoury stared down the bag across the street, his smile fading into his young cheeks.

"Could be Sergeant Khoury." Casper smiled as he lost his eyes in the dirt underfoot. "Could be."

"Lewis said you shouldn't be defusing these things at all anymore." The kid tilted his head to avoid the glare of the hot sun. "You're an officer now. You've done your part."

"I haven't made 1,000 yet." Casper tightened his lips around his cigarette. "I've still got a few left in me."

"And how about me Sir?" Sergeant Khoury shifted his feet in the hot desert sand, working off a swell of nervous energy. "How am I supposed to take over when you're gone? How am I supposed to learn my job if you never send me out there?"

Casper pulled in another drag, letting the tar gum up his blood and lungs. "Next time Khoury." He made the wretched promise knowing it might be a death sentence. Knowing that next time could be two months from now, or the next hour. "You can have the next one."

Sergeant Khoury watched the bag with the captain, keeping the explosives dead center in his line of vision, still shifting his weight from one leg to the other. "You know what I like about deployments?"

"What's that Randy?" He'd tried to stay away from first names out in the field, but it slipped out before he could catch himself.

"You don't have to worry about stupid shit." Khoury let out a hefty sigh. "I don't have to think about, did I wear brown socks with black shoes, or do I make as much money as the guy in the next cubicle, hell, you don't even have to worry about whether or not some girl likes you. None of that petty shit. You just have to worry about one thing. Am I going to die today? That's it."

Casper nodded and pinned his lips against the cigarette in his mouth, taking in the full flavor of the breezes and the dusty smells all around him. Enjoying every moment as if it were his last on this Earth.

"You got a girl back home, don't you?"

"No Sir. Not yet."

"But you got your eye on one?" Casper gave him a sly smile from the corner of his mouth. "What's her name?"

"Jasmine, Sir." The color filled Khoury's cheeks. "I didn't want to ask her until I got home. Truth be told, I'm more afraid of women than I am of these damn things." He motioned to the bomb across the street with the butt of his rifle.

"With good reason." Casper took another drag off his cigarette. "Either one will rip your heart out."

"You're all clear Sir." Sergeant Alfonso marched up the road with his M16 directed outward, approaching the Humvee with a fair confidence in his stride. "We've scouted out at least a half mile each direction. The place is deserted."

"Nice work Sergeant." Casper put his cigarette out on the toe of his boot and flicked the butt into the open air. "Let's get out the suit."

"Roger, Sir." Staff Sergeant Khoury opened the door of the Humvee and pulled out the blast suit. Casper took hold of the heavy material and stepped inside, sliding his arms and legs through the full body Kevlar. His slender limbs adjusted to the added weight, built to withstand the shrapnel and projectiles from a bomb exploding between his fingers. He grew hotter inside the suit, covered in layers of overlapping foam that were meant to protect his lungs from the incoming blast waves. Staff Sergeant Khoury stood behind him, fastening the open ends and ensuring that nothing was left exposed, with the exception of his tanned hands and fingers, which he would need to examine the wires and blasting cap of the IED. Khoury came around to the front and lifted the heavy helmet over Casper's head, attaching the breathing hose and giving him the thumbs up once all was secure.

"Take care out there Sir. I want to see your ugly face again."

Casper responded with his own thumbs up, lifting an arm that was weighed down by the additional layers of protection. A forgotten string of cadence ran through his head.

"When I get to Heaven!" His muffled voice echoed through his helmet

"When I get to Heaven!" Khoury repeated back.

"St. Peter's gonna say!" He called out before he started his long walk.

"St. Peter's gonna say!"

"How'd you earn your livin' boy?"

"How'd you earn your livin' boy?"

"How'd you earn your pay?"

"How'd you earn your pay?"

Randy's voice grew fainter as he stepped away from the Humvee, one solid step at a time. He felt anchored by the false security of the 80 pound suit on his back, and the steady hum of the cadence in his head, keeping time with his footsteps as he marched towards the unexploded bomb.

"I'll reply with a whole lotta anger!"

*"I'll reply with a whole lotta anger!"*

"Made my living as an Army Ranger!"

*"Made my livin' as an Army Ranger!"*

# Part Seven:

# Lilacs and War Crimes

# Chapter 31
## Charlottesville, VA (2012)

The smells and sounds of the cafeteria surrounded Casper as he blinked off the memories. The vibrations of old cadences still pulsed through his fingers. He sat alone at an empty table with his back to the wall, a plate of forgotten food growing stale in front of him. His eyes cleared and focused on the bodies moving around him, congregating in wide circles and streaming through the cluttered space.

His beret was laid out on the table and he was wearing his dress uniform. A short-sleeved white collar shirt, with his rank displayed on the shoulders. Dark blue pants with a thick yellow stripe down the sides. And an uncomfortable pair of dress shoes in place of his combat boots. He'd moved his dog tags from their favored place inside his laces and they lay loosely around his neck. It could only mean that another week had passed and he had forced himself into the formal wear that was required on Fridays.

Every week after the ruck march, he found himself lost in the foreign material, unable to recognize the image that stared back at him from the mirror. Just another reminder that he wasn't a soldier anymore. He was nothing more than another staff officer, processing paperwork while the young recruits were out in the field, working on battle maneuvers and kicking in doors.

He held onto the gruff strains in his head, the simple tunes that had carried him through some of the longest marches and coldest days he could remember. He found a small dose of comfort in the echoes of old platoons, recycling the tired lines back to him, warding off the creep of restlessness now that the bombs had stopped and silence was his worst enemy.

When I get to Hell!
*When I get to Hell!*
Satan's gonna say!
*Satan's gonna say!*

How'd ya earn your livin' boy?
*How'd ya earn your livin' boy?*
How'd ya earn your pay?
*How'd ya earn your pay?*
I'll reply with a boot to his face!
*I'll reply with a boot to his face!*
Made my livin' sendin' souls to this place
*Made my livin' sendin' souls to this place!*

He pushed his dried lunch around on his plate and tried to shake off the ugly history that had ripped new grooves in his brain, never to be scrubbed out. He seemed to have no choice over what memories were erased and which ones continued to haunt him. He had practically no recall of some of his sweetest moments with Grace before the war, and yet the worst experiences of his life were hard-wired into his chemistry.

What he wanted was a drink. A more effective numbing agent than a store of old tempos and refrains from a previous lifetime. The tingling and the stress were building enough to frighten him. He wasn't in control of his memories. He wasn't in control of his thoughts. The past was living in his blood and demanding retribution. Coming to collect on sins he couldn't atone for.

He was ready to dump his tray and bolt for the exit, when he picked up the distinct sound of heels on linoleum. An unbalanced click-clack that suggested a woman who was walking with a slight limp. Or maybe even a few blisters. One on the right heel, and a definite hot spot forming on the side of her large left toe.

Casper lifted his eyes from the plate and watched Lieutenant Sharon circle through the lines of the crowded cafeteria. She fit her dress uniform better than he ever would. Her white collar shirt feeding into a navy blue skirt that hugged her hips. Her blistered feet balanced into a pair of black heels. Her uniform was pressed and dignified. She stood straight and rigid, artfully masking any pain in her neck and shoulders. She kept her chin tight and her face flawless, with the exception of a very subtle wince every time she stepped into her shoes.

He might have pushed her too hard this morning, but he wasn't usually wrong about soldiers. They weren't always solid or ripped. They could be small and ordinary, even a bit scrawny or overweight. Nothing like the stereotypes that lived in the common imagination. They were just tough. They could take a beating and a lot of discomfort. Some of the hardest men in his ranks had fallen apart on him the second he took them away from an air-conditioned gym and three square meals a day. Outlasting the elements, with nothing but instincts and drive wasn't something that could be taught to someone who didn't have the mental stamina to survive. Physical fitness only took you so far. Soldiering was an entirely different concept.

Lieutenant Sharon paid the woman behind the cash register and carried her tray into the dining area, the broken clack of her heels once again filling up his head. Sharon had some toughness to her. He saw it on the first day, when she stood outside in the cold without so much as a grimace. She could take the pain from a few blisters and sore muscles.

But she had a distinct look of surrender in her eyes this morning.

"Lieutenant Sharon." He waved her over, looking for subtle clues that she'd been broken. She nodded at him from where she stood and headed towards the table. She treaded lightly as she stepped, concentrating on easing the pain in her feet, and still carrying some unexplained weight around her shoulders.

"How are your feet?" He asked as she sat down beside him.

"My feet are fine Sir." She hid everything in the seemingly simple response. She opened a bottle of water and hid her discomfort in a long swallow.

"Looks like you're limping."

"It's the heels Sir." She pointed to the dress shoes under the table.

"And the blisters." He glanced at her feet and suppressed a thin smile. He could have predicted everything about her response. Right down to the way she tried to dismiss the pain, blaming the shoes to cover up for something she perceived as an embarrassing weakness. "You should see Doc Morgan if they continue to bother you."

"I'd rather not be put on a profile over a few blisters." She glanced up at him with clear eyes, then picked up a fork and began dancing around the salad on her plate. She rummaged through the lettuce and croutons as she strung together her next words, digging deep to humble herself. "I owe you for this morning."

Casper shook his head. "You don't owe me anything."

"I wouldn't have finished if you hadn't forced me. I may not have been very grateful at the time. But I appreciate it now." She swallowed hard and reached for her water bottle to wash it all down. Recovering a small slice of her pride when it was all over. "Thank you for not giving up on me."

Casper gave a slow and settled nod. There was a lot of history in that statement. He'd never asked what had drawn her to the Army. What it was she was hoping to find here. A structured space where you weren't allowed to disappear into the darkness, even when you wanted to. Where you weren't allowed to give up or to be less than your best.

The Army had saved him from himself so many times. It had taught him, intentionally or not, that the best feeling in the world was to wake up to a morning you never expected to see, after you'd been pulled out of harm's way by people who ignored your protests, to stare into the sudden sunrise and realize that you didn't want to die after all.

He crossed his hands under his chin, his wedding band pressed against his bottom lip. "So what happened this morning?"

"You saw what happened Sir. My ruck was lopsided and my feet weren't dressed right." She dropped her eyes to the salad on her plate. She wasn't the sort of person who was moved by shallow compliments. She needed sincerity.

"Your problem was mental this morning. It wasn't physical. If it were the other way around, I wouldn't have bothered." He watched as she reclaimed her fork and began picking about her salad. He spun circles in the mess of potatoes that lay untouched on his own plate, more interested in what was going on behind her eyes. "It's not like you to give up."

"I won't let it happen again." She lifted a hand to her neck and massaged a tender spot near her left shoulder.

"Just tell me it's not the dogsitter." He was getting closer to the mysterious something that was eating at her. Not the blisters or the sore muscles, but the emotional tenderness, the sour feeling that you were alone in a mass of people, with all your vulnerabilities exposed. "Something got to you."

A subtle shadow clouded over her clear blue eyes. She shook her head and answered with tight lips. "They're just emotions, Sir. They can't hurt you."

She left a lingering space. The ellipsis at the end of a sentence. Somewhere in the messy patchwork of her heart there was a problem. Some evidence of scars that weren't healing properly.

"Emotions are the only things that can hurt you." He answered.

He clasped his hands in front of his chin a second time, amazed at how comforting it was to simply watch her, picking through her salad and holding her fork in her mouth, watching those tumultuous emotions cycle through her eyes. The cafeteria rustlings had receded to typical background noise. The twitching in his fingers had stopped.

"I have something for you." Casper reached into the bag at his side and pulled out a manila envelope. It jingled with an unexpected weight.

"What's that?"

"Dog tags came in today." He grabbed a few of the chains from the top, glancing over the tags until he found the right one. "I had them put an inscription on the back for you. A gift from a former Red Bull to another."

He passed the chain across the table and Sharon took it from his hand. She checked her name and other info before turning it over to read the inscription. "I will always place the mission first. I will never accept defeat. I will never quit. I will never leave a fallen comrade."

"That's the Warrior Ethos. It's gotten me through some pretty dark days."

She looked up at him with pale blue eyes that revealed very little. But he thought he saw a subtle spark, a transient optimism that hadn't been there before.

"Thank you."

Casper watched as she brought the chain over her head and hid the plates under her blouse. He glanced down at his wedding ring. He never bothered to hide it from her. Dishonesty only soured the connection. He craved sincerity as much as she did.

He found himself getting lost in her sadness. The last remnant of his anxiety had broken in her pale blue eyes. Yet he was terrified that the moment she walked away, the sound and the fury would all come rushing back. He reached across the table and took her free hand in his, relishing the soft feel of her fingers. He felt the urge to run with her, somewhere far away from the explosions and the guilt and the twisted dreams of so many mistakes. So many regrets.

"He's mad if he wants this miserable life more than he wants you." He squeezed her fingers in his, drawing in enough calm and tenderness to stop the chaos in his heart. "I would gladly give it all up for you."

Sharon's fingers curled around his, returning the supple touch until her skin connected with the silver band on his left hand. He watch the pleasure vanish from her face, and a gray discontent fill her calming eyes.

"As far as the Army's concerned, falling in love with either of you is criminal." He felt the pressure release as her fingers went cold in his hand. "As long as you have that ring on your finger Sir, you're no more available to me than he was."

# Chapter 32
## Charlottesville, VA (2012)

Captain Mann held a bottle of wine in his thick hands, a large gold watch dangling from his wrist. He reached for the open bottle of Cabernet on the makeshift bar and refilled his empty goblet with a generous flush.

He caught his reflection in a set of double glass doors to his right and looked himself over with a critical eye. He wore a white polo shirt that hugged his biceps and slenderized his midsection, and a sleek pair of khaki pants. His stance was a little looser, brasher out of uniform. A habit that helped hide the jarring pain and fluid that had filled his ankle since last Friday's ruck march. The pain was rough and unpredictable when he walked, but at least it was something familiar. Nothing like the sharp burn of being wrong.

"You handing out drinks?"

Mann turned towards the lieutenant in front of him, trying to remember the kid's name. The one who forgot his hat that first day of class.

"We got beer and wine. Take your pick." Mann leaned into the countertop, waiting for the name to come to him. He was surprised at how many of them were still strangers. How little effort he'd put into getting to know the ones that didn't matter. An odd assortment of characters with mismatched personalities, each them with their private reasons for spending the holiday in Charlottesville, instead of returning to wherever it was they called home.

"Just a beer, I guess."

Randall. The name came to him as he reached into the cooler at his feet and pulled out a cold bottle of beer. He offered himself a silent congratulations as he popped the top and handed it across the bar.

"Happy Thanksgiving Randall." He forced a phony smile for everyone, whether he remembered their names or not. There wasn't much warmth in their faces. Just a nod and a cool response.

"Cheers." The kid took the drink and ambled about the crowded room.

Captain Mann brought the dry cabernet to his lips, looking about the room for a friendly smile. Someone who hadn't heard how he'd humiliated himself in the parking lot, digging through Hunt's ruck sack in a sad attempt to bandage his own ego. Someone who didn't hold it against him for having suspicions.

The walls around him were lined with large windows and the open space was full of old lounge chairs. He scanned the scattered clusters of his unknown classmates, all dressed in civilian clothes. They looked a little lost and sheepish from his position behind the bar. Struggling for some sense of purpose or belonging now that the orders had stopped and they were temporarily free.

Lieutenant Sharon leaned against a lonesome pillar beside the wall. She held a fresh glass of wine between her slender fingers and was staring off at nothing in particular. She was dressed in a light blue sweater that matched her eyes, her dark hair falling loose around her shoulders. She offered Mann a thin smile and raised her glass slightly, but her mind was clearly bent on something heavier than ruck marches and runaway egos.

The sullen major sat alone in a circle of old armchairs, the last of the winter sun beaming through the windows behind him. His rank and deployment patches had been replaced with a worn t-shirt and gray hoodie, and his hazel eyes were hidden behind a bottle of cheap beer. Nothing to distinguish him from any other lost soul waiting out the holiday season in some expressionless trance. No indication that he was anyone that mattered. Other than the smallish bit of silver peeking out from the tongue of his left shoe, where he habitually hung his dog tags.

Mann's eyes eventually settled on the imposing redhead who'd bruised him. She sat alone in the folds of a well-used sofa, her nails grazing the tinted glass of the beer she'd walked in with. She was almost unrecognizable out of uniform. Her red hair was tied in a simple ponytail, still tame and professional, but just a touch softer. She wore a loose green hoodie and a worn pair of old blue jeans. There was still so much heat and ambition tucked away inside her. A ferocity that allowed her to do things you'd never guess she was capable of.

She looked up at him with a feverish stare, and the same piercing grey eyes that had broken his selfish resolve. For the first time he saw that there was real beauty in them. Something victorious and alive. A dizzying mixture of jealousy and spite ran through his veins.

He dropped his eyes into his wine glass and took another long swallow, trying to get himself drunk enough to apologize. He might need to swallow another pint before he was able to face his own ugly behavior. His ruined pride. He probably owed her something a little more dignified, but he wasn't the sort of man who could humble himself sober. His chipped ego would fight every precious word unless he lulled it to sleep. He could feel her severe eyes on him wherever he looked. She was waiting for it. And he knew there was no escaping it.

The stairwell door clicked open across the long room and Captain Aaron Cade stepped into the mild crowd. He wore a simple black t-shirt and a pair of shorts that fell just above his gangly knees, one of which was as minced and burned as the rest of him. He moved through the room like a shadow, the pink markings on his neck and face half hidden beneath a graying baseball cap. He approached the bar and leaned his forearms over the cluttered countertop, blocking Mann's view of Lieutenant Hunt.

Cade was maybe the biggest mystery of them all. No one had the nerve to ask him about his face or his history. And he seemed content to pretend that the scars weren't there.

"Glass of wine Captain?" Mann grabbed a wine glass from the bar and turned it upright.

"Beer is fine." Cade responded.

"Beer it is." Mann forced a smile as he put down the wine glass and pulled a cold beer from the cooler at his feet. He tried not to ask himself meaningless questions about how Cade had fallen behind. Whether it was an injury or the sprint or something more devious. But the uncertainty kept pitching through his head the longer the gangly captain stood in front of him.

Mann reached for his bottle opener as Captain Cade glanced around the room, smooth and fluid, taking stock of the company and the moment. He eventually caught the eye of the redhead across the way and a dizzying smile grazed his lips.

Mann tightened his fingers around the bottleneck in his hands and watched the possessive way that Cade looked at her. The liberty he took with exploring the contours of her face and the curves of her hips, as if she suddenly belonged to him.

He was hit with an unexpected shred of envy as all of his unhealthy suspicions were confirmed. Cade had never been motivated by pride or patches. And he never saw Hunt as the competition. She was his prize.

Mann's chipped ego bristled and flared, and he stared at Cade's tortured skin with a sudden revulsion. He popped open the beer in his hands and passed it across the bar to the distracted captain. He reached for what was left of his own glass of cabernet and swallowed all of it, waiting for the heavy drink to dull the pain in his leg. To bury the sudden realization that he'd been played.

Captain Cade coiled his fingers around the cold bottle. There was a dim smile reaching into the deep pink of his burned face that was both surreptitious and eager. He brought the beer to his lips and doused the offensive smile with a confident swig, almost as if he'd forgotten both his strange appearance and his brutal failure.

"So that's what you were after this whole time?" Mann felt the slow creep of the wine catching up to him as his head began to float and spin. He darted an unmistakable glance towards Lieutenant Hunt as the accusation stirred and solidified. "You never fell out of formation."

"What difference does it make?" Cade smiled a non-descript smile, a calm satisfaction in his eyes and a sheen of alcohol lining his bottom lip. "You got what you wanted, didn't you? You're going to Airborne school."

"And what about you?" Mann stumbled over his words, staring across the bar with an abrasive stare. "You really let a woman embarrass you like that just to get laid?"

"What makes you think I'm embarrassed by any of this?" A thin film glazed Cade's eyes. He traced the mouth of his beer with a slippery finger, remembering something strange and private.

"Just give me a straight answer." Mann's tongue slackened with wine and anxiety. There was a bitter flutter in his stomach as he realized he was more concerned with the suggestion of sex than the idea that Cade had thrown the competition.

"What do you care Mann?" Cade crooned.

"Because she should have to earn it like the rest of us." Captain Mann reached for the bottle of wine on the counter and poured himself another generous flush. He brought the glass to his lips again, letting the alcohol soothe his frightened ego into a calm and ignorant dream.

"And what makes you think she didn't?" Cade took a sharp swallow.

The curious question rifled through Mann's ears. He relived the aftermath of that last half mile, shaking off the boorish shame of finishing with Hunt tight on his heels.

Mann had been sick with embarrassment when he hauled her things through the school, forced to knock on her door with her disheveled ruck sack in his tired arms. To look her in the eye after he'd called her a cheat and a liar, and come up with nothing to back it up. He'd been relieved that she never answered the door. That he was able to leave her abandoned gear in the hallway without stumbling through an inefficient apology for something he still hadn't reconciled in his mind.

It never occurred to him that she might be just across the hall, with Cade's awkward and sweaty hands all over her.

He was reliving that same nauseous feeling now. The same vulgar distaste for his own shabby self. He was nearing that delicate place of humility where contrition was born. His thick fingers worked the flimsy stem on the glass in his hand, and he was forced into an awkward pause. He swayed a bit as he looked around the room, finally bringing himself to focus on her expressionless eyes. Some of the most frightening and exhilarating eyes he'd ever known.

"I need to know if I owe her an apology."

"You owe her an apology." An undefined wave broke across Cade's face and a loaded simplicity slipped from his taut lips. "Regardless of what I did or didn't do. You underestimated her. We both did."

Mann swallowed the uncomfortable truth with a dram of red wine that stung his cheeks. He still didn't know if this gangly man with the raw face had somehow beat him into a woman's bed. Made love to the fierce redhead across the room that was suddenly rattling his senses. "You don't think she's a bit out of your league?"

Mann watched the nasty slight sink into Cade's seared flesh, who pushed a wrecked smile past his teeth.

"Why don't you get me another beer?" Cade's eyes betrayed a deep loathing that sent an unnatural chill up Mann's spine. He reached into the cooler at his feet, and opened a second bottle, setting it on the open countertop between them.

"I don't need a pair of Airborne wings to prove that I'm a man." Cade shook his head with a cool indifference, a measure of condescension built into every word. "My sacrifice is etched into my face."

Mann felt the insult burn in his chest. He watched Cade toss back another swallow of beer. There was something grotesque and vulnerable in his swagger.

"You enjoy your wings, Mann." Captain Cade stepped back from the bar with both beers in his hands. "I got something better."

He turned with a polished grace towards the red-haired lieutenant behind him, approaching her with a soft familiarity. He took the empty bottle from her fingers and put his second beer in her open hands, caressing the inside of her wrist with a subtle movement of his fingers. A gesture that was certainly lost on everyone but Mann.

Mann's ankle seemed to swell as he watched them, the bitterness gathering in the most vulnerable spaces. He felt his raw ego cool and harden, the first step in an irreversible process that would end with the brittle thing splintering off into a thousand broken pieces.

# Chapter 33
## Charlottesville, VA (2012)

"Excuse me everyone. May I have your attention?" The delirious words poured from his mouth before she knew where they were coming from, but she had a dark, trembling suspicion. "I'd like to propose a toast."

Captain Mann headed towards the center of the room with a slight limp in his step. Hunt watched him struggle, her fingers sliding around the thin neck of the bottle in her hands. He winced as he straightened his posture, and the blurred and misshapen eyes of all their colleagues fell on him.

"Welcome, Ladies and Gentlemen and Happy Thanksgiving. Glad to see so many of you could make it." He sounded drunk, sloppy and out of sorts. He attempted a showy smile as he lifted his voice, but there was something lax and bent in his dimpled face. His deep brown eyes made a long sweep of the room and rested on her simple grey eyes.

She shared a smallish space with Captain Cade on a sunken old sofa, gripped in a strange energy. She felt Cade tense up beside her, his fingers twitching and his eyes creeping over her in a possessive embrace. She felt the same singular distress she'd felt when he approached her in the hallway, like a piece of meat dangling in front of a pair of hungry wolves, one with large, prying eyes, and one with pearly white teeth.

"Many of you are new to the Army, and this may be your first Thanksgiving away from home, so I'm glad we could offer you some sort of celebration, even if it isn't quite what you're used to."

She watched Cade's twisted expression as Mann slurred his words. His sad eyes rippled with contempt and unease.

"If this is your first Thanksgiving away from home," Mann swirled the purple wine in his glass, his eyes and intentions hidden from view. "I guarantee you, it won't be the last. Hopefully in time you won't think of these holidays as time spent apart from your

185

family, but as time spent with extended family. Because the military is your family now. We'll look out for each other. We'll take care of each other."

Mann's words stung like so much cheap nonsense. Trite and insulting. His perfect face was well suited to petty lies and vanity. He wore it well. Deception and strategy was in his blood, and to a small degree, she envied how easily it flowed off his tongue.

She wondered if he recognized just a small sliver of himself in her. If he was reminded every time he stepped on his swollen ankle that she'd kept up with him, right up until the very end. Or if he still thought of her as just another overconfident and entitled little girl. Someone who'd readily exchanged her sexuality for an impressive consolation prize.

"I just want you to know that I'm grateful for this opportunity to have gotten to know you all. To study with you. To train with you." He swallowed roughly. There was a noticeable dip in his tone. "Now for the hard part."

Her stomach dropped. Her fingers slipped around the edges of the cool glass in her palms. Mann swayed and stuttered through his speech with his intoxicated eyes fixed on her, trying to get something foreign and uncomfortable past his throat.

"I think it's appropriate that I take this opportunity to make a long overdue apology."

Hunt drew in a hard breath, steeling herself against his illicit song. There was a terrifying simplicity in the way the anger flooded into her cheeks, painting them red and hostile.

"Every day since we arrived in Charlottesville, Lieutenant Pamela Hunt has been working towards a chance to go to Airborne school. And every day since she raised her hand and volunteered, I've been trying to undermine her."

She watched the wine in his glass tilt and tremble, surprised at the sudden steadiness in his words. The raw edges of her stare softened against her will, her heart pumping as much human blood as it did frost and venom.

"I've lied to her about her chances. I've kept information from her. I've demeaned her in front of her colleagues. But in spite of all of this, she's continued to work hard and proven herself to be one of the most committed and capable soldiers I know."

Somewhere between the ruck march with Mann and her lurid morning with Captain Cade she'd shed the bitter ashes of her former self. She was alarmed to find that her heart was still soft and pliable underneath, like wet playdough. That it could still be molded into something whole and vital.

Cade reached for her fingers and wrapped them in a protective embrace, almost confirming that he'd recognized the same penetrable softness. She watched the winding lines of his matted flesh against hers with a gruesome pain. She'd never been afraid of his scars. But she was terrified of how they'd come together. That he didn't fully understand her fever for glory. For perfection.

"I'm standing here now, to apologize for the way I've treated you." Mann fixed his bloated stare at her and she felt the true weight of each staggered word. "You didn't deserve any of it. You deserved to have my encouragement and support, but my ego wouldn't allow it. I want to let you know that you've earned my respect for all you've accomplished over the past few months. And I'd like to ask for your forgiveness."

There was a long, somber silence that followed as she chewed through the sullied atmosphere. He'd somehow found the nerve to ask for the cruelest sort of thing he could ask of her. She preferred the insults and curses. Anything but this rank powerlessness.

She took a long swallow from her bottle and let it warm her from the inside out. She couldn't tell if any of it was sincere. Or if he'd simply found a way to manipulate her into feeling the sort of slippery softnesss that she didn't want to feel. He wore a subdued expression as he watched her watching him, his posture bowed and servile.

There was still enough darkness left in her to turn him away. To retreat back inside herself where she was safe and protected. But for the first time in a very long while, she had a choice.

"It may take some time Sir." The coldness of her response made her tremble. There was far more emotion than logic in her answer. Signaling that there was still something in her that responded to humility and sincerity.

"I can live with that."

Mann's wobbly words echoed through the room, and she saw a pained expression graze Cade's face. He squeezed her hand to the point of grief.

"As for the rest of you," Mann shifted his weight again, trying to keep the pressure off his tender joints. "I can tell already that you're fine lawyers. And you're going to make fine soldiers. I'm proud to serve with each and every one of you."

He raised his glass and the wine sloshed back and forth, making him appear dizzy and reckless. Hunt's fingers rattled against the cold glass as she waited for him to finish his toast, fighting a burgeoning need to down the whole thing at once.

"So without further ado, to the JAG Corps!"

"To the JAG Corps!"

# Chapter 34
## Charlottesville, VA (2012)

Cade lifted his beer bottle to his lips and held the bitter ale on the back of his tongue. The sunlight was fading in the windows around him, turning Mann into a talking silhouette, a faceless nobody from some lost moment in time. He swallowed the dram of alcohol and felt it tingle in his stomach.

"Give it a rest Mann." Cade's voice was hard and impatient. He'd spent half his evening trying to drown out the captain's tired voice. "First its rape-shield rules, now you're attacking the Geneva Conventions."

He watched the redhead next to him, playing with an empty bottle of beer in her lap. He was wracked by the possibility that she'd only come to his room because she was drunk on pheromones and adrenaline. That she'd only stayed because she thought he'd made some meaningless sacrifice. That the tragic mess on his face never seemed to buy him the same sort of gratitude from women.

"The rules were written by people who've never seen combat. Who've never been caught in a firefight." Mann stood in the center of their half-circle of armchairs, preaching like someone who still believed his personal experiences with war meant something to outsiders. That they might change policies or end campaigns. He flashed his perfect teeth in Cade's direction, chasing down his smile with a swallow of red wine. "That's why we have these impractical limitations and things like 'unnecessary suffering.' Whatever that's supposed to mean."

"I think it's perfectly obvious what it means." Cade rolled his eyes. He watched Mann stumble around on his bruised ankle, finally drunk enough to move past the pain. He wasn't a legitimate threat. Just an arrogant captain who'd nearly run himself into the ground for a patch on his uniform. To make himself larger by trying to beat out a woman who wouldn't break.

"I'm just pointing out the absurdity of it all." Mann swayed a little as he smiled, either a little too engaged or a little too drunk to hold himself steady. "The Geneva Conventions are an agreement that war is necessary. And a sad attempt to make it less brutal. Making the enemy suffer is a legitimate military strategy. But 'unnecessary' suffering is a war crime. If I make the enemy go blind, I could be court-martialed. But if I shoot the guy in the fucking head, I'm a war hero."

Cade bristled at the word 'hero.' His pride pinched a bit every time he heard it minimized and borrowed. He watched Hunt from the side of his face that was still appealing, desperate to know what was happening behind those deep grey eyes. To help her see past the putty that dragged across his face. She was careful to keep her opinions close and intimate. She remained still through all of this.

"The idea is to try to maintain some sense of civility."

"I get that, but it's war. It's war. The very purpose is to kill." Mann raised his wine glass, swirling the purple juices all about the inside curves, coating the glass in a rich, delicate film. "Seems to me that we just want to feel better about what it is we're doing by calling it a 'just war' or a 'humane war.' That way we can go home to our wives and children without feeling guilty about the blood on our hands."

"That's a pretty shallow analysis." Cade took another sip of beer, keeping Lieutenant Hunt in his peripheral vision. She was the most beautiful thing he'd ever had on the bed beneath him. Strong and resilient and careful with who she let inside. She had no reason to trust someone like Mann. Someone who'd abused and humiliated her the way he had. Unless she truly believed his sloppy, drunken apology. "Obviously no one here agrees with you."

"I agree with him." Hunt's steady voice finally broke through the silence, a flush of alcohol tinting her cheeks.

Captain Mann stopped swirling his wine glass and looked directly at her.

190

Cade felt a dull pain between his eyes. Something foreign and hot. The beer in his mouth went stale and bitter. "You're really going to agree with him?"

"I agree with his argument." Hunt held a straight face, her grey eyes dark and unrecognizable in the diminishing light. He noticed that same stiffening in her spine that he'd seen on the first day, when she raised her hand to compete against people who were far larger and stronger than herself. "It's not personal."

Somehow everything about it was personal. He'd kissed her naked skin and brought her to warm tears after miles of exhaustion. He'd reminded her what pleasure felt like. But that kind of mid-morning euphoria never lasted long. Perhaps there was a part of her that enjoyed the bruises. Craved the broken bones and the healing that went along with them. It was a painful reminder of the distinct difference between physical and emotional scarring.

"It's no different than humane slaughter laws." She rolled her beer bottle in her hands, dragging her pretty nails around the brown glass. "We pass a lot of laws regulating how cattle and poultry are slaughtered, so we don't have to feel guilty about eating the steak on our plates. It's a moral salve, but doesn't change the fact that someone is in the slaughter yard severing arteries to keep us fed."

Every now and again he could still feel a slight burn in his charred skin. It crept up on him now, growing angry and hot. She was every bit as gripped by competition as Mann was. And he couldn't quite drown out the burgeoning fear that they had more in common than he wanted to believe.

"That's pretty cynical, don't you think?" Cade leaned back in his chair and let a sour feeling creep into his stomach, opening up a vulnerable space buried behind all his physical cravings. It stung in the most sensitive places.

"I just think there's some sense in admitting that what we're doing is brutal and bloody." He felt her eyes settle on the raw side of his face, then drop down towards the bottle of beer in her hands. He saw the flurry of half-drunk arguments careening through her mind. "We need protein to live. Sometimes we need war to protect us. But I don't try to fool myself into thinking there's no violence or suffering involved. That's just the way the world was put together."

Mann smiled behind his raised glass of red wine. He took a generous sip to try to hide his satisfaction, but his large white teeth betrayed him as always.

He was a fool if he took this for forgiveness. He was a fool if he believed he would let her go that easily.

# Chapter 35
## Charlottesville, VA (2012)

Sharon lifted her eyes above the rim of her wine glass, watching Casper dive into his fourth, possibly fifth bottle of beer. She watched the bulging vein in his neck as he swallowed. The strangeness in his eyes that told her to keep her distance.

The sky outside the long windows had transitioned from deep orange to purple, then from purple to black. The room had emptied into a few handfuls of people, lounging in quiet circles. The sounds of clinking beer bottles and drunken chatter spun around her ears.

*"So what about nerve gas then?"*

She could no longer distinguish the sotted voices around her. She was focused on the ghosts gathering around the narrowed corners of Casper's eyes.

She watched his chapped hands, the simple wedding band on his fourth finger curiously peeking in and out of view. She wondered where this invisible woman was. What it meant that he carried her around with him on his finger, but didn't run to her for comfort.

Her fingers tingled with the memory of his touch. His casual promise that he'd gladly give this all up for her. The military and all the memories that it carried. Maybe even his marriage and his future. Fidelity was a hard sell when everyone was lonely. And everyone around her seemed to be lonely.

*"What about biological weapons and atom bombs?"*

Sharon finished the last of the wine in her glass. Casper took another long swallow from the bottle in his hands. His face was layered in shadows. The room was too dim to tell the difference between drunk or dangerous.

*"What if barbaric warfare ends the war sooner?"*

Invisible images seemed to dance in front of him, flickering like tiny flames behind his eyelids. She saw herself kissing the pain from his eyelids, holding him close to her beating heart. Sharing his fears and regrets. Helping him heal.

Given enough time, he could easily work his way into her most sensitive places. She would grant him access to all her private dreams and disappointments. Whatever it was that had drawn her to this life. To the idea of hard days and lonely nights. The wicked allure of hopelessness and terrifying freedom. He could find his way to that damaged part of her and pull out some deep-seated truth. Make her believe that he could massage it, soothe it, heal it. The temptation was strong and potent, hidden under layers of scar tissue. She still craved that promise of being understood. Of somehow being made whole.

*"What if it saves lives?"*

He closed his fingers around the bottleneck, his muscles tightening and contracting as he squeezed the fragile glass towards the breaking point. The birth of a unique pain built behind his dark eyes.

*"You have to ask yourself, what do you care about more, dead children, or dead soldiers?"*

Sharon saw the pressure in his fists. The impenetrable fog in his eyes. Some gritty transformation was tearing through him. A shock of madness and violence that sent tentacles of fear sliding up her spine.

*"The rules were written for another time. When the enemy wore a uniform and didn't hide behind women and children. Today it's just a matter of chance. You trust the wrong person at the wrong time and you get blown to hell."*

"Stop laughing!" Casper spat as the glass bottle shattered between his fingers. Beer and glass shavings covered his hands.

Sharon gripped her chin and neck, and heard the subtle smash of her wine glass hitting the floor.

Casper's palm closed around a large slice of broken glass and he lunged towards Captain Mann. He knocked the surprised captain to the floor, the wine in his hand flying towards the dark windows. Casper wrestled Mann under his control as the rest of the room shot up from their chairs and turned towards the desperate scuffle.

194

"You think this is funny? You sick fucker!" The mist in Casper's eyes burned like sulphur. Hot tears collected and swelled in the rims of his bloodshot eyes. In seconds Casper had an elbow around Mann's neck, and was holding the sharp sliver of glass against the base of his chin.

Sharon's heart sank into her stomach, pulsing and thumping like a wounded animal.

"Let go!" Mann choked out a reply, his brown eyes trained on the sharp instrument at his throat. A thin stream of blood oozing between Casper's clenched fingers. "What's wrong with you, let me go!"

"Jesus, Sir, what's got into you!" Cade gasped in place, unable to move

"My God, let him go!" Hunt shouted.

"Let him go Sir!" Sharon's voice broke through the thick silence in her head. She pushed her way past Cade and Hunt and got down on the floor with the major.

"Sharon, get away from him! He's not thinking straight!" Cade yelled to her.

"Sir, it's Lieutenant Sharon. Listen to me. It's Jamie." She ignored Captain Cade and reached towards Casper's shoulder without touching him, careful to balance herself between the here and now, and whatever lost memory had engulfed him. She skated along the periphery of time and space, sounding out his name with a gentle urgency. "Ben. You have to look at me."

He looked at her with violent eyes that chilled the blood in her heart. He didn't see her, but someone else that he once trusted. Someone from another time in a far more hostile place.

"Ben, let the captain go. Give me your hand." She extended her hand with a terrified breath, taking the gamble that she could bring him back before his defenses engaged.

"Drop the weapon Ben. You don't need it here. Take my hand instead."

"Jamie?" He breathed the soft syllables of her name. His respirations slowed and he focused on the soft contours of her face. "Is that you?"

"I'm here." She moved her perfumed wrist under his nose, drawing him back to reality.

Casper unclenched his bloodied fist and let the glass fall to floor. He planted his hand in the warmth of her palm and Sharon felt the stark reality of her skin against his. She watched the way it changed the dark color of his eyes. The desert seemed to evaporate around him. He loosened his grip on the captain's neck, who writhed away and scrambled to his feet. Casper glanced at his fingers locked inside hers, a smear of blood uniting the two. The sight seemed to both frighten and calm him.

"Whose blood is this?" He stared at the red mess in his hands.

"Just yours." Sharon's voice broke, a surge of hot adrenaline rushing through her. She held tight to his shaking hands, trying to keep them both grounded.

Her heartbeat slowed and the rush of adrenaline cooled. She felt herself drowning in disproportionate swells of horror and compassion.

She drew some ritual comfort from the strength in his fingers, trying to sort through her fears and her cravings. To keep from being drawn into his broken world. To stop the emotions from feeding and swelling. He was an uncommon mystery. The miserable sort that already carried too much weight around his heart, but was still willing to take on more. There was a curious undercurrent to his wounded soul. The sort of thing that had swept her up and broken her against the rocks so many times.

His eyes bore into her, bringing her past, present and future bubbling to the surface, alive in her eyes and unavoidably transparent.

"You damn near killed me." Mann glared at Casper as he tried to rub away the feel of Casper's elbow locked around his windpipe.

Casper pulled his hands away from Sharon and stared up at the string of faces, all watching him like they would a sick animal. He had a pained look on his face. As if he could feel their pity eating into his bones. He looked down at the deep gash in his palm, oozing red. His eyes filled with the terror of not knowing the next time he would snap.

"Next time I may." The words slipped out under his breath, but they reverberated across the room like a tidal wave.

# Chapter 36
## Charlottesville, VA (2012)

Jamie stood over the sink, watching the cool water run over her bloodied fingers. It turned pink as it slid off her skin and disappeared down the drain. She toweled off her hands and stared at her reflection in the mirror. Her hair had flattened and her lips had lost most of their sheen. She was still nauseous from the adrenaline, or maybe a little tipsy from the wine.

She splashed her face with cold water, scrubbing away the leftover make-up and lavender perfume. It would take more than a quick rinse to wipe away tonight's memories and mistakes. She turned on the shower and watched the steam fog up the mirror, clouding out the wearied expression that stared back at her.

The shower and the wine helped her tune out the last few hours. She focused on the warm spray hitting her shoulders, on the soft sound that enveloped her, on the feel of her fingers in her hair, massaging away the stress and grime that had followed her back to her room.

She dried off and slipped into a pair of loose fitting pajamas, threw her hair into a sloppy ponytail at the back of her neck and reveled in the comfort of being safe, warm and alone. She glanced at the clock on her bedside table. 9:15 p.m. For the first time in a long while, she was free to sleep through the dawn. No morning formation. No five mile run. Just empty hours begging to be filled. Her body was tired, but her mind was full. She stared up at the white ceiling, wishing she'd had a chance to finish just one more glass of wine.

The phone rang, cutting into the blinding quiet. She reached for her cell phone on the bedside table and glanced at the screen. Another unexpected late night call from Matthew Chase.

The days had crept by in a stilted silence. His last goodbye lingered in the stale air she breathed in every night. The heavy loneliness he'd left her with had calcified in her bones.

She exhaled the last of her regrets and answered the phone.

"Hey Sergeant Chase."

"Hey LT." There was an unmistakable bustle in the background. Sounds of family, dinner and cheerful conversation. The combination was both foreign and universal. Some of the most recognizable images that she'd never truly seen. "How are the ruck marches treating you?"

"Still difficult, but I'm getting stronger." She swallowed. "A little stronger every day."

"Glad to hear it." She remembered the soothing tone of his voice and she missed it. Perhaps her head was still reeling from the mess that had taken place upstairs, but she wanted to reach through the phone and touch him. To hold his fingers in hers without the smell of blood and fear overpowering her.

"How's Reese?"

"He's good. I think he misses you." His voice was soft and almost apologetic. She could feel the weight of so many unspoken words hovering between them. "We both miss you."

"I miss you too." Sharon caught her breath. She fought the familiar burning in the back of her throat. That dizzying calm that he gave her.

"Every day I think about the fact that you could've come home for the holidays." His distant voice sounded over the open airwaves. "And every day I think about how I talked you out of it."

"You don't need to explain yourself anymore." She finally let go of all the anger and confusion, the last stirrings of resentment melting into the heavy air. "You were right about duty and sacrifice and courage. You were right about everything. I think I understand what the Army means to you now."

"The Army means the world to me Ma'am." His words were like an involuntary confession, almost lost in the background noise. "And I'm going to miss it a lot."

Sharon bit her lip. Her heart flooded with a thousand unexpected tremors. She felt a painful tightening in her chest as the ugly knot she'd been harboring began to unravel.

"I never should have kissed you before you left." His words were enticing and strange, an impossible warmth weaving its way under her skin. "I can't stop thinking about it. I'm not signing my re-enlistment papers this spring."

"You can't do that Matt." She choked back a broken string of runaway emotions, chaotic and untethered. "I can't let you give this up for me."

"You're worth it Jamie." His voice curled like soft smoke through the airwaves. "I've already made my decision."

"I don't want you to regret it." She listened to him breathe, hearing the rush of air over the hum of warm voices behind him.

"I've had my chance to serve my country." His voice bent and swayed in such a pretty, stable rhythm. "Now I have my chance to be with you. What is there to regret?"

Her defenses crumbled, leaving her exposed and vulnerable. She found herself caught up in an unfamiliar temptation to hope for something stable and secure. The feeling was terrifying.

"Jamie, are you okay?"

"How can you be sure?" The words slipped past her lips before she had a chance to stop them.

"Because I'm in love with you." His words came out smooth and sure, breaking her barriers and pulling a sharp sigh from deep in her chest. The sound startled her, just as she heard a tapping noise in the outside hallway. Someone knocking at her door.

"Matt, there's someone at the door. I'll be back."

"Jamie."

"No, I'll be back." She headed towards the door with the phone curled in her hand. "Just give me one second."

Sharon opened the door to see Major Casper standing outside her room, still dressed in his t-shirt and hoodie. She glanced down at his hands. Most of the blood had been washed away, with the exception of a small red dab on his left knuckle. She felt another unhealthy tremor in her heart as she looked up at him.

"Sir." The word rattled through her ribcage and the major winced at the sound. The formality seemed to cut tiny slivers into his heart. Like glass.

"I'm sorry if I woke you." He spoke slowly, his tongue still heavy with alcohol and the taste of twisted memories. "I wanted to apologize for what happened tonight."

"You don't need to apologize, Sir." Sharon slid her fingers over the microphone on the cell phone in her hands, hoping to block out the conversation. "You had a bit too much to drink."

"I have to explain what happened." He insisted as he set his sliced palm into the doorjamb, his wedding ring cloudy and molded into his slack skin. "To somebody."

"You don't have to explain anything."

"I want to explain, Sharon." He raked her over with a set of distressed and terrified hazel eyes. "I don't like the way you looked at me tonight. I'm not an animal, and I want you to know that. Can I come inside?"

"I can't let you inside Sir." She glanced between the desperate look in his eyes and the blood smears dotting her doorframe every time he moved his right arm. "You need to get that cut taken care of."

Casper followed her eyes and saw the tiny splotches he'd left on the wood frame. He retracted his arm and lowered his eyes, inspecting the small slice in his palm. He seemed truly surprised at the sight of it, as if the daze from the alcohol was finally wearing off. "Are you afraid of me?"

"I'm not afraid of you." Sharon watched as he jammed his thumb into the thin cut in his palm, holding the skin closed to stop the bleeding.

"Then why won't you look at me?"

He lifted his eyes again. There was a challenge in them. An open invitation to remind him of the dire spectacle he'd made, of how close to the brink he really was.

"Sergeant Chase is on the phone, Sir." She lifted her hand that was still curled strategically around her cell phone. "I should probably get back to him."

"The dogsitter." Casper nodded, his eyes drawn back towards the cut in his palm.

"I want to help you through this," Sharon practically whispered, glancing at the live phone in her hand. "Whatever it is that this is, but there are some things I can't give you."

"I get it Sharon." Casper looked up again. His eyes were full and cold, hiding some bitter darkness begging to be released. The sheer weight of it seemed to be dragging him under. "Give my regards to the sergeant."

Casper turned and headed into the empty hallway. Sharon watched as he tended to the gash in his right hand. His face tensed as if the sensation was finally coming back and the pain ripped into him.

Without warning he let out a grunt and smashed his powerful arms into the wall. He collapsed after them and fell against the sheetrock, holding himself mute and immobile. In time, he peeled himself away and ambled down the dark hallway towards his room.

Sharon stood in silence, frozen in the doorjamb dotted with spots of fresh blood. Casper disappeared into his room as another door opened across the hall.

Captain Mann stood across from her with one hand around his neck. He glanced down the hall after Casper, then looked at her with an unmistakable concern. The sort of look that told her he'd been standing there for quite some time.

"You okay over there LT?"

"I'm fine. Thanks."

Sharon shut the door and hurried back towards her bed. She put the phone against her ear and listened for the comforting sound of Matt's breathing. She wanted to tell him she loved him too. That she trusted him. That she was ready to come home.

"Matt? Are you still there?"

The soft breathing had stopped. The family bustle was gone. The line was dead.

# Part Eight:

# A Reasonable Doubt

# Chapter 37
## Fort Leavenworth, KS (2014)

Jamie Sharon leaned against the headboard of her borrowed bed, propped up by a stack of firm pillows. She wore a pair of drawstring pajama pants and a loose t-shirt. Her dark hair was finally let loose, curled and soft around her shoulders. She folded her legs in front of her, her bare feet freed from the heaviness of her combat boots, and balanced Casper's file in her lap. She read through the investigation in the dim lighting, sliding her dog tags up and down their plated chain as she flipped through the pages.

She tried to forget the things she'd seen in Charlottesville and view the facts with fresh eyes. She took notes on dates, times and trivial details. She went through every item piece by piece, looking for patterns and cracks in the evidence. Some subtle inconsistency that CID might have missed. Something to confirm the storm in her heart that told her Casper wasn't lost completely. That there was still something left inside him that was worth fighting for.

She picked through the photos of his soiled clothing. A U.S. Army hoodie and a pair of faded blue jeans, speckled with someone else's blood. She pulled out the photos of the crime scene and forced herself to stare at Mann's lifeless body, wrecked and broken on the cold ground. She hoped she still had something to learn from his glossy eyes. She heard the whispers of gunshots in the back of her mind, imagining each impact and speculating as to which one finally made him fall.

"C'mon Mann. Tell me what happened that night." She placed the tiny beads of the chain around her neck between her teeth. "If Casper didn't kill you, then who did? What were you doing on post? Who were you here to see?"

She leaned forward and placed the photo flat against her comforter. She re-read the police reports and witness statements, every specious observation from the coroner and the senile old man who owned the Eagle Lounge. She toyed with her dog tags and chewed the end of her pen. She scanned Captain Hunt's list of witnesses, recognizing each of their names and functions. The jogger who found the body. The crime lab detective who analyzed the blood and the fingerprints. The CID agent who conducted the search of Casper's home. Then the familiar name at the bottom, staring back at her from the black and white print.

Captain Aaron Cade. The name brought back the sound of a glass bottle shattering beside her. The slippery feel of Casper's bloody hands linked with hers.

She kneaded her skin to try to wipe away the memory, finding a gentle comfort in the realness of Matt's ring around her finger.

She released a long breath of stale air. Cade would give up every damning detail of Casper's breakdown. Regardless of how rare or irrelevant it was. Her only hope was to object to every speculation. To find enough clutter and confusion in the details to break down the suspicion.

She reached for her phone on the nightstand and checked the time. It was past 2000. She didn't know where he was stationed or what the time difference was, but she dialed Cade's number and hit send. The phone sounded twice in her ear before he picked up.

"Aaron here."

"Sir, it's Lieutenant Jamie Sharon." She held the phone against her ear with her free hand. "I'm calling from Fort Leavenworth."

"I had a feeling I'd be hearing from you." His voice was a bit deeper, heavier than she remembered it. There was a dull pause as he digested the memory of her voice. "Still a lieutenant?"

"The paperwork is being processed." She brushed aside the distraction and focused on the photo laid out on her bed. The fragments started coming together as she stared at the punctures in Mann's chest. Then the round hole in the middle of his forehead. The redness in his swollen eyes. His broken jaw. Small clicks began sounding in the back of her brain. "I'm calling about Captain Mann's homicide."

"Still trying to protect Major Casper from himself?" It might have been a simple observation more than outright mockery, but it was hard to ignore the subtle derision in his voice.

Sharon kept her eyes fixed on the photo, cycling through the possibilities as they danced through her head. The actual truth of the matter hit her for the first time as the words lifted off her tongue. "It's possible that he didn't do this."

"Who else would've done it Sharon?" There was no sympathy left in his deflated voice. No pleasant memories of either the victim, or the accused. "He nearly killed Mann in Charlottesville. Christ, you're probably the only thing that stopped him."

"That may be true." Sharon let the admission spill from some deeply guarded place. "But anyone could've attacked Mann that night. Someone who wasn't a very good shot."

Sharon pulled out Casper's personnel records, flipping through the stack of documents until she came across his weapons qualification records. She scanned the numbers for the 9 millimeter ranges, where he averaged 39 out of 40 every time.

"Casper's shot expert with the 9 mil for the last three years." She spoke more to herself than to Cade. "It wouldn't have taken him three shots to take Mann out from this distance."

"He was too drunk to remember Sharon. He was probably too drunk to stand, much less shoot straight." She heard the tone in his voice shift, his patience thinning and a note of concern slipped in with the swagger. "If you really want to help Major Casper you need to request a sanity board. You'll have a lot easier time convincing a board of psychiatrists that he's crazy than convincing a panel of officers that he's innocent."

"What if he's both?" Sharon almost whispered the question to herself. "What if someone else was there that night?"

"I wouldn't waste your time looking for other suspects." Cade pressed her. "Major Casper is the one that shattered Mann's jaw and broke his ribs. Major Casper is the one with a violent and unpredictable case of PTSD. And as much as you don't want to believe it, Major Casper is the one that pulled the trigger."

"Are you really so sure of that Sir? Or are you doing this for her? For Pam?" Sharon fed the sound of Hunt's first name into the receiver with a certain weight and significance.

"I don't owe her anything." His words rang back, dry and severe. "I don't owe Casper anything and I sure as hell don't owe Mann anything."

A crude silence filled the receiver, as if he was weighing the advantage of being pulled into so much forgotten drama.

"You and Pam are skating dangerously close to some ethical boundaries. I can promise you that I'll testify to what I saw and nothing more. You may be willing to risk your career over this, but I'm not."

"You know as well as I do that what happened in Charlottesville doesn't prove that Casper did this." Sharon felt her throat swell.

"That's for the panel to decide." Cade brushed aside her inept argument. "I'll see you in Fort Leavenworth Lieutenant."

Without another word, the line was dead.

Sharon held the phone tight in her fist, glancing around her at the gray, windowless walls. She wasn't any closer to a solution. She had no plausible defense strategy, other than searching the weapons qualification cards of everyone on post for the few incompetent soldiers who couldn't take out a 50 meter target in less than three shots. She dropped her phone on the bed and made a quick note to herself, the first solid piece of hope in her network of calculations. *Casper would have taken him out on the first shot.*

She went back to the file on her lap and flipped through more documents, looking for more oddities, trying to scrounge up enough imperfections to create a reasonable doubt.

She turned towards the back of the investigation file and landed on Captain Mann's phone records. She scanned the cold list of data, looking for the names and numbers of the people he'd spoken with the night he was murdered. One of the last entries in the phone log was to his wife, who was still living on post at Fort Riley. He made the call at 10:32 p.m. almost an hour after he'd left the bar. He made his last phone call to CID almost an hour later.

Sharon glanced back at Hunt's witness list, noting for the first time that Cynthia Mann's name was missing. She turned back towards the front of the file and pulled out the statement that Mann's wife had given to the police. She read through the clumsy wording twice. An empty recitation of dry facts, explaining nothing more than a routine phone call between unhappy spouses. And a succession of denials regarding where Captain Mann kept his firearm, or if she had seen it since the night of the murder.

Sharon paged through the police reports and pulled out an arms registration form from Fort Riley, listing a fourth generation Glock 21 that belonged to a Captain James Anthony Mann. Another .45 caliber handgun that seemed to have disappeared.

Sharon picked up the phone from her bed and glanced at the time again. A heavy feeling spread through her empty stomach. The only way to take the suspicion off Casper was to prove that Cindy Mann was hiding something. Speaking with her would be intrusive and uncomfortable. She would be overly protective, defensive, hostile. The best Sharon could do is hope to pick up on some subtle inconsistency. To hear the tick in her voice as she masked emotions or twisted facts.

Sharon glanced at the photo of Captain Mann's body. She tried to imagine a healthier version of him, the same chestnut skin and smoky eyes, with three less bullet holes in his head and chest. "Alright then Sir." She turned a page in her legal pad and held her pen tight in her fingers. "What does your wife know that she hasn't told the police?"

She dialed the number listed on the police form and listened as the phone rang in her ear, preparing for the resentment and hurt she would hear on the other end of the line.

"Hello, this is Cindy." The voice was surprisingly light and soft.

"Mrs. Mann, my name is Lieutenant Jamie Sharon. I'm with the JAG office." Sharon pushed out a breath of pent up air. "I'm working on your husband's homicide case."

"The police said that you would be calling." Some of the levity in her voice deflated. "You're the prosecutor?"

"I'm the defense."

Sharon felt the clip of silence on the other end of the line. The dull thud of a heartbeat.

"I don't have anything to say to you Lieutenant Sharon." The response was curt but respectful. She sounded tired and spent. Like someone who'd done most of her crying before her husband was murdered and had little left to offer now that he was gone.

"I'm trying to find out what happened to your husband Ma'am." Sharon's answer was both terse and sincere. "If Major Casper is guilty, I need to know that as much as you do."

"I already talked to the police."

"I just have a few follow up questions." Sharon felt her heart pumping in the deep center of her chest. She had to be ready to hurt the woman. To pull out answers in agonizing detail if it would lead to the weapon that killed Captain Mann. "I need to know why your husband was here at Fort Leavenworth. If there's anything you can tell me it might help find the man who killed him."

Or woman, Sharon considered the possibility for the first time.

"James didn't tell me much of anything anymore." The confession was slick and manageable. A familiar way of cooperating without truly cooperating. "We had an argument and he left home. The next day the police called and told me he had been killed. That's all I know."

"I know this is difficult for you." Sharon knew the clock was ticking. There were only so many questions a widow would endure. So much she would repeat before she forgot about being polite and remembered that her husband was dead. She tried to keep her questions safe and unassuming. To reach out for some small, undiscovered fact that would lead her to the truth. "You were the last person he spoke with before he died. Did he say anything unusual? Did he say where he was going or who he was with?"

"It was a lot of rambling. I probably would have paid closer attention if I had known . . ." She cut herself off midsentence. The reality hit again. Perhaps for the first time that day. Perhaps for the hundredth. Her voice loosened and a sliver of regret worked its way between each breath. "I told him I would see him when he came home. That was the last thing I said to him."

Sharon tried to picture the face on the other end of the line. The human eyes behind the ugly details she was recording in the notebook under her fingers. "Did he give any indication that he thought someone was after him or his life was in danger? That he was planning to call the police?"

"He gave me permission to file for divorce." There was a heavy pause on the other end of the line, filled with tight, gritty breathing. The sliver of regret morphing into hostility. The window for frank and honest discussion was all but closed. "After nearly three years. He acted like he was doing me a favor."

It was a beginning. An unexpected break in the ice that might clear the way to the murky bottom. "Any idea why he would say that?"

"He'd been drinking." Her response was quick and lifeless. "James always got depressed when he drank."

"Did he say anything about taking his firearm with him when he left Fort Riley?" Sharon dug into the heart of the matter, the missing truth that was just beyond her reach. "Did he say anything about suicide?"

"I wish I could help you Ma'am, but that's all I know." Her final words were tense and gruff, as if it pained her to spit them out. "You have a nice day."

Sharon heard the painful silence of the phone disconnecting.

"Damn it."

She glanced again at Mann's picture and resisted the urge to apologize. She took down another note, hoping to collect enough fragments of data to build a plausible theory of how Mann ended up on the side of the road and riddled with bullets. *Mann also had a .45 caliber revolver that went missing.*

She picked up Mann's phone records, scanning the weeks and days before what looked like a spontaneous trip to Fort Leavenworth, looking for patterns or surprises. Repeated missed calls that might signal an argument, a frequent midnight caller, long conversations at odd hours. The only break in his routine was one unidentified call to an East Coast area code that lasted exactly one minute. She made her way through the list of numbers, flipping through the scattered remains of Captain Mann's empty social life, until she reached the night of the murder, where the numbers abruptly stopped halfway down the page.

"Another dead end." Her cell phone felt sticky in her grip. "Nothing left but the old marine from the Eagle Lounge."

She paged forward to the scattered witness statement, peppered with forgetfulness and irrelevance and inconsistencies.

She turned back to her phone and began punching Mr. Winston Cooper's number into her keypad when a text message interrupted her. She backed out of the phone call and tapped the icon at the bottom of her screen. A photo loaded in front of her. A high resolution image of a washer and dryer, with the tail of a frightened border collie dangling from the half open door.

*"Reese's new hiding spot. Come home soon."*

Sharon smiled at the image, a welcome relief from the grisly photo sitting on top of her comforter.

"Working on it." She sent Matt a quick reply, then backed out of the photo and took in the long list of recent text conversations. She meant to place her phone call to Mr. Cooper when something caught her eye. Staring back at her, from the display in her personal cell phone, was the East Coast phone number that Mann had called only 6 days before he left for Fort Leavenworth. It was attached to an otherwise unremarkable text message, naming the time and location of Casper's pre-trial hearing.

# Chapter 38
## Fort Leavenworth, KS (2014)

"He called you." Jamie Sharon swept into Hunt's office with the investigation file in hand. She dropped the evidence in the center of the prosecutor's cluttered desk and stared at her with fueled eyes. Her heart pulsed at the idea that she'd been made the victim of some vicious game. That Casper's future lay twisted and broken in a bitter colleague's hands.

Pamela Hunt glanced at the folder in front of her. A flurry of falling snow filled the window behind her, framing her face in a muffled calm.

"What are you talking about?"

Sharon opened the folder and pulled out the disorganized pages of Captain Mann's phone records, pointing to the highlighted phone call in the center of the first loose page.

"Six days before he was murdered. It's right here in his phone records." Sharon slammed her hand down on the pages under Hunt's nose, looking for some sign of anxiety. An indication that she had discovered something significant and real. "Why wasn't this in the CID report?"

Captain Hunt dropped her eyes towards the long list of numbers under Sharon's fingers, barely taking the time to scan the data. She gave Sharon a cool glare, her greyish eyes defensive and brash.

"Congratulations. You found a needle in a haystack." She took the phone records from Sharon's hands, tapped them on the desk to straighten the stack and handed them back to her. "Now let's see how you can twist it to pretend that it means something. Clearly CID didn't think it was worth investigating."

"CID didn't know that this was your number." Sharon glared at the neat stack of papers in Hunt's outstretched hand, the last of Captain Mann's petty conversations, his last polluted words to his wife, the final seeds of his brief existence hidden beneath her manicured nails. She grabbed the records and stared at the obscure

212

phone call that was buried among the long rows of digits. "What did he say to you?"

"He said nothing to me Jamie." Hunt remained settled in her chair, unshaken by the blip in the phone records or the passion in Sharon's voice. "That was an unanswered phone call. They always register as one minute calls on the phone logs, but I promise you we never spoke. He didn't even leave a message."

Jamie Sharon stared at the misleading information piled beneath her fingers. She had no reason to trust Hunt more than the black and white print in front of her, and yet there was only so much meaning that could be pulled from such a bare fact as an unanswered phone call. It said everything and nothing all at once. Entire volumes of unspoken truths were hidden in such a wicked and deceitful little events.

"You shouldn't have kept this from me. It's evidence."

"Evidence of what Jamie? What are you accusing me of?" Hunt's grey eyes flashed against her pale skin, washing out against the backdrop of snow and ice. "You must be getting pretty desperate if you really think that one unanswered phone call is enough to rescue Casper from a lifetime in Leavenworth."

"It's enough to cast some doubt on the prosecutor's impartiality." Sharon had underestimated how much spite one person was able to carry over an intangible vanity. How deeply the loss of rank and status could sour one's judgment. "You had an obligation to disclose this."

"There's nothing to disclose." Captain Hunt rolled her eyes, an exasperated surrender rippling through her face and down towards her fingers. "Captain Mann misdialed a number that was still stored in his phone from over a year ago. I ignored it, and as you can see, he didn't call again." She pointed to the list of numbers that Sharon still clutched between her fingers. "This has no bearing on anything."

"Then why did you keep it a secret?" Sharon watched her every motion, every muscle twitch with suspicion.

"You oughtta know the answer to that." Hunt firmed up her eyebrows, as if covering up some dark understanding between the two of them.

213

"I can't begin to imagine." Sharon shook her head.

"Because I want to be the one to put Casper away!" She shouted. "Because he owes me. You owe me."

Sharon shoved the phone records back into her file and stared at the impish determination in Hunt's glare. She started to suspect that there was something more malicious at stake than the loss of a pair of wings on her right shoulder. "For Christ's sake, a man's life is at stake. This isn't an opportunity for you to right some wrong that you think was done to you."

"Justice is justice." Hunt's expression was cold and passionless. Whatever she meant by the ambiguous phrase, it was clearly something she'd believed for a long time, and wasn't willing to question. "It catches up with you one way or another. Casper should've been put away a long time ago for what he did at Charlottesville."

"That's not for you to decide." Sharon felt her temperature rising, her voice trembling inside her throat. "You know better than that."

"What are you going to do, move to have me dismissed?" There was an undisguised challenge in her words. The subtle hint of a threat. "You really think you can pass for neutral in this case? You want me to dig up some dirt and question your impartiality? Your integrity?"

Sharon suddenly felt the absurdity of the charade they'd created, and it sunk in like poison. She saw the blurred ethical boundaries that Captain Cade had alluded to. That threatened her career as much as any fraternization or adultery charge. The simple fact that they had kept the past quiet. That they'd been allowed to work through the evidence as if they weren't part of it. As if they didn't know things about the man on trial and the man who was murdered that made it impossible for them to see things clearly.

Hunt dropped her eyes towards Sharon's chest, channeling the weight of her contempt on the lone Lieutenant bar where her Captain rank should've been, burning a hole in her uniform like a contemporary scarlet letter.

"I can't even begin to understand your loyalty to him." The passion crept back into her voice, soft and suggestive. "You claim to be so bent on integrity and yet the one time they asked you to step forward and do the selfless, courageous thing, you kept silent. I wonder why that is?"

Hunt's eyes seemed to pulse with a dark sense of pity. Something more precious than hate, and harder to control.

"You can't begin to understand how hurt he is." Sharon shut her eyes and dropped her voice, her energy trapped in the thickening muscles in her throat.

"Whatever helps you sleep at night." Hunt shrugged her off. She sat down at her desk and massaged around her knuckles, working around the delicate edges of her nails and displaying their non-regulation finish with an intentional grimace. "You know this trial really isn't about you or me Jamie. It all comes down to evidence. If the jury believes that Casper's guilty, it will be nothing but his own fingerprints that put him there. My personal feelings can't convict him any more than your twisted sense of pity can save him."

Sharon watched Hunt work away the knots in her hands, while a hot surge of anger pulsed in her own. She tightened her grip on the manila folder in her hands, concentrating on the ten hidden digits that swam in and out of focus on the battered pages of Mann's phone records.

"You want to stay on this case as badly as I do." Hunt took her eyes from her hands and directed them at Sharon, a bold warning making its way through her bloodstream and making a delirious rush off the end of her tongue. "The phone call from Mann isn't a conflict. No one has to know about it but you and me."

# Chapter 39
## Fort Leavenworth, KS (2014)

Benjamin Casper had lost track of the exact date. Time slowed and blended inside the gray walls of the disciplinary barracks. There were subtle distinctions between the workweek and the weekend. He separated the mornings from the evenings based on shift changes and mealtimes. He knew the weather was changing by the hats and coats of the staff and visitors. He knew that it was almost Christmas.

There was little rhyme or reason to when Grace came to see him. Her shifts at the hospital were irregular. And her emotional tolerance for the gray walls was unpredictable. She sat across from him now, at the same old table in the center of an otherwise empty room. Her hair falling in messy layers around her cheeks and jawline. She was unusually quiet, her green eyes blank and emotionless.

"Your attorney's been calling me." She finally said.

"For what?" Casper looked up from the predictable curves in the woodgrain. He heard the rattling of belts and badges outside the door as footsteps echoed down the hall.

"She said I couldn't be called to testify against you because I'm your wife. But she'd still like to talk to me about what I know."

Casper nodded, trying to take his concentration from the subtle noises just outside the door. "Have you called her back?"

"I don't know anything." Grace shrugged her shoulders. "No more than I knew the day you were arrested."

There was no mistaking the resentment in her voice. He'd kept things from her. Things that broke trust and fractured marriages. He questioned why she was still holding on. If her quiet presence on the other side of the table was a final kindness. If there wasn't a secret drawer in their old bedroom where she hid the divorce papers, waiting to be served until after the trial, the moment his sentence was delivered.

The door to the smallish room creaked open and a young specialist in combat fatigues stood on the other side. Lieutenant Sharon's shaded silhouette was positioned just behind him. She was fitted in her own fatigues and combat boots, with her hair swept from her face and secured behind her head, a large file fixed in the crux of her left arm.

"Your attorney is here to see you Sir." The specialist still did him the courtesy of addressing him as Sir.

"Send her in." Casper waved towards the door.

Grace closed her eyes and Casper felt a dull pressure, like her heart sinking into the floor.

Sharon edged past the guard and stepped directly into the tension. The specialist disappeared and the door fell shut with a long empty sound, latching securely behind her.

"They didn't tell me that you had company." Sharon stood in place, her eyes darting between him and Grace.

He found himself face to face with yet another woman that might have loved him once. A long time ago. That hadn't abandoned him yet, for reasons he couldn't begin to understand.

"I can leave." Grace pushed her chair away from the table and moved to stand.

"I want you to stay." Casper set his hand on the table in front of her. He looked up at her with a soft invitation in his eyes, silently asking her to sit back down.

"Are you sure Sir?" Sharon's gentle voice stirred the air. She stepped up to the table and set the thick investigation file on top of it, still clinging to a plain manila envelope. "We have a lot to go over."

He got up from the table and offered Sharon his chair. "Nothing's going to come of this that Grace doesn't already know."

Grace stared back at him with her quiet green eyes, regaining some sense of lost comfort. She lowered herself back into her chair, and folded her hands in lap.

"I take it this is the CID file?" He reached for the accordion file on the desk and pulled it towards him, opening the evidence against him for the first time. His fingers danced over the folds of paper with the muscle memory of a prosecutor digging through the dirt on the accused. He hesitated when he considered what kind of damning information he might find inside. Answers to the ugly voids in his memory that he'd rather keep closed.

"It is." Sharon sat in the chair he had vacated, setting the manila envelope on the table in front of her. She watched him handle the police file with a shade of caution in her pale eyes.

He still hadn't found the courage to pull the investigation from the accordion file. He listened instead to the slap of the paper as he ran his thumb along the edges. "What's in the envelope?"

"Your alcohol assessment." She opened the flap on the envelope and pulled out another degrading stack of paperwork.

"I'm not interested in that."

"The counselors determined that you have a significant substance abuse problem, and a strong likelihood of PTSD." Sharon ignored him and read off the cover sheet. "They also believe you're experiencing significant short term memory loss. The medical issues are beyond the scope of their expertise, and they're recommending that you seek treatment from a qualified professional. I know a doctor who can help with this."

"I'm not seeing anymore doctors Jamie." Casper shook his head, shifting his eyes to the concrete walls and stains on the floor. "I told you I'd take the assessment, I never agreed to anything beyond that."

"I've already scheduled a flight home to talk with him." Sharon insisted. "There's a reason you can't remember things. There's a link between being that close to all those blast waves and memory loss."

"What about evidence?" He pulled the folders and paperwork from the accordion file and spread it out on the table in front of them, burying the alcohol assessment in pieces of the CID investigation. "What have you found in here that will keep me out of Leavenworth?"

Sharon leaned forward in her chair and looked over the array of paperwork. She opened the tri-fold binder in the center, with a loose memo lying on top of the center fold. The only sheet of paper that hadn't been pinned down to a proper location.

"Hunt is calling Captain Aaron Cade to testify." Sharon picked up the sheet of paper and handed it to him. "I'll make a motion to suppress, but if it comes in, he'll tell the panel everything that happened in Charlottesville."

Casper scanned the document and recognized the format of a standard witness list. He went through the names one by one, finally focusing on the familiar name near the bottom.

"What happened in Charlottesville?" Grace interrupted, reminding Casper that she was still in the room. "Who is Aaron Cade?"

Casper covered his mouth with a rough hand as his mind started churning through the rules of evidence. "I guess I was wrong." He stared back at Grace with a thin apology escaping between his fingers. "Things are going to come up in here that you don't already know."

He dropped his hand from his mouth and put the witness list back on top of the center tri-fold, turning towards Sharon. "What's your objection?"

"It's past misconduct. It can't be used to prove additional criminal behavior."

"But it can be used to prove intent. Motive. Just about anything else."

"I'm going to file the motion regardless." Her response was quick and dry.

"What else have you found?"

"I spent all weekend going through Captain Mann's phone records." Sharon stood up from her chair and moved towards him, close enough to smell and touch. Her arms criss-crossed under his as she dug through the file, finally pointing to a single phone number highlighted in yellow, at the end of a worn sheet full of logged calls. The dizzying smell of lilacs followed her every movement. "He called his wife when he got back on post. They spoke for about 10 minutes. She didn't give me much information over the phone."

Casper turned back towards the witness list, stumbling over the names again as he looked for Mann's wife. "What did you expect her to tell you?"

"Mann had a .45 caliber handgun registered to him at Fort Riley." Sharon flipped backwards through the phone records, looking for more lost information. "Mrs. Mann claims she doesn't know what happened to it. CID never tracked it down. Which means it might not have been your weapon that killed him."

"If you put her on the stand you'll look like a monster." Casper mumbled.

"She's the only one who can tell us what Mann was doing on post in the first place. Someone must have had a reason to hurt him. He may have had unpaid gambling debts. Maybe he had gotten into drugs."

"That doesn't sound like Mann." Casper shook his head.

"His wife mentioned drinking, depression and divorce all in one breath."

Grace stiffened and her chair knocked against the concrete floor. The sound helped to break up the smell of lilacs weaving through his brain.

"That describes half the soldiers on post." Casper responded.

Sharon stopped flipping pages when she came across a second highlighted phone number, in the center of the page. Her breathing changed, as if some unknown pressure was filling her lungs from the space below her fingertips.

"There is one more thing about the phone records Sir."

Casper followed her eyes towards the highlighted number, sharing the tension that was building in the silent space that followed.

"Tell me." He looked into her pale blue eyes. He felt the blood thicken in his veins, inviting her to break down any false hope that was still beating in his chest.

"This is Captain Hunt's number. Mann called her about a week before he came into town."

Casper wrinkled his eyebrows. For the first time since Sharon came into the room, he lost his focus, trying to make sense of the sudden spinning in his head. "Captain Hunt, why?"

"It may be nothing." Sharon admitted as she pulled her fingers away from the file. "She claims she didn't answer the phone. But that's her cell number."

Casper paged through the list of telephone records, flipping forwards and backwards before coming back to the one instance in the entire log where Hunt's phone number appeared. "That's it? He only called her this one time?"

"CID only pulled phone records for November, but based on what we have, this is it. No more phone calls, no text messages. Nothing."

Casper brought his hand to his lips a second time, losing himself in the palpable shift under his feet. He released the stack of paper in his hand, watching the pages flutter back into place, hiding the aberrant phone call again under layers of distracting data. He bent his eyes on the fluorescent lights overhead. "It could be a simple coincidence."

"It could be." Sharon nodded blindly. "But Captain Mann only reached out to three people the week that he was killed. His wife, Captain Hunt, and you. One of them knows more about what happened that night than they're telling me." She looked at him with a strange curiosity, wavering between concern and suspicion.

"Have you told anyone about this?" Grace interrupted again, a sliver of urgency crystallizing in her voice.

"Not yet." Sharon's tone was flat and neutral.

"Well what are you waiting for?"

"Permission." Sharon looked at Grace with heavy eyes. "If I bring this to the Commanding General's attention I can get Hunt dismissed from the case. But the prosecution will still go forward." She turned her eyes towards Casper, a swell of hidden thoughts restrained behind her quiet stare. "I'll probably be dismissed from the case as well."

"Forget about it." Casper responded.

"Ben." Grace moved to stand, but a serious look from the corner of his eye stopped her.

"This is an important decision Sir." Sharon warned him. "I want you to think about it."

"You can get another lawyer." Grace shook her head, a thin mist lining the rims of her eyes. "This is your life we're talking about."

"You're making too much of this Grace." Casper closed his eyes and tuned out the sound of her strained voice. "It raises some questions about Pamela Hunt. About her ethics. But it doesn't get me off the hook."

"How can you say that?"

"Because only two people know why he called her that night and one of them is dead. It doesn't prove anything." He flipped through the file and found the crime scene photos of Captain Mann lying in the dirt, blood and debris covering his face and chest. Death folded around him and erased everything he once knew. Everything he might have divulged. Casper's heartbeat slowed and his fingers relaxed. "It's not going to make a difference if we can't prove I didn't pull the trigger."

"It took three separate shots to take him down." Sharon leaned into the table and he could feel her next to him again, shoulder to shoulder, pointing out the fragments that didn't fit. "I already spoke with the coroner. She agrees that he was shot twice in the chest and didn't actually fall to the ground until he was shot in the head. It shouldn't have taken you three shots from this distance, depending on how much you'd had to drink."

"I could've made that shot on a full bottle of Captain Morgan." Casper stared at the photo, resisting the spark of a promise.

"How can you be sure?"

"Because I've done it before." He pursed his lips, realizing the limitations of this simple truth.

"What about the gun Ben?" Sharon's voice was distant and blurred. "Where is the gun you brought home from Iraq?"

"I don't remember Jamie." He felt the sting of her warning about blast waves and memory loss. All of the lost moments that he blamed on alcohol or carelessness, all of the pointless missed appointments, stores of unidentified names and faces, petty echoes and social conventions that he'd just as soon dismiss. And then those few indestructible moments in time, that could cost him his life or his freedom, vanished in the recesses of space. The sound of a distant IED blast resurfaced and reverberated through his bones. "I honestly don't remember."

# Chapter 40
## Fort Leavenworth, KS (2014)

Grace stood for a long while outside the open door to the borrowed legal office, holding a small box in her arms. She wore a loose winter jacket and a pair of ankle length boots. Her hair was pulled back in a high ponytail with stray hairs falling around her ears and neck. She watched the brunette lieutenant bent over a cluttered desk in the far corner. Her office was crammed with discarded furniture and old law books. Dusty files and paperwork spilled over from the cramped shelves onto the floor. The walls were gray and windowless. The air was stale and the lighting was dim.

Grace found the nerve to step forward into the open doorway and rapped on the solid wood with a closed fist.

The lieutenant looked up from her notes, a clean look of surprise washing over her pretty face. "Grace."

Her voice was lost in the crowded space. She stood and made her way around the desk, her combat boots bumping up against a stack of old boxes that had been stored underfoot. She shoved them aside with one foot and lifted a large box from one of the nearest chairs. "Come in. Have a seat."

Grace stepped inside and shut the door behind her, weaving through the scattered boxes and furniture towards the desk in the corner. She set her own small box of secrets on the floor while she removed her jacket and reached for the folding chair that Sharon had cleared. She wiped it clean with a swipe of her hand before sitting down, lifting the small box from the floor and guarding it in her lap. A lone envelope skirted the top of the old folders, marked with the word "ISOPREP" and stuffed with an intimidating stack of loose-leaf pages.

"I didn't think I'd ever hear back from you." The lieutenant sat down behind her desk.

"I thought of everything I could to avoid coming here." Grace's eyes focused on the toxic envelope inside the box, full of confessions and suffering and final words that she wasn't ready to hear.

"Can I ask what changed your mind?" Sharon began flipping through her scattered notes as she spoke, appearing both distracted and awkward.

"I just need an honest answer what his chances are."

Sharon looked up from the messy file beneath her fingers, her lips firm and suspicious. "I wish I knew how to answer that. There's not a lot of evidence against him. But he doesn't remember much. And he doesn't seem willing to put up much of a fight. He still won't tell me what started the fight at the bar. Or how his fingerprints ended up on your pepper spray."

Grace lifted the box from her lap and set it on top of the lieutenant's desk. "I brought you everything I have on Ben's military career. Deployment orders, military schools, awards, transfers, every piece of military paperwork since the day we were married." She ran her fingers over the frayed edges of Ben's paperwork, a surge of resentment hidden just below the surface of her skin. "I'm not sure if anything in here will be useful to you."

"It's worth a look." Sharon stood and glanced at the collection of mismatched folders, then casually moved the box from her desk to the floor before sitting back in her chair. "If there's anything you can tell me that you haven't told CID. Anything that might help fill in the gaps. Now would be the time."

"I really don't know anything." Grace brushed the loose strings of blonde hair around her neck, repeating the same lifeless story she had told the police so many weeks prior.

"Are you sure there isn't anything the investigators might have missed?" Sharon played with a pen as she spoke, the glint of a silver ring standing out among the colorless gray walls. "Did he have a routine before leaving the house? Before going to bed? Did he leave his shoes out or set an alarm? Anything that would help prove when he came home that night?"

Grace felt her heart pumping louder and faster. She had stepped into a minefield of invisible slights and misplaced anger. And so much that was better left unsaid. She reminded herself that she had come because she loved her husband. There was nothing suspicious or calculated in that.

"I came home and the house was dark. His car was gone. But I went through the house to see if he was there." Grace brushed a loose strand of hair behind her ear. It always seemed easier to start with the innocent facts. To inch towards the darker matter in the hopes of making it brighter. "I carried my keys with me when I checked the rooms. Just in case. The house was empty, so I had a few glasses of wine and I went to bed."

Grace saw a small suspicion creep into the lieutenant's expression. She tapped her pen against the notebook on the right side of her desk. Fast at first, and then slowing to almost a dead stop, as if she could sense the missing details hiding under her sloppy words.

"Did you hear him come home that night?" She leaned forward in her chair and set her palms face down on her desk. "Did you notice what time he came to bed?"

"We haven't shared a bedroom for some time." Her words came out slowly, heavy and humiliating. She looked towards the ceiling with tight lips, a hot wind expanding in her lungs. She waded deep into that dark matter that she'd rather keep hidden. "Ben couldn't have taken my keys that night, because I brought them into the bedroom with me."

She wanted to curl up and hide from the heavy silence that came next. She dropped her eyes and found the lieutenant staring at her with large, probing eyes.

"Do you always sleep with your keychain by you?"

"I do." She nodded. "And I take it with me into the kitchen every morning."

She watched the simple statement sink past Sharon's parted expression and settle into her stomach. The subtle hints collecting and merging into an unpleasant truth. "Any idea how your husband's fingerprints ended up on the keychain if it never left your side?"

"He grabbed them by accident on his way out the door that morning." Grace replayed that bitter morning when CID showed up at her door, not knowing how one thoughtless gesture could irreversibly upend their lives. That the moment he agreed to go in for questioning and reached for his keys, he was implicating himself in the very crime they were investigating. "He was in a hurry to catch his flight to Minneapolis."

Sharon brought both hands up to her lips. Grace watched the look on her face turn sad and sour, like someone wrestling to believe in an unfortunate coincidence.

"That damn pepper spray." Grace opened a valve deep in her heart and the tears started spilling over her checks, fast and reckless. "I can't remember how long it's been. Sometime between Iraq and today. He mistook me for an insurgent. Pulled me out of bed by my hair, threw me to the ground and wrapped his hands around my neck. Things went dark around the edges." She reached for the ponytail at the back of her neck, twisting it in her hands as she forced out the wretched memory. "I was too terrified to scream. I was sure he was going to kill me. And then, just like that, he let go. The ringing in my head stopped and I could hear him crying. Shaking and sobbing in the corner. I'm not sure who was more frightened, him or me. That's why he bought me the pepper spray. That's why I started sleeping in the other room."

Grace stared across the room, a chilling sadness gripping her entire body. The lieutenant was pale and quiet, absorbing more and more of the complicated story that was Ben Casper. She pulled a box of tissues out of her desk drawer and passed them to Grace, a little too awkward and a little too late to be of much comfort. The silence swelled around them, stealing the oxygen from the air.

"Does anybody else know about this?" Sharon's voice cracked in the dry air. "Did either of you tell anyone?"

"Agent Hartman." Grace whispered. She closed her eyes and brought herself back from the edge of nowhere. She focused her attention on the details of the unpleasant storage room. The musty smell in the walls and the thin layer of dust that had settled all around. Little hints to tie her to the present and convince her that she was safe. She reached for a tissue and cleaned up her face. "Ben called Agent Hartman to turn himself in. He confessed that he tried to kill me. He begged to be arrested. Leon came by and calmed him down. Promised to keep everything quiet if we would get Ben some help, but he just started drifting further and further away. The next thing I knew, CID was at my door."

Grace coiled her hands around themselves, staring at the tightness in her fingers and wrists. She barely heard the lieutenant's shaky response.

"I should've done something after he attacked Mann in Charlottesville." Sharon set her fingertips along her forehead, looking lost and uncomfortable in the dangerous flood of details. "I should've known that it was going to happen again."

"I have the gun." Grace blurted the last of her secrets into the open air, squeezing the used tissue in the empty palm of her hand.

Lieutenant Sharon's eyes went wide and her fingers quivered. She wore an impossible stagger in her soft face.

"He used to wake up in the middle of the night, looking for his M16." The memories slipped from her lips like molten metal. "I never took it to be anything more than a memory or a dream that he couldn't shake. But something about that morning seemed so real. He was looking for an old shoe box he brought home from Iraq. As soon as CID left I rummaged through the basement and found it."

"Where is it?" There was a desperate expression in the lieutenant's face.

"I can't tell you that." Grace shook her head, firm and unflinching.

"They have casings and bullet fragments from the crime scene." Sharon tried to stare her down with those icy blue eyes. "Testing could prove that that it wasn't his gun."

"It could also prove that it was. I can't take that chance." Grace tilted her head to the side, bending her eyebrows in a sophisticated stare. "You act like it's your job to prove that he's innocent, but you have as many doubts about that as I do."

"This is no way to help him Grace. This is criminal."

"You want to make sure that you're the hero." Grace felt a jealous sting rise up through her throat. She tried to keep the pain out of her voice, but slivers kept flying like daggers. "But I loved him before you knew him. I remember who he was before he was

228

broken. I may not be a soldier, but I know what fear is. I know what loyalty is."

Grace stood up from her folding chair and reached into the box of military records that Sharon had set on the floor. She pulled out the loose envelope that had caused her so much pain and anxiety, happy to be rid of it. "I found this in the shoe box with the handgun. It could be a confession, or a suicide note or the proof you need to set him free. I can't tell you because I don't dare open it."

She passed the envelope across the desk. Sharon took it into her small hands and opened the unsealed flap. "This looks like an ISOPREP letter."

"What's an ISOPREP letter?"

"Some units require it before a deployment." Sharon shut the flap of the envelope, as if realizing she'd stumbled upon something dark and personal. "It's a final goodbye letter to family. In the event that a soldier is killed or goes missing during combat operations. It's a way for soldiers to tell their families how much they meant to them. Where to find wills and other important documents. He must have written this during his last deployment."

Sharon tried to hand the letter back to her, but she shook her head and pushed it away. "I don't want to read what's in that letter. He had that it tucked away with that gun for a reason. I don't want to know why."

Sharon tucked the envelope into the side pocket of her trial binder. "I'll make sure you don't have to."

Grace grabbed her jacket and threw it around her shoulders. A heaviness trailed her as she leaned into the back of the old chair, sending a complicated glare in Sharon's direction.

"I know about the adultery charges." Her voice was flat and controlled. The naked honesty sent an unrecognizable quiver down Sharon's spine. "I see the way he looks at you. But I can also see that he trusts you, and if you can get him out of this, we'll call it even."

"What did he tell you about us Grace?" The lieutenant's shaky voice cut through the air. "What did he say?"

"It's not important now." Grace cut her off. "Until you pulled out those phone records yesterday, I was convinced that my husband had killed somebody. He still may have. But at least you've given me a reason to hope for a little while longer. I'm grateful for every hour."

# Chapter 41
## Minneapolis, MN (2014)

Jamie unpacked her uniforms and set them on top of the washer. Just as it was nearing the end of its cycle, Reese crawled inside the dryer, his restless panting blending in with the low hum of the wash.

"Honestly Reese." She called to the frightened dog, the sound of each erratic breath echoing through the hollow interior. "I have laundry to do, go hide under the bed."

"I warned you not to start your laundry this late." Matt called from the kitchen.

She'd only been home for a few hours, but already felt pressured and bent. She didn't feel safe or rested here. Not with all the unspoken confusion slinking through the narrow hallways.

"How long is he going to be in there?"

"All night." Matt appeared in the entryway between the kitchen and the tiny laundry room closet. He offered her a cold piece of sausage to lure the dog out of the dryer. His eyes were vacant and dry, with no smile behind them.

"He can't stay in there all night." She grabbed the sausage from Matt's hand, little ripples of stress already wrinkling her forehead. "I have all these uniforms to wash."

"I've started doing my laundry a little earlier in the day. He crawls in there around six or seven and he doesn't come out until morning."

Jamie dangled the slimy meat in front of the appliance door, trying to coax out a dog that wasn't budging.

"Do you want some coffee?" Matt asked. It was his first attempt at real conversation, but it only made her feel vulnerable, twisted, afraid.

"C'mon Reese. I have an entire smoked sausage with your name on it."

"Jamie." Matt spoke again with a new sense of urgency.

"What?" She turned and looked at him, the sound of Reese's scratching and the tumbling of spin cycle echoing behind her.

"Do you want some coffee?" He asked again. Gentle. Serene.

"Yes." Her voice softened, embarrassed by the tension in her last response. "That would be nice."

"You should let him be." Matt motioned towards the heavy breathing escaping from the open dryer door. "He feels safe in there. It's warm. You can do your laundry in the morning."

"I'm meeting with Dr. Brock in the morning." The wind deflated from her lungs. She pulled herself to her feet and followed him into the kitchen, blindly wading into whatever it was that came next.

"From the VA?"

"Yes."

"You're going to ask him to testify?" There was an element of judgment in his question. The first sign that he was growing tired of the trial and the toll that it was taking. He pulled a bag of coffee grounds from the cupboard above the sink and scooped out enough for a strong pot of coffee.

"Yes." Jamie tossed the cold sausage into the garbage can and fell into a familiar chair at their cramped kitchen table.

"Is that part of some sly defense strategy?" She watched Matt fill the coffee maker with two generous cups of water and set the device to brew. He kept his eyes and his unhappiness hidden from view. "Or is this guy bona fide outside the wire?"

"I don't even know what you mean by that." She brushed off the subtle insult. It was finally coming. The stale suspicion over that dropped phone call in Charlottesville, and anything else that hadn't quite settled. He wasn't typically insensitive or harsh. It was Casper. It was personal.

"You know what I mean." The coffee pot buzzed behind him, adding to the rapid spinning of the washing machine in the next room and the panting of the dog in the dryer. The white noise was fast overwhelming the space between them. "Is this some make-believe battle trauma to get a get out of jail free card or is this the real deal?"

"It's the real deal." Jamie spat. She didn't know what he'd heard during that phone call. How he'd filled in the gaps between things he didn't understand or hadn't seen. But he seemed ready to talk now. Just as she was on the verge of losing Casper. "Certifiably outside the wire."

She tried to find some comfort in the smell and feel of the old coffeemaker on the kitchen counter. The slow sound of percolating water slowed and then stopped. The coffeemaker buzzed again and the warm smell overtook the gurgling of the grounds brewing. Matt reached into the cupboard for two mugs that didn't quite match and poured them each a cup. He set a full cup on the table in front of her, complete with two packets of sugar and a stirring spoon.

"What if I told you I thought he was innocent?" She murmured. She tore open the sugar and sprinkled it into the dark brew. Then stirred the crystals until they were fully dissolved, an invisible sweetness lost inside the bitter drink.

"When did you decide this?" Matt rested against the kitchen counter with a steaming mug in hand, his eyes narrowing as he stared into the dark drink.

"I've looked at the evidence Matt. I've been over it more times than I can count." Jamie brought the mug to her lips, feeling the warmth stream up into her nose and mouth, tasting the familiar flavor without taking a sip. She thought back on her conversation with Grace. The loaded confession that explained so much, but only led to more questions and recollections that weren't likely to result in happy endings. "He wouldn't have needed to fire three rounds from that distance. Not off of three beers. He blacked out because of the bombs, not the alcohol."

She took her first sip of the sweetened coffee, the brown syrup coating her lips in a comforting way. Drowning out the unfortunate sounds from the other room.

"His wife slept with the pepper spray on the nightstand by her bed. He couldn't have taken it without waking her. But I can't have her testify about the keys without making him look like a madman."

Matt watched her from across the room, a painful resentment buried in his eyes. There was so much she didn't dare tell him about Casper. So much he would never understand.

"I think you're far too close to this to think rationally." He spoke quietly.

"You're wrong." She set her mug down on a stack of unopened mail, the bulk of her melted sugar sinking to the bottom. "It was the emotions that made me think he was guilty. It will be emotions, not evidence that convict him."

"Jamie, is there something you want to tell me about him?" Matt looked up from his cup of coffee and sought out her eyes. She felt him trying to pull her down an unventured road, to clear the mines and other debris that was waiting for them.

"There's nothing to tell." She kept her eyes hidden in the mug in her hands, swirling the contents in repetitive circles.

"Was it you and Casper?" His slippery voice rippled through the dark drink in front of her. She swallowed some air and raised her eyes, watching as he chose his next words with surprising alacrity. "The adultery?"

The rumbling from the spin cycle in the next room slowed and then stopped. The room was wrapped in a dull quiet, with the unmistakable sound of Reese's terrified panting.

"I need to check on Reese." She left her coffee mug on the table and stood up from her chair.

"When are we going to talk about this Jamie?" His voice was tired but severe.

"There's nothing else to say." She headed towards the laundry closet, leaving his ugly suspicions hovering in the air. She distracted herself with unloading her wet uniforms as Matt crept into the room behind her.

"Was it before or after I told you I love you?" She could feel his eyes bearing down on her as she sorted through the wet t-shirts and fatigues. "Why won't you tell me what happened?"

234

"Because you've already made up your mind." She dropped a handful of wet clothes into the basket at her feet with a soggy sploshing sound. "Just like everyone else."

Jamie finished unloading the washer. She reached into the dryer and took a hold of Reese's collar, attempting to drag him out of his makeshift foxhole. "C'mon out of there Reese. I have to get in here . . ."

Reese let out a sharp whimper and bit deep into her hand.

Jamie yelled in pain. His teeth pierced the softest part of her skin, then released at the sound of her scream. Jamie pulled out her hand, punctured in two places and oozing a thin red streak from each open wound.

"Jamie, what happened?" Matt rushed forward and reached for her injured hand.

"It's okay. He bit me." Jamie covered the broken skin with her other hand to stop the bleeding.

"Reese!"

"Don't, Matt! Don't yell at him. He didn't mean it." Jamie moved in front of the dryer to shield the dog. "He's just scared. I was pushing him too hard. It's fine."

"Here, let me see." Matt took hold of her hand. She watched him delicately pull aside her fingers and assess the damage. "That's a lot of blood for just a small bite."

"It doesn't hurt that much." She insisted.

"I'll have to take your word for it." He closed the wound with his own fingers, his eyes mixed with alarm and concern. "Come into the kitchen. Let's get you bandaged up."

She followed Matt into the kitchen and let him run her hand under cold water. The blood slipped away in an easy pink trickle, just as it has done in Charlottesville.

"Here, keep putting pressure on it." Matt covered her hand in a clean towel and turned to rummage through the cupboards, eventually pulling out a first aid kit.

Jamie sat down with him at their kitchen table, moving aside her abandoned coffee cup and watching in silence as Matt unwrapped her bitten hand. He was tender and calm as he covered the open wound with an antibiotic ointment, then re-wrapped it in a sterile gauze.

She glanced at the syrupy ring her cup had made on the week old bills and advertisements on the table. She pulled a thin postcard from the pile with her free hand, turning it over once or twice before she recognized the logo and the name attached to the front. The bridal shop in Blaine from the newspaper clipping all those weeks ago.

*"Congratulations Jamie Sharon! You are the winner of one free bridal gown, to be chosen from our beautiful selection of designer dresses."*

"What's this?" She showed him the postcard with the coffee stain dotting one corner.

Matt looked at the postcard with a tempered grief, full of both longing and remorse.

"I wrote them our love story." There was a dim light still flickering in the guarded corners of his eyes, low and steady. "You don't have to claim it. I just wanted you to have the option."

"Matt, . . ." She was both lost and bewildered by him. His simple way of caring out loud, and then shrugging it off as if there were nothing extraordinary about it. Nothing remarkable about loving someone and wearing your heart on your sleeve, naked and exposed to the elements where it was liable to get burnt or broken.

She watched as Matt applied a continuous, gentle pressure to the open wound, staring back at her with full and serious eyes. "Should I be worried about you?"

"What is there to worry about?" Jamie raised her eyebrows.

"You said this is the real deal." He kept his sharp eyes focused on her, repeating himself to make sure the impact of the question sunk in. "Should I be worried about you?"

She couldn't tell if he was talking about love or violence. She buried the queasy feeling that Grace had given her when she talked about Casper's fingers around her throat. The loose memory of Casper's bloody hand on her doorjamb on Thanksgiving night.

"Casper wouldn't hurt me if that's what you're thinking. He's not that kind of unstable."

She might never be as brave as he seemed to be. Might never find the courage to tell him everything she felt. Not in words. Not in deed. Even after all he'd given up for her, the thought was still too terrifying.

Matt picked up the pretty announcement from the bridal shop and set it aside with the rest of Jamie's unopened mail. He took her wrapped hand in his and placed a gentle kiss against her undressed skin.

"It's your decision. But for what it's worth, I think you'd look great in a wedding dress."

She watched a genuine smile play across his eyes, while the dismal sound of Reese's cries filled up the background.

# Part Nine:

# A Toast for the Departed

# Chapter 42
## Charlottesville, VA (2013)

Major Casper stood in front of his classmates in his dress blues, his sandy blonde hair settled against his high forehead. His jacket was clean and pressed, and decorated with awards from healthier days. The uniform made him taller and straighter, hiding the frailty behind the branch insignia on his collar and the gold blossoms on his shoulders. Everything down to the embossed name plate that suggested he was little more than a ghost, still walking among them.

The fifth floor of the JAG school was dressed for the formal dinner in thick white tablecloths with deep blue runners. Small tea lights flickered alongside polished silverware and delicate vases with silk bouquets. Elegant champagne flutes whispered as they were raised and filled with sweet bubbles that tickled going down. The room was full of delirious captains and lieutenants, oblivious to the frost forming on the windows and the cold that surrounded the building. They huddled together in the warmth of forged friendships and the promise of bright futures.

"Your attention please." Major Casper sounded off by clinking a fork against the champagne flute in his hands. He waited for the room to settle. His vacant eyes were fixed on a small, empty table near the front of the room. It was set for one, with an unlit candle, and a thin vase holding a single red rose, centered on the pristine white surface.

"At this time it is customary for us to remember those who cannot be with us tonight."

A stillness settled over the room as that one isolated table took on a life and import far larger than its simple mass.

Casper dug a lighter out of his pants pocket and flicked it with his thumb, igniting a small flame that he carried towards the tall candle in the center of the table. His hands were steady. An eerie calm settled in his eyes as he stared at the empty seat in front of him and proceeded through the timeless ritual.

"Those who have served in the United States military are ever mindful that the sweetness of enduring peace has always been tainted by the bitterness of personal sacrifice."

The solitary flame reflected in Casper's eyes as he echoed the words of the dedication, sounding out each syllable as if it carried the weight of the injured, missing or departed on its back.

"We are compelled to never forget that while we enjoy our daily pleasures, there are others who have endured and may still be enduring the agonies of pain and internment. Before we begin our activities this evening, we will pause to recognize our POWs and MIAs."

Casper glanced out over the sea of faces, loosely connecting with the time and space that they shared. A draft had followed him from his seat beside the window. It nipped at his hands and bristled about the table, nearly extinguishing the small flame at the top of the lit candle. He watched the fire falter in the invisible wind. It danced until it disappeared, snuffed out by the sudden chill. Then, in the space of a moment, the golden light recreated itself, growing along the sides of the wick and wax. Soft and steady as a heartbeat.

"We call your attention to this small table, which occupies a place of dignity and honor. It is set for one, symbolizing the fact that members of our armed forces are missing from our ranks. They are referred to as POWs and MIAs. We call them comrades. They are unable to be with their loved ones and families tonight, so we join together to pay humble tribute to them, and bear witness to their continued absence."

Casper looked past the heads of his classmates, mesmerized by the falling snow outside the dark windows. He hadn't been back to this room since late November, when his cruelest memories took over, forcing him to face a flurry of buried feelings. He watched the snow spin and collide, the way that memories of his last convoy and Thanksgiving night had merged into one fantastic nightmare.

"This small table is set for one, symbolizing the frailty of one prisoner alone against his oppressors. The tablecloth is white, symbolizing the purity of their intentions in responding to their country's call to arms."

Casper looked across the blended faces again and picked out Captain Mann's humbled expression. A grim vision flashed in front of his eyes, of that same face locked in the pit of his elbow, helpless and terrified.

"The single red rose signifies the blood they have shed in sacrifice to ensure the freedom of our beloved country. This rose also reminds us of the family and friends of our missing comrades who keep the faith, awaiting their return."

He wandered into Jamie Sharon's clear blue eyes, standing only a few feet away, a bewildering pity twisting her fingers. He pushed all thoughts of her to the back of his mind as he stood in front of that barren candle. It symbolized hope for so many people who still had loved ones out there somewhere. But for him, it was a last opportunity to remember the fallen.

"The yellow ribbon on the vase represents the yellow ribbons worn on the lapels of the thousands who demand a proper accounting of our comrades who are not among us tonight. A slice of lemon on the napkin reminds us of their bitter fate."

He looked into the empty seat in front of him, fighting an impossible craving for the distant echo of a dead friend's voice. An echo that might disappear if he didn't keep it burning fresh in his mind. If he forgot, even for a moment, the distinct sound of its chord and tenor.

"The salt sprinkled on the plate reminds us of the countless fallen tears of families as they wait. The glass is inverted, they cannot toast with us this night. The chair is empty, they are not here. The candle is reminiscent of the light of hope which lives in our hearts to illuminate their way home from their captors, to the open arms of a grateful nation. Let us pray that all our comrades will be back within our ranks. Let us remember and never forget their sacrifices. May God forever watch over them and protect them and their families."

As he whispered the last words of the dedication, Casper lifted his right hand in a revered salute to the empty seat in front of him. He closed his eyes and tuned out the sights and sounds of the company around him, concentrating on keeping a fragile peace with the lone ghost that he'd brought back from the dead.

# Chapter 43
## Charlottesville, VA (2013)

"Ladies and Gentlemen of the United States JAG Corps, welcome and congratulations."

Captain Fassbender stood in front of the class for the last time, raising his glass to offer them a gracious farewell. His simple address was dwarfed by the presence of the three star general standing behind him. The Judge Advocate General of the Army, who had come to offer her congratulations to the new graduates. To meet the fresh young lawyers who'd joined her elite corps. She brought the crisp smell of winter indoors with her and a chill ran through the room, making the tiny candles along the dressed tables flicker and dance.

"You've made it through the early morning runs and the ruck marches. The powerpoints, the mock trials, the lectures, the exams. You've proven yourselves to be committed to the values of the United States Army. And most of you are in a little better shape than when you arrived."

A loose laughter rippled through the class. They stood with their champagne glasses held high, rising and falling on command like an ancient order of monks or clergy. The temperature had dropped in Charlottesville, and a thin layer of frost coated the edges of the windows. The class lined up along long tables that ran the length of the room, the mass of warm bodies concentrated in the center to avoid the cold drafts slipping through the windows.

Captain Cade stood in the center of the mass, his glass raised alongside the others. He stood proud and poised in his dress blues, decorated with legendary colors that seemed to make other men envious and insecure. But there was a deep prickle in the pink burns across his face, a solemn reminder that he was no longer the stunning officer he once was.

"Those of you who have already been through basic training will move on to your duty stations after the ceremony tomorrow. The rest of you, will go on to Fort Benning to complete your testing on basic soldier skills. Marksmanship, land navigation, combat lifesaver training and everything you've been prepping for during your stay here in Charlottesville. Some of you will struggle more than others, but I have no doubt that you'll rely on each other as you've done here. You'll come together as a team, and I expect that all of you will graduate with flying colors. The best to you."

Captain Fassbender raised his glass and took a hearty sip. A sweep of hurrahs rippled through the class as they tipped back and tasted the champagne in their sparkling glasses.

"Please, take your seats." Captain Fassbender extended his arm and the shuffle of thick uniforms filled the long room.

Cade could feel the body heat of the redhead beside him. He watched with simple pleasure as she took her seat, her stiff uniform transforming her into something bold and intimidating. He might have played a risky game to attract her, and he might not be able to keep her, but for the time being, she was his.

He could smell her nervous sweat beneath the bravado. He watched the pulse of her heartbeat graze her neck. He zeroed in on the few thin strands of red hair that had worked themselves loose from their ties and lay quietly against her neck.

His thick fingers reached for her hand under the table and gently squeezed.

"Before we begin with dinner, General Taylor would like to take this opportunity to recognize a handful of students who deserve special mention for their outstanding performance in physical training. These students got up earlier, ran faster and longer, trained harder than the rest of their peers. Because of their dedication, commitment and personal strength, these 20 individuals have been selected to attend Airborne school following their training at Fort Benning."

Cade joined in the short round of applause, despite the discomfort that hit his soft center. He wasn't ready to let her go. To send her mucking through the swamps of Fort Benning, climbing towers and jumping from deafening aircraft with Captain Mann lurking beside her.

He cut off his applause early, watching the lustrous sheen in Pamela Hunt's eyes as she clapped along with the others. He took in a small drink to calm his nerves and keep the cold out of his bones.

Captain Fassbender held up his hand to quiet the room. General Taylor took a step forward, taking easy control of the room, the noise from the crowd subsiding to a quiet hush.

"As is customary," The General began. "I would like to personally congratulate each of you for this outstanding achievement. Captain Fassbender, would you call off the names?"

"Yes Ma'am." Captain Fassbender reached for a folded notecard, hidden in the inner pocket of his dress uniform. He cleared his throat as he opened the folds and began reading names off the list.

". . . Lieutenant Alden."

Fassbender's voice echoed through the room. Lieutenant Alden stood at attention in the front row, tall and dignified. He pivoted in place and marched to his right, around the tables and through a rehearsed route to approach the Lieutenant General at the front of the room.

"Captain Brannigan."

Captain Brannigan straightened and turned on cue, immediately following in Lieutenant Alden's footsteps. Cade watched the procession with a sick feeling, while Pamela Hunt emptied her champagne glass, a bright anticipation shining in her cheeks.

"Lieutenant Dalton."

Lieutenant Dalton stood at attention and moved in line with the others. His footsteps echoed against the floor as he marched, a sterile reminder that Cade's own name wasn't among them. He would be forced to look the other way as the boundaries between Mann and Hunt blurred and disappeared. His control had ruptured the moment he dropped from formation. The same morning he finally felt her naked body move and sweat beneath his, and convinced her to find some solace in his dark energy and burns. He remembered how soft she was underneath all that forced strength, the curves that covered the muscle and grit.

He glanced towards Captain Mann, only a few seats down on his right. A slick smile lined his lips, as he waited for the sound of his own name.

"Lieutenant Gonzales."

One by one, the selected Airborne candidates marched to the front of the room, passing in front of their peers to accept the heavy handshake of the three star general.

"Captain Harvey." Fassbender's roll call was slow and constant. Cade could almost feel the race of Hunt's heartbeat beside him, as if there was just enough dry air between names to begin making her nervous.

"Lieutenant Hunt." Fassbender announced her name and she slipped her hand out of Captain Cade's grip. She moved a little unsteady, bobbing quickly through the space between the tables to fall in behind Captain Harvey. She wore an unmistakable confidence as she fell in line with the male officers, her skirt and heels making a definite break in the procession of blue pant legs with solid yellow stripes.

"Lieutenant Lewis."

Cade kept his eyes on Lieutenant Hunt as she walked, approaching the general with an auspicious grace. She took her hand with a flutter of adrenaline and entitlement, her lips uttering an unintelligible "Thank you Ma'am" as she offered her congratulations.

"Captain Mann."

The delirious captain finally stood as his name was called, his posture straight and unwavering. He took a powerful and pretentious step forward, blissfully unaware of how small a piece of military history he owned. As if a pair of wings on his uniform was going to transform his character or fix the broken pieces of his ego.

"Lieutenant Miller."

Hunt's steps were light and proud as she moved back through the crowd, the promise of her unfurled wings raising her up. She wove her way back to him, her face heating up to match the auburn color of her hair. She brushed her warm body against him as she found her seat, too distracted by the tempo of her own breathing to see the sheepish grin on Mann's face as he took the general's hand and showed the world his flashy teeth.

Cade tried to see the enormity of this moment through her eyes. All the sweat and pain and hostility that she'd volunteered to take on, it all came down to the pleasure of this exhilarating moment. Her face was flush with the same endorphins and adrenaline that had brought her to his room that morning.

"I don't want you to go." His voice was low, but loud enough for her to hear him. Firm and real.

"It's only for a little while." Her smile was sweet and caressing, missing the severity in his mood. "I'll only be a few hours away when I get to Fort Leavenworth."

"I'm not worried about the distance. I'm worried about Mann." His words seemed to break up the glow in her cheeks. He watched her pretty smile dry against the contours of her face.

"Captain Novak." Captain Fassbender's voice sounded across the room, and the interruption gave her just enough time to regroup. To find an appropriate and accommodating response.

"You're worried about nothing." She reached for the bottle of champagne on the table and poured herself another flute of dancing bubbles.

"You took a lot of abuse from him." He reminded her. Gently. Urgently.

"He's apologized." She tipped the glass to her lips and brushed away his concerns. Each and every one of them. "Maybe it's time to let it go."

"I don't trust him."

"Maybe you don't trust me." Her grey eyes turned cool and icy. Almost colorless.

"I've given things up for you." He said plainly, without explanation or justification. The dull prickle in his skin grew sharp and distracting.

"I never asked you to." She swallowed with a sharp, sick sound. "I never wanted you to."

"You never would've come to my room if I hadn't done what I did." He felt suddenly sheepish and weak, stripped of whatever honor and heroism adorned his face and uniform.

"Bullshit favors and lies are the only way that girls like you look at guys like me."

"Is that what you think?"

"Captain Parcell." Captain Fassbender's voice broke the stalemate again. Cade watched her twirl her champagne in the silence that followed. The ice in the air crystallized in her grey eyes and a deep injury flashed across her face.

"I came to your room because you treated me with respect and you took me seriously." She kept her eyes focused straight ahead. She didn't dare look at him, but there was a definite soreness in her skin. "It had nothing to do with the ruck march."

"Are you sure about that?" He shook his head with renewed conviction, nursing a twisted and absurd hope that it wasn't true. That he hadn't misjudged her and manipulated her for no rational purpose. "Because you want this in the worst way."

"Captain Rainey." Fassbender continued calling names. Continued breaking up their argument with his low drawl and flimsy accolades.

"You said I didn't owe you anything." She stammered, her words becoming more and more fragile.

"You don't."

"So why are you doing this?" Her voice broke in the cold air, turning a few heads and shattering the thin veneer of privacy. "Why do you want to take this from me?"

"Because it's nothing more than a patch on you uniform." Cade finally spat. "That's all it is."

He'd meant it as a warning. But nothing in her posture or her bearing seemed to be taking it that way. There was a dismal fear in her stormy eyes, and his own patchy skin started to burn and tingle. He was losing her. Every time he opened his mouth she slipped further out of his hands.

"Why do you want it so badly?" He shook his head slowly, legitimately confused and bewildered.

"So people don't think I'm weak." She bit her lip and he saw every tremor reflected back in the crystal glass. Distant memories rising with the slow mist of the slippery champagne, bringing back a deep, violent hurt. "So people don't use me."

248

"A patch isn't going to protect you from that." He whispered in vain.

"Lieutenant Sellers." Captain Fassbender called off another name and one more officer shuffled to his feet to shake the general's hand.

"Awards and patches only matter to people who have nothing underneath." Cade reached for his own champagne glass, feeding himself a guilty taste of the sweet, sticky drink. "That's not you. I'm sorry for being one of the people who convinced you that you need this."

He swallowed a long, reckless gulp of champagne, and closed his eyes against the stinging in his tangled flesh.

# Chapter 44
## Charlottesville, VA (2013)

Pamela Hunt reached for an abandoned champagne bottle in the center of the nearest table to refill her glass. She tipped it skyward and watched a few fizzy drops fall to the bottom of her curved flute. The bottle was empty. She glanced at the scattered champagne bottles that lined the long tables around her, wondering if any of them had enough champagne left in them to reverse time and make her feel proud again. The sweetness of the weighted bubbles tempted her to douse her overworked muscles with something other than protein and adrenaline. And put her in sudden danger of losing her military bearing in front of a three star general.

She stood next to the frost-lined windows, snow coming down in torrents behind her as the dining staff cleared dishes and broke down tables. Her classmates crowded into comfortable social circles and the faculty ushered General Taylor about the room, making meaningless introductions that she would never remember. Hunt stared at Captain Cade from across the room, taking the general's hand and introducing himself with a serious smile. The warm center of her palm was imprinted with his fingers. She could still feel his hand wrapped around her heart and squeezing.

"Care for a beer instead?" Captain Mann stepped into her line of vision, setting a plastic cup of draft beer in front of her. He stood across the table sipping from his own cup, his celebrity smile muted behind the cheap plastic.

"Where did you get this?" She glanced at the cup and then back at his loaded smile.

She'd lost sight of Cade and lost her feel for what was honest and sincere. She'd trusted Cade in ways she never should have. Let him deep insider her and he twisted her confidence into tight, frayed knots. He had no way of knowing how much she'd enjoyed the discomforting feel of his twisted skin beneath her fingers. How much she'd needed to feel that kind of fluid intimacy again.

"The bar just opened. Beer is free, while it lasts. I'd take it while you can get it."

Hunt circled the cup with her fingers, pausing before she drank. Her eyes wandered along the smooth skin of Mann's perfect face, already missing the broken ridge along Aaron's cheekbone.

The poor fool still thought she'd clung to him out of some sense of obligation. That she wouldn't have seen past the burns if he hadn't paid her some grotesque favor. He planted a cruel seed of doubt that crept up her spine and sunk into her neck like the bite of an unseen predator, polluting the one moment that should have given her nothing but satisfaction and pride.

"Is this some kind of peace offering?" She weighed her words carefully. Still cautious. Still reserving judgment. Almost frightened of her own rude emotions.

"You could call it that." She didn't like the feel of Mann's eyes on her skin. There was a different sort of heat in them now that could melt her very bones. "You said it would take some time to forgive me. Perhaps it hasn't been enough time?"

She took her first sip of the stale ale, pinched by the bitterness after so much sweet champagne. "You were drunk when you apologized, Sir. How am I supposed to believe that you meant any of it?"

"I'm not drunk now." Mann looked at his feet, still hiding behind a cunning smile and an ambiguous phrase that didn't necessarily mean all that it implied. "I think you understand me better than you admit LT. I'm sorry that I treated you the way I did. But you're just as ruthless and mean as I am. And you wouldn't hesitate to tear me down if I was in your way."

She looked into Mann's wide eyes, hoping that he wasn't right. Something about the snow falling behind him and the unkindness in the air made her curious and reckless. She thought about what peace might taste like. How it might feel going down and settling in the warm pit of her belly. She decided that it might be something like this moment. Strangely poetic and satisfying.

"Do you really think I deserve to be here?"

Cade's self-serving sacrifice threatened to change her heart into a mess of regrets. Ugly, unwholesome anger that he'd taken such a crucial piece of herself. That she couldn't sit beside him without seeing her own shortcomings reflected back at her.

Mann set his drink on the table and held on to the back of the chair between them. He didn't bow his head or mince words, and almost seemed to draw strength from the peculiar opportunity. "I haven't questioned it since the ruck march."

"I guess we'll never know what might have happened." The loose words fell from her lips like so many lost pebbles. Spontaneous confessions that she couldn't simply slip back inside her mouth and hide beneath her crafty tongue. "If Cade hadn't given up and let me take his place."

"Just like we'll never know if Cade really let you take his place." Mann had a queer expression buried in his face. An uncommon mixture of confusion and amusement. His eyes still seemed treacherous, tricky. He took a bold swallow from his drink and she lost sight of his greedy, manipulative smile.

She tried to remember what exactly Cade had told her that morning. What specific words had led her to believe that he'd done it intentionally, for her. But there was nothing precise or damning in his words. She'd been manipulated with suggestive turns of phrase and calculated omissions.

"What makes you think he didn't?" She chased her ominous suspicions with another hard swallow from her plastic cup. She concentrated on the features of Mann's face, the fine lines that replaced that egotistical smile of his. She felt the anger loosening and breaking up as the beer hit her belly. His peace offering slipping into her bloodstream like candy. It felt surprisingly good to let go of some of that anger. Even if the anger was the only thing that had kept her going so long.

"Cade never gave me a straight answer one way or another." Mann's answer was smooth and forceful, but nowhere near trustworthy. "He just said that we both underestimated you. And he was right."

Hunt tightened her fingers around her plastic cup to keep from dropping it. Cold eddies circled through her bloodstream.

"He asked me not to go." She mumbled to herself, staring through the amber drink to the bottom of her plastic cup. "Because he doesn't trust you."

She worried that he might find something soft and vulnerable inside the hard exterior she'd been wearing. Her first instinct was to clamp down and protect it. But the peace swimming through her blood suddenly urged her to let it go.

"Don't let him take this from you." Mann almost looked concerned. Thrown off guard by the wrecked look on her face. "Whether he dropped on purpose or not, you stuck with me till the end. No one did that but you."

Hunt looked around at the rest of her classmates. They had formed distinct social circles all around the compact room. They swapped stories and drinks. They shared memories and laughs. They seemed to see beyond the ranks and patches sewn into their uniforms and tapped into some common human element underneath. The very thing that Aaron had warned her about. He'd told her that the only people who care about patches are those that have nothing underneath. The sudden revelation sent an electromagnetic pulse through the calloused muscle that beat in her chest.

"You were an asshole to me, Sir." She shook her head and stumbled over the deep fear rising in her chest. "Why should I believe anything you say now?"

"Because you want to." Captain Mann stood for a moment longer, rolling his tongue around as if he were looking for some other sharp and flawless response. Then let the loaded arguments die in his mouth.

"Try to have some fun tonight LT." He turned away from the table, leaving her alone with her small cup of improbable peace. "I'll see you in Fort Benning."

# Chapter 45
## Charlottesville, VA (2013)

Lieutenant Sharon drew in a tight breath as she shook the General's hand. General Taylor offered her routine congratulations, her expectations for the future and her hopes that Sharon would consider going active duty. Sharon smiled as brightly as she could, offering her own version of small talk and gracious thanks. She balanced a nearly full glass of champagne in her hands, the pretty bubbles disappearing with the slow creep of time.

From the corner of her eye she saw Major Casper lift a bottle of champagne from the end of a long table and pull up a chair to the sacred Table of Remembrance. An empty champagne flute dangled from his limp fingers, with just enough carelessness to cause concern. She bent her neck to keep a cautious eye on him, wondering what sort of obscene performance might erupt if he were allowed to get lost in his memories again. If her soft hands and tender voice weren't enough to bring him back.

General Taylor offered a simple farewell, finally stepping around her and moving towards the next crowd of lieutenants. Sharon released a hot breath as the general passed by. She threw back a grateful swallow from her glass and trained her eyes on the sullen major who'd sat down to have a drink with someone invisible to an easy heart.

He upended the champagne flute in front of the empty chair and filled it with the crystal white drink, then set the glass down in the glow of the solitary candle. He lifted the champagne bottle to toast the lost soldier before him, and then drank straight from the end. Jamie watched as his fingers curled around its neck, worried that it might snap at any moment. She had been watching for some time when he lifted the champagne bottle for the last time, tilting his head back and draining the last of the drink into his empty heart.

He set the bottle down with a sick thud. His eyes glossed over as he stared into the empty space across the table, lost somewhere between the past and the present, ruminating on the fate of a friend who never made it home.

Sharon waited for a long time, wondering if it was safe to intervene in this kind of grief. She took a final swallow from her champagne glass and set it down on a table beside her, steeling herself against the possibility of spilled champagne and broken glass. She stepped towards the table with a quickening pulse in her neck.

She reached for a chair from close by and sat beside Casper. She followed his eyes to the empty space across the table, trying to see what he was seeing.

"Who is it you're remembering tonight, Sir?" She almost whispered.

"Staff Sergeant Randy Khoury." He glanced up at her, and for a brief moment seemed to welcome the softness in her eyes. Then turned back towards the untouched glass of champagne. "He served with me in the EOD unit in Iraq. We were investigating a blast site outside Mosul. He was only a bit farther away than you are right now, when the blast ripped him apart." Casper held tight to the empty bottle in his hands. He tried to take another sip, bringing the bottle all the way to his parched lips before he remembered that it was empty. He brought the bottle back down and held it tight against his chest. "Don't you have some celebrating to do before you head back to your civilian life? Ease back into your routine as a part time soldier, fraternizing with the enlisted and whatever else you get away with in the National Guard?"

Sharon watched the slow rise and fall of his chest as he breathed. She could almost feel the cool rhythm of his heart as it struggled to digest the slivers of so much unprocessed grief. "Is there anything I can do for you Sir?"

"Yeah." He tilted the empty champagne bottle towards her. "I could use another drink."

She hesitated. She saw the pain gathering behind his eyes, concentrated, toxic and potentially lethal. "I don't think a drink's going to do you much good."

"I never said it would LT." He cast a sideways glance at her. "But I can't leave the good Sergeant to drink by himself, now can I?"

Sharon concentrated on the familiar tick in his hazel eyes, wondering if this would be the last time she'd see him. If he'd find a way to vanish into obscurity like the soldier in the empty chair.

"I guess not." Sharon nodded quietly and got up from the table, making her way towards the bar at the far end of the room. There had been no spilled champagne or broken glass, but there was a certain sort of violence. She ordered two light beers and glanced back at Casper, still clutching the empty champagne bottle, trying to understand what it was that kept him pinned to that chair.

The bartender set two plastic cups in front of her. She took a long sip as she watched Casper, sharing the loose glow of candlelight with a ghost. The sparkling champagne still misting in the Staff Sergeant's drink.

Sharon took her drinks and walked back towards Casper, setting the plastic cup on the table in front of him.

He glanced at the brown ale for a short time, then stared up at her for far longer than he should have, the light from the candle dancing across the whites of his eyes.

"Don't leave me here to drink this alone." He said to her as if she was a long way away. "Stay and have a beer with Staff Sergeant Khoury. This man lost his life in a god awful desert far away from home. The least you can do is say hello and drink a toast with me."

Sharon nodded. She sat back down at the table and raised her glass, offering a sincere toast to the fallen Staff Sergeant.

"Staff Sergeant Khoury, thank you for your bravery, your loyalty and your sacrifice. I wish that you could be with us here today. Cheers." She lifted the plastic cup to her lips and took a long, dry swallow.

"Will I ever see you again?" Casper asked through dry lips, playing with the wedding band that was still tight around his fingers. "After you go home to this miserable sergeant who's waiting for you?"

"It's anyone's guess Sir." She tried to tame the promises and emotions that collected under her tongue.

"Would you mind if I called you by your first name tonight?" He seemed barely aware that there was anyone else in the room. He gave in to a natural tendency to let protocol slip. The combination of alcohol and loneliness took him out of himself and made him brasher than usual.

"No, I don't mind, Sir."

"Jamie." Her name sounded and felt better rolling off his tongue. Substantial, smooth and bordering on intimate. "You're going to need to stop calling me Sir."

# Chapter 46
## Charlottesville, VA (2013)

Jamie Sharon stumbled as she stepped off the elevator onto the third floor. She told herself it was from the heels as much as the beer she'd put down while making conversation with an empty chair. She was fighting the exhaustion from an entire evening spent in her stiff dress uniform in the company of a three star general. A levity and recklessness spread through the class as the hours wore on. The promise of tomorrow's graduation loosened tongues and broke down decorum. They were heading home soon, or at the very least, into the final leg of a long, tiresome journey.

Sharon's feet were sore and her head was dizzy. She took care as she stepped down the hall towards her room, looking forward to collapsing into bed.

The hallway was full of loud voices. A handful of her classmates lingered outside their rooms in sweats and pajamas. They were already making themselves far too comfortable with each other, passing around beers and exasperated congratulations.

She could hear Captain Mann from halfway down the hall. He stood just outside his door, in a pair of clean gray sweatpants and a worn tank, revealing a pair of thick, toned arms and a set of dog tags hanging around his neck. He leaned against one arm, scanning the hallways as he shouted into his cell phone. "Yeah, c'mon down. We're on the third floor. Hey Sharon!" He called as she approached, his cell phone still pressed against his ear. "Yeah, it's room 311."

He silenced the phone and sank it deep into the pockets of his sweat pants before turning back towards her.

"Hey Sharon, can you do me a favor?"

"What favor?" She tried to settle the buzzing in her head, concentrating on stopping the swaying in her unsteady heels."

"Can you look after Lieutenant Daniels? She's had way too much to drink and someone needs to put her to bed."

"Yeah, I can take care of her." Sharon could taste the alcohol clinging to the back of her mouth and wished she could undo the last few swallows. "Where is she?"

"She's in my room." He nodded his head towards the open door behind him.

"Just let me change my clothes first." Jamie reached into the pocket inside her suit coat for her room key. She turned and slid her card key into the lock and slipped into the quiet of her empty room.

She closed the door behind her and fell back against it with a tired sigh, the tingling still working its way through her brain. She dug her cell phone out of her jacket pocket and noticed a missed call from Sergeant Matthew Chase. She turned up the volume and hit redial, turning on the speakerphone as she removed her jacket. She set the phone on the bed and opened her empty closet, pulling out her uniform bag as she listened to the quiet ringing behind her.

"Congratulations Ma'am." Matt's voice echoed through the room. "How was your last night in Charlottesville?"

"It's almost over." She unbuttoned her blouse and unzipped her skirt, speaking slowly to avoid sounding sloppy. "Graduation's tomorrow at 10:00."

"I wish I could be there for you."

"You won't miss much. A couple of predictable speeches and a lot of formalities." She lined up the pieces of her uniform as she undressed and placed them on the coat hanger, the last item to be packed up and shipped to Fort Benning.

"I am proud of you though. I hope you know that."

"It's nice to hear." She zipped up her uniform bag and hung it in the closet, then rummaged through her dresser drawers for a pair of loose pants and an old t-shirt. She felt an unrecognizable warmth as she closed her eyes and imagined her homecoming, the comfort of feeling his full arms around her. "As long as you and Reese are waiting for me when I get back."

There was a loud knock at the door, and the muffled voice of a drunk Lieutenant Daniels leaked through the walls.

"Jamie, are you in there?"

"Will you be up for awhile Matt?" Sharon slurred into the phone, forgetting to focus on her words and giving in to the heaviness in her head. "I have to go take care of someone who's had a bit too much to drink." She pulled her t-shirt over her head and tightened the drawstring on her pants, grabbing for the phone and holding it next to her ear.

"Just call me when you can. I'll wait up for you." She heard the smile in his voice and it warmed her cheeks and forehead.

"I'll talk to you soon."

Sharon hung up the phone and set it on the nightstand by her bed, heading towards the voice on the other side of the door that broke and slurred even more than her own. She opened the door and found Lieutenant Daniels wandering away from her room and towards the elevators.

"Carrie." Sharon headed down the hall after her. She grabbed the lieutenant by the wrist, just as she was reaching to send for the elevator. "Where are you going?"

"Jamie!" Lieutenant Daniels' eyes lit up. "I was going upstairs to find you."

"There's no one upstairs anymore. C'mon. I'll take you to your room." Sharon led her back down the hall, stopping in front of room 322 and trying the door. "Do you have a key?"

"Yes, it's in my sock." Lieutenant Daniels bent over to retrieve the room key. She stumbled as she felt for the plastic card. Jamie caught her before she fell over.

"Careful."

"I'm being careful." Daniels tried to stifle a loud giggle.

"Just hold on to the door, I'll get the key." Sharon fished the card out of Daniels' sock and slid it into the door lock. The green light pulsed and Sharon opened the door, leading the drunk lieutenant into the room ahead of her.

"Jamie, I don't want to go bed yet."

"Everyone else is going to bed." Sharon brought the lieutenant towards the bed and sat her down. She opened a bottle of water that was sitting on the nightstand and handed it to her. "Here, drink this. You're going to have a headache in the morning."

260

"I have a headache now." Daniels took a couple of quick swallows. Her head bobbed from side to side as the fatigue started to catch up with her. "Why can't we stay in Captain Mann's room?"

"Because General Taylor is still upstairs. We have to be quiet alright." Sharon took the water bottle from her. She took a long swallow herself before she re-capped it and set it back on the nightstand. "We have a big day in the morning. Where is your cell phone? Is your alarm set?"

Lieutenant Daniels reached into her pockets and pulled out her cell phone. She handed it to Sharon without answering. "Jamie, are you nervous about Fort Benning? I'm worried about the swamps and the marching. I don't know if I'll be able to do it."

"You'll do fine, alright. We're all going to do fine." Sharon set the alarm on Daniels' phone and placed it on the nightstand beside the bed. "Now stand up for a minute."

Daniels wobbled to her feet as Sharon pulled down the covers. She sat Lieutenant Daniels back down on the sheets and lifted her legs into the warm bed. "Alright, now go ahead and lay down. I'm going to sleep too as soon as you're in bed."

"I'm super dizzy." Daniels re-positioned herself on her side. "Is your boyfriend coming to graduation tomorrow?"

"No." Sharon answered as she pulled the covers up over her friend, wondering how many of her classmates had their suspicions by now. "No, I don't have a boyfriend."

"I know it's a secret because he's a sergeant, but I promise I won't tell anyone." Lieutenant Daniels looked up at her with wide, spacey eyes. "He must be proud of you."

"Shhhh." Sharon tried to quiet the questions. "We have six more weeks and we go home. That's it. Just six more weeks. Now get some sleep. I'll see you in the morning."

"Goodnight Jamie."

"Goodnight Carrie."

Sharon set Daniels' room key on the nightstand next to her phone. She turned out all the lights and headed back into the hallway, making sure to close the door behind her.

Sharon made her way down the hallway towards her own room. She reached towards her hips to dig out her room key, suddenly realizing that her pajama pants had no pockets. She stopped in front of her room, relieved to see that she had left the door cracked open.

"Jamie." She heard Lieutenant Hunt's voice in a loud whisper behind her. She turned and saw Hunt standing behind her with an open bottle of beer in her hands. Her red hair was unrestrained, the long layers falling loose about her face, her grey eyes swimming in alcohol and spent anger. "I have to ask you something."

"I told Sergeant Chase I'd call him back."

"You don't need to call him tonight. Your dog is fine." Hunt took a long swallow from the bottle in her hand, the drink going straight to her glossy eyes. "It's important."

"What's important?" Sharon was pinned to her position in the hallway, torn between keeping her promise to the sergeant back home, and keeping him a secret from the tipsy redhead in front of her.

"You're supposed to be the smart one." Pamela Hunt swept a long flush of red hair from her sad grey eyes. "How can I tell which one is lying to me?"

"Give me five minutes." Sharon insisted softly. "I'll be over in five minutes."

"I'll be waiting for you."

Pam Hunt disappeared down the hall as Sharon gently pushed open the door to her room. She shut the door behind her and flipped the light switch as she walked into the room, a cold flush washing through her bloodstream as her eyes fell on Major Casper, drunk and shaken, sitting on the edge of her bed.

"Sir, what are you doing in here?" She hadn't intended to whisper, but the sound got lost in her throat.

He looked up at her, with lonely, bloodshot eyes and responded as if there was only one, obvious answer. "They keep coming back." The vibrations from his flat response went straight to the marrow of her bones. "I can't get rid of the dreams, they won't stop."

262

The tingling in her head accelerated, blocking electromagnetic impulses dead in their tracks. She was afraid to step either forward or backward. "How did you get in here?"

"You left the door open." He seemed preoccupied with his hands, studying every line and soft spot, running his fingers across the crude scar in his palm like an old fortune teller, confronting a hopeless and decaying future. "I don't hear the blasts in my head when you're close to me. I need to stay here with you tonight."

"I can't let you do that Sir." She stepped closer to the bed and placed a firm hand on his shoulder. She looked down on him with nervous eyes and a subtle shake in her voice. "I have someone waiting for me at home. So do you."

"They don't need to know Jamie." He reached for the white hand that was on his shoulder and drew it close to his chest. He held it there, like a wounded bird, studying the ancient lines, the lost story that was written in her tender flesh. "You won't see me again after tonight. Just do me this one small favor."

"Ben, please . . ." She shook her head, blood pumping ominous notes against her temples. She tried to pull her hand out of his cool fingers, but felt his grip tighten around them. Her stomach dropped and her legs went numb. She felt her simple heart grow cold and slow. It's soft meat waiting to be crushed by intangible nothings like rank, duty and patriotism.

"Just one small favor Jamie." He whispered out loud, not taking his eyes from the promise in her hands. "I need one now."

# Chapter 47
## Charlottesville, VA (2013)

"I don't know why you're making a big deal of this." Captain Mann stood outside his room with his cell phone pressed against his ear. He leaned into the wall and tapped his room key against his thigh, as the voice on the other end rambled. "It has nothing to do with you."

The footsteps and voices started up again. It wasn't the first time he had heard them, and they were definitely coming from Sharon's room. He tuned out the voice on the other end of the line as the muffled sounds moved closer to the door.

"Shhh. Hold on a minute." He tried to quiet his phone call. He slipped his card key into his door lock and disappeared inside, waiting and watching from behind his cracked door.

Sharon's door creaked open and Major Casper stepped into the hallway, a slight wobble in his gait. Sharon was half hidden in the darkness behind the doorway, but he could make out her face and hands as she moved in and out of the light. The woman on his cell phone called his name for the second or third time. He tapped a button and ended the call, straining to make out the conversation in the hallway.

"You worry too much." Casper's voice was deep and slow. He lingered outside the doorway, staring back at the smallish lieutenant, who had never really appeared all that small until this very moment

"I have a lot to lose, Sir." Her voice was shaky.

"You really don't know what you've done for me." Casper looked down at the floor. He seemed lost in the intricate design of the carpet. His head was too heavy and his soul too weary to look her in the eye. "You saved me tonight."

"You have to leave now Sir. Before somebody sees you."

"You're still planning on calling him aren't you?" Casper looked up, a sad epiphany rushing across his tired face. "You think he's still waiting for you? What are you going to say to him?"

"Please, just go."

Mann heard the tell-tale break in her voice. The catch and swell between words. He'd made enough women cry to recognize the change in pitch. The stress between syllables betrayed everything from surface fractures to a distress that was buried deep in the fibers of the heart.

"It's going to be tough to say goodbye to you tomorrow." Casper placed his fingers beneath her chin and lifted her head. His eyes flashed as if capturing the image of her face in his hands. He leaned forward and took her lips in his. She stood perfectly still as he kissed her, like a deer in a hunter's crosshairs, a thin stream of tears running down her face.

# Chapter 48
## Charlottesville, VA (2013)

Lieutenant Hunt clutched her patrol cap in her fingers and marched down the hall. Her head ached and her throat was dry. Her red hair was rolled up in a tight knot at the back of her head, pulling on her scalp and doubling the pain in her head.

She had tried to sleep through last night's pain, but it was still there when she woke up. The sting of betrayal tightening and twisting in her stomach.

"Formation in ten minutes." She knocked on the doors as she headed down the hall, calling out the new report time to those who were still in bed. "In full uniform. Hurry up."

She passed her classmates in the hall, most of them hungover and confused. She glared at each of them with suspicion, heartless bystanders that didn't have the nerve to tell her she was being played. To let her sink into the lies of a selfish man whose only intention was to use her for his own gratification.

"What's going on?"

"I don't know. Just get dressed and get downstairs."

Hunt stiffened as she knocked on Captain Mann's door. The contact sent strong vibrations through her wrist and arm, and an eerie dread began settling under her skin. "Formation in ten minutes."

Someone had crossed a line last night, and the entire class was about to get shredded for it. The fog in her head was lifting and she started to connect the dots. That's why they were being dragged out of bed on graduation day. So Fassbender could lay into them one last time before he sent them off to Fort Benning.

Hunt turned around and saw Lieutenant Sharon standing in her doorway, still dressed in her drawstring pajama pants and t-shirt from last night. A surge of questions embedded in her face.

"Fassbender wants everyone downstairs in ten minutes. In your fatigues."

"I've already packed them." Sharon sounded as if she'd forgotten where she was. She looked worse than the rest of them, puffy skin and red lines crossing the whites of her eyes.

"So unpack them." Hunt's response was short and gruff.

Sharon disappeared from her doorway, stepping back into her room in jerky movements, listless and hollow.

Hunt scanned the hallway for anyone she'd missed, watching the last minute commotion build around her. Sick and dehydrated officers scrambled out of their rooms, still zipping up their uniforms, slapping on patches and arranging their disheveled collars. She caught sight of Major Casper halfway down the hall, heading towards her in sweatpants and a t-shirt. He held one hand against his right temple, as if he were trying to massage away the imprint of last night's alcohol.

"Formation in 10 minutes Sir." She repeated as he stopped in front of her.

"So I heard." He made no attempt to hurry back to his room and into uniform. His speech was slow. He glanced around at the sound of doors shutting and elevator doors sliding open. She couldn't tell if he was still drunk. "I'm missing my cell phone, can you call it for me?"

"We don't have time Sir." Hunt curled her fingers around the brim of her patrol cap, controlling the roughness in her response.

"It will take you two seconds LT." He glanced down at her with a clear indication that he wasn't moving until she complied. "My wife will be calling."

Hunt pulled out her cell phone and began scrolling through her contacts. "I will find it for you Sir. Just get in uniform and get downstairs."

She hit send and dialed the number.

"Yes ma'am." Casper nodded his thanks and turned back towards his room, just as the unmistakable buzz of a vibrating phone sounded inside Sharon's open door.

Casper stopped in place, a sudden stiffness gripping him as he turned towards the sound.

Hunt glanced from the ringing cell phone in her hand to the noise inside Sharon's room. She stepped past the threshold with Casper following her, tracing the sound into the open room, where a black cell phone was vibrating on top of Sharon's dresser.

Sharon stood and backed out of her open closet, where she was digging through boxes of packed combat uniforms. She looked up at Hunt and Casper, then towards the vibrating phone on her dresser.

"We're looking for Major Casper's cell phone." Hunt's voice was low and mangled.

Sharon nodded, her swollen eyes closing against the dizzying noise that seemed to grow louder the longer she stood without speaking. She moved to grab the vibrating phone from her dresser and handed it to the major with stiff, locked joints, turning as if she were facing a firing squad.

"Is this it?" The words cracked and died in her mouth.

Casper glanced at the phone in her hand, a dim recognition washing over his face. He raised his eyebrows in a long arch, and stared at her outstretched hand. "It is."

"You stopped in for a bottle of water last night," Sharon dropped a loose explanation before anyone had a chance to ask. "Don't you remember?"

"I don't remember much of anything last night." Casper reached for the phone and turned to look at the glowing screen. It flashed and then faded into oblivion as the call ended and the light dimmed. "Let's hope I haven't lost anything else."

Casper slipped the phone into his pocket and turned back towards his room. His casual gait interrupted after only a few short steps as he lifted his head over his shoulder to look back for answers to some mystery that was buried in last night's alcohol.

Hunt turned towards Lieutenant Sharon. She stood in the doorway with a pale expression, and no indication that any words or thoughts were forming inside her rattled cage.

"You never came by last night." Hunt tried to coax it out of her. Even a brief acknowledgement of the hurricane that had just swept across her face. "Long talk with the dogsitter?"

"Yeah." Sharon responded on cue, following a simple and predictable pattern. The obnoxious clog in her throat. The selfish note of shame that followed an expected and unrepentant infidelity. "I fell asleep on the phone."

Hunt twisted her patrol cap even tighter between her fingers. "Hurry up and get dressed."

# Chapter 49
## Charlottesville, VA (2013)

Major Casper marched out to the field, a cold rain soaking into the ground under his feet. The sky was still dark, hiding the puddles that had collected overnight. He slunk through them as his liver churned through liters of unmetabolized alcohol. His memory was shrouded in a thick fog, the color and consistency of the mud gathering on the soles of his combat boots.

He found his place in the back of 2nd platoon and watched the formation assemble in front of him. The squads lined up in straight rows, heavy heads bowed to keep the rain off their faces. Sharon stood in the center of 1st squad, her small frame almost buried in the bodies and camouflage between him and her. She stared at the ground like the others, still and guarded. She didn't turn and smile. She had distanced herself from every element of her environment, including the falling rain and the gray morning air.

A disturbing feeling seized him. He felt the weight of his cell phone deep in his uniform pocket and wondered how it had ended up in her room. What he had said and done with her last night.

The rain picked up as the last of the stragglers crossed the parking lot and filled in the holes in the formation. Hunt was one of the last to step in place, her fists clenched at her sides and her jaw locked. He'd learned to recognize each of them by height, size and hair color. By the way they held their hands at their sides and balanced their weight. Casper focused his blurred vision on the names on the backs of the patrol caps in front of him, Harris, Swanson, Wagner, Nelson, Hunt, Sharon. He'd heard them laugh or complain each morning. He'd come to know their personalities, their home states and individual breaking points. But this morning there was an undeniable coldness in the ranks. They conducted themselves like strangers, quiet and unkind. The call to formation had sent a dark tremor through the class. Because it meant that someone had fucked up, and everyone was going down for it.

A chill climbed up his spine as the pieces started coming together. He squeezed his fingers to feel the embrace of the wedding ring on his left hand. He played and replayed the spacy look in Jamie's eyes when she handed him his cell phone. It might have been them. The reason for the sudden call to formation.

"Hey Nichols, where's your hat?" A voice broke through rain.

"I couldn't find it. It's packed up somewhere."

"Are you serious?"

"That's just fucking great."

"Calm down, they won't keep us here that long." Capser tried to quiet the coming storm, even if he wasn't entirely convinced of his own words. "Graduation's in a few hours. Someone embarrassed Fassbender in front of General Taylor and we're going to get one final ass-chewing, that's all."

Captain Fassbender stepped through the schoolhouse door, bundled in a heavy gortex jacket. The class straightened as he approached, all eyes following him as he strode through the rain. The ugly emotion on his face looming larger as he crossed the distance. He stopped in front of the formation, pacing in front of all three platoons, watching the lot of them freezing in cold morning rain.

"Put your hat on soldier!" He spat at Lieutenant Nichols.

"I don't have it, Sir, I've packed it."

"Then all of you get down on the ground and push until I tell you to stop!" The captain shouted and the class dropped to the ground. Casper saw a number of patrol caps fall into the mud as they descended. He set his hands and knees in the wet earth and began an unknown set of repetitions, the rain assaulting him as he lifted his heavy torso up and down. "I bet you're all wondering what you're doing out here in the rain on graduation morning! Most of you anyway. You have seriously, seriously messed up! And I'm not talking about Nichols' hat! You've got a lot more problems than showing up to formation out of uniform!"

Casper listened to the squish of Fassbender's boots as he walked the length of the formations and shouted. He strained against the sick feeling from last night's recklessness, dropping his face inches from the muddy ground.

"I received a phone call this morning, from a woman whose husband is a JAG officer in this class. She told me that she called her husband late last night and a strange woman answered the telephone. When she confronted her husband, he confessed to the adultery and told her not to come to the ceremony today. Because he'd found someone that meant more to him than her." Casper could smell the dank earth as Fassbender's words hit his pounding head. His muscles starting to shake. He watched his classmates hit their knees, their arms giving out under them. "For fear of destroying her husband's career, she wouldn't tell me her name. She just thought I should know what was going on in my school. Get on your feet!"

The class crawled out of position and raised themselves from the ground, splashes of mud coating their hands and uniforms. The rain had begun to soak through their fatigues and clung to their hair and faces. They re-positioned themselves and replaced their patrol caps, as suspicious eyes started darting through the ranks.

"Now I am demanding to know which one of you it was." The captain glared at the officer in front of 2nd platoon with his head exposed to the elements. "Was it you Nichols?"

"No Sir, I don't even have a wife."

"Shocking." Fassbender responded. "How about you, Anderson?"

"No Sir."

"O'Brien."

"No Sir."

"So who was it?" Fassbender continued to pace in front of the formation, scanning the tired faces for subtle traces of guilt. "At least two of you know the answer. This is an exercise in integrity people! You did the crime you pay the price! No one wants to step forward? Take responsibility for you lack of judgment? Your lack of character?"

Casper glanced at the rain-soaked faces around him, every one of them determined and hard. He felt heavy stares, both real and imagined, raking him from head to toe. He looked to his left and caught sight of a drenched Captain Mann, staring straight ahead with an unrestrained heat. The disturbed look was almost enough to make Casper break the silence. To raise his voice and confess to something he couldn't remember.

The phone in his pocket still stored any relevant evidence that had vanished from his memory. The exact time of any midnight phone calls from Grace. Any answers it held were right at his fingertips, and yet completely out of reach.

He focused on Sharon, standing straight and resolute in front of him. He couldn't see her face or gauge her reactions, other than the goosebumps forming on the back of her neck. He waited for her to speak up, or give some indication of a struggle. Of grappling with an incriminating truth buried deep in her stomach. She remained dead silent.

"You will stand here until I have a confession, do you hear me?" Captain Fassbender continued. "Have you learned nothing over the last four months? Are you really going to make your classmates pay the price to save your own skin? Your family members will be arriving in a matter of hours, ladies and gentlemen! Your mothers and fathers, your spouses, your children, your grandparents! Traveled from all over the country to applaud the honorable men and women that you've become! Are you going to do this to your classmates?"

The silence stretched and solidified. Fassbender walked back and forth before each of the platoons. The longer it dragged on, the less likely that the guilty parties would emerge. The gravity of the offense thickened and settled. The initial promise of clemency was replaced with a hard and intensifying instinct for self-preservation. Within the span of a few long minutes, the offenders had found themselves inexplicably locked in, committed to their passive dishonesty.

"How are you going to protect each other on the battlefield?" Captain Fassbender shouted. "If you're willing to sacrifice your comrades for your own selfish needs? Are you truly going to stand here, silently, to let all of their hard work be done in vain? Believe me when I tell you that this will catch up with you! It will haunt you! You will have a reputation and you will not last long in the United States Military! This is a better test of your abilities as leaders than any of the training we could have provided! I ask you to do the honorable thing and come forward! To be an example! What are the Army values ladies and gentlemen? Loyalty. Duty. Honor. Respect. Selfless Service. Personal courage. Am I forgetting one?"

Captain Fassbender scanned the ranks again, looking for some chink in the armor. Some break in the impossible impasse. "Integrity, ladies and gentlemen! Integrity! Does that mean anything to you?"

The captain's appeal was met by the same firm and unyielding silence, the empty sound of the rain echoing through the space between him and his officers.

"You have until 1000 hours to turn yourselves into my office. You will stand out here until you do."

Captain Fassbender turned from the front of the formation and headed back towards the school. He disappeared through the same double doors that he had come from, leaving the formation to stand, unattended and exposed, as the first streaks of dawn began winding around the horizon.

The drops fell. The mud thickened around their boots. Soldiers stood at attention, shivering, faces forward, their eyes moved about the ranks, each one silently forming a list of suspects. Each one cursing beneath their breath as the day got brighter. No one came forward.

"For the love of God, whoever it is, will you just turn yourself in so the rest of us can get on with our lives?" Nichols moaned.

"Shut up Nichols, you can't even remember to bring your friggin' cap!"

"Screw you."

"Boy, whoever it is I hope it was worth it. This is pretty fucking pathetic right here."

The company stood until the rain stopped. Intermittent patches of bright sky broke through the cloud cover and a sharp breeze crept through the air.

Cars began to fill the parking lot. Families in suits and dresses filed into the building, glancing curiously at the soaked soldiers standing in formation, not recognizing their own.

"What are you smiling at, Tibbs?"

"This, this whole goddamn thing."

"It ain't fucking funny asshole! My grandma flew out here from Texas!"

"We signed up for this shit! Volunteered to be treated like a bunch of children. That's fuckin' hilarious."

"You think this is hilarious, I'll turn you in right now, I don't care if you did it or not!"

"Everybody shut the fuck up! If you did it, get in there and take it like a man."

Bodies shifted in wet fatigues as they watched the last of the arriving guests make their way into what was certainly an auditorium full of confused families. The company stood soaked and miserable.

"This is goddamn ridiculous! Why the hell can't they just confiscate cell phones and find out who the hell it was? It ain't that fucking difficult!"

"That's not the point." Casper's voice was low and bent.

"What the hell is the point, Sir?"

"The same as always, Marshall. Honor and integrity."

Casper lifted his chin and scanned the cluster of bodies around him. He saw the tension wane from their hands and faces, tight jaws and stiff shoulders beginning to slacken. The anger had worn through them with the rain. Their heads and bodies were tired and sore, and the first signs of defeat were percolating to the surface. The Army had intended to teach them to look out for one another, but here and now, the unjust punishment was spreading through the group like a poison.

"I can't believe nobody knows who the hell it was! I sure as hell hope I never have to deploy with the asshole who's going to screw over his buddies so he can get laid."

"The women aren't exactly innocent either. One of you bitches is behind this."

"Watch the language, Nolan!"

"That's some Mary Poppins bullshit! If I catch the son of a bitch who did this . . ."

"At ease, soldier!" Casper stopped him, glancing at the watch on his wrist. "It's too late now anyway. It's just about 1000."

Almost on cue, the company commander stepped through the JAG school door. He marched across the parking lot and stood before the formation, a dire expression etched into his face.

"You are not fit to be officers in the United States Army! You know who you are! You're a disgrace to the uniform! You disgust me! You can go in there and tell your family members that they can now go home. Your graduation ceremony has been cancelled."

The sun broke through the clouds and a touch of warmth fell over their broken faces, but the cold had already seeped through their skin and settled in their bones.

"I've also been in contact with Fort Benning and removed all of your classmates from Airborne School. All of the work you have done since you arrived in Charlottesville. You can forget about it. It's done."

Casper saw Lieutenant Hunt's chest heave and then deflate. She seemed to sink deeper into the mud under her feet, the heavy sentence physically weighing her down. He glanced towards 3rd platoon and searched Captain Mann's face for some sign of shock or anger, but encountered only a focused stare, as if he'd heard none of the company commander's harsh punishments.

"Those of you who are awaiting promotions to captain, your promotions will be delayed for one year. Because you have failed. As a class, you have failed to look out for each other. You have failed to keep each other on track and you have failed to live the Army values. You have dishonored the JAG Corps, you have dishonored the United States Army. You have dishonored your family and friends, your teachers. You have dishonored me and

276

most of all, you have dishonored yourselves. You are now dismissed."

Captain Fassbender walked away from the class without a second look. Officers staggered where they stood, fracturing the formation as they took their first dismal steps out of the wet field and towards disappointing confrontations with families. Casper held firm to his place in the rear of the messy ranks, watching the remainder of his classmates skulk and scatter. He reached one hand deep into his uniform pocket and curled his fingers around his cell phone, terrified at the prospect of scrolling through the recent calls log, and finding his reputation shredded in between the million errant pixels of data.

# Part Ten:

# U.S. v. Casper

# Chapter 50
## Fort Leavenworth, KS (2014)

Lieutenant Sharon leaned against the wall outside the door to the courtroom, hugging a bloated file close to her chest. She closed her eyes and swallowed a pound of air. She wore the stiff dress uniform that she hadn't seen since she packed it up and sent it home from Charlottesville. The same day she'd stood outside in the rain while Fassbender shouted about integrity. She could still feel Hunt staring at her from the corner of her grey eyes, filling with suspicion and venom.

The corridor was wide and open, and echoed with the footsteps of clerks and.paralegals. They moved in and out of the offices lining the hall, making copies and last minute preparations as the time wound down.

Sharon was warm in the thick jacket, despite the frost lining the glass door and the lingering feel of Christmas clinging to people's faces. A nervous sweat was building under her clothes. She stared down at the sheen of her black heels, waiting for the noise of the MPs' badges and keys to interrupt the routine flow of business. Some cue to reflect the severity that was thumping through her heart.

She honed in on the sound of recycled breathing and felt the heat of an extra set of eyes. She looked up from the floor and saw Grace Casper standing in the open doorframe of a witness room across the hall. She wore a gray wrap dress that hugged her hips and long arms. Her hair was swept from the sides of her face and pinned in place, the loose locks falling lightly behind her ears. She looked stronger and healthier than her former self, working her nerves into a piece of wasted chewing gum. There was a stiff optimism playing off her pink cheeks. She seemed both sturdy and scared for her life. Sharon felt the dual weight of all that hope and dread settling about her shoulders.

Somewhere behind Grace a heavy door slammed. Sharon heard the echo of two separate sets of footsteps and looked down the hall. She saw Casper walking ahead of his police escort. He was still tall and built in his dress uniform. She focused on the stack of deployment honors pinned to his chest. Simple trinkets given in exchange for the damage his body and his mind had endured. She bent her eyes on him for a moment that felt like a broken slice of forever, trying to preserve the image of a pristine war hero, before it was gone.

He slowed his pace as he approached the open doorway where Grace was standing. He stopped in front of her, taking in the sight with eyes hungry for something comfortable and familiar. Grace stepped forward, placing her arms in the shallow indent where his neck merged with his jawbone. She looked into his eyes for a long spell, then pitched forward and planted her lips against his.

Sharon felt like a voyeur, trespassing into an intimate moment where she didn't belong.

Grace lowered herself back onto her flat feet, still holding the base of his neck. "I still love you, Ben. Whatever they decide today." She straightened his collar and moved her nimble fingers down his thick arms, taking a strong grip on his hands. "I know you. You may not remember everything, but I'll always know you."

He wrapped his fingers around hers and squeezed, then lifted her hands to his lips. He pressed her skin against his cheek for a cool moment, drinking in the sensation before he surrendered her back into the open hallway.

Casper glanced over at Sharon, then stepped towards her without looking back. His wife disappeared into the witness room and the flash of intimacy was gone. Casper stepped up beside her, close enough to break the professional space between them.

"Are we ready, counselor?" He tugged at his sleeves and straightened his jacket.

Sharon nodded and directed him toward the courtroom doors. "This way Sir."

She reached for the solid handle and forced the door open, stepping into the heavy atmosphere of the wood paneled room. She surveyed the high desks of the judge and the panel members, getting caught on the colors of the flag in the center and the silver seal on the left. The sights and smells brought her back to the first day that she'd arrived at Leavenworth, when they led him out of this very room in handcuffs.

"Why isn't Grace allowed in the courtroom?" Casper's voice was low and subdued.

"Because she's a witness." Sharon answered as she stepped forward, moving through the gallery and reaching for the swinging door into the courtroom.

"You're asking her to testify?"

"I need her to explain that the pepper spray on the keychain was hers, not yours." She moved to the left side of the courtroom, setting her file on the desk just under the JAG Corps seal and directly under the bench of the military judge. She opened her binder and saw the edge of the envelope that Grace had given her, peeking out from underneath the stack of papers. She'd never asked him about the unopened letter. She'd never explained what Grace had done to protect him. "She's doing it because she loves you."

Sharon lifted her eyes and absorbed the tumult in the courtroom. She felt the rush of bodies moving through the formal space and the creep of feedback sounding through microphones as they were connected and adjusted. She tried to sort through the white noise and cling to the essentials. Facts, procedure and the burden of proof.

"As I was getting dressed this morning, it occurred to me that this may be the last time I ever wear this uniform." Casper began fidgeting with his cufflinks, adjusting little imperfections in his uniform. "It's amazing how much we wrap ourselves up in novelties. I'm not even sure I know who I am without this uniform."

"Don't give up on me just yet, Sir."

Sharon opened her trial binder on the defense table. She heard the cheap plastic creak between her fingers as the courtroom doors opened behind her. She felt a prickle ride up her neck. She turned her head to see Captain Pamela Hunt pass through the gallery to the other side of the bar, her auburn hair and crimson nails dancing like a red flag in front of a tormented bull.

Sharon thought back to the first day they had met, when Casper had ordered the class to remove their gloves and Hunt had tried to hide her covered hands behind her back. Every day she got away with that awful nail polish she seemed to grow bolder. Started believing she could push the rules and hang on to that lingering sense of individuality and entitlement. That sort of mindset that had no place in the armed forces. It might not catch up with her today or tomorrow. But it would not go unnoticed forever.

Sharon anchored herself in her seat, gripping the edges of the binder in her hand. She knew she would never be a sharpshooter. She would never have the physical strength or stamina for dangerous field work. But she still had her opportunities to perform her own sort of heroics. This was her service. This was why she wore the uniform.

"All rise." The bailiff bellowed from behind her and she stood with the rest of the courtroom.

"Please be seated." The military judge stepped through his chamber door and seated himself in the elevated box directly across from her and Casper. He scanned the room and paged through the memoranda on his desk, adjusting a pair of thick black frames over his nose.

"Good morning everyone. My name is Judge Hirsh, I will be presiding over the case of the United States v. Major Benjamin Lee Casper. Counsel for the government and for the defense both being present, are there any issues to be addressed since we last adjourned?"

"No your honor." Hunt stood and answered.

"No your honor." Sharon did the same.

"That being the case, we are now prepared to proceed to trial. Bailiff, you may bring in the panel."

The bailiff opened the heavy courtroom doors and one by one, a line of six aging officers entered the room. They walked stiff and proud, all donned in their formal attire. They sported elevated ranks and prestigious titles, passing through the gallery and filing into the raised seats on the far right side of the courtroom. They had stone faces, lined with war stories and hard egos. They settled themselves into their places, looking resolute and untouchable, as if encased in glass.

The president of the panel sat in the center, a full bird Colonel's rank fixed to his shoulders. A pair of Lieutenant Colonels sat on his right and left hand sides, with a line of Majors filling up the rows behind him.

Sharon felt their severe stares falling down on her. Every officer in the room around her, from the major that sat beside her to the red-haired captain that aimed to put him away, wore at least one rank above her. She found herself at the bottom of an intimidating food chain, but still recognized that she wasn't the one with the most to lose.

She was still collecting her thoughts when the military judge snapped his gavel and called the proceedings to order.

"The panel has now been convened. All parties are present. Is counsel ready to proceed?" He asked the two attorneys.

"Yes your honor." Hunt responded.

"Yes your honor." Sharon followed with a swift intake of stale air.

"Very well then. This court martial has been convened to determine whether the defendant, Major Benjamin Lee Casper, is guilty as charged of the following crimes under the Uniform Code of Military Justice, Article 118, Homicide, by intentionally firing a weapon three times at Captain James Anthony Mann, now deceased. We will begin these proceedings with opening remarks from the government counsel, to be followed by defense counsel at their election. Captain Hunt?"

Captain Hunt stood and found her way to the podium in the center of the courtroom. She set a large binder full of notes on the stand and curled her hands around its edges, hiding her unauthorized nail polish from the president and the panel.

"Mr. President, members of the panel." She looked towards the panel with flat, detached eyes and opened to the first page in her notes. "As I look at your uniforms, I can see that all of you have served overseas. Some of you have commanded troops. And more than likely, all of you have lost soldiers in combat. The pain that comes with this kind of loss is intense and surreal. And tragically, it's something that we've become accustomed to. As members of a professional military, we learn to cope and we carry on. But as tragic as it is to lose a soldier in combat, the circumstances that have brought you all here today are equally tragic. Because this soldier, Captain James Mann, wasn't killed by enemy fire." Her voice vibrated with the slightest touch of trauma as she sounded out the familiar name. "He was beaten and later murdered by one of our own. By someone who never learned to cope." She turned towards Casper and her corneas narrowed into calculated slivers. "The defendant, Major Benjamin Lee Casper, has also served multiple tours overseas. He's also lost people who were close to him. But unlike most of us who wear the uniform, he wasn't able to put the trauma of war behind him. He let it ravage his mind until he could no longer tell the difference between friends and enemies, between combat and civilian life. And ultimately, gave in to his delusions, killing a fellow soldier."

Sharon's pulse thumped as she listened to Hunt speak about strength. About coping and dealing with loss. She hadn't earned the right to wear a combat patch on her right sleeve. She wasn't pinned with any combat awards. She had no battle scars. Her nails were perfectly manicured and her uniform was pressed and clean, with no concerns about a screaming mortar coming through the window and shattering her world.

Sharon set her hand on top of Major Casper's. She felt his fingers flinch beneath her touch, almost as if stung by the simple kindness.

"The evidence that will be presented at trial today will convince you that Major Casper had the inclination, the opportunity and the ability to murder Captain James Mann, first beating him in the parking lot of a bar on Veteran's Day and then hunting him down on post and killing him in cold blood." Hunt's narrative was full of stark images and every word hit like a loaded fist. Every member of the panel could visualize the weight of Casper's clenched fingers breaking against a tender face, his long reach connecting with a fragile ribcage. Already, Sharon could imagine the sounds echoing in the space between her ears. "The defendant had no reason, no justification for taking Captain Mann's life. In fact, he has no memory of the events at all. Because in his mind, he's still wandering the streets of Mosul, hunting invisible killers and mistaking innocent people for terrorists."

Hunt closed her notes and glanced towards the panel, cool and satisfied. "I thank you for your attention."

"Does the defense counsel wish to make an opening statement at this time?" Judge Hirsch spoke as Captain Hunt reclaimed her seat behind the prosecution table.

"Yes Your Honor." Sharon stood and advanced towards the podium, her heart beating a steady flutter that she could feel in her neck and fingers. So many times she'd come to the defense of soldiers who were war weary, who'd been torn to shreds by the things that they'd seen and experienced. They'd been broken by war. Only to be accused by the brass at the top of being soft. The very people who surrounded themselves in sheltered bunkers and heavy security as they ordered others in harm's way, shaking their heads at the damaged souls that came back to them. She coiled her fists and let the anger well up in her fingers.

"Your Honor, Mr. President and members of the panel." She opened her notes on the podium in front of her. It was her job to dilute the sharp images that Hunt had created. To dull the edges and immerse the picture in a fog of chance and uncertainty. "With all due respect, this prosecution is nothing more than a witchhunt."

The words ripped a solid tear through the proceedings. Sharon wavered a bit on her heels, the sudden pitch in her voice surprising even herself. "Major Casper joined the service at eighteen years old. Because he believes in this country. Because he believes in the values that it stands for. He's put his life on the line over a thousand times, in order to protect those values. And yet there are those who would hold it against him that he cares about the soldiers that he's lost. That he's damaged from the things he's seen. That he's guilty of some unbearable weakness because he's not 'coping and carrying on.'" She glanced back at Hunt, a lost flame re-igniting under her skin.

"Captain Mann was murdered on Veteran's Day, but even after a thorough investigation the prosecution doesn't know who killed him. They simply aim to point the finger at someone with a checkered history, who's suddenly become disposable due to his war trauma.

The government will present plenty of evidence today that Major Casper is unstable. But they will not present to you any evidence definitively tying Major Casper to the scene of the murder, because there isn't any.

It is my job to prevent you from confusing the issues that are presented to you today. To prevent you from letting your emotions or your instincts guide your decision. To prevent the automatic jumps in logic that serve us so well in every other context from putting an innocent man in prison. To prevent you from filling in gaps with expectations or assumptions. To remind you that evidence of hostility or trauma, without more, is not evidence of murder. Those are the values that Major Casper fought for. That is the reason that we all wear the uniform."

Sharon closed her notes and returned to the defense table, her fingers still shaking as she took her seat beside Casper. His eyes were warm like bright stones melting into the center of his pale skin, and for a brief moment she felt like something she said had reached him and reignited some buried impulse to fight.

# Chapter 51
## Fort Leavenworth, KS (2014)

"It was still pretty dark when I got to the trail. It was cold. I didn't see any other runners that morning." The tall sergeant major swiveled in his chair with every response.

"About what time did you reach the trail?"

Captain Hunt asked a string of routine questions. Lieutenant Sharon took simple notes on the responses. Major Casper tried to tune out the thousand irrelevant sounds and details colliding all around him. The soft scratch of papers rustling, the hush of chairs on rollers sliding across the sleek floor, the smell of Grace's strawberry chewing gum filling up his wandering mind.

"It must have been around 5:00 a.m. I usually make it to the trail by 5:00."

"And what happened when you reached the trail?" Hunt continued.

"I noticed a few broken branches near a bend in the road. Looked like something heavy, maybe a deer or some large animal, had barreled through. I slowed up to take a look and that's when I saw the body."

There was a repetitive tick coming from behind the witness stand, likely nothing more than the wristwatch of the sergeant major who had discovered Mann's lifeless body. An anxious beating that pulled Casper into a senseless trance.

He tried to detach himself. To step outside his body and lose himself in the white lights overhead. He scanned the room for possible escape routes. Unguarded doors or windows. Distracted security detail. Furniture that might stop a stray bullet. Pens and office equipment that might be converted into weapons.

"Did you recognize him?"

"No Ma'am. I'd never seen him before. But I knew right away that he was dead."

"What convinced you that he was dead?"

"I saw the bullet holes. And his eyes." The sergeant major's voice dropped a full octave and he played with his ticking watch as he answered the question. "I've seen dead men before. Overseas. There was nothing left behind his eyes. He just looked dead. He was cold and stiff and looked like he'd been dead for at least a few hours. Been beaten up pretty badly too."

Casper inhaled and he felt his body drop back in his chair, the stiff leather confining him to the earth and floor. He watched Sharon's white hands criss-crossing the paper in front of her. The silver sparkle of the bright ring on her finger danced in front of him. It occurred to him that she should be the last thing on his mind. That the questions and answers unfolding in front of him would determine the rest of what remained of this borrowed life. And he was still tormented with how she felt about him. He could spend the rest of his days locked away in Leavenworth Penitentiary and consider himself saved if she would only lift the darkness that had gripped him since the night he attacked Mann in that filthy bar.

"You don't have to cross-examine this guy." He leaned in and whispered.

"I'm going to cross-examine everyone." Sharon continued jotting down fragments of questions.

"He doesn't know anything. It's a waste of time."

"Will you just let me do my job?"

Casper straightened himself. He toyed with his own wedding ring, tasted the hint of strawberry that had wrapped around his brain, mingling with the lilacs and the dust of the desert. He felt as if the earth were shifting, all his fears bubbling to the surface and merging with the constant ticking that buried the sergeant major's testimony. He slid one finger over the tiny scar in his right palm, where the bottle had left its indelible imprint. He let the stored breath out of his lungs and leaned towards Sharon again, closer. His voice quieter and almost frightening.

"Did you really mean what you said in your opening?" He looked into her placid eyes, searching for the smallest sign of redemption.

"Why are you asking me this now?" She turned her eyes from him, burying herself in the notes in front of her.

"You made it sound as if it didn't matter if I were guilty. That you'd still be here, even if I'd done something, . . . truly unforgivable."

"I don't know what you're talking about Sir." She refused to lift her head.

"How can you still pretend to not know what I'm talking about?" His eyes flashed and she froze in place, bent over her marked up folders and papers. "You really think war is an excuse for doing something unforgivable?"

He watched an eerie chill grip her. She was sucked into a sharp silence that was barely broken by the sound of the judge's gavel.

"Lieutenant Sharon." The judge shouted. "Does the defense wish to question the witness?"

"Only a few questions, your honor." Sharon flipped the pages in her scrambled notebook and stood to address the sergeant major. The unavoidable ticking surged and filled up his head, the dark matter still swirling around, waiting for an answer.

"Sergeant Major Patterson. You said you were wearing headphones, while you were jogging, is it fair to say you wouldn't have heard any passers-by on the trail ahead of or behind you?"

"Yes, Ma'am. That's fair."

Tick. Tick. Tick. Tick. The sound came louder. Stronger. Fiercer.

"And it was still dark when you reached the trail. So is it safe to say you might not have seen if there was anyone on the trail ahead of or behind you?"

"Yes Ma'am. There may have been someone there. But I didn't see or hear anyone."

Thump, Thump, Thump, Thump. The ticking became footsteps of infantrymen on a road march, weighed down by decades of pain and forgotten sacrifice.

"You said you noticed the bullet holes immediately, but did you take the time to sweep the area for the weapon that had fired those bullets?"

"Believe me Ma'am, I searched the woods in all directions while I was waiting for CID to arrive. There was no trace of it."

Bang, bang, bang. The comforting sound of boots on gravel became the unmistakable ringing of three round bursts and enemy fire, encapsulating him on all sides.

# Chapter 52
## Fort Leavenworth, KS (2014)

"Did you perform an autopsy on Captain James Mann?" Captain Hunt focused on the gangly woman behind the witness stand. She was dressed in a navy blue pants suit. She had short dark hair and a pair of wire-rimmed glasses, balanced awkwardly on the bridge of her nose.

"I did." Dr. Nelson lifted her glasses as she answered.

Hunt tucked a loose strand of red hair behind her ear. She could see Casper out of the corner of her eye. He sat guarded in his chair, his eyes darting across the room at invisible ghosts. His hands coiling open and shut as tension filled his muscles.

She hoped he was frightened. That he could feel the walls finally closing in on him. She didn't concern herself with whether he was guilty. Justice didn't have to be perfect. It didn't have to be immediate or precise or even completely understood. As long as it restored balance. The rest was just details.

"And what did you determine was the cause of death?" She turned back towards Dr. Nelson.

"Captain Mann suffered three gunshot wounds, two in the chest, and one in the left side of the forehead just above the inside corner of the eye. Based on my review of his injuries, I was able to determine that Captain Mann's death was principally the result of this gunshot wound to the head. My examination revealed that the bullet pierced the premotor cortex, which would have led to loss of motor functions, possible seizures and extensive blood loss. In my estimation, the damage done would have led him to expire within 20 to 25 minutes, if not sooner. The bleeding from the other two gunshot wounds was significant, but the most immediate trauma and the most life-threatening was the shot to the head."

"May I approach the witness, Your Honor?" Captain Hunt spoke directly to Judge Hirsch, who nodded once over his bifocals.

"You may."

Hunt stepped out from behind the podium and walked towards the witness stand, her slim fingers pressed against three grisly photos of Captain Mann's corpse. She'd stared at these same photos over and over again until she was numb to them. Until she'd burned away every feverish emotion they might have inspired. She felt an immature satisfaction in handling them now. In channeling the discomfort they carried to those who hadn't yet scrubbed themselves of their ugly import.

"I am now showing you what has been marked as Government Exhibits 15 through 17 for identification purposes. Do you recognize these photographs?"

"These are photographs I took of the victim prior to performing the full autopsy."

"Can I have a projection of the images please Sergeant Cole?" Hunt nodded to her paralegal in the gallery, and the woman quickly moved through the courtroom and turned on the projector. In a short moment, the three photographs were displayed in crisp detail on the white screen beside the coroner.

The panel of six officers absorbed the shadows of the soldier's death, their stoic jaws hiding a dulled sense of empathy. Hunt saw the way the images made even hardened emotions swell and stir, momentarily paralyzing rational thought. She was pleased with the way she'd immunized herself against those very same feelings. The way she'd convinced herself that she could make everything right by putting Casper away.

"Can you describe for the panel what you see in these photos?"

Dr. Nelson adjusted her glasses as she turned to look at the images, taking her time to read every bruise and feature before speaking. "You can clearly see the three gunshot wounds here. The two chest wounds are indicated in photos 1 and 2. Photo 1 depicts the points of entry, in the front of the victim's chest. Photo 2 depicts the exit wounds on the victim's back. The head wound is pictured in photo 3. There was no exit wound, as the bullet fragmented and remained lodged in the brain. All three wounds have a clean, round point of entry, with more ruptured flesh near the exit wound. I was able to identify minimal traces of gunpowder on the victim's skin. There was a very faint residue near the chest wounds, and a larger amount surrounding the head wound. Which can be accounted for by the fact that the victim's shirt would have shielded much of the residue. But the fact that any residue was identified at all tells us that the victim was shot at a fairly close range."

"Did the victim present any injuries besides the three gunshot wounds?"

"Yes. The victim clearly had some significant lacerations to the face, consistent with what was documented in the police report. The victim's jaw was broken and his ribs on the left hand side were cracked in several places."

"Did you uncover anything else during your examination?"

"Yes, I also discovered a significant inflammation of the capillaries in the skin surrounding the victim's eyes and mouth. This is consistent with exposure to an inflammatory agent, such as that found in most pepper sprays. There was some slight swelling of the soft tissue in and around the eyes and throat, likely a reaction to the chemical agent."

"Your honor, I'd like to enter these photographs into evidence as Government Exhibits 15, 16 and 17." Hunt recited as she returned to her place behind the podium.

"Does the defense have any objections?" Judge Hirsh turned towards the defense table.

"No, your honor." Sharon stood just long enough to answer the judge and then sat back down, still scribbling notes into her paperwork.

Hunt watched with a grim curiosity, trying to grasp what perverse understanding of patriotism kept bringing her to this man's defense. She was built with the same muscles and tendons as everyone else. And somewhere, in some unacknowledged corner of her heart, she felt the same nasty feelings of spite, jealousy and vengeance that everyone else felt.

"Exhibits 15 through 17 are accepted into evidence."

"I have no further questions your honor." Hunt nodded to Judge Hirsch and returned to her seat, a curious anxiety spreading through her veins as Lieutenant Sharon shuffled her notes.

"Does the defense wish to question the witness?"

"Yes, your honor." Sharon stood on cue and moved with steady steps towards the podium. "Dr. Nelson, you mentioned in your testimony that the victim had been shot at close range. Can you estimate how close the shooter was when he or she pulled the trigger?"

"I couldn't say for sure." Dr. Nelson adjusted her glasses again and stared intently at the photos beside her. "In my experience, you wouldn't see this amount of residue on a victim if the shooter was more than 10 or 20 feet away."

"And you're fairly certain that it was the head shot that killed him?"

"Yes. When that bullet hit, the victim would have fallen fairly quickly and he would not have gotten up again."

"So there would be little need to shoot the victim twice more in the chest if he had already been shot in the head?"

"That's correct."

"So it's fair to say that the victim was shot twice in the chest and that the shot to the head came last?"

"Objection, your honor." Hunt stood from her chair the moment she saw where Sharon's questions were leading, forming the initial building blocks of a shaky defense. "Speculation."

"I'm asking for Dr. Nelson's expert opinion, your honor." Sharon lifted her eyes from her notebook to answer Judge Hirsch. There was an unrestrained energy in her response. That overdeveloped passion for the underdog that was still swimming in her veins and working over her sense of reason.

"Overruled." Judge Hirsch responded. "You may answer the question Dr. Nelson."

The doctor's response time was slower. She seemed alarmed at the possibility of her words being twisted and used against her. "Yes, assuming that the shooter intended to kill Captain Mann, and barring any unnecessary emotional or good measure shots to the torso, I'd say it's likely that the shot to the head was the final shot. There would be little need to continue shooting once the bullet pierced his skull as it did here."

294

"And if the shooter was only 10 to 20 feet away," Sharon continued in a calm cadence from behind the podium, "and still had to fire off three shots in order to take the victim down, it's safe to say the shooter was a pretty bad shot, wasn't he?"

"Objection, your honor." Hunt stood again, a little fiercer and less controlled. "Outside the witness's area of expertise."

"Sustained." Judge Hirsch agreed. "I gave you a pass on the last one counselor. From now on you'll stick to the witness's area of expertise."

"Yes, your honor." Sharon nodded and returned to her notes.

Hunt turned her grey eyes toward the detached panel of officers. She could sense the electrical activity firing behind their closed eyes, making the exact connections that Sharon had intended. She didn't need Dr. Nelson to answer the question. The suggestion had already made its way into their calculations.

"Dr. Nelson, you discussed the victim's broken nose and cracked ribs as being consistent with the fist fight described in the police report, isn't that correct?"

"Yes, that's correct."

"Were you able to determine when those injuries were sustained in relation to the shooting?"

"I was not. There was substantial bruising that occurred around the affected areas. It would have taken some time for this degree of swelling and discoloration to appear. I wasn't able to determine the exact time of death, but I'd say that the other injuries, the broken nose and cracked ribs, likely occurred anywhere from 6 to 12 hours prior to the victim's death."

Hunt watched Casper straighten in his seat. He seemed content to watch Sharon. His eyes flooded with mysterious emotions that popped and danced against his colorless skin. His posture, his mannerisms, everything about him looked guilty. But he also looked remorseful when he stared at Sharon. Perhaps even traumatized. At times he appeared to lose control of his own mind and body. At times he was pitiable. But not innocent. Nothing about him suggested innocence.

"Based on your examination, did the victim have healthy bones?"

"They were typical of a man in his age group, yes." The doctor answered.

"Would it take a good deal of force to break Captain Mann's ribs and jaw?"

"Yes, it would have taken a series of fairly strong blows to inflict this kind of damage."

"So, whoever broke Captain Mann's bones like this was a fairly effective fighter?"

"Yes I would say that's that case."

Hunt was ready to spring from her seat a third time. She couldn't see the end of Sharon's questioning or the invisible seeds that she was planting in the panel members' minds, but her confidence was powerful and unnerving.

"I have nothing else your honor." Sharon closed her notebook against the podium, leaving Hunt with the sinking feeling that something had slipped by her. That she had missed a crucial opportunity to shape the minds of the panel. To mold them in favor of her own dogma and keep them from seeing things she didn't want them to see. "No further questions."

# Chapter 53
## Fort Leavenworth, KS (2014)

Sharon never believed that Casper was telling her everything. That he hadn't recovered slivers of memory that he preferred to keep to himself. But she wasn't prepared for a confession, if that's what he meant when he whispered in her ear that he'd done something *truly unforgivable*." His secrets had cost her the opportunity to insist on a sanity hearing and claim that he was too damaged to appreciate right from wrong. Now she was left with nothing but to argue against science and DNA.

"For the record, please state your name and organization." Hunt had already sworn in her next witness. Sharon could still feel the archaic formality echoing across the courtroom walls, as if it somehow insulated the proceedings from deceit. But she felt it, swirling and vibrating all around her. Heard it breathing in the chair next to her.

"Special Agent Simon Dang. CID, crime lab." He had tame brown eyes and a tuft of deep black hair near the front of his forehead. His pale skin had a sleekness to it that suggested most of his time in the Army had been spent behind desks rather than out in the field. He was dressed in a suit and tie, still shielded behind the civilian attire that hid his rank and pay grade from the rest of the courtroom.

"What do you do for CID, Agent Dang?"

"I specialize in Forensics. Our lab analyzes physical and biological evidence collected during criminal investigations. DNA samples, fingerprints, weapons' tracing, all of that comes through our office. I've been with the crime lab for about four years now."

"And did you personally perform forensics work for the homicide investigation of Captain James Mann?"

"I did."

Sharon tried to focus on the busy notepad in front of her, looking for traces of undisputed logic in the strings of smeared ink. She listened to Casper breathe beside her. Watched his fingers dance along the desk and his eyelids twitch as if he were preparing to shut out the world.

It was possible that Matt was right about her. That she was too close to be objective or rational with the facts. She didn't even realize how immersed she was until Casper's cryptic questions had shattered her crystalline fortress.

"Can you tell the panel what that forensics work consisted of?" Hunt reached around the edges of the podium again, her gaudy red nails clashing against the cherry wood.

"CID detectives recovered three pieces of evidence that were sent to our lab for testing. A black Army sweatshirt that contained traces of dried blood, a small canister of pepper spray containing latent fingerprints, and some bullet casings and fragments recovered from the crime scene and from the victim's body."

"May I approach the witness your honor?"

"You may." Judge Hirsch watched Captain Hunt step across the courtroom, an oversized evidence bag clutched between her manicured fingers.

"Special Agent Dang, I am now handing you what has been marked as Government Exhibit 24 for identification purposes. Do you recognize this?"

Hunt offered him a sealed plastic bag with a black Army sweatshirt inside. He turned the bag over a few times, feeling the soft fabric between his fingers.

"Yes. This is the black Army sweatshirt that we received from Special Agent Leon Hartman, who was the senior investigator on the case."

"What specifically tells you that this is the same sweatshirt?"

"It's been labeled with the case number, along with a brief description of the evidence and initialed by both myself and Special Agent Hartman, in accordance with CID policy."

"Is there anything noteworthy about this sweatshirt?" Hunt kept her questions clipped and brief, allowing her witness to do most of the talking.

298

"Across the front and along the zipper you can still see traces of dried blood. We were able to lift DNA samples from three different locations of the soiled fabric and perform a comparison with DNA samples obtained from both the accused and the victim. From that comparison we were able to conclude that the blood on this sweatshirt belongs to Captain James Mann."

Sharon closed her eyes as the agent walked them through the biological evidence that Captain Mann had left behind. A fragile trail to track down his killer. She fought off the flashes of gun bursts in the back of her mind. Unprovoked visions of bullets piercing Mann's chest.

Captain Hunt held out her hand to retrieve the evidence bag from the witness. "Your honor, I would like to introduce this sweatshirt into evidence as Government Exhibit 24."

"Does the defense have any objections?" Judge Hirsch turned towards Lieutenant Sharon.

"No your honor." Sharon pushed out a quiet response and returned to her seat.

"Government Exhibit 24 is accepted into evidence."

"Agent Dang, I am now showing you what has been marked as Government Exhibit 25 for identification purposes. Can you tell the panel what this is?"

Captain Hunt placed a second plastic bag in Agent Dang's hands. "This is a pocket sized canister of pepper spray that was recovered from the accused's home. It's fitted with a key ring, and had been fastened to a set of keys at the time it was recovered."

"Are you able to positively identify that this is the same canister of pepper spray?"

"Yes I am. Once again, It's been labeled with the case number, a description of the evidence and initialed by both myself and Special Agent Hartman."

Sharon found herself re-living that chilly Veteran's Day in early November, when Casper sat across from her in an empty coffeehouse in Minneapolis and told her he was being court-martialed. She remembered the clammy feeling in her palms. That same slickness coming back as Agent Dang turned over the evidence bag in his hands.

"What sort of analysis did you perform regarding this canister of pepper spray?" Hunt asked him.

"We were able to identify three intact fingerprints and a partial thumbprint. All of these were lifted and compared against the accused's prints on record. From our analysis we concluded that two of the four prints belonged to the accused."

"Your honor, I would like to enter this canister of pepper spray, recovered from the defendant's home, into evidence as Government Exhibit 25."

"Does the defense have any objections?" Judge Hirsch adjusted his glasses over the bridge of his nose.

"No objections, your honor." Sharon responded. She realized that somewhere between that distant coffee shop and the courthouse in Fort Leavenworth, she'd swallowed her own arguments. She'd lost herself in the tiny discrepancies she'd uncovered and blown them up to be bigger than they were.

She watched the expressionless faces of the elevated panel of officers, looking for hints of skepticism or bias. Any indication that they were likely to put two and two together before she had.

"Government Exhibit 25 is received into evidence."

"Special Agent Dang, I am now showing you what has been marked as Government Exhibit 26 for identification purposes. Do you recognize this?"

Captain Hunt handed him a third evidence bag that contained two bullet casings and two ugly slivers of metal that had been recovered from Captain Mann's corpse.

"I do." Agent Dang responded as he turned the bag over and examined the metal pieces. "These are the bullet casings and bullet fragments that were recovered from the gunshot wound to the victim's head. They were removed during the autopsy and sent to the lab for analysis."

"Are you able to positively identify that these are the same fragments?"

"I am. The evidence bag is properly labeled in accordance with CID policy. It contains the case number, a description of the evidence and has been initialed by both myself, Special Agent Hartman, and Dr. Nelson."

Sharon felt a metallic taste in the back of her throat that reminded her of those early morning ruck marches in Charlottesville. She remembered the long stretches of dark, winding roads with a terrific load on her back, trying to hug the heels of the person in front of her. All the while knowing that she was falling behind. She remembered the way that Casper had lifted the weight from her shoulders and helped her to find her way back, wishing that there was some way he could do the same for her now.

She watched the shake in his fingers. The way his lips moved in time to some gentle noise in his head. He'd come all this way with her. Only to give up on her as they were climbing the last hill. To unload some horrible truth that he hadn't had the courage to tell her all this time.

"And what can you tell us about these items?"

"Unfortunately they don't tell us much. We were able to identify a series of markings that are typically associated with .45 caliber revolvers, which is a fairly common class of firearm. We were unable to determine the specific make or model. CID was unable to locate a suspect weapon from the crime scene or the defendant's residence, therefore we were unable to perform the necessary test fires to identify a specific weapon."

Sharon thought about the unregistered weapon in the shoebox from Iraq. The filed off serial number and the three rounds in the chamber. The missing piece that would have sentenced Casper to life in prison, had CID gotten to it before Grace did.

"Your honor, I'd like to enter the two casings and bullet fragments identified as Government Exhibit 26 into evidence."

"Does the defense have any objections?" Judge Hirsch asked.

"No objections, your honor." Sharon mouthed the words, but little sound escaped. She had agreed to defend him because he needed someone to fight for him. Because he'd fought for them. Because he'd been broken and someone needed to take responsibility for him now. None of that had changed. And yet she couldn't shake the feeling that she'd been used and deceived.

"Government Exhibit 26 is received into evidence." The judge watched Captain Hunt retrieve her third evidence bag from the witness, focusing his attention on the unauthorized splash of color at the ends of her fingers.

"I have no further questions your honor."

"Captain Hunt." Judge Hirsch called her name before she had a chance to make it back to the prosecution table. Sharon saw a strange tightness in his jaw. He glared again at the color on her nails, a rigid curl crossing his forehead.

"Yes, your honor?" She turned towards the bench.

"You care to tell me how you get away with that fingernail polish in the MP Brigade?"

His eyes went straight to her hands, a self-incriminating statement painted across the tips of each and every finger. Hunt froze in place, her trim nails coiled around the evidence bag. Her auburn hair melting into the sudden flush in her cheeks.

"I suppose, Sir, that it's because I'm the only female officer in the Brigade." The blood pulsed in her face. She sweated under the heavy stares of the six court-martial officers, distracted by the patent proof of insubordination.

"It ends today." Judge Hirsch instructed her. "The next time you step into my courtroom I want that nail polish gone."

"Yes your honor." Captain Hunt returned to her seat with a bowed step.

In one unexpected moment, she had lost favor with the judge and jury that held Casper's fate in their hands. It wasn't enough to change facts or perceptions, but it meant that details mattered, and gave Sharon a small reason to hope. Even if the idea of real justice had gone sour. Even if it had morphed into a raw hurt that she would be forced to carry on her conscience.

"Does the defense wish to examine the witness?"

"Yes, your honor." Sharon stood in place, retrieving her papers and heading towards the podium. She opened her notebook on the flat space and focused on the pale CID agent, looking to expose every seedy ambiguity that had fooled her into believing that Casper was innocent. "Agent Dang, on direct examination, you identified a black sweatshirt that was taken from Major Casper's residence?"

"Yes. That's correct." He answered.

"You told the courtroom that this sweatshirt contained traces of dried blood that belonged to Captain James Mann?"

"Yes, that is what the DNA test revealed."

"Were you able to determine, based on any of the tests you ran, when the blood came in contact with the sweatshirt?"

"No Ma'am, we don't have a reliable method of determining that."

"Were you able to determine how the blood came in contact with the sweatshirt?"

"Not in this case. At times we can examine the size and shape of the blood spatter to determine what direction the blood came from, what sort of weapon was used or how much force was behind it. In this case there was a significant amount of smearing and no reliable pattern was left for analysis."

Sharon blinked off images of those incriminating red droplets, smattering the front of Casper's sweatshirt. She still cared for him, guilty or not. She still felt a surge of tenderness when she was near him. She still felt a pang of injustice at the thought of him sentenced to life in Leavenworth. Locked away in a gray cell, with nothing to fill his hours but memories of IED blasts and soldiers who didn't make it home.

"So there was no determination as to whether the blood spatter came from a bloody nose, versus a gunshot wound to the chest?"

"No, there was not." Agent Dang responded in simple sentences that made him easy to control.

"Is it the case then, that the blood stains on the Army sweatshirt could be the result of the fist fight at the Eagle Lounge and not the shooting?"

"Yes, that is a definite possibility."

"Did you test the sweatshirt for traces of gunpowder?" Sharon flipped to another page in her trial notebook, catching sight of Captain Hunt out of the corner of her eye, re-positioning herself in her cushioned chair and trying to hide her fingernails under her desk.

"Yes, we did."

"And what were the results of those tests?"

"The results were negative. We were unable to find any trace of gunpowder on the clothing."

"Are you typically able to detect traces of gunpowder on clothing after a shooter has fired a handgun?"

"Not always, but it is something we do see. It depends on how recently the weapon was fired and how carefully the clothing was handled prior to collection."

"And in this case, considering the fact that there was no gunpowder found on Major Casper's clothing, and the blood may very well be due to the fight at the Eagle Lounge, is there anything about this sweatshirt that definitively ties the defendant to the shooting of Captain Mann?"

"Objection, your honor." Hunt stood with a loud charge. "Defense counsel is putting words in the witness's mouth."

"Overruled." Judge Hirsch lowered his eyes in Hunt's direction, still full of petty contempt. "You may answer the question Agent Dang."

"Not definitively, no." The CID agent gave a crisp response.

Sharon made a quick notation in her notebook and flipped forward to another page full of draft questions, dates, times, and other facts in evidence. She watched the lined faces of the six officers processing the witness' testimony, working her way towards a firm and reasonable doubt.

"Agent Dang, you previously identified what has been accepted into evidence as Government Exhibit 25, a pepper spray canister taken from Major Casper's home, is that right?"

"Yes, that's correct."

"You stated that you lifted three fingerprints and a partial thumbprint from the canister. Two of those prints, were compared against Major Casper's and found to be a match?"

"Yes, that's correct." Agent Dang nodded.

"Do you sometimes handle your wife's keys, Agent Dang?"

"Objection." Captain Hunt stood again. "Relevance."

"Overruled, Captain." Judge Hirsch silenced her a second time, nodding to the witness to proceed.

"Frequently." He answered with a dry throat.

"And do you imagine that by doing so you leave your fingerprints on some of the keys and attachments." Sharon flipped to the next page and worked through her last set of questions. She could hear Casper's breathing behind her. His lungs stirring up the air between them like smoke signals, trying to communicate something unspoken and unspeakable in the midst of a crowded room. The sound was enough to convince her, if only momentarily, that he was still capable of lifting some of the weight from her shoulders.

"Yes, I imagine that I do."

"And in your opinion is there anything unusual about finding a man's fingerprints on his wife's keys?"

"Objection, your honor." Hunt stood again, her grey eyes pulsing and the tips of her fingers gripping the underside of her desk. "This is opinion testimony."

"Agent Dang is a subject matter expert, your honor." Sharon responded.

"Overruled." Judge Hirsch ruled again without even looking in Hunt's general direction. "Take a seat Captain."

The red haired prosecutor sat down with fire under her breath.

"Not necessarily." Agent Dang answered.

"Were you able to determine when Major Casper handled those keys?" Sharon looked towards the panel of officers, trying to identify unique characteristics in each of their faces. Traces of individuality or emotion that told her they could relate to human error and random chance. Soft spaces that she could appeal to. For a moment, that glimmer of hope grew stronger. It started to feel palpable and real.

"No, that couldn't be determined."

"So it's entirely possible that Major Casper didn't handle those keys until after the shooting, isn't that correct?"

"Yes. That is possible."

"I have no further questions your honor."

Sharon closed her notebook and lifted her eyes from its thick, worn pages, just as she heard the echo of Casper's voice spinning across her membranes a second time.

*"You really think war is an excuse for doing something truly unforgivable?*

# Chapter 54
## Fort Leavenworth, KS (2014)

"Do you recognize the defendant in this case?"

Agent Hartman's breakfast swirled in his stomach. He recognized Ben's pale face and blonde hair. The curious eyes and familiar shape of his old friend, but not much beyond that. Ben was seated on the wrong side of the courtroom, with an inexperienced first lieutenant at his side. A pretty face who didn't even have enough sense to demand a psych evaluation before she put a man's life on the line.

"I met Ben Casper when we were a lot younger. We went through Ranger School together, met up again in Mosul and then again when he moved out to Fort Leavenworth with his wife. He was assigned as the Chief of Military Justice here on post. He was a good prosecutor and a good soldier." Hartman felt the accidental use of the past tense scratch across his throat. He made a conscious effort to craft his next words differently. "I have a lot of respect for him."

Captain Hunt turned in her eyebrows as she flipped through her notepad. "What can you tell us about the investigation you performed this past Veteran's Day?"

"I received a phone call, alerting me that a body had been discovered in the woods, about a mile or so from the rec center. It looked like a homicide, so I came into the office."

"And what did you learn when you came into the office?"

"We learned that the victim was a soldier. Captain James Anthony Mann. A JAG officer stationed at Fort Riley, Kansas. His wallet was left in his pants pocket with his credit cards and identification on him, so it didn't look like a robbery. Because we hadn't located a suspect weapon at that time, I also did a quick registration check to see if the victim owned a personal handgun. He had, in fact, registered a fourth generation Glock 21 with arms registration at Fort Riley."

"And what caliber handgun is a fourth generation Glock 21?"

"It's a .45 caliber Ma'am." Agent Hartman nodded.

"Were you able to locate the victim's personal handgun?"

"No Ma'am. We obtained a search warrant for the victim's home and the defendant's home, but the weapon was never found."

"What steps did you take after that?"

"I reviewed the police blotter to find out if there had been any recent activity that might give us a clue who this guy was or what had happened to him. Sure enough, we found that a man matching the description of the victim, was in a bar fight earlier that evening. An ID check confirmed that it was the same individual."

"And did the police blotter identify the assailant from the bar fight?"

Hartman straightened in his chair, feeling the unwelcome sting of the prosecutor's stare. He turned towards Ben for the first time, who lifted his eyes just enough to make every word a struggle. He sat waiting, patiently, for the honest assessment of an old friend to fall down around him.

"The police blotter identified Major Benjamin Casper as the assailant." Hartman forced the answer past his jaw.

"Were you surprised to see Major Casper's name on the blotter?" Captain Hunt continued.

"I was."

"Were you given any indication that Major Casper might be prone to violence or acts of aggression?"

Hartman felt a warm knot of guilt tightening in his stomach, pulling him in opposite directions. He needed some ambiguous way to answer truthfully, without abandoning someone he loved behind a cold iron door. "I knew that Ben was struggling. He never talked about it, but I saw it in him. Sometimes I worried about him."

"Were you worried that he might hurt someone?"

Hartman glanced down at Ben, a soft apology in his eyes. "I was more worried that he might hurt himself."

"That's not what I asked you, Agent Hartman." There was a stiffness in the captain's voice. An overwhelming lack of sympathy. "Were you worried that he might hurt someone else?"

Hartman took his eyes off Ben and stared at the floor. He fell back in time to that merciless day in August, when Ben called to confess that he had attacked his wife. He considered the reckless chance he'd taken in keeping the entire thing off the record. How lucky he had been that Grace's body hadn't been pulled out of the woods, instead of some unknown captain.

"Never intentionally, Ma'am." Hartman answered honestly. "Never like this."

Captain Hunt leaned over her notebook and made a simple swipe with her wrist, no doubt dotting her notes with checkmarks over all of her necessary admissions.

"How did you respond to the news on the blotter?" She continued.

"I sent some of my agents to bring Major Casper in for questioning."

"Did you, at any point, start to reassess whether or not Major Casper was capable of intentionally hurting another soldier?"

"Objection your honor." The inexperienced lieutenant finally jumped to her feet. "Leading the witness."

"Overruled." Judge Hirsch responded. "You may answer the question, Agent Hartman."

He knew exactly how the captain expected him to answer. He was silent just long enough to make her anxious. To make her question whether the little checkmarks she'd been collecting were enough to label a man a murderer. "Yes. It crossed my mind that he might be more troubled than I thought."

"What steps did you take after you questioned the defendant?" Captain Hunt turned back to her notes.

"I instructed Major Casper not to leave post and I obtained a search warrant for his residence."

"Why did you instruct him not to leave post?"

"It's standard practice to place an administrative hold on someone when they're involved in a criminal investigation. It ensures that the person will remain available for questioning and charging if necessary. It's also a measure against interference with potential witnesses and the loss or destruction of evidence."

"And did the defendant leave post against orders?" The woman lifted her cool, grey eyes towards him.

"Objection your honor. Irrelevant and prejudicial." The lieutenant stood and bellowed another futile objection. At least she had some fight in her.

"The evidence shows that the defendant had a motive and an opportunity to dispose of evidence in the case, your honor."

"I'm going to allow it. Your objection goes more to the weight the evidence should be given, Lieutenant, but it is admissible. You may proceed, counselor."

"I'll repeat the question for you Agent Hartman." The prosecutor turned a set of unfeeling eyes in his direction, waiting impatiently for him to answer. "Did the defendant leave post against orders?"

"Unfortunately he did." Hartman watched Captain Hunt make another bold checkmark on her notepad. "He had already booked a flight for the Veteran's Day weekend. He boarded the flight and left the state against orders. I accompanied the investigative team to his home, which was searched while he was AWOL."

"Is it possible then, that while you were searching the defendant's home for the handgun that killed Captain Mann, that the defendant was disposing of that same handgun in another state?"

Hartman felt his muscles tense in the soft leather chair, forced between admitting an obvious, un-redeemable truth or sacrificing his credibility. All in the hopes of rescuing someone he'd already lost, months or possibly even years ago. "I'd have to say it is possible."

"I have no further questions for this witness, your honor." Hunt closed her notebook and stepped away from the podium with a grim satisfaction dancing along the edges of her lips.

"Does defense counsel wish to question the witness?" Judge Hirsch turned towards Lieutenant Sharon.

310

"Yes, your honor." The first lieutenant headed towards the podium with her own stack of paperwork and unchecked boxes. She looked towards him with a guilt ridden determination in her eyes. The sort of look that told him she wanted Ben to be innocent as much as he did. But she knew too much to believe her own arguments.

"Agent Hartman, you stated on direct that when Major Casper left the state against orders, he had already booked a flight for the Veteran's Day weekend, is that correct?"

"Yes. That's correct."

"So there would be no reason to suspect that he left the state in response to being brought in for questioning?"

Agent Hartman was relieved by the simple question. For the opportunity to redeem a small piece of his previous testimony. "Unless he knew that he was going to be brought in for questioning months in advance, I don't see how that's possible."

"Are you aware of the reason he left the state?"

"Yes Ma'am. Every year on Veteran's Day Major Casper goes home to put flowers on the grave of a soldier he lost in combat. He never misses it." Agent Hartman felt the words flutter off his tongue. He watched the faces of the stoic panel members for some trace of softness or sympathy, and found nothing but stale curiosity. "For the past five years, since Staff Sergeant Khoury was killed, Major Casper's been there on every Veteran's Day. Every Memorial Day. And anything you can think of in between. This Veteran's Day was no exception, homicide investigation or not."

"You stated earlier that you attended Ranger School with Major Casper?"

"Yes, that was just before he transferred into the EOD."

"Can you explain for the panel what kind of training you received during Ranger School?"

"Lots of intense training. Long days and long nights in the field, very little food and very little sleep. Long patrols, marches with heavy equipment, reconnaissance missions, defending against ambushes, performing tactical raids, Airborne and Air Assault missions. It was a hard environment, but Ben was good at it."

"Did you receive training in hand to hand combat as part of your curriculum?" The lieutenant looked up at him with sharp blue eyes.

"We did." Hartman nodded easy.

"Is it fair to say that Major Casper had the training and skills to break someone's jaw and crack their ribs in a fist fight?"

Hartman drew in a long breath before he answered. He was guarded and skeptical, but somewhere between her first objection and the calm determination in her eyes, he found a way to trust the young lieutenant. "Yes he did. And more if necessary."

"Can you think of any reason why someone as highly trained in hand to hand combat as Major Casper would need to pepper spray his victim to take him down?"

The question sank into his skin and he closed his mouth mid-breath, suddenly recognizing the inconsistency.

"Objection, speculative." Captain Hunt stood from her seat.

"Overruled." Judge Hirsch responded. "You may answer the question."

"Given what I know of Major Casper," Hartman's answers came a little lighter. More gracious. "He could've taken that captain down without much effort. Let alone a canister of pepper spray."

"You stated that you worked with Major Casper when he was Chief of Military Justice?" The lieutenant flipped forward in her notes, her eyes buried in layers of dates and facts and other baseless assumption. "What sort of a lawyer was he?"

"He was one of the better prosecutors I've worked with." Hartman nodded. "He saw details that others missed. Things that seemed irrelevant. Some of that extreme focus came from deployments. You have to be very mindful of your environment during combat operations. Because you never know what might save your skin or get you killed. He never really lost that ability when he came home from Mosul. He still sees and hears everything around him."

"With that kind of attention to detail," the lieutenant briefly looked up from the scribblings in front of her. "And the legal training Major Casper's received as a JAG officer, how likely is it that he would forget to wipe the fingerprints off a canister of pepper spray that he'd used while committing a murder?"

"Objection, your honor!" Captain Hunt stood again, her voice echoing through the open courtroom.

"Sit down Captain." Judge Hirsch responded. "I'll let him answer."

Hartman waited for the easy nod of the first lieutenant across the room, resisting the urge to hope or feel too much as he fished for an answer. "In hindsight, it doesn't seem likely at all that he'd forget something so simple."

"In all your years of training with Major Casper," the lieutenant wore a convincing confidence, almost erasing the deep doubts that he recognized when she first approached the podium. "How often did you see him fire a weapon?"

"Many, many times." Hartman nodded soundly. "Too many to count."

"And how was Major Casper with a handgun?" She pursed her lips as she waited, hanging on his next words.

"He was an ace with both the M16 and the M9. Shot an expert almost every time we qualified."

"And based on what you know of Major Casper's proficiency with a handgun, was he typically able to hit a 50 foot target on the first shot?"

"Major Casper could typically hit a 100 foot target on the first shot." The answer fell easy from him lips. Quick and potent as he realized the implications of the question. "At 10-20 feet, there's no way he would've missed."

He watched the subtle glow in her skin subside as she closed her notebook, swallowing a familiar and enduring discomfort. She was cool and adept at pointing out the flaws in logic. The empty conjectures that might have made a difference in any other case.

If he could shake the vision of Ben's hands around Grace's neck, it might have been enough to convince him.

# Chapter 55
## Fort Leavenworth, KS (2014)

"I met Captain Mann in Charlottesville, Virginia. We were classmates." Aaron Cade raised an eyebrow towards Pamela Hunt, remembering every vivid detail about her. The hint of a smile danced across his placid eyes. "I didn't get to know everyone, but a few of them left lasting impressions."

"Did you know Major Casper?" Hunt kept her grey eyes buried in the notepad under her fingertips, avoiding the lurid smiles and intimate shadows that moved between them.

She'd left Charlottesville without saying goodbye. Without even looking in his direction. She brushed the mud from her uniform and walked away from that final formation before he had a chance to call her name.

"I knew *of* him more than I knew him. Major Casper wasn't very social. He never came out for dinner or drinks with the rest of the class. He would go for a run, or he'd drink by himself in his room."

Cade glanced towards Major Casper, calm and disinterested behind the defense table. He looked for echoes of the lunatic that had attacked Captain Mann back in Charlottesville, and saw very little trace of him. Just a cool, detached stare.

"Did you consider Captain Mann a friend?"

"A friend?" Cade mangled the word as he pictured Mann's pretty face before the bullets hit. "Not really. There were only a handful of us who had any real military background. Who had actually seen combat. We had that in common, but not much else."

Mann had found a way to turn her against him. It was the only palatable explanation. He'd recognized the way he twisted facts the morning she came to his room, hot and begging for someone to lie to her. The one petty falsehood that he'd fed her. Everything else had been genuine.

But it was enough. It gave her an excuse to go running into his arms like every other shallow girl he'd tried not to care for.

She'd chosen that pretty demeaning face over something wholesome and real.

"What sort of things did you talk about with Captain Mann?"

"Nothing of any substance. We worked out in the mornings and sometimes we would go out for drinks after class. Sometimes we'd exchange war stories or argue about things we were studying in class. We didn't talk about family or religion or anything important. We just passed the time together. That's all."

"How about after graduation?" Captain Hunt finally looked up from her notes. Her face as pretty and complicated as he remembered it. Firm and steady on the surface, while hiding some unpredictable fury just below the skin. "Did you keep in touch?"

"No more or less than anyone else I met in Charlottesville." Captain Cade sat upright in the witness chair, waiting for the redhead to start digging into the small bits of information that she wanted from him. A part of him wanted to keep it from her as long as he could. Tease her with it. Make another polluted trade that would transform her into something delicate and tender in his arms again. The way it had once been.

"Were you aware of a history of violence or animosity between Major Casper and Captain Mann?"

Cade watched Sharon's eyes flash as the question filled the room. She didn't object or stir from her chair. She'd already fought and lost the battle to keep Charlottesville out of the courtroom. He was the only one that could keep it out now.

They were both there when it happened, but held some silent conspiracy to keep their personal involvement hidden from the court. With Casper's sorry soul caught in the crossfire. He hadn't expected to feel any sympathy for the major piled in the chair beside Sharon, but he could see the invisible wounds that he was still fighting. The psychological equivalent of the twisted skin along his face. "They weren't particularly fond of each other. But to the best of my knowledge there was only one instance when it became violent."

"What can you tell us about that instance?" She needed him to give the court some sort of proof. Something to make their burden a little lighter. So they could dispose of a man's life without feeling the weight on their consciences.

Captain Cade had never fully realized how small these courtrooms were. How easily a trained prosecutor could stare down a witness, intimidate them into caving, lying or lashing out.

"It was over the Thanksgiving holiday." He saw the weight of his answer hit the air with the force of a three round burst. There was a painful anticipation in Hunt's dancing fingers. A recoil suspended in Sharon's eyes. "Those of us who didn't go home got together for pizza and beer on the fifth floor. There were only a handful of us there. Captain Mann was one of them. So was Major Casper."

"What happened between Major Casper and Captain Mann that night?" Pam stepped out from behind the podium, taking a dangerous step towards him. It reminded him of the way she'd reached for his hair and pulled his lips into hers.

"Major Casper had been drinking. Everyone had. He seemed a bit dazed. Mostly staring off at nothing. He was like that. He always seemed a little unpredictable or off balance."

"At what point did things become violent?" Her hungry eyes were making him warm and uncomfortable. He was still surprised at what he was willing to do for her.

"I don't remember anything about the conversation that night. I don't remember what provoked it, if anything. I think we were talking about the Geneva Conventions or war crimes. Something like that. But at some point, Major Casper busted open a beer bottle and pounced on Captain Mann. He knocked him to the floor and wrestled with him until he had his arm around his neck. He was holding a piece of broken glass next to Mann's throat."

He saw the change in the faces of the panel members. The thick breaths that followed their first taste of unambiguous evidence. The first hint of motive and delirium that would color their judgment and taint the rest of the evidence.

"Do you remember what specifically Major Casper said to Captain Mann at that time?"

"Objection, your honor." Sharon stood from her chair, reaching for the only source of protection she could find. "Hearsay."

"It's an excited utterance, your honor." Hunt snapped back.

"Overruled." The judge nodded towards him. "You may answer the question Captain Cade."

It dawned on him for the first time as he watched her fight the objection, why she was so hell bent on putting Casper away. Why she was so willing to abandon her principles and her career for this moment. He saw the snap in her eyes. The reckless thirst for vengeance. It wasn't the stalled promotion or the clipped wings that had inflamed her. It was every traitorous feeling she had for Mann. The sick beginnings of love.

"None of it made sense." He turned his eyes back towards Hunt, mixing pieces of anecdotal truths between the facts and omissions. He knew it was love because it didn't seem to matter whether it was intentional. It didn't even matter if he was guilty. Someone had murdered the last pretty face that she trusted, and she needed justice. "He was just rambling like a lunatic having a flashback."

"Were you afraid that he would hurt Captain Mann?" Her grey eyes looked suddenly cool and sad, and he wondered if she was still grappling with the fact that Mann was dead. Coming to terms with the fact that her surviving spite was so petty and irrelevant.

"I think all of us were. I think he very well would've if one of our classmates hadn't reached out and calmed him down. Brought him back to reality." Cade looked directly at Lieutenant Sharon, a visible chill running up her spine. "Too bad she wasn't around when Casper found Mann at the lounge that night."

"What happened after Casper 'came back to reality?" Hunt set her eyes into him.

"He just sort of looked around him like he had no idea where he was or how he got there." Cade's eyes glazed over as he revisited everything he had seen and heard, trying to pick apart the relevant details. He lifted a hand towards the permanent scar on his face, coming to terms with a brutal reality. "He wasn't there with us that day. He was in Basra or God knows where, but he wasn't in Charlottesville."

"Did Casper say anything when he realized what he'd done?"

"Objection, your honor." Sharon stood from her chair again.

"Overruled." Judge Hirsch responded and nodded towards Cade to proceed.

"Mann was standing behind me with his hands around his neck, shouting about how Casper had nearly killed him." Cade let the words out dark and slow, watching the incriminating phrase leave its mark on the panel of officers. "Casper said, 'Next time I may."

Cade saw Casper's chest deflate at the sound of his own abandoned threat, and a futile surge of pity moved through him.

"No further questions, your honor." Hunt closed her notebook on the podium with a loud slap, the sound leaving an indelible imprint across the room. His twisted craving for her swelled and burned. He was still captivated by the fire in her, but was recognizing for the first time just how dangerous that fire could be.

# Chapter 56
## Fort Leavenworth, KS (2014)

Sharon pulled Casper's bar tab from the night of the murder and labeled it as Defense Exhibit G. She stared at the fading blue ink, a simple tally of three draft beers, priced at 3.25 each. Two of them had been subtracted from the total bill with an abbreviated justification under the reduced subtotal. *Veteran's Day.*

"The prosecution calls Mr. Winston Cooper."

Sharon listened to the slow footsteps of the old marine moving through the gallery. He walked with a slight limp and a brave attempt to hide it. He waddled towards the witness stand and turned towards Captain Hunt, his right arm raised as if he'd been through this process before.

"Do you swear that the evidence you give in the case now in hearing shall be the truth, the whole truth and nothing but the truth, so help you God?"

"I do."

Mr. Cooper never gave the same account of the assault at the bar. Pieces of information were always lost or rearranged. Miniature facts and details distorted by the fading memory of an old man. He didn't remember anything about a girl that started the fight, if there ever was a girl. All he could do for her was confirm that Casper hadn't had any more to drink than what was listed on his bar tab. That he wasn't so drunk he couldn't shoot straight.

"And for the record you are Mr. Winston Cooper of Leavenworth, Kansas?"

"I am Ma'am."

"Please be seated."

The old man took some time positioning his bad leg in the witness chair, then nodded towards the prosecutor, indicating that he was ready to begin.

"What is it that you do for a living, Mr. Cooper?"

"I own the Eagle Lounge just outside Fort Leavenworth. I've been bartending out there since I left the marines." Mr.

Cooper had the raspy voice of an old marine, worn, gray and proud. "I wanted to do something that kept me close to the military, and the bar was right off the installation."

"Do you recognize the defendant as one of your customers?"

Mr. Cooper stared across the courtroom towards Casper, sparks of recognition settling in the corners of his eyes. "I do Ma'am. He was one of the only officers that came into the lounge. Most of the guys were enlisted men. He came in about two or three times a week. Never caused any problems. He asked that I call him Ben, so that's what I called him."

"Do you remember a particular night that Ben did cause you problems, Mr. Cooper?" Hunt was restrained behind the podium, still trying to hide the unnatural color of her fingertips from the rest of the courtroom.

"I do. It was Veteran's Day weekend." The old man put a hand against his forehead, pressing his memory for the broken details. "Didn't expect anything like that from Ben, but I suppose that all of us have a history somewhere. Guess it just caught up with him."

"Do you remember how much Ben had to drink that night?"

Sharon reached for the bar tab in front of her and glanced up at Mr. Cooper. He didn't always remember what day it was. He didn't always remember Ben's name. He was more lucid today. It could only work in her favor.

"I couldn't say Ma'am." He shook his head, the clouds re-assembling behind his eyes. "It was Veteran's Day, I usually gave the soldiers a free drink or two."

Sharon suppressed a relieved smile. The free drink or two had already been annotated on Casper's bar tab. She scribbled out a simple note to herself to follow-up with some additional questions on cross-examination.

"Is it also possible that Major Casper had a few drinks before he showed up at the lounge?" Hunt tried to build in some additional ambiguity, some way to discredit her own unpredictable witness.

320

"It's always possible Ma'am." The old man nodded. "But I didn't suspect it."

Sharon watched Casper's thick hands, balanced on the table in front of them. She was compelled to reach for him. To warm his cold fingers in hers. To comfort him. To promise him that they would walk out of here together. But it was too soon. They were still too many questions and too many arguments from the end.

"Do you remember Ben getting into an altercation that night?" Hunt bit her lip, hanging on the hope that the man's borrowed memory wouldn't give out before she reached the end of her questions.

"Yes Ma'am. There were quite a few soldiers that came in that night, but I remember the one that started the trouble." His face lit up with the parade of sudden memories, lifting the tired wrinkles around his eyes and mouth.

"What do you remember about him?" Hunt leaned into the podium.

"Well I noticed that he was an officer as well. A captain if I recall correctly, from out of town." Mr. Cooper reached again for his forehead, grasping his long eyebrows in his fingers as he spoke. "I didn't catch his name. He wasn't too talkative, with myself or anyone else."

"May I approach the witness your honor?" Hunt raised her eyes towards Judge Hirsch, who nodded back in response.

"You may."

"Mr. Cooper, I am now handing you what has been marked as Government Exhibit 29 for identification." Hunt handed exhibit 29 across the witness stand to Mr. Cooper, a polished photo of Captain Mann in his dress blues, before his jaw was broken and his forehead was shattered. "This is a photograph of the victim in this case, Captain James Anthony Mann, can you tell us if this is the gentlemen you saw at the Eagle Lounge that evening?"

"Yes Ma'am." Mr. Cooper looked over the photo with certainty in his eyes. "That's him alright."

"Thank you Mr. Cooper." Hunt retrieved the photograph with a twisted relief and returned to the podium. "Can you tell the panel how the altercation between Captain Mann and the defendant started?"

Sharon felt her heart skip, alarmed that she might finally hear some new detail that she wasn't ready to hear. About the woman or the words that had lodged under Casper's skin, turning him from just another morose veteran, into something untamed and lethal.

"I can only tell you what I saw Ma'am. And I didn't see everything because I was tending bar." Mr. Cooper reasoned in his same raspy voice. "I didn't notice much of anything until I heard a bit of shouting coming from the end of the bar. I turned and saw this captain harrassing Ben."

"Can you describe what you mean when you say 'harassing,' Mr. Cooper?"

"He was up in Ben's face, Ma'am. Talking real close and heated. I couldn't quite hear what he was saying, but it looked like things might get physical." Mr. Cooper leaned forward in his chair, shaking his head as the images flooded through him. "I waved to my bouncer to come over and break it up, but things escalated before he got there."

"How did things escalate?" Hunt gripped the edges of the podium, her red nails still exposed and unnatural.

"Ben got up from his chair and laid a solid hit across the captain's jaw. I remember it now." Mr. Cooper's fingers lay still on his wrinkled forehead, a lost memory creeping across his sour face. "The captain called him a racist. That's what triggered it."

The unexpected word echoed through the walls and drummed hard against Sharon's ears. She felt the sound sucked out of the air around her. The courtroom muffled in a thick blanket of silence.

"Did you say racist?" Captain Hunt was as stunned as everyone else.

"Yes, I believe that's what started it." Cooper nodded without hesitation.

"Ben." Sharon reached for Casper's sleeve and whispered into his ear. "What is he talking about?"

"He's not talking about anything." Casper's voice was flat and abandoned. "He's just an old man with a bad memory. And bad hearing."

"I have to do something." Sharon started flipping through her trial binder, searching through his earlier statements for something to break apart the unexpected twist in his testimony.

"Let it go Jamie." Major Casper shut her binder and held it closed.

"The captain fought back as best he could. They started knocking into things, people, chairs." Mr. Cooper was still talking, remembering things that he shouldn't be remembering. "My bouncer and a few others finally stepped in and dragged the two of them out the door. By the time I made it to the parking lot the captain was already beaten up pretty badly. He was on the ground and Ben was sort of hovering over him, with his collar in his hands, like he didn't know what to do with him. He looked dazed. Maybe even a little scared."

"Did you speak to him?" Hunt started digging for more information. More brutal facts from the opened stores of the old man's memory.

"I told them both that they best get off the premises before the police arrive." The old man answered, a distant, wispy sound returning to his voice. "I know what it's like to lose your military career over a mistake, Ma'am. I didn't want that to happen to these two officers."

"Did you have any concerns that the defendant might attack the victim again once he left your bar?" Captain Hunt lay her brutal question at the old man's feet, with little regard for what he might answer.

"No, he seemed to have snapped out of it, whatever it was that got a hold of him."

A wave of unhealthy suspicion flooded Sharon's limbs and throat. She stared down at Casper's heavy hands, weighing down her notes and evidence. The simple gold ring the only bright spot in the folds of his calloused skin. He had told her the fight was over a girl. But something far darker was hidden in details below his hands. Something that he didn't want her to see.

"I have no further questions, your honor." Hunt closed her notepad and returned to her desk. Her face had a rare quiet to it, her skin coated in a slippery sweat from the unanticipated testimony.

"Does the defense wish to cross-examine the witness?"

"No, your honor."

Casper's voice echoed beside her, though she couldn't truly tell if the words rang throughout the courtroom the way they did in her head. He kept his hands locked over her trial binder, warning her not to question one of the most toxic pieces of evidence against him. To walk away and let it hover in the air, unraveling everything she'd woven together. She waited in the barren silence for the judge's gavel to strike as she fumbled for a string of words that might save him.

"What haven't you told me Ben?" She shook her head and the room spun about her. "If it wasn't over a girl, then what was it?"

"We have nothing further to offer your honor." She heard Hunt's voice break through the silence and the gavel strike the solid wood beneath the judge's sturdy hands. "The prosecution rests."

# Chapter 57
## Fort Leavenworth, KS (2014)

"What are you hiding from me Ben?" Her voice faded in and out.

He tried to contain the shaking in his fingers. He paced about the confined space like an animal who's suddenly realized that's he's trapped. Still searching for some way to climb or burrow his way out.

He felt Jamie's eyes following him as he moved. He felt her bare nails tapping against the binder in her hands. He tasted the scent of lilacs that wafted from her wrists. Sights and sounds that he might not hear again after closing arguments. He realized how little time he had left with her. To tell her the things that mattered. To confess what he needed to confess. It was down to a small handful of hours.

"I'm trying to help you! Why the hell won't you let me?" He heard her voice ring through the room again. Time and space expanded and contracted in his brain.

He continued pacing the floor, noting every loose cord, every soiled coffee mug, every discarded pen. Trappings from prior cases. Previous defendants who always thought they'd have more time. Who didn't start to feel the government's grip around their neck until the end date was staring back at them, definite and inflexible.

"Why did you ask me here?" He watched her lips move as she berated him. "What do you want from me?"

He gauged the length of the walls, the height of the ceiling, the distance to the unguarded slit beneath to door. He listened to the busy sounds of footsteps and whispers on the other side. The heavy wood was solid and thick.

"I needed this time with you." He shook his head towards the floor. "I needed to find out if it was true."

"If what's true?! I'm not here to hold your hand as you hang yourself!" He heard a dull thud as she dropped her binder on the table in the center of the room. The sour notes in her voice rattled the cold chambers in his heart. "You think Randy would be proud that you're using him as an excuse to ruin what's left of your life? You think that's what he wants his legacy to be?"

The shaking in Casper's hands spread to his chest. He reached for the comfort of the weapon slung over his shoulder and found it wasn't there. The emptiness weighed on his fingers. His heart muscle was heavy and bloated with the blood of his dead staff sergeant.

"Why did Mann call you a racist?" Jamie's lips were dry and angry.

The trial, the testimony had all hit far too close to the bone. He'd been wandering this one-way road since that last explosion in the desert that completely dislodged his future. The sleepless nights that followed. The cold sweats. The times that he'd woken up in the middle of the supermarket, or on the front lawn, with an invisible weapon drawn, the grass under his feet no match for the hot sand in his head. The merciless memory of the last night he'd spent in Grace's bed. When he'd awoken just in time to find her soft neck in his hands. To see the glossy fear in her eyes and feel the soundless pulsing under his fingers. It was all inevitable after that. The separate rooms with the locks on the doors. The pepper spray and the midnight trips to the bar. The blood on his clothes belonging to a dead man in the woods. The questions and charges. There was no other way for this to end but to find himself standing in this very room, staring down his former life.

"He didn't call me a racist Jamie. He called me a rapist."

He finally forced the words past his stomach and watched her slowly pull away. Her skin turned a milky gray as she wrapped her arms around her midsection and drew back towards the cement walls. "What are you telling me Ben?"

"You have to tell me what happened that night." He moved towards her, finally ready to give up the uncertainty for a firm, immutable truth. The jury outside the heavy door was no match for the judgment in his own head. Holding things against him that he couldn't remember or couldn't face. This was his last chance to force the answer out of her. Even if the sentence was as ugly as he suspected.

"What did you do? To who?" She looked at him with a dark trembling in her throat.

"Did I hurt you that night?" He reached for her shoulders, felt the soft tissue give beneath his rough fingers.

"You're scaring me Ben." She shook her head.

"Did I hurt you?!" He shouted out loud and the words came out like bricks, falling and smashing against the ground at her feet. He slipped to the ground with them, losing himself in the mash of rubble and broken stone.

"It's me, isn't it?" She looked down at him amazed. "Mann was talking about me."

Casper couldn't find the words to answer her. His mouth was full of powder and lye. He reached for the holster on his belt and connected with the cold 9 millimeter pistol that hung at his hip. He slid his finger along the metal grip of the weapon at his side. The weight felt good in his hands. Comforting and safe. He understood now why Randy didn't want to leave it behind. Why he couldn't bury the temptation to use it.

"We were never even together." She practically whispered.

The sound broke across his back like blast waves carried by a lost wind, breaking up molecules in his brain. He felt the sting of sand and saltwater stirring in his empty eyes, blurring his vision. He'd been waiting for an explosion that didn't detonate. That stalled and sputtered and smoked in the hot desert sun.

"It's not possible." He nearly choked on the words, afraid of the hot swell of relief that threatened him. "He told me how frightened you were."

"I was terrified." She nodded, the gray in her skin dissolving as the words formed like tiny bubbles beneath her breath. "You were drunk and you were lonely and I thought you might be desperate enough to do something awful. But that wasn't what you came for."

"What did I come for?" He felt a slick trickle of sweat run down his face as the cramped spaced grew warm and unbreathable.

"For solace." She whispered. "For hope. I touched your shoulder and you wrapped your arms around me. I held you against my chest and you cried with me. You told me about the day that you lost Randy."

The subtle lavender scent was the only thing that kept him anchored in the present. The only thing that could compete with the pull of the desert and the very real sensation of his finger resting on the imaginary trigger of his old M16.

He felt the heat swell around him, and without warning he was back in the desert, reliving that same five miles of wasted terrain. His mind was caught on the last lonely ride with Sergeant Khoury, recycling the footage in a never-ending loop. The convoy would never reach its destination. He would never complete the mission. It would never give him peace.

# Part Eleven:

# Blast Waves

# Chapter 58
## Mosul, Iraq (2008)

"Sir." Randy's voice pulled him upright just as the nausea was beginning to set in. He felt a hand against his shoulder and turned to see the staff sergeant looking at the bloody, smoky mess underfoot. "You shouldn't be doing this alone Sir."

"Lewis has got security."

"That's not what I meant." Sergeant Khoury had a familiar shake in his eyes as he looked about the wreck. "Were you able to find anything?"

"Nothing you should see." He reached into his pocket and pulled out the dog tags he'd retrieved. "Take these. I know you and Hestler were close."

Casper handed the burnt dog tags to his staff sergeant, who closed his fist over the curled metal. He stifled a slight gag as the smell hit him.

"Did you finish clearing the area?"

"Yes Sir," Khoury buried his hand in his pocket, hiding the disturbing trinket where he wouldn't have to see or think about it. "I think I found something."

"Take me to it."

Khoury stepped away from the destroyed MRAP and moved in the direction of one of the larger side streets. Casper followed, his rifle muzzle pointed towards the surrounding buildings, the infantry squad assembling around them as they moved. The streets were smoky and quiet as the sun started its long descent into the sandy horizon. Casper glanced at the grim faces lining the streets, wondering if this was the last sunset of his unremarkable life.

"Alright Khoury. Let's see what you found."

"Just about a quarter mile up the road Sir." Sergeant Khoury started down the long road, the infantry following in quick succession, rifles out and focused on the windows and rooftops all around. "It looks like some kind of dead animal balanced on the curb."

The squad filed down the street until it came into view, coming to an abrupt halt about 100 meters down the road from the suspected IED.

"Good catch, Sergeant." Casper laid eyes on the carcass up ahead, the hollowed out shell of a stray cat, small and deadly.

"How do you want to handle it, Sir?" Lewis asked.

"Vang, I need you to call in the Humvee. Give him our location and the location of the bomb so he doesn't come from the other direction."

"I can put the suit on." Randy made the calm announcement. His voice was steadier than it had been on the way in. As if the burnt dog tags in his pocket had given him the resolve he needed. Far more motivating and far more effective than carrying around an unregistered handgun. "You said the next one was mine. I want to take it. For Hestler."

"There's too many people around for the suit." Casper brushed passed him, ignoring whatever idle promises he'd made. "We'll try the robot first."

Private First Class Vang radioed the Humvees and dispatched them to the unit's new location. Casper kept his eyes trained on the moving bodies in his periphery, sliding in and out of view. He focused on the sounds of flies buzzing about him as his body armor swelled with the heat. He waited for the usual cues that preceded a firefight. Odd shouts, backward footsteps, the telling clank of a round being dispatched into an empty chamber. All three came at once.

"Captain, I think we have company." Sergeant First Class Lewis called over his shoulder. His rifle was pointed towards the men and women who loitered in the streets, their movements listless and strange as they wandered in and out of range of the explosive. They were angry and bewildered, and passively threatening. An old woman cried and a young man shouted in incomprehensible panic and confusion. In the distance, a middle-aged man stood alone and detached from the gathering crowd. Any one of them could trip the device from where they stood, but only one of them was waiting just outside the edge of the blast radius, as if he were the only one aware of the danger.

The young man moved towards the team with harsh Arabic sounds coming from his mouth. He moved forward until Lewis gave a loud and convincing order that stopped him in his tracks.

"What the hell's he want from us Lewis? Talk to me." Casper hollered with his eyes still set on the isolated man in the distance. He wore a long, brown and yellow desert garb and his skin was tanned and leathery, half hidden by a thick beard and a reddish head scarf.

"I'm not getting all of it Sir. I think he said he's looking for his son."

"His son is dead. And I think he knows that." Casper shifted his focus between the foreign faces, trying to discern a legitimate threat from a desperate and bereaved father, as if there was any real difference.

Lewis hollered back a quick, unintelligible phrase in the man's native tongue. The shouting continued and Casper felt the hairs on the back of his neck bristle.

"He wants to see him Sir." Lewis shouted back. "He wants to see where the boy's at if we know."

"We can't do that Sergeant. He needs to leave the area unless he wants a bullet in his head. You can tell him that from me." He scanned each of their war worn faces, trying to ferret out the bloodthirsty from the unfortunate stragglers. "All these people need to leave."

Lewis kept his rifle trained on the young man's chest as he hollered the captain's message. The bereaved man took one steady step back, mixing in with the rest of the crowd that lingered around them. They all swayed and stared and made no movement to disburse.

Casper re-focused on the idle man in the red turban, standing awkwardly still and distant from the eerie crowd. Casper thought he saw a vulgar crease form along the man's brow, wearing an indelible groove into his forehead. There wasn't much pain or suffering in his expression, but it was infused with over

100 years of rebellion. He stood in that same defiant posture just long enough to convince Casper that he was their triggerman.

Unless the desert heat and adrenaline were toying with him. Making him see hatred and terror when there was only uncertainty and suspicion. Casper felt for the drop gun in his holster beneath his body armor. The only insurance he needed to put a bullet in someone's head right then and there.

He took a sincere look at his surroundings. The Humvee appeared around the corner with its heavy wheels crushing the gravel as it pulled up. The infantrymen fanned out around him and the vehicle, each man keeping their weapons trained on the loose bodies around them. They lurked in dark corners and broken windows that lined the streets. There simply weren't enough of them to cover every potential threat.

"Khoury, put your weapon on that man and don't move it." Casper spoke into Randy's ear and motioned towards the man in the red turban. "He's the only one who's standing at a safe distance from the explosive and that makes me nervous."

"Roger Sir."

Casper watched Randy lift his rifle and aim it at the center of the man's red turban, the weapon moving up and down with his breathing. Randy was still young enough and sensitive enough to hesitate before pulling the trigger. The veins in his neck were filling and emptying quickly. Sweat lined his forehead all the way to the back of his neck.

"Just try to keep your weapon steady Khoury. Breathe. You got this."

"Yes sir." Khoury echoed.

Casper slung his weapon over one shoulder and opened the door of the Humvee. He pulled out a sturdy case full of equipment, opened the lid and began assembling the delicate arms of the IED robot. His big fingers were slippery with sweat and fumbled with the precision gadgets. He filtered through the sounds around him as he worked, tense soldiers chewing the insides of their cheeks, boots stepping back and forth in the gravel, heavy breathing, the repetitive clanking of metal on metal, minutes ticking by on his stopwatch as the daylight waned.

The young man was hollering again, emotional and stricken. The garish notes exploded around him, filling his head and breaking his concentration.

"Lewis can you keep him quiet?!"

Lewis shouted back at the man and the heated words melted into the background. Casper powered on the robot and set it down in the center of the gravel road, then picked up the remote and dispatched it towards the IED on the right hand side.

The little robot wheeled down the street in front of all the sunken eyes, its whimsical whir rising through the heavy desert air. The robot rolled forward about 60 meters, closing in on the dead animal parked against the curb when it dipped into a small divet in the road and fell on its side.

"Fuck!" Casper spat and nearly dropped the remote in his lap, watching the tiny machine flail its useless arms in the desert air. He saw a sullen dread fall across the dry faces all around him. He felt their resignation settle into the sand.

"Let me put on the suit Sir." Randy called back.

"Not now Khoury. Your job is to keep your weapon trained on that man's head."

"Then let me get the robot."

"I can't let you do that." Casper shook his head.

"I got this Captain." The conviction in the kid's voice was almost convincing. "Someone's going to have to step into the blast radius. Either to diffuse the bomb or to grab the robot. I'll move twice as fast without the suit weighing me down."

Most days Casper was able to convince himself that his crew was the best at what they did. That they were smarter than the bombs. Smarter than the insurgents. That was what had kept their casualties so low. Training. Discipline. Maturity. Skill. Most days he believed it.

Then there were moments like this. When all of the bluster melted away, and all he was left with was dumb luck.

Casper watched the man with the red turban nestled in the shadows, caught in the crosshairs of Khoury's rifle. He narrowed his eyes against the bitter crowd and the lost father begging to see the scorched remains of his son. He glanced ahead at the dead cat on the side of the road with explosives hidden in its skin. They weren't going home until that bomb was either defused or detonated. And the triggerman would never give them the chance to diffuse it.

It wasn't too late to take him out, based on nothing more than the truth in his gut. To put a bullet in his head and leave the drop gun behind as evidence of something that everyone knew, but couldn't prove until he reached for the trigger. To end this thing before he was forced to make a decision that would end someone's life.

The suit was no guarantee that the blast wouldn't kill you. In some cases it just made you a broader target, slow and bulky and pressure-cooked inside your own personal oven. But stepping into the circle without the suit was suicide, unless by some miracle you were able to make it out before the wave hit.

Casper knew he couldn't hold off a man who was willing to die for a cause. But the man in the red turban was standing at a distance for a reason. He intended to live to fight another day. He wouldn't pull the trigger as long as Casper kept him in his sights.

"Alright, Khoury." Casper turned towards his young Staff Sergeant. "You're going to go in and out on my orders, do you hear me?"

"Roger Sir."

Casper honed his rifle on the man in the distance, his large, dangerous hands were determined and steady, unshaken by the smell or the blood in the streets.

"Alright, I'll cover you. Go."

Casper kept the man's leathery hands between his iron sights as Randy took his first step out of the security of his squad and towards the downed robot.

"Lewis, you tell that guy he keeps his hands where we can see them. He moves his hands a fraction of an inch and he's a dead man."

Lewis began shouting to the man across the blast radius, but the sounds were swallowed up in the hot wind blowing through the streets.

Casper kept his weapon ready to fire, watching out of his peripheral vision as Staff Sergeant Khoury stepped into the blast radius. He crept quick and low, crouching towards the dirt until his gloved fingers connected with the thin metal of the robot's mechanized arm. He uprighted the tiny machine with one motion, and breathed out as the wheels connected with solid ground.

"That's it Khoury, you got it. Now get your ass back here." Casper yelled.

The triggerman's leathery hands were still idly perched in front of him. His fingers twitched lightly as he watched the EOD team from a shady recess, a little over hundred meters in the distance. Staff Sergeant Khoury stood in place as he adjusted his rifle, stepping forward and then backward again, and knocking the robot back to the ground.

Casper heard the dismal sound of the robot hitting the dirt a second time. He watched the faces around him turn grim and ugly. He felt a numbness in his throat as the time crept by, and the odds started stacking against them.

"Let it go Sergeant." He shouted. "You need to get out of the blast radius, now."

"I can get it Captain." Khoury shouted back.

"I said get back here now! That's an order!" Casper kept his weapon fixed on the hands of the man with the trigger as he edged into the blast radius after Khoury.

The harsh Arabic picked up again, demanding and defiant. The sharp, guttural sounds echoed through his ears as Staff Sergeant Khoury lowered himself back to the ground, reaching for the body of the robot, when soundlessly, the triggerman slid his hands out of sight.

It took only the flick of a wrist, the fraction of a second to trip a button.

Casper saw the simple movement as he stepped into the edge of the blast radius. He pulled the trigger, dispatching his first round toward the man's forehead.

He saw the waves tear Randy in pieces, solid fragments of flesh were hurled towards his feet, and a thick stream of dark blood whipped across his face. He felt the gooey mix hit the back of his tongue and swallowed before his reflexes kicked in.

The next thing he heard was a horrible ringing in his ears as a wave ripped through his hands and feet. He felt the heat and pressure of being scorched in a microwave, the molecules in his body mixing and colliding. A sick, painful shock.

He fell to the ground coughing and sputtering. When the ringing subsided he heard boots and metal shuffling across the heavy air. The shrill sound settling into his bones as he lay helpless in the blood-soaked dirt.

"Captain! Jesus! Sir, all you alright?!"

He felt hands and arms falling across his head and torso. He was raised up onto his knees, where he could see the mess of pulp in front of him. Randy's torso had melted and oozed from inside his body armor, still intact enough to resemble his shape and size, without limbs or head. Casper's hands felt slick and oily. He glanced down at the blood, none of which was his, then he tasted it.

## Part Twelve:

## Soldier's Heart

# Chapter 59
## Fort Leavenworth, KS (2014)

"Ben. Ben, look at me!" Sharon held Casper's face in her hands, kneeling on the ground beside him and applying the softest pressure to his temples, massaging away the bad memories. Her fingers were cool and flighty against his hot skin. She made tiny, repetitive circles as she lost pressure in her chest, like her heart was leaking. A slow, rhythmic drip.

Casper was still dragging his hands along his face and forearms, trying to wipe away the phantom blood that stuck to his skin.

"You're safe here." She grabbed his hands and pulled them aside. "I'm here with you. It's over."

She watched his pupils dilate as his eyes adjusted. He stared back at her with a haunted expression. A sudden trickle of déjà vu crept along her neck.

All this time he'd believed he assaulted her. Abused her in the harshest way. She was the something '*truly unforgiveable*' that he'd confessed to. Not murder. Not anything real.

"You're not a ghost Ben, do you hear me?" She firmed up her grip along his wrists. "Look at me, feel my hands. You're still here. I'm still here."

Casper grabbed her hands and squeezed her thin fingers, slowing the anxious dripping in her heart.

"I killed him." The sound broke through his parched lips. His sturdy frame shook and the words seemed to scorch him from the inside. "I sent him out there knowing he wouldn't come back."

"What happened to Randy is not your fault." She shook her head and held tight to his hands. She could almost see her firm voice wrapping around him, cradling him in a soft, soothing embrace. "You did what you were asked to do. You're not responsible for any of this."

"I had his gun in my holster Jamie!" He looked up at her with tired, unforgiving eyes. "All I had to do was pull the trigger and he would've come home with us."

"You don't know that! There were too many hands and too many faces all around you. You'll never know that." She pulled his head against her chest and held him close, weaving her soft fingers through his blonde hair. "You have to see a doctor Ben. For me. For Grace. You have to talk to her."

"I can't do that." His voice shook as he pulled himself away and got to his feet. He stood motionless in front of her, distant and unsettled. "I don't want to hurt her."

"You have to try." She stood upright and shook her head again, watching a liquid calm return to his blue-green eyes. The rage and the hurt giving way to a deep and listless void.

"I can't ask her to forgive all of this." He stared at his own thick fingers, swelled with so much regretted violence. "I can't expect her to understand what this is."

"She understands more than you think." Sharon saw a raw strength moving beneath his muscles as he made tight circles on the worn carpet. He was still capable of healing. Still hungry for the trace of faith in her voice. "She told me about the flashbacks Ben. About the pepper spray and the separate rooms. She knows what it's like to live in fear. She knows what it's like to have dreams that won't go away."

He seemed to sink into himself as she spoke, realizing that the last of his secrets had crested and fallen. That there was nothing left between them but open air.

"She found the drop gun in a shoe box in the basement." Sharon let another intricate confession slip. There was no time left for guarded words and lies. Their last minutes together were waning away, and her heart couldn't take any more silence. "Just before Hartman came back with the search warrant."

Casper watched her with wide-open eyes, vacillating between an unwieldy shock and solid understanding. "I tried to tell her she couldn't protect me this time. But she finds her ways."

Sharon stepped towards the table and reached for her trial binder. She opened the cover and pulled the worn ISOPREP

340

envelope from its side pocket, feeling the weighty creases between her fingers. "Your ISOPREP letter was still inside with the gun. She was afraid to open it. I promised her that she wouldn't have to."

Sharon held the thick envelope out to him and he took it in his rough hands, passing his fingertips delicately across the seams. It looked as though the words of the old letter were seeping through its paper shell, making their way to the center of his pulsing heart.

"Why are you doing this for me?" Casper's words seemed to scratch like sandpaper. There was a glossy sheen to his eyes that told her his heart was either opening or breaking. "I would have gladly spent the rest of my life in Leavenworth if I had hurt you."

"You never hurt me Ben." She looked in his hazel eyes and tried to lift the sadness from his soul. "You kissed me goodbye when you left my room. That was the first and last time you kissed me."

It was more than a small tragedy. She felt the sting of regret over all that lost passion. That she never felt his lips and skin and sweat beside her. That she'd lost the opportunity to know him, soothe him. To share just a sliver of his pain.

"Why didn't you tell me?" Casper's eyes were hungry and open, feeding off the pulse of her leaking heart. "All that time standing in the mud. Thinking through everything I couldn't remember about your hair and your skin and your smell. Why didn't you tell them that it never happened?"

"No one would've believed me." She had spent too much time avoiding looks and suspicious words to believe the truth carried that much weight. She was always indicted by the traitorous lieutenant bar on her chest, calling her out for her make-believe crime. "Grace would never have believed it. You didn't even believe it."

"I didn't remember." The low notes in his voice resounded against the walls and ceiling, his hands still tenderly pressed against the envelope in his hands.

"Why did you tell her about us?" Sharon felt an old fire flare in her throat. A hot confusion that never seemed to settle or wane. "What did you say to her that night? Why did she think that we'd been together?"

"I never told Grace anything Jamie." His voice was dry and brittle, but almost frightening in its sense of conviction. "She wasn't the one who called the school."

Sharon felt more pressure release from her lungs, her leaky heart dripping faster and echoing in her ears. "How do you know?"

There was a swift, bold knock at the heavy wood door and a solid voice rang through the walls. "Five minutes. Session is scheduled to resume in five minutes."

"I would have turned myself in if Grace had made the call." Casper's eyes were strangely calm and deliberate. "I made a few phone calls to find out for sure. About a month after we were dismissed I got a copy of the school's phone records in the mail."

"How did you get a hold of that?" Sharon felt her heart ricochet inside her, capillaries and blood vessels bursting with every breath.

"I'm a major. Specialists and sergeants tend to do what I tell them."

Sharon's palms went warm and clammy, a strange pulse beating at her fingertips. His overdue confession was both ruthless and telling.

"I went through that list line by line looking for Grace's phone number. But I promise you Jamie, it wasn't there."

Sharon was silent, her blue eyes melting into a pool of confusion.

"You and I may not have been together that night, but somebody was."

# Chapter 60
## Fort Leavenworth, KS (2014)

Grace watched the solid oak door that had swallowed her husband, armed escorts standing at either side.

"Five minutes." One of them rapped his knuckles hard against the heavy door. "Session is scheduled to resume in five minutes."

Everything around her was unfolding in slow motion. The creak and moan of the courtroom doors, the steady parade of people filing past her. She closed her eyes and offered a sincere prayer to anyone that might care. It was a practice she'd abandoned somewhere between deployments, but the words came back naturally, like a sudden rush of energy bubbling up from a hot spring.

She heard the distant echo of a door latch springing and opened her eyes to see Ben step into the hallway. His uniform collar was bent and the lapels of his jacket were uneven. She couldn't allow herself to ask what had happened behind those closed doors. He may have broken down into a ball on the carpeted floor. He may have pressed his pretty lawyer up against the wall and locked her in an earth-shattering kiss. Or a choke hold. Jealousy and fear mixed through her veins like silt, slowing up the blood supply. Her fingers tingled as she lost circulation.

"Ben." She shouted across the hall and hurried towards him.

Ben lifted his head as she approached, a hint of recognition and comfort swelling in his hazel eyes.

His escorts seized up as she stepped towards him.

"I just need to straighten his collar." She ignored their stares and nudged past them, reaching for his neck and flattening the folds in the stiff fabric.

She went about her familiar routine, straightening his jacket and adjusting the creases to comport with proper military regulation, taking advantage of the opportunity to touch him again.

She resisted the urge to embrace him. Fought back the realization that his body might be taken from her at the end of the day. That she would have to adjust to an entirely new sort of emptiness. Regretting all the nights she might have had with him, had she not been so afraid of what he might do. She was finishing with the sleeves just below his wrists when he grabbed her hands.

"I never wanted to hurt you Grace." He whispered, a cool flame burning at the back of his eyes. "I need you to know that."

"I know." She held back a small fire in her voice.

"You don't have to testify." He whispered.

"Yes, I do." She breathed softly as she centered the wedding ring on his right hand. "I don't want to sleep alone anymore."

"Sir, I'm going to need you to make your way back into the courtroom." The sergeant beside them placed a hand on Ben's shoulder and began ushering him towards the courtroom doors. "Ma'am, the bailiff will come for you when you are called."

The procession of stiff bodies filed through the open doors, the slow motion speeding into a flurry of footsteps and erratic heartbeats. She jumped at the sound of the tall doors closing. Her entire being was lost in the silence the followed.

# Chapter 61
## Fort Leavenworth, KS (2014)

Casper tested his sleeves and collar, noting the care that Grace always put into her minute adjustments. His chest burned as he settled into the stiff chair behind the defense table. He reached for a swig of water.

*"I don't want to sleep alone anymore."*

The impossible phrase echoed like white noise through his ears.

The judge smacked his gavel on the desk and called the room to order. He couldn't make out any of the words that were spoken, but he felt the vibrations they made in the air around him. Every syllable passed through the tiles underfoot and sent tremors into the soles of his feet.

"The defense calls Mrs. Grace Elizabeth Casper to the stand."

Major Casper closed his eyes and waited until he heard the creak of the doors opening behind him, and the clack of Grace's shoes hitting the floor of the gallery.

"Please approach the witness stand." Captain Hunt opened the swinging door that separated the gallery from the rest of the courtroom. The folds of Grace's gray dress swept past him, her body blurring as she walked. She came into focus as she stepped behind the witness stand and turned towards the red-haired prosecutor waiting to swear her in.

"Raise your right hand." Hunt instructed her.

Grace raised her right hand, then turned and looked at him, her eyes cloudy and ancient.

"Do you swear that the evidence you are about to give in the case now in hearing is the truth, the whole truth and nothing but the truth, so help you God?"

"I do."

"And for the record, you are Grace Elizabeth Casper?"

"Yes Ma'am."

"You may be seated." Hunt turned towards Lieutenant Sharon and offered a simple nod. "Your witness."

He watched Sharon rise from her chair and straighten the folds of her uniform. She reached for the trial binder where she had hidden his lost isolation letter. Stuffed in a shoe box with the unregistered weapon that could have saved so many lives. The weight of that letter was in his hands now. He laid it out in front of him and stared at the frayed edges.

"Mrs. Casper, do you know the defendant in this case?" Sharon stepped up to the podium and spoke calmly to Grace.

"Yes Ma'am. He's my husband."

There was a disturbing sense of conviction in her voice. The sort of conviction that could only come from a woman who'd tampered with evidence and more or less gotten away with it. A woman who somehow, when she came to the end of all the unanswered questions and brutal tears, arrived at some implausible reason to hope. The very thought started a dull pressure building behind his ears.

"How long have you been married to your husband Mrs. Casper?"

"It's been eight years now. We moved out to Fort Leavenworth a few years ago, after Ben came home from Charlottesville."

Home. The word stung and burrowed its way under his skin. He tried to fight off a wave of buried memories, both warm and sweet. A terrible longing began boiling in the pit of his stomach.

"Were you living with your husband over the Veteran's Day weekend?"

"Yes, I was." Grace's hearty voice echoed through his ears. "Other than deployments and trainings, we've always lived together."

"What can you tell us about that weekend?" Sharon's question left her lips and lingered for a short spell, potent and real.

"I remember that it was a Friday night." Grace lifted her green eyes from her hands. She seemed to be looking for somewhere comforting to rest her heavy gaze. "Ben was supposed to meet me at the high school to watch the fireworks. I texted him a few times, but he never responded."

"Did you have any reason to worry about your husband at that time?"

"I assumed he forgot that we had made plans. It wasn't unusual for Ben to forget things." A string of unwanted shadows followed the broken statement. "His memory has been spotty since his last deployment to Iraq. Sometimes it's better than others. Sometimes I let it go because I don't want him to feel embarrassed or broken. Sometimes it hurts me, because I can't tell if he's really forgotten something, or if he's just stopped trying. A lot of his memories of our life together seem to be missing. I'm still trying to adjust to that."

Casper looked for the courage to imagine himself walking out the courtroom doors with his wife, working to rebuild what was left of their shattered life.

He closed his eyes and tried to scare up old memories from the locked vault in the back of his brain. He imagined what coming home might have been like. Not today or yesterday, but some obscure date in the past. When Grace was still young and in love. He was newly enlisted, in peak physical condition. A mechanic with no specialized knowledge of explosives or chemical agents. No experience with evidentiary rules or burdens of proof. Randy was still alive, trying to flirt with some oblivious girl during a history lesson in a far away high school. There wasn't the slightest whisper of war.

"What time did you leave the high school that night?"

"I didn't stay for the fireworks, so it must've been around 8:00 or 8:30. I didn't want to argue with Ben about not showing up or not responding or the problems with his memory. I just wanted to go to bed."

"Do you remember how you got home from the high school?"

"I took my car. It's about a 15 minute drive."

"Can you describe your car keys for the panel?"

"There were five or six different keys on my key chain. One for the car, one for the house, and a few different keys for the filing cabinets at work." Grace's voice dropped to just above a whisper, as if she were giving away some intimate secret. "I also had a small container of pepper spray on my key ring."

"Can you tell the panel what you did when you got home from the high school on Veteran's Day?"

"I went to the kitchen and poured myself a glass of wine." Grace's eyes started to fill with a familiar mist. "I sat up for about an hour waiting for him. After a second glass of wine Ben still wasn't home, so I went to bed."

"And where were your car keys when you went to bed that night?"

"On the nightstand next to my bed."

Grace let out as little as possible, without exposing the dark details to the panel. It all sounded awkward enough to be true, even if they'd already made up their minds that she was put on the stand to lie and protect him.

Casper dropped his eyes to the envelope on the table. He wondered what had gone through her mind when she found the loaded gun in the shoe box. How long it had taken her to decide that it could destroy him? That it had to be hidden some place where no one would find it.

"Did you hear your husband come home that night?"

"I didn't. The wine put me right to sleep." There was a heaviness in her voice that sounded like guilt. An involuntary quiver at finally having the opportunity to confess everything out loud. "I wouldn't have had that second glass if I thought Ben was in any danger. I didn't hear anything that night."

Casper closed his eyes and pictured Grace's young face, smiling and waiting for him on the other side of a long nightmare. They had dreams once. Macchu Picchu, the Himalayas, Southeast Asia. All those adventurous things a young couple could imagine, when they were brazen and untested. Before the war and the first deployment orders came. Maybe it was still possible. Maybe there was still time.

"What's the next thing you remember, Mrs. Casper?"

He opened his eyes and his future evaporated.

"I woke up around 7:30 and went looking for Ben. I found him sleeping in the guest room. He slept better in there."

He marveled at the way she slipped the lies in with the truth, seemingly benign and unassuming. It all blended together in the end, a mix of facts and emotions that were no more or less reliable than a pair of fingerprints or an old blood stain that couldn't be pinned to a particular time or source.

"What did you do after you found him asleep?"

"I went into the kitchen to start some coffee and make breakfast. I brought my keys with me and set them on the center island."

Sharon turned a page in her notebook, leaving intentional holes in Grace's testimony. She was taking a dangerous gamble that Hunt wouldn't ask the right questions. That the panel would look past the peculiarities of Grace's story and dig no deeper than the surface of her words.

"Did you see your husband that morning, Mrs. Casper?"

"Ben woke up and came into the kitchen just as I was finishing the eggs. He was pretty groggy and out of sorts. He didn't remember much, like always. CID showed up shortly after that. They told Ben that he was wanted for questioning. That he'd been in a fight and someone had been killed. I don't remember the details. I do remember that Ben grabbed my keys as he headed out the door, thinking they were his. He handled them only for a moment before he put them back down and grabbed his own."

"And you're certain that this was after CID arrived at your house?"

"Yes Ma'am." Grace nodded. "Long after the captain had been killed."

"Objection your honor." Captain Hunt stood up and faced the judge. "The witness has no personal knowledge of when Captain Mann was killed."

"Overruled." Judge Hirsch responded. "If CID had arrived to question the defendant regarding the murder it was clearly after the victim had been killed. You may proceed counselor."

"I have no further questions your honor." Sharon turned another marked page in her notepad and returned to the defense table. The muscles in her jaw and face were stiff and unsettled. Casper watched as Captain Hunt moved towards the podium, closing in on an undefended witness, with too many undisclosed details to count. Everything inside him wanted to protect her. But he was locked behind a table and surrounded by rules and formality. His skin grew warm and his breathing tightened.

"Mrs. Casper, you were fairly clear on direct that you didn't hear your husband come home the night of the murder?" Hunt stepped out from behind the podium and pinned her eyes on Grace, bent on intimidating and breaking her.

"No, I didn't." Grace responded.

"He didn't wake you when he crawled into bed, because he was no longer sharing a bed with you, isn't that the case?"

"He didn't wake me." Grace clung to her version of events. She was as loyal and proud as any of his soldiers. No matter how trite and irrelevant, she wouldn't give away anything. She wouldn't admit to the separate bedrooms, even if it bolstered her credibility or explained her erratic behavior.

"Isn't it possible that your husband came into your room that night and picked up your keys without you hearing him?"

Casper watched Hunt move behind the podium, soft and flawless like a desert snake. A serpent hidden inside her proud uniform. The smell of hot sand hit his senses.

"Ben has his own car and his own keys." Grace's response was quick and tight. "He had no reason to take mine."

"Unless he just needed the pepper spray?" Hunt narrowed her eyes from beside the podium. "Is there some reason you bring your keys to bed with you at night?"

"Ben didn't kill that man." Grace looked as if she were shouting, but the sound hit him like a thin whisper.

"You have no way of really knowing that, do you Mrs. Casper?" Hunt took a dangerous step towards his wife and Casper felt his lungs narrow, his entire body filling with fever and adrenaline. "You have no way of knowing what your husband was doing while you were sleeping."

"I know who he is." Grace's singular answer echoed overhead, and her pretty face faded out of focus.

"Mrs. Casper, is it safe to assume that you carry the pepper spray on your keychain for protection?"

"Yes, that's correct."

Casper watched her shaken form roll and morph from worlds away, slivers of dismal memories flashing behind his eyes.

The prosecutor paused as she turned a page in her notebook, reading between the lines and finding the truth in everything that had been left unsaid. "Protection from your husband?"

Casper's fingers began to twitch, hungry for the invisible trigger of an M16. He could hear the blood in his ears and felt the sweat breaking across his forehead.

He slid his along the desk, reaching for the reliable weapon that always hung at his side.

"Objection your honor!" Sharon pinned Casper's hand to the desk as she stood, shattering the delusion before it was fully formed.

Casper opened his eyes and saw her slim white fingers on top of his, her warm skin and familiar smell pulling him back to reality. It was as if she'd known where his mind was racing. All the vicious things his body wanted to do.

"Is that why he slept in the other room?" The prosecutor continued her vile questions as Casper shook off the delirium, waiting for his racing heart and tingling senses to come back down. "Why you kept such close tabs on your keys with the pepper spray? Because you knew exactly how dangerous he was?"

"Objection, your honor!" Sharon called out again, still anchoring Casper's hand to the table. "The government is trying to compel the witness to testify against her husband."

"Do you care to re-phrase counselor?" Judge Hirsch finally silenced the satisfied captain.

"I'll withdraw your honor." She closed her notebook with a smooth exhale, unaware of how close he'd come to wringing her neck. "I have no further questions."

Casper felt the air re-filling his lungs. Sharon let go of his fingers and he watched the blood creep back into his skin, restoring the human color to his tingling hand.

# Chapter 62
## Fort Leavenworth, KS (2014)

The courtroom felt smaller, emptier, after Grace was gone. Casper felt for the gold band around his finger, still tying him to the woman in the gray dress. There was an overwhelming comfort in recognizing how much she still loved him, despite the confusing specter he'd become.

He closed his eyes and drank in his last breaths of lilac perfume, before the handcuffs closed around his wrists and he slipped further and further into his delusions. Perhaps he should have allowed her to ask for a sanity hearing. To finally admit that something was going on inside him that he couldn't control.

"Can you tell the panel about some of the work you've done concerning soldiers with PTSD?"

Sharon stood a few feet in front of him, introducing the seasoned doctor that she'd tried to force on him. He was lucid enough to realize that there was no magic serum to apply to his ruined psyche. But he also knew that Sharon had brought him back from the brink more than once. And if he could come back, there was hope.

The doctor gave the panel his long list of credentials. He had no real evidence to offer. He was only here because he was Sharon's last real chance to gain some sympathy for him. Because emotions are far less predictable than facts. And under the right circumstances, even the suggestion of a misunderstood diagnosis might do as much to sway a panel as a bloody knife. The difference between guilty or not guilty could depend on how much loaded testimony she was able to get in front of the panel before Hunt presented a proper objection.

Casper opened his eyes and focused on the doctor, a short, hefty man with graying curls and kind eyes. He was slow and deliberate with his speech, stringing his words together with a simple rhythm and a precision.

"Your honor, at this time I'd like to offer Dr. Brock as an expert witness in the field of combat related psychological disorders." Sharon announced to the court.

"Any objection from the government?"

"Not at this time your honor." Hunt ran her thumbs across her bare nails, stripped of all color and shine.

"Dr. Brock, based on your research on PTSD, how long have soldiers been suffering from combat related trauma?"

"Soldiers have displayed symptoms of war-related trauma as long as there have been wars." The doctor's answer was vague and sentimental. "PTSD is a modern term, but other cultures, other time periods have had their own labels for the same psychological illness. The Swiss used to call it 'Nostalgia.' The Germans and the French referred to it as 'Homesickness.' The Spanish used the term 'estar roto,' which means 'to be broken.' During the American civil war it was sometimes called 'Irritable Heart' or 'Soldier's Heart.' After that we used terms like 'shell shock' and 'combat fatigue.' Today it is PTSD. All different names for the same disease. The same symptoms. The same cause."

The different labels fell on Casper's ears, each of them leaving their impact. Each of them describing a piece of how he felt. Homesick, broken and mired in the past. He'd never heard the term 'Soldier's Heart,' but it resonated through him. The noble sound was something that he could own. That belonged to his brothers and sisters in arms alone. Something that commemorated him for the humanity that he'd lost. That took the shame out of the hurt that he felt.

"What, if anything, is distinctive about the trauma you've seen as a result of the Iraq and Afghanistan wars?"

"Very little, to be honest. The disorder has stayed the same throughout history. It is society that changes." The doctor nodded to himself and focused his soft eyes on Major Casper, seeming less aware of the panel listening to his words, or even the purpose of his speech. "During Vietnam, our young men were drafted into the Army. The pain of warfare was spread among the entire population. Most Vietnam veterans served one combat tour, though many were exposed to terrible amounts of violence. For Iraq and

Afghanistan veterans of course, there is no draft. A far smaller number is taking on a greater responsibility and the repeated exposure is taking its toll. Soldiers from the Iraq and Afghanistan wars are also surviving events that would have killed soldiers in previous campaigns, due to advances in medicine and equipment. As a result, we're seeing far more men and women coming home with significant brain injuries. We're also seeing far more women soldiers and far more orphans. Overall the violence is the same. The trauma and the repercussions are the same. But the numbers and the demographics have shifted."

Casper's hands grew clammy and warm. He watched the faceless panel of officers taking in the raw data. He read the implications in their apathetic stares. At the end of the day he was nothing more than a madman wearing a Major's rank, with an arbitrary history of violence towards the victim. There was little Sharon could do to change that.

"And in your research, have you found any clear association between soldiers suffering from combat trauma and criminal behavior?"

"Without question. Crime waves have followed every major war throughout history." There was both pedigree and conviction in his words. "The American Civil War gave rise to a period of stagecoach banditry and outlaws like Jesse James, who had significant combat experience fighting for the Confederacy. World War II gave rise to biker gangs like the Hells Angels. We've repeatedly seen soldiers turn into criminals when the wars end and they have no outlet for their aggression."

Casper was only hours away from becoming a statistic. A hidden piece of unsavory national history. Part of the lost, the lonely and the forgotten. Like Randy. Like the soldiers buried beside him. He felt a rumbling in his core. The regret and grief hardened in his arteries, turning into hot anger. For the first time since the blast he understood what it meant to be responsible for Randy's legacy. To prevent him from falling into obscurity.

"And in your opinion, what role does society play in helping soldiers grapple with these issues?" Sharon flipped another page in her notepad. "In encouraging them to seek treatment for their conditions?"

"Society's acceptance and acknowledgement of the soldier's condition is critical to their recovery." The doctor turned towards Casper again, a color of compassion and wisdom in his eyes. "In the western world, the blame has generally been placed on the soldier. He is marginalized and degraded because he was not tough enough to withstand the trials of war. In other cultures, we see a complete reversal. Many Native American societies, for example, would host rituals for returning soldiers, during which the bloodguilt that they had incurred was transferred to the whole of society. Everyone shared the blame for the killing that took place in the name of national defense. And the warrior was not returned to society until he was fully healed, physically, mentally and spiritually."

"Objection your honor." Hunt rose from her chair. "Nothing in this man's testimony is relevant to these proceedings. If the defense is trying to argue that the accused is not guilty as a result of some combat related psychological condition, the proceedings should be referred to a sanity board."

"Defense counsel?" Judge Hirsch turned towards Lieutenant Sharon. "You had the opportunity to request a sanity board before trial, is there a reason you're bringing this evidence in now?"

"The defense is not requesting a sanity board your honor." Sharon answered simply.

"Then what is the relevance?"

"Your honor, the government has produced evidence suggesting that my client intentionally assaulted the victim. That he hunted him down and murdered him in cold blood. This witness's testimony supports an alternative theory that the prior assaults were not out of personal animus, but as a result of delusions brought about by PTSD."

Casper watched the pristine faces of Lieutenant Sharon and Captain Hunt, practicing an academic craft in pleated uniforms in an air-conditioned room. They wore no deployment emblems. The ranks of soldiers that could remember life before the wars were dwindling. New enlistees were young, barely old enough to remember 9/11, with an ignorant thirst for adventure. Unscarred.

He was part of an outgoing class of lost warriors.

"Your honor," Hunt's eyes were fierce and direct. "This testimony is clearly meant to create sympathy for the defendant. This is similar if not identical evidence that would have been introduced at a sanity board. I see no difference."

"What is the difference, counselor?" Judge Hirsch asked Sharon with a firm voice.

"The difference, your honor, is that I'm not arguing that Major Casper wasn't in his right mind when he killed the victim, I'm arguing that he didn't kill him at all!"

Sharon's argument echoed across the courtroom, shaking up the unspoken assumptions that flowed through the stale air. Casper saw a subtle change break across the faces of the panel of officers, waking them out of their complacency. Their faces were suddenly alert and open. Their eyes waiting to be filled with uncertainty.

She'd broken through. Found her way to the warm heart of their pre-conceptions and shattered the glass.

Hunt steadied herself against the prosecution table. The conviction in Sharon's voice must have alarmed her. Made her question what hidden truths Sharon had uncovered in her folder of notes and theories.

Judge Hirsch sat back in his seat. He shifted his weight from one side to the other, adjusting his glasses before he gave his ruling. "I'll allow it."

"Your honor, you can't possibly." Hunt shouted.

"Take your seat, counselor, I'm not going to warn you again."

Hunt lowered herself back into her seat, her hands still gripping the edge of the table.

"You may proceed, counselor."

"Thank you, your honor." Sharon gave a grateful nod to the judge and released a long breath of nervous air. "Dr. Brock, can you explain for the panel, how combat trauma can lead to criminal activity?"

"It begins with combat training." The doctor answered firmly, leaving little room for doubt or interpretation. "Soldiers learn to take out the enemy. With bullets, with explosives, with their bare hands if necessary. The training they endure is specifically designed to overcome the natural, human reluctance to engage in this sort of violence, because it helps them survive on the battlefield. But they are rarely, if ever, deprogrammed when they return from combat."

Dr. Brock turned towards Casper again, silently assessing the awards on his chest as if they were clues to what had gone wrong with his chemistry.

"Soldiers suffer unimaginable hardships. They watch their friends bleed to death in their arms. They survive events that should have killed them. They detach from the things they see and hear. They struggle to justify the things they're asked to do. They learn to think very little of human life."

The doctor's eyes were calm and forgiving. He saw straight through Casper's rough exterior to the knots of pain under his skin. His words softened pieces of scar tissue around his heart, exposing the raw flesh to the open air.

"Some soldiers are so numbed by their experiences that they turn to high-risk behaviors just to experience some form of emotion again. To relive the adrenaline rush they experienced in combat. Others survive combat, in part, because they are so adept at staying hyper-vigilant. They take in every element of their surroundings. They hear things, smell things, taste things that our brains typically filter out. They become so skilled at processing all that extra sensory data, that they appear almost superhuman. They often misinterpret the intentions of those around them, construing everything as a possible threat. Many of them self-medicate with drugs and alcohol, which frequently leads to petty crimes, if not larger issues. They experience depression, insomnia, suicidal thoughts, and rarely allow themselves the space they need to cope. To heal."

A spring burst deep inside Casper's core. He bit his lip to hold it back, but his eyes welled with hot tears.

"What experiences have you had with EOD personnel?" Sharon continued.

"EOD personnel frequently have problems with memory. Combat medics and the media tend to focus on burns and shrapnel wounds, things that you can see. But not all of the damage is visible. When a soldier is close enough, the blast waves can shake up some of the hard-wiring in the brain, causing significant long and short-term memory impairment."

"And is it possible, Dr. Brock, for a soldier that's experiencing some of these problems to black out completely? To assault someone and have no recollection of it after the fact?"

"Yes, that very thing has happened with a handful of my patients." The doctor's eyes went blank for a brief moment, as if he were cycling through stores of personal tragedies. "It's not common, but in cases of intense trauma, patients do experience dissociative flashbacks. They are reliving a traumatic event from combat, often while sleeping, but sometimes certain cues or excessive alcohol can trigger the episode. They may act out against persons around them, believing them to be an enemy target."

Sharon turned a final page in her notebook and marked off the last bit of information she needed to make her closing argument. "Thank you Dr. Brock. I have no further questions."

"Government, do you wish to cross examine the witness." Judge Hirsch asked Captain Hunt.

"I do, your honor."

Casper watched Captain Hunt approach the podium, an abysmal strain etched into the contours of her face. She looked desperate and worn, as if she felt her steady hold on him slipping.

"Dr. Brock, you've testified that a soldier experiencing a dissociative flashback might assault another person and not remember it. Is it also possible that a soldier could kill another person and not remember it?"

Captain Hunt was counting on the panel to make assumptions where her evidence fell short. The blood stains and fingerprints that couldn't be pinned down to a time or place. The easy distance between the shooter and the victim. The missing weapon that had fired the three deadly rounds. Nothing in the faces of the empaneled officers told him if it was enough. Their features remained half hidden and lifeless as marble.

"Yes, that's entirely possible." Dr. Brock answered.

"Is it the case then, that someone who's experiencing these sorts of afflictions presents a significant danger to those around them?"

"Yes, I'd have to say that's true. The dissociative state is unpredictable and can be incredibly volatile."

"I have only one more question for you Dr. Brock." Hunt paged through her own collection of notes, circling gaps and looking for some strategic advantage. "Have you seen patients in your practice exaggerate their symptoms to avoid criminal penalties?"

"Many of my patients don't seek help until they're in some sort of legal trouble." The doctor responded, showing his first signs of being defensive. "That doesn't make their trauma any less real."

"That's not the question I asked you, Dr. Brock." Hunt tapped her pen against the podium with feverish energy. "What I want you to tell the panel is, has there ever been a circumstance where you've believed the trauma to be invented in order to avoid legal consequences?"

Casper watched the pulse of Hunt's breathing in the thin skin of her neck. He watched the impatient faces of the panel members. She needed the doctor to tell them that their previous assumptions were legitimate. She needed him to give them permission to make the leap from assault to homicide.

"It's rare, Captain, but yes. It has happened."

"Thank you, your honor." She made a swift mark in her yellow notepad. "I have no further questions."

# Chapter 63
## Fort Leavenworth, KS (2014)

A cold hand closed around Sharon's wrist, and she startled at the unexpected touch. She turned towards Casper who was standing beside her, his heavy hand weighing down hers. There was a small, but noticeable gap between their fingers, created by the rough edges of the stone on her engagement ring. He stood over her, trying to communicate something for which he couldn't find words. She felt slivers of fear and love. Gratitude and regret. Even hope. A tangle of emotions, both intricate and common, all transmitted through the tips of his fingers.

"It's not over yet Sir." She gave his fingers a slight squeeze.

"I should have trusted you." He turned his hazel eyes on her, rich and pure and almost as calm as the day she met him. "If it's not too late for me, I think I'm ready to face it now. All of it."

"All of what?"

"Soldier's Heart." He moved his hand over his heart, as if covering up the hurt that had spilled to the surface.

Sharon let herself slip inside this temporary serenity, until she felt the heat of a pair of grey eyes boring into her. She turned to see Captain Hunt standing across the table, a critical stare embedded into her pale flesh.

"What is it Pam?" The informality slipped from the end of Sharon's tongue.

"I've come to ask you not to force Mann's wife to testify." Hunt glared at her with a thousand unproven assumptions. "You already have your reasonable doubt. Let the poor woman alone."

Sharon started at the sudden appeal to compassion, sounding flat and insincere coming from Hunt's reddish lips. She was almost dizzy at the idea that Hunt was conceding something. She wanted to feel Casper's grip in her fingers one more time, to draw a few more strands of strength and hope from his warm hands. "I still don't know how those officers are going to vote."

Sharon nodded towards the court-martial panel. "I have to do everything I can to get them to not guilty."

"And what do you think you're going to get out of this?" Hunt demanded.

"I'm entitled to ask her a few questions about the night her husband died." Sharon stared back, unflinching. "I'm surprised you didn't bother to do the same."

"Are we ready to proceed counselors?" Judge Hirsh knocked his gavel against his desk.

"I am your honor." Sharon reported from where she stood. She felt the weight in the air shift as Hunt turned away and headed back across the aisle.

"The defense calls Cynthia Jane Mann." Lieutenant Sharon spoke aloud and she heard Hunt scratching her chair against the courtroom floor.

The courtroom doors opened wide and the bailiff escorted Mrs. Mann into the room.

She was a slight Asian woman in a shapeless white dress. Her hands were distracted with a silver chain around her neck, and she lifted a pair of morose eyes towards the deep shine of the witness box ahead of her.

She seemed both meek and beautiful, neither of which were surprising considering Captain Mann's arrogance and taste. They must have made a breathtaking couple when standing side by side. It was her sense of frailty, more than anything else that caught Sharon's eye. She still needed to study the details, find out more about who this woman was. She still had unanswered questions about the night that Mann was killed, and this woman might have some of the answers, if she was willing to engage in a small bit of cruelty to pry it from her.

Hunt stood before the gallery and opened the swinging door for Mrs. Mann to pass through.

"Please make your way to the witness stand, then turn and face me."

Mrs. Mann moved through the gallery with her eyes fixed on the floor. She looked tired from waiting, agreeing to move through the painful motions only so she could put her demons to bed.

Hunt directed the small woman towards the seat at the center of the courtroom. Mrs. Mann walked the length of the room under the abstract eyes of Judge Hirsch and the panel of officers. She turned and faced Captain Hunt, who was standing beside the podium, stiff and rigid. She held in a stale breath, almost as if she'd forgotten, in the heat of the moment, how to exhale.

"Please raise your right hand." The air poured out as she spoke, but her body refused to relax. "Do you swear that the testimony you are about to give in the case now in hearing is the truth, the whole truth and nothing but the truth so help you god?"

"I do." Was the small response.

"And for the record you are Mrs. Cynthia Jane Mann?"

"I am."

"You may be seated." Captain Hunt looked again towards the defense table, a visible chill in her stare. "Defense counsel has some questions for you."

Hunt returned to her seat, while Sharon gathered up what was left of her paperwork and approached the podium. Her notebook had only a few remaining scribbles. More observations and curiosities than questions. She had no real plan of attack, just a suspicion and a cause.

"Good afternoon, Mrs. Mann. I know it must be difficult for you to be here today. But I need to ask you some questions about the night your husband died."

"Ask me whatever you like, Lieutenant." Her voice was clipped and distant. "I'll cooperate if it will get this business over with."

"Can you tell the panel about the last time you spoke to your husband?"

"The last time I spoke to my husband was the night he was killed. He called me at about a quarter to 11:00, so I know he was still alive at that time."

"Can you recall the conversation you had with your husband?"

"It wasn't much of a conversation. It was really just a lot of rambling. He mentioned that he had been in a fight. He wasn't making much sense at all."

Sharon listened to Cindy Mann repeat the same answers that she had before, her words growing more rehearsed and emotionless every time. She had to find some way to rattle her into slipping, into admitting something she didn't want to admit.

"What else do you remember about the phone call, Mrs. Mann?"

Cindy Mann stared into some invisible void all around her. Her eyes glazed over with a protective film that kept her emotions tight and restrained. "Nothing of any importance to this trial."

Sharon recognized the distress in the woman in front of her. Her words, her demeanor, everything down to the way she stared blankly at her hands convinced Sharon that there was something more to the story. She knew what it meant to keep toxic secrets hidden in your skin. The energy it took to keep them at bay.

"Did he ask you for a divorce during this phone call?"

"He didn't ask me for a divorce, Lieutenant." A small spring of passion bubbled to the surface. "He gave me permission to file for divorce if that was what I wanted. There's a difference."

Just a minor twist in an innocuous question to burst the dam. Sharon was close to something. To triggering the reaction she was looking for.

"My apologies." Sharon sifted through her papers, looking for the notes she'd taken during their last conversation. She read through a choppy list of facts and phrases, stopping at a half line of scribbled jargon that took on a sudden, crucial significance.

*Mann asked his wife about divorce – after almost three years of marriage.*

Almost three years. Captain Mann had been married in Charlottesville.

The realization sent a tingle through her frame. She froze in place, afraid to look at the redhead behind her. She paged back to Captain Mann's phone records from the night he was murdered, scanning the list of unknown and irrelevant numbers until she hit upon the unanswered phone call that he'd placed to Captain Hunt, six days before he drove out to Fort Leavenworth.

She felt the wind slip from her chest, and a thin gasp escaped into the air.

"Lieutenant Sharon." Judge Hirsch called out to her from his raised desk on the other side of the courtroom. "Do you have additional questions for this witness?"

"One second your honor."

Sharon returned to the defense table and whispered to Major Casper, barely hearing her own breath over the sound of the blood pumping in her temples.

"You told me that someone sent you the phone records from the JAG School." She spoke to Casper, low and urgent. "Where are those records now?"

"If they're anywhere, they're in my personnel folder. In that old box that Grace gave you."

Lieutenant Sharon picked up the worn box from the floor under the defense table. She searched through the tabbed folders until she found the academic records near the end of the file. She shuffled through the sloppy stack of papers, past diplomas and certificates with the JAG crest, finally pulling out an abused manila envelope with no markings. She opened the envelope and pulled out a stack of dated papers, lined with incoming and outgoing calls. She flipped through the heavy ledger, checking the dates in the corner until she came across January 6, 2013. Graduation day. She scanned through the incoming calls, the entries slowing as she neared the early morning hours, where one specific entry was highlighted.

Her finger stopped at the highlighted entry, the earliest recorded entry of the day. An incoming phone call at 4:42 a.m. from an out of state area code.

"Your honor, I ask that the defense proceed with the examination or excuse the witness, they've had ample time to prepare for this case." Hunt stood and objected.

"Counselor." Judge Hirsch knocked his gavel on the desk.

"Yes, your honor." Lieutenant Sharon stood upright at the sound of the heavy wood connecting with the judge's desk. She returned to the podium with the phone records in hand, setting the missing evidence down in front of her. She compared the highlighted phone number from graduation day to the 10:43 phone call Mann placed to his wife, only hours before he was killed. The records were an exact match.

"Mrs. Mann." Sharon began her question before she'd even had a chance to secure all the connections in her mind. She had a hard time tearing her eyes from the criminal footprint in her hands. "Has your husband ever cheated on you?"

"Objection your honor, relevance."

Hunt was quick and severe. The tingling grew stronger, faster, rooting her to the floor where she stood. The answer was beneath her fingertips. And Hunt knew it.

"Your honor, Mrs. Mann was the last person to speak to her husband before he died, the content of that conversation is crucial to these proceedings."

Judge Hirsch must have sensed the tension that had spiraled across the room at the mention of adultery. The Earth between her and Hunt had opened, exposing the heart of truth and innocence.

"There is no evidence of adultery in the record your honor." Hunt spoke again, a little louder and a little more desperate. "The defense is grasping at straws and trying to confuse the panel by suggesting that that Mrs. Mann had some motive to kill her own husband."

"This testimony is relevant your honor, if you'd just allow me to proceed." Sharon felt her heart beat in her chest, her neck, her fingertips. She watched the opaque eyes of the man in the black robe struggling with a dangerous decision, with the full knowledge that a man's life hung in the balance.

"You may answer the question for now, Mrs. Mann." His answer was slow and cautious.

"Your honor!" Hunt practically shouted.

"Sit down counselor!" He shouted back.

A deafening silence filled the air. Hunt reached for the chair behind her and sank slowly into submission.

"I will give you three questions Lieutenant Sharon." Judge Hirsch continued.

"Your honor . . ." Sharon began to argue, but was cut off midsentence.

"If you're not able to convince me that this line of questioning has some bearing on the defendant's guilt or innocence in three questions, I'm going to put a stop to this. Choose them wisely."

Sharon looked up at Cindy Mann, then back down at the phone records in her hands. She tried to steady the torrents swirling through her head. To boil everything down to three essential facts.

Cindy Mann's eyes were narrow and strange. Her face painted with layers of distrust. "May I approach the witness your honor?"

"You may."

Sharon stepped towards the witness stand, swallowing a dram of adrenaline and fear. Mrs. Mann turned her eyes towards the floor as she approached, the pain digging into her swollen heart. Sharon never wanted to break her down. All she could do was convince her to tell the truth for three crucial questions.

"I'm not trying to trick you Mrs. Mann." Her voice was as tender and soft as a butterfly's wings. "I am trying to find the person who killed your husband. And in spite of what you think, in spite of what you've been told, it just might not be the person sitting behind that desk."

Sharon pointed towards Major Casper, hiding in plain sight on the opposite side of the defense table.

"I need you to tell me the truth. For James' sake." Sharon continued. "Has your husband ever cheated on you?"

Cindy Mann looked at the eyes of the strangers all around the courtroom, as if she were waiting for someone to rescue her. For an objection or some sort of disruption that would stop the questioning. Her small brown eyes were forced to follow Sharon's arm towards the bowed frame of the man she believed killed her husband.

Casper had lifted his Hazel eyes towards her, his hands moored to the table, waiting on the answer to the first of only three questions that might decide his fate.

"Only once, that I know of." Cindy Mann answered the question with a subtle vibration in her words. "A few years ago. The night before he was scheduled to graduate from JAG school."

Sharon dropped her arm to her side in a cool swell of relief. She took a step back from the witness stand and drank in her first real breakthrough. The shadowy confession that could make way for a perfect rush of secrets to come spilling out after.

"I called him that morning and a woman answered the phone." Cindy Mann's answer was low and uneven. "She sounded groggy or hungover. I believe she thought she was answering her own phone. I asked for James and she hung up the phone. I continued to call back until my husband answered. He told me what he'd done. That he'd had too much to drink and that he'd been with someone else. A classmate of his. We had an argument and he told me not to come to graduation the next day, so I called the company commander."

Sharon steadied herself and collected her thoughts, pushing her second question past the tremors in her throat. "Did you ever find out who it was that was with your husband that night?"

"James never told me her name." Her answer was thick and honest. "But he did tell me that I ruined his life by making that phone call. That the entire class was punished. His selection for Airborne school was revoked. Everyone's promotions were suspended. He started drinking after that. He wouldn't speak to me. He was very angry for a long time. His reaction seemed extreme. I knew that Airborne school was important to him, but it wasn't like him to be so upset for so long. I couldn't understand what was happening with him."

Sharon reached for the dogtags around her neck, drawing strength from the simple phrase that was etched into the metal. The promise to never give up, and to never leave a fallen comrade. Everything hinged on her last question. All she had left was instinct and hope. "Mrs. Mann, did your husband tell you why he came to Fort Leavenworth that night?"

"He told me everything the night he was killed." Cindy Mann let the powerful words spill from her mouth, tangled and knotty. "He said that one of his classmates had been raped. But because of my phone call, because no one had confessed to the adultery, she couldn't come forward without being suspected. He had been carrying that guilt with him for all this time. The night that he was murdered, he told me that he couldn't live with it any longer. The only way to make it right was to confess. He was going to tell CID about the rape. About the affair. He was going to accept whatever consequences came his way so that this woman could find justice. Even if it meant his career. But before he confessed, he wanted to warn the woman that he had been with that night, whoever she was. He felt he owed that to her." Cindy Mann paused as the last of her energy was caught up in the fine details of her last statement. The subtle suggestion that his affair was based on something more substantial than alcohol and recklessness. "I believe that was your last question Lieutenant."

Sharon's chest heaved and deflated. She was rooted to the moment, unable to move beyond the immediate necessity for breath and bloodflow.

"And that woman is stationed here at Fort Leavenworth?" Judge Hirsch interrupted, taking on a fourth and final question in her place.

"I believe so, your honor. James didn't know where she was living or how to get in touch with her. But he knew that she was an officer in an MP Brigade." Her final words carried an unexpected echo. "That's all he told me."

"Thank you for your testimony Ms. Mann." Judge Hirsch gave a slow, seasoned nod, then turned his heavy eyes on Captain Hunt. He stared at her stripped fingernails, and then into the frightened eyes of the only female officer in the MP brigade. "You may step down."

"That's it? That's all?"

"I'm afraid I have to declare a mistrial, on account of the prosecution withholding crucial evidence from these proceedings." He lifted his eyes towards the red-haired prosecutor across the room, who was pinned to her chair, with a harsh, cool wind trapped in her lungs. "And in fact, may even be complicit in the crime under review. Bailiff, please see to it that Captain Hunt does not leave the premises."

Judge Hirsch slapped his gavel on the desk a final time. The sound pounded through Sharon's ears. Her legs went numb and the ground slid out from under her.

"Major Benjamin Casper, the charges against you are dismissed. You are hereby released from further confinement in association with the dismissed charges. You're free to return home until further notice."

The words echoed across the walls and Sharon found herself wrapped inside Casper's arms. She found her bearings just long enough to turn and look into his warm hazel eyes, the heavy dread around them evaporating. She heard the sound of the invisible shackles falling from his wrists. He took her into the longest embrace, more intimate than anything she'd ever known, that communicated everything from love, to longing, to goodbye.

# Chapter 64
## Fort Leavenworth, KS (2015)

There was no blood on her hands, like there was in the movies. Her palms were clammy and her fingers shook, but her hands were still as milky white as she remembered them. The first thing that hit her was the smell of sulfur. Then the vibrations echoing through the inner ears. Finally she felt the weight of the gun, anchored in the center of her pristine hands.

When she found the courage to look towards the fallen body, he was already still, his eyes wide and ghostly.

The ugly images emerged from every dark recess of her memory. She slipped between the present and the past, haunted by those brief, irreversible moments. No more than thirty grim seconds in the course of her whole life that had resulted in so much ruin.

She sat at an old table in the center of a barren room, a rights warning form lay in front of her. She glanced at the familiar words and phrases that somehow lost all of their meaning.

"Am I under arrest?" She looked across the table at Agent Hartman. He folded his hands over the table and waited for her to spill her soul.

"Yes you are." He didn't hesitate.

She could almost feel Mann's soft fingers as he slid his hand over hers that night, holding them still and secure. She had been rapt in the beauty of her pale skin next to his. As if there was something human and prophetic in the touch. Something she didn't even believe in, unraveling all around her.

She let herself be swept up into the chaos as it unfolded. The thrilling blend of fear and intoxication. She surrendered before she knew she'd surrendered. Lost herself in the simple joy of his warm body beside her, watched his chest moving up and down in calm liquid breaths, sentimental and timeless.

Until the ring of a cell phone interrupted the quiet. And the infamous moment when she hit the button and garbled into the speaker. And a woman's voice tore through the serenity.

"We've already executed a search warrant at your house." Agent Hartman's cold voice brought her back to a terrifying place, one that was as imposing as it was real. "We located what appears to be the captain's handgun on a shelf in your bedroom closet. You can either talk to me about that right now, or you can ask to talk to a lawyer."

She wanted to dismantle it into as many pieces as she could. Hide the remains all about the base as soon as the trial had ended. When she could dispose of it without a hundred pairs of prying eyes trying to unearth it.

She scanned the boxes on the form in front of her, explaining what remained of her freedom. Her final option to cease all questioning and wait silently for the walls to close in around her.

"I want to talk to Lieutenant Sharon."

"She left for home yesterday." Agent Hartman leaned back in his chair, watching and waiting as she lingered in fourth amendment limbo. "That was pretty clever what you did. You had everyone thinking he was guilty. His wife. His colleagues. Hell, even me."

"He's dangerous, Sir." She sputtered.

"He'll get the help he needs." Hartman leaned over the table again as if he could smell her vulnerability. "What's your excuse? You put a bullet in a man's head to save your career."

"He lied to me." The words bled out of her mouth. Her face was hot and she was quickly losing air. Mann had lured her away from Aaron's meaningless lies and pulled her into a nest of thorns and broken glass.

She still couldn't believe that it was her. Even while they were out there standing in the mud, waiting for someone to confess, listening to the commander take everything that she'd worked so hard for. She still thought it was Jamie. Because the selfish bastard had told his wife not to show up for graduation.

That he'd found someone who meant more to him. It was too much to believe that that kind of commitment was meant for her.

She needed to lose herself in the hard veins of Aaron's twisted skin again. To feel his forgiving arms wrapped around her worthless heart. But it was far too late for that now. That was over the moment she fell for Mann's perfect, dimpled smile.

"You could've confessed and ended this." Agent Hartman's voice receded into the background.

She had gone for a run to clear her head. Still thinking about his unanswered phone call. Still obsessing over what he might have wanted. What he might have to say to her after all this time. She turned onto the empty trail behind the rec center, breathing in the cool November air. She rounded a bend, then she looked up and he was standing there. Just as the fireworks were starting. He'd followed her from some corner of the world, and for a brief moment, her heart jumped. Just before her eyes adjusted to the shadows and her pretty fingers curled around the pepper spray in the pocket of her windbreaker.

He was drunk and bloody, with a firearm at his side. He rambled as the colored lights flashed overhead, about Casper and Charlottesville and something that looked and smelled like rape. He spun a thousand versions of the fear he saw in Jamie's eyes that night. About the delusional way that Casper caressed her face as she cried. About the adultery charges hanging over her head and keeping her silent. The accusations sunk in like hot lead, working against her misdirected anger and shaping it into cruel remorse.

"He had to be punished for what he did to her." Hunt heard her own voice echo through the empty space.

"She swears he never laid a hand on her."

"She'd never admit it." Hunt shook her head blindly. Sharon would see the good in every broken soldier until it killed her. The consequences of that blind kindness had manifested itself in a desperate captain pacing the woods, with a loaded handgun at his hips and an unshakable resolve to confess to an insignificant crime. She told him there were other ways. But nothing she said was registering. He just kept ambling back and forth as the snaps and pops went off overhead, as if he couldn't decide who the gun was meant for. Himself or Casper.

"It felt like justice." She said out loud, remembering the way that Agent Hartman had dropped the charges against Casper into her lap. If he wasn't going down for what he did to Jamie, she would see to it that he went down for Captain Mann.

She was patient until he pulled out his cell phone and started dialing. Hell bent on ruining both their careers over an enduring cruelty that happened every hour of every day, with no hope of ever being eradicated.

She reached for her pepper spray and dropped him to the ground, just as he hit send. His weapon fell from his hands and she lunged for it, just to keep him still until she could talk him down. But it fired. Again and again. Until she regained enough control to look up from her bloodless hands and see the raw bullet holes she'd left.

He'd forced her hand. Compelled her to take someone out of this world who might have loved her. Who might have made a home in her skin and hair. Who might have helped her find some way to not be broken together.

# Part Thirteen:

# Back Home

# Chapter 65
## Minneapolis, MN (2015)

Matt fished his keys out of his pocket as he walked up the front steps. In his other hand he carried a bag of Thai food from Jamie's favorite restaurant. The smell of the spices brought him back to those first few nights they'd spent together, forging a privileged, and perhaps naïve sense of security in each other's arms.

He had gotten used to coming home to her. To finding her shoes piled up near the door and her scent on the pillow. The small house seemed quiet and unnatural while she was away, as if she were a part of the very architecture of the walls around him. And yet he couldn't shake the feeling that a different woman had come home in her place. It may have been a fit of hopeless optimism that convinced him a pair of salad rolls and curry would be enough to seal up the invisible breaks that had formed in their short, unstructured life together.

He turned the key in the lock and opened the door, pushing past the pile of shoes. He lifted his head and saw her, standing in the middle of the living room, in a flurry of white satin. Her hair was piled in a messy knot at the back of her head. She held the front of the white dress against her chest and used the other to try and tame the fabric billowing out around her. She looked up with wide blue eyes, a pink tint settling into her cheeks as she pushed her eyes back towards the ground.

"I picked out a dress while you were out."

Matt set the take-out on the counter and watched her as she moved. "It looks good on you."

"You brought dinner?"

"Your favorite." He watched the smile creep back into her eyes. Some of the shyness eroding. "Isn't there some sort of rule against me seeing you like this?"

"Only if there's a chance you might change your mind." She carried a blank expression, waiting to be filled with whatever emotion came bubbling over.

"No chance of that." He shook his head.

A light smile played across her lips, while the loose beginnings of warm tears formed in the wells of her eyes. She turned back towards the mirror as she dabbed at the corners of her eyes, still fighting to hold dress in place.

"Let me help you." Matt crossed the room and stood behind her, gently brushing the hair from her neck. He traced the loose ribbons down towards the small of her back, and began weaving them into place.

"I'm sorry I didn't tell you about Casper." Her voice was both pained and distant.

"Don't apologize Jamie." He worked his fingers through the loops of the dress, still struggling to make his peace with everything that had followed her home. He fought to suppress the images of them together that night. The anger and the confusion and the pity. He wanted to tend to her bruised heart. But all he could do was trust her. Trust her word and her judgment that this was how she wanted things to end. And that it had in fact ended. "I'm sorry I didn't give you a space where you could trust me."

"I just wanted to help him."

"It's over now." He tightened the fragile ribbons and pinned them in place.

He had tried to avoid the full story for as long as his heart would allow. He'd wanted to keep her pristine in his mind. He looked up at her reflection in the mirror and recognized the bearing of a soldier. Braised in fire. Both bold and restrained. Full of fear and courage. She wasn't a porcelain doll. But a woman with flaws and curiosities. He wanted to know all of them. To grow with her.

She turned to face him, eyes wide open and aware.

He said goodbye to the dream and reached for her hand, closing her fingers in his. He felt his heart melt in the warmth of her eyes, then took her face between his hands and seeded his lips in hers, in a deep, unconditional surrender.

"I love you Jamie. Forever I love you."

She closed her eyes and nodded as the first intimate tears escaped down her cheeks. "I love you too."

He slid his arms around her waist and pulled her into his heart, with the scent of sesame and ginger flavoring the air around them.

"Welcome home."

# Chapter 66
## Minneapolis, MN (2015)

The cemetery was brighter in the spring. The grass was a mild green and the walks echoed with the sound of water running over stones. The soft earth gave way under Casper's feet as he wandered the trails towards Randy's headstone.

The Memorial Day crowds thinned as the early evening settled. Casper took a lonesome drag off his cigarette, a chorus of voices accompanying him as he walked. Morose, gritty vibrations from the ghosts of soldiers, both celebrated and forgotten. Ghosts from abandoned battlefields, from Marathon to Wounded Knee walked with him. Young men who died at Antiem or Iwo Jima. Friends from Basra and Kandahar, and everywhere in between. He listened to their off-key cadences called out with a melancholy spirit.

> I don't know why I left,
> *I don't know why I left,*
> But I know that I was wrong,
> *But I know that I was wrong,*
> And it won't be long,
> *And it won't be long,*
> Till I get on back home.
> *Till I get on back home.*
>
> Got a letter in the mail,
> *Got a letter in the mail,*
> Said 'go to war or go to jail.'
> *Said 'go to war or go to jail.'*
> And it won't be long,
> *And it won't be long,*
> Till I get on back home.
> *Till I get on back home.*

Casper stepped off the trail and turned in the direction of Randy's grave. He only made it a few steps before he raised his head and saw her. A woman in a spring jacket, arranging a handful of blue carnations along the stone that marked Staff Sergeant Khoury's bones. She stood and brushed a handful of sandy brown hair from her bronze face, revealing a set of round brown eyes.

She turned from the memorial and froze, as if the earth had sent up roots to hold her feet in place. The music swirled and swelled in his head as he stepped towards her, still questioning whether she was just another phantom he'd stored in his head.

"Are you a friend of Randy's?" The thin notes of her voice wove their way into the patterns that repeated in his head.

"I was his commander." He put out the cigarette on the bottom of his shoe and stuffed the ugly butt into the bottom of his pocket. "And his friend. Are you Jasmine?"

"He told you about me?" He saw the pulse of her heartbeat living in her eyes. Pure and simple and unafraid.

"Several times." He nodded as the old song resurfaced, blending in with the sound of wind and water humming around him.

Back home, back home,
*Back home, back home,*
Back home where I belong,
*Back home where I belong,*
And it won't be long,
*And it won't be long,*
Till I get on back home.
*Till I get on back home.*

"I have something for you." He pulled a worn envelope out of his jacket pocket, the corners bent with years and the words ISOPREP scrawled into the inner fold.

"What's this?" Her question turned to mist and evaporated in the air between them.

"Something he wrote for you before he was killed. I've been trying to track you down for awhile now. To make sure that this got to you." He felt the breeze against his skin, calling to him from somewhere beyond the horizon.

The young woman took the envelope and offered him a teary smile. "I don't know how to let him go."

The idea was strange, of a lost soul asking him how to cope. How to navigate the minefield of guilt and pain that followed a hero's death. The sort of loss that even the cosmos couldn't justify. That fell into the inconsolable space between random and planned.

"Promise him you won't cry forever." It had taken him many lost years, but he finally found the permission he needed in the curved handwriting of his old friend. "And remember him. He deserves to be remembered."

"I will." She reached out and took his hand, sharing the warmth of her small fingers. "Take care of yourself."

"Yes Ma'am." He squeezed her hand to seal the promise.

She pulled what strength she could from his solid grip and drew in a final, calming breath, holding Randy's letter up to her heart. She made a clean break from Casper's rough hand, and he was left with just the memory of her skin in his palm. His last mission for Staff Sergeant Khoury accomplished, and nothing further to fight for.

Casper watched her descend down the trail, following the line of stones until she was nothing more than a silhouette, eclipsed by the dying light.

He took the final steps towards Randy's grave and kneeled beside it. He followed the cool engravings with his fingers and thought about everything that was buried below. The incomplete remains that had been gathered from the blast site, further decomposed and broken down into nothing. He coughed on the sad memories, feeling the emptiness in the earth. Randy wasn't buried here. He was borne on the air, mixed with history and legend, a puff of vapors and molecules, riding the atmosphere into the unknown.

He had a sentimental craving for the flask he used to carry with him. There was nothing poetic or inspiring about turning in the bottle for a handful of prescription meds. They slowed his heart rate and numbed his motor skills, just like the alcohol did. And they helped him sleep at night, with every uneventful evening bringing him that much closer to inviting Grace back into his bed.

He borrowed a breath of crisp air from the ghosts around him and searched for the right words to connect with the past.

"I'm sorry I wasn't able to protect you." He almost whispered into the air. He took a second swig of fresh air and started again, firm and sincere. "I'm sorry I wasn't able to protect you Randy. That was my job out there, and I failed you. But I came here today to ask your permission to start living again. Maybe I never asked because I knew you'd give me your blessing. That's the kind of guy you were. Maybe I never asked because I was too afraid to try. I'll always remember that you took that blast for us. That you were brave enough and selfless enough to do what was asked of you, even though it cost you your life. But I know you wouldn't want that sacrifice to be for nothing. And I'm not so afraid to face the world anymore, even though it's a lot sadder place without you in it."

Casper stood above the marker and quietly raised his hand to his brow, offering a final salute to his comrade and friend until a heavy set of tears dropped from his eyes and streamed across his cheekbones.

"I'll see you on the other side Staff Sergeant."

He lowered his hand and turned from the gravesite, his heavy footsteps taking him down the worn path. His heart led him towards the flags and memorials that lined the entrance to the sacred cemetery, where Grace was waiting for him.

> Mamma, Mamma can't you see,
> *Mamma, Mamma can't you see,*
> What the Army's done to me,
> *What the Army's done to me,*
> And it won't be long,
> *And it won't be long,*
> Till I get on back home.
> *Till I get on back home.*

Done my part for Uncle Sam,
*Done my part for Uncle Sam,*
They took this boy, made me a man,
*They took this boy, made me a man,*
And it won't be long,
*And it won't be long,*
Till I get on back home.
*Till I get on back home.*

Back home, back home,
*Back home, back home,*
Back home where I belong,
*Back home where I belong,*
And it won't be long,
*And it won't be long,*
Till I,
Till I,
Till I get on back home.
*Till I,*
*Till I,*
*Till I get on back home.*

Made in the USA
Lexington, KY
24 October 2015